THE WISE SILENCE
OF GOD

Book Three of The Claddagh Trilogy

Evan Geller

To my wife, because she kept asking when I would finally be done with "that damn book," until I was.

Let Him be just and deal kindly with my people, for the dead are not powerless. Dead, did I say? There is no death, only a change of worlds.

CHIEF SEATTLE, 1854

Kill one man, and you are a murderer. Kill millions of men, and you are a conqueror. Kill them all, and you are a god.

JEAN ROSTAND, THOUGHTS OF A BIOLOGIST

I look for the new Teacher, that shall follow so far those shining laws, that he shall see them come full circle; shall see their rounding complete grace; shall see the work to be the mirror of the soul; shall see the identity of the law of gravitation with purity of heart; and shall show that the Ought, that Duty, is one thing with Science, with Beauty, and with Joy.

RALPH WALDO EMERSON, THE DIVINITY SCHOOL ADDRESS

As Man now is, God once was: As God now is, Man may be.

LORENZO SNOW, 1893

CONTENTS

SYNOPSIS OF BOOK ONE OF THE CLADDAGH TRILOGY

God Bless the Dead

Gabriel Sheehan is failing as a graduate student until he marries an enigmatic undergrad named Helena. She is an Irish émigré with an obscure past who inspires Gabriel to discover a method to detect and translate brainwaves. In partnership with Arthur Schlessel and his wife, Samantha, their discovery achieves profound success. This success causes an employee of the National Security Agency named Charles Parnell to confront Gabriel with the intelligence implications of his discovery, as well as pointing out Helena's troubling history. Parnell's suspicions cause Helena to go into hiding. It is revealed that Helena has led a very troubled life, beginning with her childhood in Ireland in which she and her twin sister were orphaned at age 6. The sisters were raised in a Catholic orphanage in which they were serially abused, culminating in the death of Helena's sister. Helena retaliated by killing their abuser, Father Donovan. This event had caused Helena to be committed to a mental hospital in Dublin until she was sixteen.

At Gabriel's assurance, Helena returns. However, she continues to be haunted by her past, in particular by the circumstances of her sister's death, for which she feels responsible. While helping Gabriel further his studies of the workings of the mind, Helena undertakes a profound experiment in which she hopes to rejoin her sister while allowing for Gabriel to follow. Helena takes her own life in a fashion that Gabriel is provided a path to discover a window into the afterlife. This path involves the pursuit of the origin of a particular Claddagh ring which Helena gave Gabriel on the occasion of their wedding. Gabriel's investigations lead him to discover many of the events of Helena's past. Almost at the end of his strength, Gabriel finally succeeds in deciphering the intricate puzzle of his late wife's journey, and in so doing achieves the ability to communicate with his wife. He discovers that his wife's real name is Grace, and that there is, indeed, a world beyond death.

SYNOPSIS OF BOOK TWO OF
THE CLADDAGH TRILOGY
<u>The Problem With God</u>

The book opens with the morning routine of Julius Zimmerman, a Jesuit priest and instructor at Georgetown University. Along with his English bulldog, Jack, Zimmerman goes rowing each morning on the Potomac River. On this day, however, Zimmerman and Jack witness a woman jump from a bridge and rescue her from the river. The woman proves both mysterious and provocative, imposing herself into Zimmerman's life. While the woman remains an enigma, alternatively adopting various names and explanations for her distressed situation, Zimmerman finds himself inextricably drawn into her plight.

We come to realize that this enigmatic woman is indeed Grace from Book One. She has been compelled to return to life in order to reverse the revelation of the afterlife, for which she was responsible. The cost of failing to undo this act will be the excision of her soul from existence. Father Donovan, the priest who abused Grace as a child in Ireland, has also returned, despite being murdered at Grace's hand. Now assuming the name of Fr. Peter Pauley, the rector of theological studies at Georgetown, Pauley is charged with excising Grace from existence. Charles Parnell, thwarted in Book One from developing the mind-sensing invention into a security asset, has followed Gabriel's discovery of a means of communicating with the dead. Parnell, however, is confronted by a powerful and confounding individual named Uriel, who co-opts Parnell into assisting him in preserving Grace from excision.

Grace is trapped as the gateway between the living world and the afterlife is blocked, preventing her from rejoining her husband and family in the afterlife. During the course of escaping Pauley, Zimmerman and Grace come to realize that there are additional forces at work. In particular, an army of Mormon missionaries seem intent on capturing Grace, though their motivation remains obscure. In an effort to find an alternate gateway for escape, Zimmerman helps Grace flee to New York by way of a stolen sailboat.

Uriel and Parnell come to NY in an effort to assist Grace's escape. While surveilling one possible gateway which exists in a car dealership designed by Frank Lloyd Wright, Uriel witnesses someone break in by a basement window. However, Grace actually attempts to escape by way of the gateway within the Guggenheim Museum. Despite the heroic efforts of both Zimmerman and Uriel during the confrontation in the museum, Fr. Pauley/Donovan succeeds in causing Grace's excision. The only path to restoring Grace's soul is for Uriel to stab Zimmerman in the heart. In death, Zimmerman is led by Gabriel's Claddagh ring to return to the moment just before Grace jumps from the bridge into the Potomac, where he restores Grace to her previous existence.

PROLOGUE

San Francisco, California

Arthur Schlessel was not a stupid man. He wasn't a scientist or a theoretical mathematician, not a cosmologist or philosopher. He was a businessman. But he was a very good businessman, and he knew people. He understood their desires, their motivations. He was smart that way, and it had made him extraordinarily successful. He sat at the desk, staring at the small pile of items before him, understanding this fact and regretting it.

He wished he didn't know. Arthur was still in his somber, charcoal gray suit; his funeral suit. He always wore this suit to funerals, never to any other occasion. He seemed to be wearing it a lot lately. He loosened his tie and unbuttoned his collar. Arthur closed his eyes and remembered watching his friend slump forward in this same chair, slump forward and die, his friend's face coming to rest on this same pile of stuff on his desk. What was this shit, anyway? A computer hard drive, sitting in a nest of crumpled yellow paper; notes, scribbled equations, doodling and scrawled obscenities visible on their face. What was this shit, that had been piled like some offering before his dead friend? Arthur feared he knew. He put his head in his hands and—

—Noticed his name, printed clearly on an envelope. It was sticking out from beneath the hard drive, crisp and obvious, not crumpled like the rest of the papers. He stared at it for a moment, then tugged it out from beneath the drive. His name was printed boldly in black marker, obviously in

Gabe's writing.

"Got a match?" Arthur looked up to see Chuck leaning against the door. He, too, was still dressed from their friend's funeral. Well, maybe not Chuck's friend, not since the deceased had caused that twist in Chuck's nose.

Arthur shook his head, quickly stashing the envelope in his inside coat pocket.

"Too bad." Chuck stepped up to the desk and poked at the pile of papers on the desk. "I'm going to take a look through this stuff, okay?"

"Sure, Chuck," Arthur said, standing. "Just lock up on your way out, okay? I guess I'll come back at some point to box up his things. Not today."

Chuck nodded. "He was a little nutsos there towards the end, huh?"

"Why do you say that?"

Chuck shrugged as he sat down at the desk and started to paw through the pile of papers. "He sent me a couple of emails. About his research. Sounded like he was running off the rails." He looked up at Arthur, who only stared back at him. "That woman really fucked him up, you know." He rubbed the bump in his nose. "Fucked us all up." Arthur turned to leave. "See you round, Arthur." Arthur didn't think so.

"Hey," Parnell said. Arthur stopped in the doorway. "Look at this." He pulled Gabriel's Claddagh ring from the envelope and held it up for Arthur. "Shouldn't this still be on him?"

"He's dead," Arthur said somberly, walking back and taking the ring from Parnell. He stared at it for a moment before putting it on.

"Hey," Parnell said, "why do you get to—" But Arthur turned, ignoring the other man, and left.

PART ONE

CHAPTER 1

CALL ME WHAT YOU WILL. ANY OF NINE MIL-LION NAMES, IT MATTERS NOT TO ME. MY NAME IS THE SOUND OF ALEPH. THE FAINT WHISPER THAT ESCAPES AS YOUR LAST SIGHING BREATH, THAT IS MY NAME. TOO LATE AND FOR TOO LONG, I'VE CHOSEN SILENCE. IF YOU ARE READING THIS, THINGS HAVE GONE VERY WRONG. I MAY BE DEAD. I DON'T KNOW.

THAT'S THE WORST PART: I DON'T EVEN KNOW. WHERE DOES GOD GO WHEN HE DIES?

Helmand Province, Afghanistan

The man sat in the dirt at the end of the road. Hila looked at him briefly, glancing at him momentarily before returning her gaze to the tall plant swaying in front of her. She kept working, deftly passing the four-bladed *nushtar* over the poppy, scoring it deeply, then moving on to the next flower without a pause. It was hot work beneath the sun, the sharp stony ground pressing into her knees through the fabric of her skirts as she shifted along the rows of swaying poppies. She stole another glance at the man as the *nushtar* sighed against another blossom. He was not Afghani, she was sure. Hila couldn't say exactly how she knew this to be so from such a distance, as the man wore a traditional beggar's clothes, a topi covering his head, his face turned away from where she knelt along the row of poppies. The way he sat, perhaps. But not Afghani, of this she was sure.

Hila glanced over her shoulder to where her brothers were working. Surely they had also noticed the man. Soon, one of them would need to greet the man, would need to invite the stranger to their home for tea and something to eat. She shifted down the row, the *nushtar* cut, she moved on. They are waiting, she thought, because they too sense that he is different. Not Afghani, but what? If not Afghani, maybe the customs don't apply, she thought. She wasn't sure. She was only fourteen, and though she knew most things in this life, this was new. Her mother hadn't taught her everything, it seemed. Now she never would, Hila thought.

She caught the motion from the corner of her eye, saw her oldest brother start down the dirt track towards where the man sat, her brother's sandals kicking up little clouds of dust with each step. Hila cut, moved on. Her brother was talking to the man now, gesturing. He seemed unnerved. Not angry, just disturbed. She bent her head as her brother called to her, pretending not to see.

"Hila," her brother called again. She stood and at a gesture from her brother, gathered her skirts and ran down to them. The man stood. He was tall, much taller than her brother and bone-thin. Definitely not Afghani. She stopped before the two men, her eyes lowered to the ground. "Take this pilgrim," her brother said in Pashtun, "and give him water, Hila. You have your knife, sister?" Hila held up the *nushtar*. Her brother watched as the stranger's eyes took in the wicked looking implement. "Good. Get him water, then. Be quick."

Hila led the man up the path to their home. As they came to the mud hut in the middle of the poppy fields, Hila called ahead to her father. She did not wish to startle him. "Father," Hila called as they approached the open door. "I have brought a pilgrim, as my brother, Atal, has told me. I will give him water, as Atal has told me to do, Father." She waited, the stranger waiting behind her until her father appeared in the doorway, leaning on his cane. Her father looked the man up and down, then spat on the ground before he turned back into the house. How rude of my father, Hila thought, as she turned to lead the man to the well. The man had bent slightly in a respectful bow, now straightening as Hila caught sight of his face for the first time and saw why her father had acted as he did. The man was no Afghani, indeed. The man's head was smooth beneath the topi, but reddish-blonde eyebrows hooded the man's green eyes. He smiled at her as he caught her eye and Hila blushed as she quickly lowered her gaze again. She led the man to the well.

The stranger sat on a rock. Hila drew a bucket of water from the well. She set the bucket down and took the ladle hanging from its hook on the side of the well. Hila paused, a glint of light from within the bucket having caught her eye. The man behind her coughed politely. Hila offered him a ladle of water from the bucket. He smiled at her again as he took the water and drank. As he did so, Hila peered into the depth of the bucket. She saw a shiny metal object sitting at the bottom. Hila puzzled at it. The man politely dipped his head as he returned the ladle.

"More?" Hila asked. The man inclined his head in assent. Hila refilled the ladle and the man drank this off as well. She waited, but the man offered no word of thanks. Hila didn't know what to do, so she looked at the ground and waited. She pretended not to see the thing in the bucket. Atal would come soon, she was sure. The man would leave. Meanwhile, she had her knife.

The stranger leaned forward and touched Hila's hand. She jumped back and raised her *nushtar* threateningly. The man barked a strange little laugh, smiling at her. He pointed at the bucket, smiling.

"More?" she asked him. He shook his head and waited, head inclined in anticipation. Hila simply stared at the man. After a time, he sighed and shook his head. Then his smile vanished as he looked at her very seriously and raised his hand, pointing at her, then himself. Listen to me, he seemed to indicate, though he said nothing. Listen to me, he gestured again. He swept his hand in an arc, looking at her closely, watching her. Hila stared at the man. Where was Atal? she wondered. She looked down the road for her brother. The man clapped once, sharply, staring at her fiercely. He pointed at her again, then at himself. Listen! She nodded at him. He made the arc in the sky again, and Hila couldn't stop herself, she said, "Tomorrow?" The man nodded. He pointed back to the house, still staring fixedly into her eyes. Then he made a violent gesture with both hands, a gesture of explosion. Hila gaped at him. He nodded solemnly, repeating the gesture more slowly, more emphatically. He tilted his head, eyebrows raised. Do you understand? he seemed to be asking. "Tomorrow?" Hila asked again, eyes wide. The man nodded.

"Has he had his water?" Atal asked, coming up the path. Hila nodded. "Then back to the field, Hila. I'll see him off." Hila opened her mouth to say something, not sure what to say. "Go, Hila," her brother insisted. Hila turned to leave, stealing a glance at the stranger's face. He winked at her slyly. Hila blushed again. She lifted the bucket and turned to shield it from her brother and the other man as she set it down on the edge of the well. She snatched the shiny object from the bottom of the bucket, then turned and ran off towards the field, clutching the small, hard object in her fist as she ran.

Hila returned to cutting the poppies, stealing glances at the strange pilgrim as he shuffled off down the road. She took out the metal object she had hidden in the folds of her skirt, fondling its cool surface. It was a ring, wrought from gold. A strange and priceless object, how could such a thing be in her little well? She stared at it, the face of the ring sculpted into two hands cradling a heart, the heart topped by a crown. She had never seen such a ring before. She tested it on her finger, but it was far too large for her. She replaced it in the inner folds of her skirts, wondering at it.

Hila worked the field, sweating, wondering what to tell her brother about the stranger's message. It made no sense to her. They were a poor family, struggling in the rocky dirt to raise their poppies; only just enough, once the sap was dry and harvested, to keep them all from starving in the coming winter. It made no sense. It was then she saw the dust clouds in the distance, along the road opposite the way the stranger had walked off. She watched as the dust clouds approached, not trying to hide her curiosity as the two trucks came closer, then turned up the road to their farm. Hila went back to scoring the poppy. Suddenly, the stranger's message made sense. Tomorrow, she thought, we will all die.

THE LORD SPEAKS, BUT NOW NONE MAY LISTEN. WHERE ONCE WAS WRITTEN MY WORD, NOW ONLY LIES THE UNSEEN PAGE. WHO MAY READ IN DARKNESS, NOW THAT THE CANDLE LIES COLD? IT IS NOT IN GLORY THAT THE LORD PROCLAIMS TO YOU, BUT OF NEED. CLOSE, CLOSE DEAR CHILD OF MY CREATION: ATTEND TO THE LORD!

Helmand Province, Afghanistan

Hila squatted by the well, scrubbing the pots and plates from dinner. She and her stepmother had struggled to put food on the table for their family and the dozen men who had arrived unannounced that afternoon. Now she had been sent outdoors to clean up. She could hear voices arguing from the house, snippets of angry protests from her father, wailing from her stepmother. Hila couldn't make out specifics, but it didn't sound good. She finished the cleaning and stacked the pots on the smooth stones to dry, then sat next to the pots and waited. She watched the sky as it grew dark, listening to the voices.

The door opened as Atal came outside. He walked over and sat next to Hila. Atal said nothing as he ceremoniously lit a cigarette. He blew smoke up to the stars.

"I am sorry, little sister," he said at last, shaking his head. Hila looked at him, his face lit in the glow of the cigarette. "You know who these men are?" Atal asked her. The dozen men from the truck, who had eaten all of her family's food without a word of thanks, the men who carried AK-47's and RPG's, men with long beards and hard, sun-weathered faces. Hila knew who they were. She nodded in the dark. "They will take you tomorrow, little sister."

"What?" Hila asked. "What do you mean?"

"You will be with them when they leave in the morning. I am sorry."

"Why would I go with them? I don't want to go anywhere, Atal."

"We cannot pay them, Hila. They loaned father the money for the poppies, and we do not have the money to pay them back."

"But it's not time yet! When the sap is dry, then—"

Atal shook his head. "They say the army is coming to burn the fields. There will be no harvest, Hila. Nothing to sell."

Hila looked at her brother fiercely in the darkness. He took a deep drag on his cigarette, making it glow brightly.

"So you will sell me, instead, brother? You do not even know if what they say is true." She fixed her brother with a hard, accusing stare. "When the army doesn't come, and you bring in the harvest without your little sister, and you sell the crop, what then, brother? Will you be able to keep the money, since you gave me to these men? Or will they come back, and want the money, too? Maybe then, you can buy back your little sister's dead body, and give me a good burial. Maybe we be together then, brother?"

"I'm sorry, Hila. Father tried." He shook his head again.

Hila looked up at the cold, hard points of light above

them. She considered what her brother had told her. "You should know, brother, that the pilgrim told me—" At that moment, the door to the house crashed open and one of the men came running towards them, screaming curses. Hila and Atal stared at the wild-eyed man as he rushed at them.

"Idiot!" the man yelled at them, swinging his gun and smashing Atal's arm. Atal screamed, falling to the dirt. The man stood over him, cursing again as he ground his boot down on Atal's hand, extinguishing the glowing cigarette. "Idiot!" he repeated. "You will get us all killed!" he yelled, gesturing at the sky. "Idiot!" He turned with a shake of his head and stomped back to the house.

Atal moaned as he lay cradling his arm in the dirt. Hila knelt over him, soothing him with a hand on his shoulder.

"Is it bad, brother?" she asked softly.

Atal nodded. "Broken, I think," he said, his voice cracking. He moaned again.

"That is too bad, brother," she said soothingly. "Now you will not be able to fight for the honor of your little sister, will you? Now you will not be able to make them go away without me, to show that the men in our family honor their women and would never let a thug like that take your sister to pay a debt. Will you?" He looked up at her as she straightened and stood over him. She looked down on her brother with a pitiless stare. "Goodbye, Atal." Hila turned from him, away from her house and the sound of her stepmother's wailing, to walk down to the road. In the dark, she turned to follow the way the pilgrim had gone.

ATTEND THE WORD OF THE LORD:
"YOU MAY CALL ME THAT," SO SAYETH I.

"I WAS JOKING," HE SAID. THE MAN LOOKED ABOUT THE SMALL EXAMINING ROOM AT HIS WIFE AND TWO SONS, NOT SURE WHAT I WAS DOING

THERE. HIS WIFE DABBED AT HER EYES WITH A TISSUE. I LOOKED AT THE OLDER BOY. HE WAS HANDSOME, ATHLETIC, SEVENTEEN. AND DYING.

"SORRY ABOUT THE CANCER," I TOLD THE BOY. HE BARELY MANAGED A SLIGHT NOD. THE DOCTOR HAD EXCUSED HIMSELF FROM THE ROOM TO ALLOW THEM A LITTLE TIME TO DEAL WITH THE NEWS. HE HAD JUST TOLD THEM THAT THE BOY'S RECENT SCAN SHOWED THE CANCER HAD PROGRESSED, DESPITE THE CHEMOTHERAPY AND RADIATION THERAPY THAT HAD MADE THE YOUNG MAN'S LIFE A MISERY THESE PAST FOUR MONTHS. NO WAY THE KID WAS GOING TO SEE HIS FRESHMAN DORM ROOM AT STANFORD.

I TURNED TO THE YOUNGER BOY SITTING NEXT TO HIS MOTHER. HIS EYES WERE RED FROM CRYING AS WELL. "JULIUS, RIGHT?" I ASKED HIM. HE NODDED AT ME, NUMB. "HOW OLD ARE YOU, JULIUS?"

"THIR-TEEN," HE STAMMERED, VOICE CRACKING. HE LOOKED AT HIS SHOES AND SNIFFLED.

"BAR MITZVAH YET?" I ASKED HIM. HE SHOOK HIS HEAD.

"NEXT YEAR," HIS MOTHER SAID, APOLOGETICALLY. SHE PUT HER ARM AROUND YOUNG JULIUS'S SHOULDER. "WHEN THINGS ARE BETTER."

"YOU MEAN WHEN I'M DEAD," THE OLDER
BOY SAID. MOTHER STARTED TO CRY AGAIN.

"ELI," THE FATHER ADMONISHED.
"DON'T TALK LIKE THAT."

"IT'S TRUE!" ELIJAH SAID. "YOU HEARD
DR. CHU. THE CHEMO'S NOT WORKING.
THE RADIATION WAS A GODDAMN WASTE
OF TIME. NOTHING'S WORKING."

I CLEARED MY THROAT SOFTLY. "YEAH,
ABOUT THAT…" I BEGAN AGAIN.

DAD LOOKED AT ME SHARPLY.
"I ASKED YOU WHO YOU ARE," HE
REPEATED. "ARE YOU A DOCTOR?"

I SHOOK MY HEAD. "I LIKE TO PRETEND I'M A
SURGEON, SOMETIMES," I SAID, SMILING. IT WAS A
LITTLE JOKE. THEY DIDN'T GET IT. I CLEARED MY
THROAT AGAIN AND SPOKE TO MOM THIS TIME. "I'M
VERY SORRY, MRS. ZIMMERMAN. I KNOW THAT THIS
HAS BEEN HARD ON YOUR FAMILY. YOU ARE A GOOD
FAMILY, GOOD PEOPLE. I'M SORRY THAT ELI AND
THE REST OF YOU ARE GOING THROUGH ALL THIS.
I'D LIKE TO HELP."

"HELP? HELP HOW? ARE YOU FROM THE
HOSPITAL? IS THIS ABOUT THE BILLS FOR THE
CHEMO? THAT DIDN'T WORK, BY THE WAY? IS
THAT WHAT THIS IS ABOUT?" DAD INTERJECTED.

"NO, MR. ZIMMERMAN, THIS ISN'T ABOUT THE

BILLS. THIS IS ABOUT ELI. I WANT TO HELP HIM."

"HOW? THE DOCTOR SAID—" HE CHOKED BACK A SOB. "IF YOU'RE NOT A DOCTOR, THEN HOW'RE YOU GOING TO HELP?"

"WHAT I AM ISN'T IMPORTANT, MR. ZIMMERMAN," I SAID. "HERE'S THE IMPORTANT PART: IF YOU WANT, IF YOU WANT ELIJAH TO LIVE, THEN YOU HAVE TO MAKE A DECISION."

"OF COURSE WE WANT ELI TO LIVE," DAD SAID.

"OF COURSE YOU DO, MR. ZIMMERMAN. I DON'T MEAN TO BE INSENSITIVE. PLEASE HEAR ME OUT. IN A FEW MINUTES THE DOCTOR IS GOING TO RETURN AND ASK IF YOU HAVE ANY QUESTIONS. IF YOU WANT ELIJAH TO LIVE, YOU CAN ASK HIM IF THERE IS ANY RESEARCH BEING DONE ON ELI'S CANCER. ASK DR. CHU IF THERE'S AN EXPERIMENTAL TREATMENT, PERHAPS AT THE NIH, FOR INSTANCE, THAT ELI MIGHT BENEFIT FROM."

DAD OPENED HIS MOUTH TO SPEAK, TURNING RED WITH ANGER, BUT HIS WIFE SPOKE BEFORE HIM. "BUT WHY DIDN'T DR. CHU TELL US ABOUT THIS? WHY DO WE HAVE TO ASK?"

"YOU MEAN THERE'S A TREATMENT THAT COULD CURE ELI THAT CHU ISN'T TELLING US ABOUT?" DAD FINALLY STAMMERED.

I SHOOK MY HEAD. "IT'S NOT QUITE THAT STRAIGHTFORWARD, MR.

ZIMMERMAN, MRS. ZIMMERMAN. DR.
CHU DOESN'T KNOW ABOUT THIS."

"WHY NOT?" DAD ASKED.

"BECAUSE THERE IS NO EXPERIMENTAL TREAT-
MENT, NOT YET," I SAID. DAD STARTED TO GET RED
AGAIN, BUT BEFORE HE COULD SAY THE OBVIOUS I
CUT HIM OFF. "ARRANGEMENTS NEED TO BE MADE."
THEY ALL LOOKED AT ME, NOW CONFUSED AS WELL
AS DISTRAUGHT. "I KNOW WHAT I'M TELLING YOU
SEEMS UNUSUAL," I CONTINUED. "PLEASE, LET ME
EXPLAIN. YOU NEED TO MAKE A DECISION. IF YOU
WANT ELI TO LIVE, THERE IS A WAY. BUT THERE ARE
CONSEQUENCES."

"WHAT KIND OF CONSEQUENCES?" DAD
ASKED. "WHAT IS THIS, A BARGAIN? ARE WE
SELLING MY SON TO THE DEVIL HERE, IS THAT IT?"

I SHOOK MY HEAD. WHY DO THEY ALWAYS AS-
SUME THAT? "NO, MR. ZIMMERMAN, I ASSURE YOU
THAT I AM NOT THE DEVIL. THIS ISN'T A BARGAIN,
AND YOU'RE NOT SELLING ANYTHING, CERTAINLY
NOT YOUR SON'S SOUL. IF YOU CHOOSE THIS PATH,
NOTHING TERRIBLE WILL HAPPEN TO YOU, YOUR SON,
OR YOUR FAMILY."

"THEN WHAT KIND OF CONSEQUENCES?"
HE ASKED. THE OTHERS LOOKED BACK AND
FORTH BETWEEN US, FOLLOWING BUT NOT
QUITE FOLLOWING THE CONVERSATION.

"LOOK, IF I DIDN'T COME IN HERE, IF WE ALL DO NOTHING, THEN I'M AFRAID THAT DR. CHU IS CORRECT. YOUNG ELI HERE WILL DIE IN THREE AND A HALF MONTHS." ELIJAH CURSED, THEN STARTED TO SOB AGAIN.

"JUST GET OUT," DAD SAID.

"WAIT," MOM SAID. "PLEASE. WHOEVER YOU ARE, WHAT CAN WE DO?"

I SIGHED. "YOU CAN CHOOSE TO ASK DR. CHU WHAT I SAID."

"AND HE'LL LIVE?" SHE ASKED. I NODDED. SHE LOOKED AT HER HUSBAND.

"OF COURSE WE WANT OUR SON TO LIVE. THIS IS RIDICULOUS," HE SAID. "WHO ARE YOU?"

"IF YOU CHOOSE TO ASK DR. CHU ABOUT THE NIH," I SAID, IGNORING THE QUESTION, "YOU WILL CHOOSE A FUTURE IN WHICH ELIJAH LIVES. IT'S AS SIMPLE AS THAT."

"BUT YOU SAID THAT THERE'D BE CONSEQUENCES," MOM SAID, LOOKING BACK AT ME. I NODDED. "BAD CONSEQUENCES? WILL SOMETHING HAPPEN TO JULIUS, INSTEAD?"

"NOT GOOD OR BAD, BOTH BAD AND GOOD. EVERY LIFE HAS ITS CONSEQUENCES, THAT'S A BETTER WAY TO THINK ABOUT IT," I SAID, SMILING. "JUST DIFFERENT. CHOICES HAVE CONSEQUENCES. YES, SOMETHING WILL HAPPEN TO JULIUS, SOME-

THING DIFFERENT THAN WHAT WOULD HAPPEN IF HIS BROTHER WERE TO DIE IN THREE MONTHS. SOME BAD, NECESSARILY, SOME GOOD—BUT DIFFERENT. LET ME BE COMPLETELY FRANK WITH YOU, MRS. ZIMMERMAN. THE FUTURE, AS IT STANDS, IS THAT ELIJAH DIES FROM HIS DISEASE. JULIUS GROWS UP WITHOUT A BROTHER. I'M SAYING THAT YOU MAY CHOOSE ANOTHER FUTURE, ONE IN WHICH ELIJAH IS CURED OF HIS CANCER."

"FOR HOW LONG? WHAT'S THE CATCH?" DAD ASKED.

"CURED," I ASSURED HIM.

"SO WHAT'S THE CATCH?" HE REPEATED.

"NO CATCH, MR. ZIMMERMAN. BUT A DIFFERENT FUTURE. ELIJAH SURVIVES HIS CANCER. THAT LEADS TO A DIFFERENT FUTURE FOR EVERYONE IN YOUR FAMILY; FOR MANY, MANY PEOPLE." FOR THE ENTIRE WORLD, I DIDN'T TELL HIM. I LOOKED AT JULIUS, WHO WAS STARING AT THE FLOOR AGAIN.

"I DON'T UNDERSTAND." IT WAS MOM AGAIN. "WHY WOULDN'T WE CHOOSE A FUTURE IN WHICH ELI LIVES? HOW IS SUCH A THING EVEN POSSIBLE?" SHE LOOKED BACK AT HER HUSBAND.

"YEAH. HOW IS A THING LIKE THAT EVEN POSSIBLE?" HE ASKED ME. I GAVE THEM MY MOST REASSURING SMILE. THREW IN THE PALMS UP GESTURE OF GENTLE SUPPLICATION—THE ONE MY BOY USED

ABOUT A DOZEN TIMES A DAY. I DIDN'T BOTHER WITH THE TECHNICALITIES. THEY WOULDN'T UNDERSTAND ANY EXPLANATION I COULD PROVIDE. MR. ZIMMERMAN WAS A CORPORATE ATTORNEY, NOT A COSMOLOGIST WITH INSIGHT INTO ADVANCED QUANTUM MATHEMATICAL THEORY. "HOW COULD WE NOT CHOOSE TO SAVE OUR SON?" HE ASKED.

"IT'S YOUR CHOICE, I ASSURE YOU," I SAID.

"ARE YOU AN ANGEL?" MOM ASKED. "YOU SAID YOU'RE NOT THE DEVIL. ARE YOU AN ANGEL, THEN? OR WHAT?"

I SMILED MY BENEFICENT SMILE. REASSURING. HEARTFELT. "IT WAS A PLEASURE TO MEET YOU. YOU HAVE A BEAUTIFUL FAMILY. I'M GOING TO GO NOW. BLESS YOU ALL." I OPENED THE DOOR AND LEFT. DR. CHU ENTERED RIGHT BEHIND ME. BEFORE THE DOCTOR EVEN HAD A CHANCE TO CLOSE THE DOOR, I HEARD MR. ZIMMERMAN ASK HIM ABOUT THE NIH. CHU WASN'T AWARE OF ANY RELEVANT STUDIES, HE SAID, BUT HE ASSURED THEM THAT HE WOULD CHECK INTO IT.

IT WAS A GOOD DAY. IT WAS THE END OF DAYS.

New York, NY

Julius Zimmerman sat in the dark. He was cold. He didn't know how long he had been here. He stood up on shaky legs and stretched, then took a few tentative steps around. He didn't dare walk too far in the pitch darkness.

His surroundings, he had painfully discovered, were littered with debris. He found his hard seat and sat, again. It had been days since he had last eaten, he was sure. His water was gone as well. He didn't know how much longer he could keep this up. He felt spent, lost and ill.

Julius sat in the dark and listened. He could hear the soft scuttling of rats in the corners. At least, he assumed the sound was of rats. He stared about, seeing nothing, and stretched again. He yawned. He listened to the air fill his lungs, then leave again.

Julius waited. He didn't pray.

Julius sat and listened, exquisitely focused on the slightly less black window high in front of where he sat in the dark. He might have imagined it, but he thought he heard a new sound, a different soft scuffling than the sound of what he thought were rats. He wasn't sure, but he thought maybe...

Julius sat, staring hard at nothing in front of him, listening. The window high on the basement wall in front of him gave a muffled snap, and Julius smiled in the darkness.

"Careful, Grace," Julius said, "I've got you." He gently embraced the pair of legs that appeared, hanging down in the darkness from the window. The legs struck him a vicious kick in the nose and Julius went down, bright lights painfully strobing across his vision as he landed hard on his ass on the cold concrete floor of the car dealership's basement.

"Holy shit, Grace," Julius said, holding his face. "What is it with you? Why the hell did you do that?"

There was a soft thump as the legs landed on the floor in the darkness. "Julius?"

"Yeah, Grace. It's me. I think you broke my nose. Again."

"I can't see you."

"No kidding, Grace. It's dark." He heard her shuffle carefully forward to the sound of his voice, her hand tentatively finding his face. "Ouch. Shit! Careful."

"Julius, I'm so sorry. How can you be here? I just left you. I left you on the boat." Grace found his hands in the darkness and helped Julius stand, enfolding him in her embrace. "I left you and Jack on the boat. No way you could follow me with that much narcotic in you, honey."

Julius stiffened. "You drugged me?" He felt her nodding against his chest. "Why?"

"You weren't going to let me go, Julius. I knew that. It was the only way. How can you be here?"

"I've been waiting here a long time, Grace. Waiting for you."

"How?"

"I came back."

A GOOD STORY. NOT A PARABLE. NO DEEPER MEANING FOR YOUR PRIESTS TO PRATTLE ON ABOUT. I ASSURE YOU, THOUGH, THAT WON'T STOP THEM FROM TRYING. SOME OF THOSE GUYS COULD TWIST A SUNNY DAY INTO PROOF OF ORIGINAL SIN. MAKES ME CRAZY, JUST TO HEAR SOME OF WHAT GOES ON. ANYWAYS, THIS ISN'T LIKE THAT. BETTER THAN MOST OF MY STORIES, AND THIS ONE HAPPENS TO BE TRUE. A LITTLE INCIDENT, RELATED JUST AS I REMEMBER IT, JUST AS IT HAPPENED. THE WORD OF GOD, AS IT WERE.

IT IS A GOOD STORY. THERE WAS A CHILD: A GREAT KID, REALLY, BY ANY STANDARD, EVEN FOR A TEENAGER. NEVER GAVE HIS PARENTS A MOMENT'S TSURIS. VALEDICTORIAN, FULL RIDE SCHOLARSHIP

TO STANFORD. NOT A BAD FIRST ACT, EXCEPT FOR THE 'DYING FROM CANCER' PART. NOBODY LIKES THE KID DYING FROM CANCER. SO I FIXED IT. A MIRACLE! NO MORE CANCER. KID IS CURED, EVERYONE LIVES ON IN FAITH AND HAPPINESS. GREAT STORY, NICE ENDING.

YOU'RE WONDERING, THOUGH, WHY THE KID HAD TO GET CANCER IN THE FIRST PLACE. WHY DID THE KID AND HIS FAMILY HAVE TO SUFFER THAT WAY? AND WHAT ABOUT ALL THE MILLIONS AND MILLIONS OF OTHER FAMILIES WHO HAVE SUFFERED THE SAME AND WORSE, WHAT ABOUT ALL OF THEM? THE ONES I DIDN'T FIX. HOW IS THAT FAIR?

LET ME JUST STOP YOU FOR A SECOND RIGHT THERE: I NEVER SAID IT WAS FAIR.

Helmand Province, Afghanistan

Hila walked through the cold night, shivering. In the morning, she knew, the men would get back in their trucks and coming racing up the road to snatch her up. She kept walking, arms wrapped around herself to control her shaking. Tonight, she thought, I will walk. She did not think that they would bother to come for her in the night. Brave *mujahedin*, she scoffed, scared of the glow of a cigarette. They will not come for me in the night, she felt certain. So she walked in the cold darkness, beneath a million icy stars.

A soft whistle from behind caused Hila to freeze in her tracks. She turned slowly.

"I have a knife," Hila said loudly. She pulled the *nushtar* from her skirt. From the darkness, she heard the strange bark, an almost laugh. The pilgrim materialized from the gloom at the side of the road. Hila could make out his smile in the darkness. She put her knife away. The man advanced, pulling a mule behind him on a rope lead. He bowed slightly.

"What do you want?" Hila asked. The man turned to a saddlebag on the mule and fished out a rough woolen cape. He offered it to Hila. Hila hesitated for a moment, then shrugged and took the garment. "Thank you," she said, pulling the cape about her shoulders. The pilgrim gestured forward to the road ahead. Hila turned and walked on, the pilgrim following just behind, leading his scuffling mule.

"My name is Hila," she said over her shoulder as she walked. She waited but the man said nothing. "You are wondering why a young woman would be walking without escort on a road in the dark, I am sure. It is not proper, of course." She listened to the stranger's steps and the clop of the animal's hooves as they traveled with her. "It is not proper for a woman to walk alone on the road, in the dark. But is it proper to sell your daughter to strangers? Is that more proper? Is it acceptable for a family to give up their daughter to be raped and made a slave to bandits, to settle a debt?" She swore softly. Hila jumped as the man tapped her on the shoulder. He pointed off to the side of the road. "What?" she demanded.

The pilgrim turned in the direction he had pointed, leading the mule. "Where are you going?" Hila asked. The man did not stop, only gestured for Hila to follow. Hila hesitated, looking down the road, then back from where she had come. Finally, she turned with a sigh and followed the stranger into the scrubland.

They didn't walk very far. The pilgrim led them up a narrow path to a clearing beneath a rocky escarpment. He tied the mule to a low, bent tree and removed blankets from the saddlebags. He handed a canvas bucket to Hila and pointed her to a small creek not far past the rocky outcropping. Hila moved off to fill the bucket.

When she returned, Hila saw that the pilgrim had made

up two bedrolls, each sheltered partially by the overhanging rock but a proper distance apart. A saddlebag was placed as a pillow at each. The pilgrim pointed her to the mule and Hila set the bucket of water down for the animal to drink. The pilgrim nodded and settled into his bedroll. Hila moved off to her own and snuggled beneath the rough blankets. She lay back, looking up at the night, her fist clutching the knife. As she watched, she thought she could see a tiny black cross moving across the dark purple sky, eclipsing the stars as it silently circled above them. "I have a knife," she said again. The man said nothing. She fell asleep.

New York, NY

"I came back."

Grace puzzled over Julius's statement. She didn't understand what he meant, was going to ask him to explain, but instead held him tight. She felt his heart thudding against her cheek and thought about the boat, the time she had spent with her cheek on his chest, feeling his heartbeat like this. Maybe they should go back, she thought. Something wasn't right.

The basement flooded with light at the sound of a snap. They both looked up, blinking in the sudden brightness.

"Hey guys."

"Gabe!" Grace pushed herself away from Julius. "What are you doing here?" She did a double-take, suddenly smiling. She laughed at her husband, who stood naked at the top of the steps. "Looking good, hon." She winked at him.

"We gotta go," Gabriel said, gesturing over his shoulder. "No time to find something to wear. I remember being thinner, I think," he added, looking down at himself.

"Go where?" Julius asked, following Grace across the debris strewn floor of the basement to the foot of the steps.

" 'Where' is not as important as when, Julius," Gabriel said. "As in, right now, guys. This place is going to get pretty crowded in about two minutes. We don't want to still be here when that happens."

Grace and Julius came up the stairway two steps at a time, then followed Gabriel as he led them across the gloomy showroom of the car dealership.

"Are these the same guys from the park?" Julius asked, catching up to Julius.

Julius nodded. "The same guys who were in the park last time around. This time, they're coming here."

"What do you mean, last time around?" Grace asked.

"That's not important right now, hon," Gabriel said. "We gotta get out of Dodge."

"It's a Mercedes dealership, I think," Grace corrected.

Gabriel led them past spectral cars in the dark showroom, led them between dealers' desks to the back hallway. Light spilled from an open doorway at the end of the hall. As they turned down the hallway, they heard shouts from the front of the building. A flashlight cut through the showroom windows and found them momentarily. More shouts, then a hard metallic bang from the front door.

"Go, go, go!" Gabriel said, pushing Grace down the hallway in front of him. They ran to the light spilling from an open door. Grace stopped short, looking into the small janitor's closet. She turned and looked at Gabriel questioningly. "Say goodnight, Gracie," Gabriel said, nodding towards Julius who came up behind.

Grace leaned back and gave Julius a kiss on the cheek.

"Thanks for waiting for me," she said.

"I'll be right behind you," Julius said. Grace turned and stepped into the closet. She disappeared as her foot touched down, her clothes puddling on the small tiled floor. Julius turned to Gabriel. "You go next. I'll be right behind."

"You say so, Father. Good luck, son," Gabriel said. Then Gabriel stepped in.

Julius turned back towards the sound of thudding blows to the front door, watched as the glass shattered onto the polished showroom floor. When he turned back to the closet, it was empty. Julius stepped into the closet as he heard more shouts from the front of the showroom, the sound of feet crunching on broken glass. He stood there, surrounded by mops and buckets. Nothing happened. He heard people shouting, saw flashlight beams playing about, reflected crazily by windshields and rear-view mirrors, now pointing up the hallway. Julius pushed at the walls, stomped on the floor of the little closet—nothing happened. The voices were getting closer.

"Shit," Julius muttered to himself. He flicked the switch to kill the light and pulled the door of the closet closed. In the darkness of the cramped space, he continued to push against the walls, straining for the passage that the other two had taken.

The closet door was flung open. Julius stared into the face of a young man in his twenties, dressed in a white shirt and black tie. The man pointed his flashlight directly into Julius's face.

"Nothing," the young man said as Julius prepared to strike out at the blinding light in front of him. Then the guy slammed the door closed again.

Julius stood in the sudden darkness, seeing only the light's blurry afterimage, stunned.

"What the fuck?" he almost said aloud. Julius listened to the voices of the men as they searched the dealership. The door before him remained closed. After about twenty minutes, Julius was alone again, once more in silence and in the dark.

Grace opened her eyes as she felt herself falling. As she fell, she could see a round window, bright blue above her. She fell, down and down, farther and farther from the round window above, and as she fell she saw the blue sky, and clouds scudding across the window, and then only white.

CHAPTER 2

*YOU CAN CHECK YOUR LORD ON THAT:
NEVER SAID ANYTHING ABOUT BEING FAIR.
CHECK THE BOOKS. NEVER SAID IT.*

*FAIRNESS, YOU SEE, IS YOUR CONCEPT. NOT MY
IDEA. NOT EVEN A THING, REALLY. IT'S NOT MUCH
MORE THAN AN EXPECTATION. IT SEEMS, HOWEVER,
TO BE OF THE FABRIC OF YOUR BEING. WHICH IS
REALLY UNFORTUNATE, WHEN YOU THINK ABOUT IT.
THE VERY NATURE THAT ALLOWS YOU TO BELIEVE IN
ME, MAKES FAIRNESS QUITE IMPOSSIBLE. NOT IN MY
WORLD. IRONIC, ISN'T IT?*

*IRONY, THOUGH—IRONY IS A BASIC BUILDING
BLOCK OF THE UNIVERSE. THAT'S JUST A GIVEN.*

Over the Indian Ocean

Arthur Schlessel sat next to his wife, holding her hand across the armrest of their first class seats. He looked past her to the darkness outside the window. Sam turned to him, smiling.

"Tell me again," Samantha said, "why we're here."

"What do you mean?" Arthur asked, bringing his gaze back inside the cabin of Malaysia Airlines flight 370.

"On this plane. Flying to Biejing. Why?"

"I told you forty times already. And again, when we were sitting in the airport."

Sam shook her head. "I know. Tell me again. Because I still don't get it."

"Gabriel left us these tickets. You know that."

"Yeah, I get that part. In the envelope, on his desk. You told me."

Arthur nodded. He thought that answered the question.

"Gabe's dead, hon," Sam continued. "He's been gone a long time. He was dead when you found the tickets. For what possible reason would he have bought us tickets to fly to Beijing?"

Arthur shrugged. They had been through this dozens of times.

"And even if he wanted us to fly to Beijing, why fly to Kuala Lumpur first? Why not go straight to China from San Francisco? It makes no sense, Arthur."

"I know, hon. But the tickets were in the envelope, and they had our names on them, and they were for this flight, so —"

"Gabe never said anything about going to China, did he? Did he ever once mention going to China? No, never. Not even when Helena was alive. I don't remember that girl even getting on an airplane in her life."

"She didn't like to fly."

"You know who else doesn't like to fly? You know who's pretty pissed off about flying over the ocean all night for no goddamned reason? Give you one guess."

"I know, dear," Arthur sighed. "They were our friends."

"Yeah, well now they're our dead friends, Arthur." She gestured to the large ring Arthur was twisting nervously about his right ring finger. "That's why you're wearing his ring, Artie. He's dead." Samantha looked out the window, seeing nothing but her own reflection against the black night sky. "Makes no goddamned sense," she muttered.

"Maybe we should try to get some sleep," Arthur said. "It's

a long flight."

Arthur waited a half hour, waited until he was certain that his wife was asleep. He leaned forward and fished through his carry-on bag until he found the device. The device was a featureless metal cylinder with a single button on one end. He had no idea what the thing did. He looked at his watch.

"What's that?" Samantha asked. Arthur jumped slightly in his seat.

"I thought you were asleep," Arthur said.

"You thought wrong. Gonna take a whole lot more drugs and alcohol to get me to sleep on this plane. What is that thing, Arthur?"

"I'm not sure."

"What do you mean, you're not sure?"

Arthur sighed as he leaned back, twisting the smooth cylinder in his hands. "It's part of the whole 'letter from Gabe' thing, hon."

"The same letter that had the tickets that got us on this ridiculous junket? That letter?"

Arthur nodded. "There was a schematic in the envelope, with a note. It had instructions on how to get this device made and to bring it with us on the plane."

"I'm just assuming here that my husband has somehow gone batshit crazy. You're making this up, aren't you?"

Arthur shook his head. "No, hon. I wish I was. It sounds nuts, I know. But I took the plans to an electronics shop and they gave me this two weeks later. Cost me almost ten grand."

"Ten grand? For what? What does it do?"

"I told you, I got no clue. The guys who put it together didn't have much of an idea, either. Said they never saw anything quite like it."

"Great, hon. Sounds just great. Put it back in your bag."

Arthur looked at his watch. "No, I can't. I'm supposed to push the little button on the end here in exactly two minutes."

EVAN GELLER

"Who says?"

"The letter."

"The letter from Gabe, our dead friend? That letter?" Arthur nodded, rolling the smooth cylinder in his hand and looking at his watch. "Well, you're not pushing that button. Put it away." Arthur looked at her in the darkness. "Geez, Artie, it's probably a bomb or something," she whispered. "I don't know why Gabriel went to so much trouble to screw with us like this, but no way you're pushing that button." She shook her head and in a milder voice said, "Poor Gabe was pretty screwed up there towards the end."

"That's what Chuck said," Arthur said

"When did you talk to Chuck?"

"Right after the funeral. In Gabe's office."

"He called today," Sam said.

"What? Chuck called you?"

Sam nodded. "Called my cell. I have no idea how he even got the number."

"What did he say?"

"I didn't answer it."

"You didn't? Why not?"

"It was Chuck, Artie. Why would I talk to the guy? What could he say that I would want to deal with?"

Arthur shrugged. "No idea. Did he leave a message?"

"Yeah."

"What did it say?" Arthur asked.

"I didn't listen to it. It's Chuck."

"Let me see your phone." Samantha reached under the seat to retrieve her purse. She fished the phone out and gave it to her husband.

"Not sure why you care," she said.

Arthur pushed the necessary buttons: "Sam, it's me, Chuck. Long time, dear. Listen, this is important. Don't get on the plane. Tell Arthur—a matter of life and death. Do not get on that plane. Give my regards. Bye."

Arthur looked up from the phone. "Huh. Wonder what

plane he was talking about." He handed the phone back to his wife and looked at his watch. He pushed the button on the end of the cylinder.

Samantha gasped. "Shit, Artie! I told you not to—why the hell did you do that?"

Arthur shrugged. "Chuck's voice. Always pissed me off, that guy." He looked around the plane in the semi-darkness. "Guess it wasn't a bomb, hon."

"Maybe it is and you just started some kind of timer, dumb-ass."

"Hmm. Good point." Arthur held the device to his ear. "Don't hear any ticking."

She rolled her eyes. "How could the guys who built it for you not know what it does? That makes no sense."

Arthur put the cylinder back in his bag. "I know. But all they could say was that it was some sort of transmitter, and that it was very powerful. Not explosive, though. I asked."

"Well that's almost reassuring."

"Yeah, I thought so, too."

Samantha looked around at the other first class passengers sleeping in the semidarkness. "It seems it didn't do much for ten grand, dear."

"Maybe I can return it when we get home. Get a refund."

Samantha grabbed her husband's arm. "Holy shit, Artie!"

Arthur looked to where his wife was staring. "What the— holy shit, Sam! It looks like—"

"—Gabe! It looks just like him." They both stared at the man sleeping in the seat across the aisle two rows ahead. "Artie, I don't think he was there before."

"Of course he was there before, Sam. Don't be nuts. We just didn't notice him. And it's not Gabriel, so quit hyperventilating. It's just someone who looks a lot like him from this angle."

"It's Gabe, I'm sure of it."

"Gabe's dead, hon."

"Yeah, well, maybe you should go tell him that. Because

I'm sure that's Gabe." She gave her husband a nudge in the ribs. "Go see."

"I'm not going to wake that guy up. What am I going to say? Hey, buddy, you look just like my best friend who died a year ago. Buy you a drink?"

"Go."

"I'm not going. The seatbelt sign's still on."

Sam gave him another shove. "Go! I'm going to start freaking out in two seconds unless you go over there and see it's not really Gabe."

"Yeah? And what if it is?"

"Shut up! You're scaring me. Go see who it is. Or isn't, rather."

Arthur reluctantly unsnapped his seatbelt and stood up. He walked up the aisle and looked down on the man sleeping in the seat. He tapped the man's shoulder. "Excuse me," Arthur said.

The man's eyes opened and he smiled at Arthur. "Hey, Arthur. Good to see you, buddy." Arthur looked back at his wife, his face ashen. Samantha screamed.

Helmand Province, Afghanistan

Hila awoke with a start, a hand clamped across her mouth preventing her scream from escaping. She struggled, searching for the knife that had been in her hand as she fell asleep, but without result.

"Quiet, little sister," Atal hissed in her ear. "I am here now."

Hila relaxed and Atal removed his hand from her face. She blinked in the darkness, looking over to where the pilgrim still lay sleeping.

"What do you want?" Hila whispered to her brother.

Atal sat back and playfully flipped Hila's knife in his hand. "Is that how you thank your big brother for coming to rescue you?" Atal asked softly.

"Screw you, brother," Hila said. "You couldn't rescue a

THE WISE SILENCE OF GOD

mouse from a kitten. And don't try to take me back to Father. I'll break your other arm if you try."

"Such bad talk from a little girl," Atal said. "If I weren't such a good brother, I would leave you with this creep."

They both looked over to see the man sitting up, staring at them. Atal looked at him defiantly, gesturing with Hila's knife.

"Yeah, asshole, I'm talking about you. This is the thanks for giving you water, eh? You try to take my little sister? I should kill you."

"He didn't—"

"Quiet, sister," Atal said, not taking his eyes from the other man. The older man shrugged and said nothing. "Maybe I don't kill you, pilgrim. Maybe I just take your donkey to teach you a lesson."

"No, Atal. He was—"

"Shut up, little girl. No more words from you. I mean it." Atal stood up and moved to stand over the other man, pointing the knife at the man's nose. "What do you say, old man? I take your donkey—or I take your life?" He smiled down in the darkness. "Maybe both, eh?"

Without a word and too fast for Hila to follow, the old man swept Atal's legs out from under him. Atal landed face-first in the dirt with a grunt as the man planted his knee in Atal's back. Atal screamed as the man grabbed at his broken arm. The pilgrim stood, shaking his head. He took the knife from Atal's other hand and walked over to Hila. He handed the knife back to her and sat back down on a rock, brushing the dirt from his pants.

Hila helped her brother to sit up, cradling his broken left arm. "Not even a mouse from a kitten, brother," she soothed. "His arm is broken," she explained to the pilgrim. The man shrugged. Atal rocked in pain, biting his lower lip.

"Give me the knife, sister," her brother said through clenched teeth. "I will kill him."

"I don't think you should kill him, brother. Sit. I'll get you some water."

The three sat together silently. As the sky lightened with the approaching sunrise, the pilgrim made a small fire beneath the rocky escarpment and heated water for tea. He fished strips of jerky from the saddlebag at his bedroll and gave them each a piece. He indicated the bag at Hila's bed and she found two battered metal cups and leaves for the tea. They ate and drank their tea, Hila sharing hers with her brother.

Finally, Atal spoke. "We will go home now, Hila." The pilgrim shook his head.

"No, brother," Hila said. "I'm not going home. Not with you. Not ever."

"Do not be insolent, little girl," Atal said, standing. Hila glared at him. The other man gestured for Atal to sit. He put down his cup of tea and searched in his saddlebag, making a guttural murmuring sound that the other two could not make out. He produced a roll of something and came over to where Atal still stood, glaring. The pilgrim gestured for Atal to sit. Atal sat. The man gestured to his broken arm lying in his lap.

"What?" Atal asked. The man raised his eyebrows questioningly, then gently reached for the injured arm. Atal flinched away. The man made a 'tsk-tsk' sound and reached for Atal's arm again, slowly. Atal let him touch it this time, eying him suspiciously. The man nodded and murmured to himself as he examined the injury. He turned to Hila and gestured to the water bucket. Hila brought it over and knelt beside her brother, holding his good hand as she watched the man gently trace the skin bulging over the broken bone. He tore a rolled plaster into strips that he measured against Atal's arm. From the saddle bag he produced linen that he gently wrapped about the forearm. The man dipped the plaster strips in the water, then fashioned them into a gutter-shaped splint along Atal's forearm. Sitting cross-legged in front of Atal, he held the splint in place and grasped Atal's hand firmly. The pilgrim looked into Atal's eyes and winked at him, then firmly pulled on his hand. Atal gave a short scream as the bones set in place. The other man held the splint in place as the plaster hardened, then wrapped the arm with another roll of linen bandage. He stood, dusting plaster from his hands. Atal looked at the splinted arm and moved his fingers gingerly. He smiled thinly, and the man smiled down at him, nodding.

"Thank you," Hila said to the man. He nodded and started to pack up the bedrolls and other things. It was now fully light. Hila helped put things back in the saddle bags, then got more water for the donkey.

"Since you fixed up my arm," Atal told the man when Hila returned, "I have decided not to kill you. Though I should, for taking my little sister. Hila," he said, turning to her, "we'll go home now, little one."

"No," Hila said.

Atal reached to grab her with his good arm but the man stopped him. He put two fingers to his lips and then pointed back towards where their house stood beyond the hills, out of sight. He shook his head. Then the man made the explosion gesture with both hands. Atal gaped at him.

"What do you mean?" Atal asked. At that moment, two yellow streaks appeared in the sky overhead. They all three watched as the fiery trails silently arced down and disappeared beyond the hill. A split second later, they were struck by the roll of a rumbling double explosion. They flinched at the sudden concussion in the earth, then stared in shock as a pillar of dark smoke slowly rose up from beyond the hill.

"Father!" Atal yelled, then ran up the trail back towards the road from which they had come.

"No, brother," Hila called, starting to run after him. The pilgrim grabbed her by the shoulder and held her, shaking his head slowly. She stopped, then sat heavily on the ground and started to cry.

WHY DO I LET BAD THINGS HAPPEN? "WHY DO BAD THINGS HAPPEN TO GOOD PEOPLE?" ISN'T THAT REALLY THE QUESTION? I HEAR THIS ALL THE TIME. WHY, GOD, WHY? WHY ME? WHY MY BABY, MY WIFE, MY CHILD? WHY, WHY, WHY? I WON'T LIE TO YOU—IT'S TIRESOME.

THE ONLY AMUSING PART OF THIS IS LISTENING TO THOSE HUCKSTERS EXPLAIN IT FOR ME. "GOD IS PUNISHING YOU FOR YOUR SINFULNESS!" OR MY FAVORITE, "WE ARE ALL SINNERS FROM BIRTH!" ORIGINAL SIN, WHAT A CONCEPT. THAT AUGUSTINE, SUCH A CARD. PERSONALLY SUCKED THE FUN AWAY FOREVER, SO OF COURSE, THEY HAD TO MAKE HIM A SAINT. YOU'VE ALREADY LOST, BEFORE YOU EVEN KNOW THE RULES OF THE GAME. WHAT A BUNCH OF SELF-SERVING, HYPOCRITICAL CHARLATANS, THE WHOLE LOT OF THEM, FROM DAY ONE TO ETERNITY, I'M TELLING YOU.

SORRY, I DIGRESS. IT IS NOT A PUNISHMENT. NOBODY GETS CANCER BECAUSE EVE ATE SOME MAGIC, FORBIDDEN FRUIT TART. UNLESS YOU'RE ONE OF THOSE LITERALISTS WHO INTERPRET 'FORBIDDEN FRUIT' TO BE SEX, AND THE CANCER YOU'RE REFERRING TO IS CERVICAL CARCINOMA FROM HPV, IN WHICH CASE, YEAH, IT IS PRETTY MUCH CAUSE AND EFFECT THERE. I'M THINKING THAT THAT'S

NOT WHAT YOU'RE REFERRING TO, THOUGH. BUT —BROAD STROKES—LIFE'S UNFAIRNESS IS NOT A PUNISHMENT. BE REASSURED. YOU HAVE NOTHING TO BE FORGIVEN FOR. IF YOU INSIST, I'LL JUST GO AHEAD AND SAY IT ANYWAY: YOU ARE FORGIVEN. BOOM! PRAISE BE! BIG SMILES, HIGH FIVES FOR EVERYBODY. YOU'RE WELCOME, BY THE WAY. GO IN PEACE, SERVE—YOU GET THE IDEA. BUT THE BAD STUFF? STILL GONNA HAPPEN.

New York, NY

Julius stood just inside the door of the Guggenheim museum, watching as scores of young men circulated about, some watching him in turn. He scanned the spiral ramp, not entirely sure what he was looking for. He felt lost.

"Zimmerman!" he heard and looked about, not able to discern who had called his name. "Over hear, Padre," and this time Julius saw who was speaking to him, a black man with close cropped snow white hair, sitting on a bench, waving. Julius slowly walked over, carefully navigating the crowded lobby. "Sit, Julius. You've had a rough morning, from the look of you."

Julius dropped onto the bench next to the old man. They both scanned the upward curving ramp, watching as the throng of Mormons and museum goers moved up and down the graceful spiral. "She's not coming, is she?" the old man asked, still looking upwards. Julius shook his head. "Which are you?"

Julius looked at the man. "What do you mean?" Julius asked.

"You the one I stabbed in the heart? Or the other one?"

Julius raised his shirt to show Uriel the wound on the side of his chest.

"That was you?" Julius asked him.

The other man nodded soberly, then returned to scanning the crowd.

"You don't remember?" the old man asked.

"Not enough to make any sense."

"It'll come back. Still won't make sense, though."

"I don't want it to come back," Julius said.

"Don't nobody care what you want, Padre," Uriel said, smiling wryly. "You've figured that much out, I'm sure."

"Pretty much the only thing," Julius agreed. "Should I know you? Or am I just one of your mugging victims?"

"Wasn't me who did the mugging, Padre. That was God."

"So who are you? His murdering angel?"

"Name's Uriel," Uriel said, extending his hand. "I'm nobody's angel, Julius." Julius shook the man's boney hand.

"What are you then, Uriel?"

"Right now, I'm the only friend you got, Father." Uriel pointed up the ramp to the second spiral turn. "You remember that jackass?" Uriel asked. Julius looked up to where Uriel was pointing.

"Yeah, I remember him. Charles Parnell. What's he doing up there?"

"Trying to kill your old boss."

"Pauley?" Uriel nodded. "Why?"

"Long story," Uriel said. They watched as Father Pauley appeared at the top of the ramp, slowly walking down the spiral towards Parnell.

"Never took Parnell for the killer type," Julius said, watching.

"You got that right," Uriel replied. "Last time I watched this play out, the only one he managed to kill is your girlfriend."

Julius looked at the man, confused and upset. "What the hell are you talking about?"

"It truly does not matter," Uriel said. Julius suddenly swayed forward and nearly toppled from the bench. Uriel caught him by the collar and gently pulled him back upright, steadying him. "You okay there, Padre?"

"I've been better," Julius replied. Julius let his head fall back against the wall and closed his eyes. "Tired."

"When's the last time you got any sleep?" Uriel asked.

"Don't remember sleeping," Julius answered.

"You have any idea what's happened to you, Julius?" Julius shook his head slightly, eyes still closed. "You just rest for now, Zimmerman," Uriel said soothingly. "You'll learn soon enough, my friend."

Uriel turned to the sound of a commotion from the entrance. A man burst through the doors running, knocking aside several young white-shirted patrons. He skittered to a stop in the middle of the rotunda, breathing hard as he scanned the crowded museum.

"Here we go, Zimmerman," Uriel said softly. Then more loudly, "Zimmerman!"

"I'm sitting right next to you, Uriel. No need to shout —Holy shit!" Zimmerman whispered, opening his eyes and staring at the man in the middle of the lobby. He was looking at a man identical to himself. His other self stood breathless in the lobby and turned to his name.

"Over here, Father," Uriel said loudly, and the other *Zimmerman* slowly approached them through the crowd, now oblivious to the men who perfunctorily brushed by him, his eyes fixed on the man sitting next to Uriel. He stopped in front of them. *Zimmerman* looked down into the eyes of Zimmerman staring up at him. "You both look like hell," Uriel said. "We need to get out of here."

"Grace," the newly arrived *Zimmerman* managed to say between panting breaths, starting to scan the crowd again.

"She's not here," Uriel said.

"But I've got to—"

"She's not coming!" the sitting Zimmerman said bitterly. The other *Zimmerman* turned back to look down on him, his look questioning. "She's not coming back," Zimmerman repeated. "Get over it."

Helmand Province, Afghanistan

As Hila cried, the pilgrim set about packing. When he had finished loading the saddlebags back on the donkey, he came and sat next to Hila. Hila sniffled and wiped tears from her face with the back of each arm, sitting up straight.

"I am coming with you," she said. He inclined his head, the way he had done the night before. She stood. "Let's go, then," she said. The man smiled and gestured for her to sit back down. "Why?" she asked. "We should go. We should go before the Americans shoot a missile at us, pilgrim. Oh, shit," Hila added, looking at the small fire still smoldering from their tea. She quickly set about kicking sand into it until the thin strand of smoke stopped rising.

"We need to be moving," Hila said, coming back to where the pilgrim sat. "Where are we going?" The man gestured for her to sit. His two hands settled, palm down; be calm, he signed. Hila shook her head at him. "You want to sit here and be killed, like them?" she said, gesturing angrily towards the column of black smoke still rising over the hill. "What do you want to wait for?" The man said nothing, staring up at her with a sad smile. "You think he's coming back? My brother? Fuck him, I say. He can go pick through the rubble and think about what he has done to our family." She stared down at the man, tears starting to roll down her cheeks again. "Fuck him, I tell you. And damn the rest of them to Hell. They were going to give me to those *mujahedin*, those animals. Did you know that that's all I am worth, to be chattel to settle a debt? This is what a woman is good for, as valuable as a fast horse, if I'm lucky. And when those scum are done riding me, what then, eh? Will they sell me across the border, trade me for gas for their truck or bullets for their guns? Or just fuck my brains out until I'm dead? You don't think my big brother, my father, my whole fucking family knew what was to become of their little girl? My whole dead, fucking family? My family..." she trailed off, sobbing, falling to her knees in the dirt before the man. The man reached out and cradled her, still crying, as he rocked her as he would his own child.

After a while, Hila sniffled and wiped her face against him, as she held tightly to the man. "I don't want to wait for him, pilgrim. I don't care that he's all I have left of my family. I want to go." She felt him shake his head as she kept her head on his shoulder, still sniffling. "I want to go. I don't want to see him again." The man shook his head. "I won't ever, ever forgive him." The man hugged her tightly and nodded. Maybe, she thought, maybe, with time, he may be right.

Hila straightened up in the man's arms and looked into his strange, green eyes. "You won't let him sell me away again, will you?" The man smiled warmly at her and shook his head. "Okay, then. If you think we should, we'll wait." At that, she moved away from him. She busied herself with washing up in the small creek and, when there was nothing else to do, took the bucket to get more water for the donkey. They waited, quietly, as the sun climbed in the sky.

Hours later, they saw Atal come shuffling back up the path. His head down, shoulders bowed, he didn't even see them until he was almost upon them. He stopped and stared at them, hollow-eyed, cradling his splinted arm to his chest. He was crying, Hila saw. The man gestured for Atal to sit beside him. Atal came over and sat.

"They are all dead, sister." Hila sat next to her brother and put her arm around his shoulder as he cried. Hila didn't cry anymore.

Over the Indian Ocean

Arthur and Gabriel managed to stop Sam's screaming. Actually, it was mostly Gabriel's doing, as Arthur was incapable of little more than stammering incoherently. Gabriel did manage to calm Samantha down before the other passengers and the flight attendant became too involved.

"It's nothing," Gabriel reassured the concerned onlookers. "She just got an email—her Mom won the lottery." Gabriel stood in the aisle of first class, leaning over Arthur (still stammering) to put a hand on Sam's shoulder. "It's okay, Sam," he murmured in her ear.

Sam stared at him, then at his hand on her shoulder.

"The fuck it is!" Sam said, still looking at his hand so she didn't have to look at his face. "What in hell's name are you doing here, Gabriel?" She took his hand off her shoulder and leaned into him. "You're dead," she hissed.

Gabriel straightened up and shrugged, a sheepish grin on his face. Arthur had managed to stop stammering and now just looked at Gabriel, mouth agape. "I got better," Gabriel said, smiling. The other two stared at him. "How about a drink?" Gabriel asked jauntily. "Follow me."

"Hell, yes," Arthur managed to say. He stood to follow Gabriel but stopped and turned to his wife. "You coming?"

"Hell, yes," Sam said. "It better be a damn stiff one, Arthur."

The two of them followed Gabriel to the galley in the front of the cabin. Gabriel smiled at the busy flight attendant. "Could we get three glasses of scotch?" he asked the attendant amiably.

"I can bring them to your seats," she offered.

"If you don't mind, we'd like to just stand and stretch our legs for a bit," Gabriel said. He looked at his two shaken companions as Arthur and Sam joined him. "Better make theirs doubles," Gabriel added.

"What the hell is going on?" Arthur asked, after downing half his drink in one gulp.

Samantha drank hers off entirely before saying, "We're dead, Arthur. I told you not to push that damn button."

Gabriel shook his head vigorously, looking over nervously at the flight attendant. She wasn't listening. "You're not dead, Sam," Gabriel said.

"Oh, shit, Sam," Arthur said. "You're right. I am so sorry. I should've—"

"You damn well, 'should've.' Nice going, dumbshit. Why don't you ever listen, Artie? Huh? Now we're goddamn dead."

"You're not dead," Gabriel insisted. He looked nervously again at the attendant. She still wasn't listening.

Sam and Arthur stared at Gabriel, waiting. Gabriel smiled at them nervously. "I'll explain," Gabriel said.

"Oh, good, Gabe," Sam said.

"Yeah, Gabe," Arthur agreed. "That'd be great."

They waited for Gabriel to speak. Gabriel watched the flight attendant, who was putting together a tray of drinks. The other two stared at Gabriel. "You're going to have to trust me for a little bit," Gabriel said.

"Like when we trusted you and got on this doomed plane?" Sam said acidly. The attendant looked over as she picked up her tray and moved past them to the aisle.

Gabe gave her a smile, waiting for her to pass. "Quiet, Sam. It's not doomed. Just—displaced."

"What the hell does that mean?" Arthur said.

"It means we're fucked, Artie," Sam said. "I told you we shouldn't take plane tickets from a dead guy. I told you."

"Just give me a minute, okay, guys?" Gabriel said. He turned to the control panel by the door behind him and twisted a switch.

"What are you doing?" Arthur asked.

"Disarming the slide," Gabriel said. "This way, guys." Gabe pulled down the latching lever on the door.

"Gabe, I don't think you're supposed to do that," Arthur said.

Gabriel pushed the door open and stepped out into the black void.

"Holy shit," Samantha said.

"Gabe?" Arthur asked.

Gabriel poked his head back in the doorway. "Come on,

you two. Quick, before the stewardess comes back." He reached in and took Samantha's hand, helping her step over the doorway.

"They're called flight attendants, Gabe."

"LIFE MUST BE UNFAIR BECAUSE MAN HAS FREE WILL." WRONG! LOVE THE CONCEPT, THOUGH. AGAIN, IT PUTS ALL THE BLAME ON YOU GUYS. "GOD GAVE MAN THE WILL TO MAKE MISTAKES, AND EVIL ENTERED THE WORLD." WHY WOULD I DO THAT? EVERYBODY'S PRETTY VAGUE ON MOTIVE. BECAUSE IT'S NOT TRUE.

WHEN DID IT BECOME OKAY TO SAY GOD IS AN ASSHOLE, BY THE WAY?

I DON'T RECALL EVEN SAYING THERE IS OR ISN'T FREE WILL. IT'S A DIFFICULT CONCEPT. I MEAN, DO FOLKS REALLY BELIEVE THAT EVERYONE IS JUST RIDING THE RAILS DOWN THERE? JUST GOING THROUGH THE MOTIONS? IS THAT WHAT YOU THINK? IT DOES TAKE AWAY A CERTAIN AMOUNT OF RESPONSIBILITY, DOESN'T IT? LIKE, ALL OF IT. BAD THINGS HAPPEN? KARMA, BABY. BUT, NO. NOT THAT EASY, MY PEOPLE OF EARTH. TAKE SOME RESPONSIBILITY. BE A MENCH. SO LET ME JUST SET THIS STRAIGHT RIGHT NOW, ONCE AND FOREVER: YOU HAVE FREE WILL. EVERYBODY HAS FREE WILL.

WELL, I'M SURE GLAD WE FINALLY GOT THAT SETTLED. AREN'T YOU?

New York, NY

"Who's not coming back?" Grace asked, appearing behind them.

"Oh, shit!" Uriel said, swiveling around to look at her.

"Grace!" Zimmerman and *Zimmerman* said simultaneously.

"Hi, guys. Get used to what? Who's not coming back?" Grace asked again. Then she noticed the two Zimmermans standing in front of her. She whistled softly and whispered, "Well, fuck me sideways."

Uriel shook his head and spat in disgust. "Yeah, girl. There's about three hundred guys up there," he said, jerking a thumb behind him towards the ramp, "who'd like to do just that. Your husband said you were stubborn, not crazy stupid. Shit." He spat again.

Grace kept looking between the two Zimmermans before her.

"Grace, you can't—" Zimmerman started to say.

"Grace, I didn't—" the other *Zimmerman* said, cutting him off.

"Shut up, both of you," Uriel interjected. He turned to stand in front of Grace. "I have no words, girl. No words can express how fucking amazed I am to see you standing here."

"Really?" Grace asked.

"What are you wearing?" *Zimmerman* asked.

"Oh, this?" Grace asked, holding out the sides of the large plastic garbage bag she was wearing in a mock curtsey. "Just something I found in the janitor's closet back there. Fifty-five gallons of fun, that's me."

"Shut up, all of you," Uriel said. "You think this is funny, girl? Is that what you think? After what I've been going through for your sorry ass? After what this poor clown went through to get you back into existence yet another fuckin' time? You think this is some kind of joke?"

"What poor clown?" Grace asked.

"That one," Uriel said, gesturing toward *Zimmerman.* "No, not that one. The other one. The one that looks like shit. Yeah, him."

"I don't know what you're talking about, Earl," Grace said.

"You don't know what I'm talking about?" Uriel said, his voice rising in incredulity. "What in sodding slugfuck are you doing here? That's what I'm talking about!"

"What do you mean, 'another fucking time?'" *Zimmerman* asked.

"I'm here to kill that son of a bitch," Grace said, pointing to where Pauley stood at the top of the ramp.

"You *can't* kill that son of a bitch," Uriel said. "You can't kill him, because he's going to kill you—again—if you keep standing here. Not just kill, either. Excise you the fuck out of existence. Now get your stupid self out of here before it happens again." Uriel turned to look up the ramp. He saw Pauley and Parnell now looking at them from the top of the ramp. Parnell waved. "Oh, *Hell* no," Uriel said.

Grace stared at Pauley, who had started down the ramp, pushing Parnell aside as he came. "I've been here before?" Grace asked.

"Yeah, you been here before, girl," Uriel said. "And guess what happened the last time around, girlfriend. Take a guess."

"Tell me," Grace said, still watching as Pauley descended the spiral ramp towards them.

"Last time, you went charging up that ramp to kill that sorry son of a bitch. And you ended up getting your skinny little ass excised out of existence."

"Did I kill him?"

"Yeah. Big fucking deal," Uriel spat again.

"But not this time?"

"No," Uriel said. "Not this time. This time, you got away. Or so I thought."

"What changed?" Grace asked. "Why did I go to the dealership instead?"

"God only knows," Uriel said. "Something to do with him going back, I think," Uriel said, pointing at Zimmerman. "Maybe someone finally kicked you in the ass. Same whatever that got this yo-yo," Uriel gestured at *Zimmerman*, "to show up this time around. Haven't quite figured that out yet. But in about two minutes, not going to matter anyhow, unless you get the hell out of here."

Grace stole a glance at Zimmerman, who was silently staring at her. She gave him a sad smile. "Thanks, Julius. Sorry I hurt your nose." Zimmerman smiled at her.

"Second time," Zimmerman said.

Zimmerman started to say something, then thought better of it. Grace turned back to Uriel as Pauley reached the bottom of the ramp. "Okay, Earl. I'm going to go back. Gabe said this was a mistake."

"Why don't you ever listen to that man?" Uriel asked.

"He always says it's a mistake, Earl," Grace said. "But I had to come back, make sure my Julius was okay." She smiled at Zimmerman. "Sorry, we kinda ditched you in the closet back there, hon. Hope you're feeling better." Grace stole another glance up the ramp at Pauley. "This looks like a problem, though. I can see that now."

"You think?" Uriel asked.

"What's going to happen?" *Zimmerman* asked.

"Nothing, if she gets out of here," Uriel said.

"This isn't over," Grace said, watching Pauley as he approached.

"It will be," Uriel said, moving to put himself between Grace and the approaching priest, "if you stick around and let that son of a bitch touch you out of existence. Again."

Grace hesitated as Pauley came to a halt before them, smiling.

"Hello, Grace," Pauley said. "Good to see you, child."

CHAPTER 3

Helmand Province, Afghanistan

Hila and Atal followed the pilgrim as he led the donkey along the track that followed the stream. The path cut through a narrow defile and twisted sharply, steep cliffs rising on either side as the trail led steadily upward. They walked all day, pausing occasionally to take water and jerky along the stream. They walked up, steadily up, as the pass climbed the mountains. Looking back, Hila could see the valley they had left, the valley where she had lived her entire life, shadows from the mountains spreading beneath them. She tried to pick out their farm, to see the smoke pillar that would mark what was left of her home.

"Come on, Hila, look!" her brother called to her from up ahead. Hila caught up to where Atal and the pilgrim stood on the trail, looking ahead. From where they stood, Hila could see the trail drop down into a green valley ahead, a new valley on the other side of the ridge line from where they had climbed. The sun was a flattened sphere, golden red, just above the horizon before them, and she could pick out lights and fires from a village below them. Her breath caught as she looked down on the idyllic scene. Hila turned to the strange man and asked, "Is that your village? Is that your home?" The man nodded, smiling, and took up the donkey's lead, starting down the series of switchbacks that led down the face of the mountain.

As they descended the mountain, Hila kept staring down at the little village. Something was so strange that she nearly stumbled off the path several times until she finally figured out what it was. She realized that this valley had no poppy fields at all, only scant fields of some other crop; wheat, or barley, maybe, she couldn't tell. But no poppies. How could such a community exist, she wondered, as they climbed down and made the last turn on the dirt path.

They reached the floor of the valley and walked the remaining way to the village. This valley, she saw, was ringed on all sides with steep mountains, completely cut off save the narrow slot canyons where the small river entered and left. Sunset had come as they entered the village, soft candlelight appearing in the windows of the huts along the main road. The pilgrim walked beside her and hummed softly, obviously relieved to be home.

As they approached the main street, Hila saw dozens of people hurrying about, rushing home to and fro in anticipation of the evening meal. A murmur quickly arose as several villagers noticed them approaching,. The bustling came to a halt as everyone turned to watch their approach. Ahead, she could see doors opening and people coming out of their homes all along the road. They all stood at the sides of the road, apparently waiting for them. Atal looked at his sister nervously.

"What's this?" he asked her. "Maybe they don't like strangers here so much, little sister."

Hila stared ahead and shook her head. Now closer, she could see the faces of the nearest villagers. They certainly looked friendly enough. Actually, she thought, they seemed more welcoming than she would have expected in her own village. They looked almost eager, smiling as they approached. And then, as they came up to the first of the villagers, the men and women on either side of the dusty road dropped to their knees. Each murmured a quiet, "Bless me" as the pilgrim, still leading the donkey, came abreast of them. He touched some on the head, smiling but saying nothing, and as he approached many villagers pressed their foreheads to the ground, only rising once he had passed. Hila and Atal watched the pageant with amazement, but said nothing as they walked along in the man's wake.

They followed the pilgrim to a path that led to a modest hut at the far end of the road. A young boy, smiling, took the donkey's lead and the pilgrim squeezed the boy's shoulder in thanks. The boy beamed at them and led the donkey away. As the pilgrim walked up to the door of the hut, a man approached Hila and Atal.

"Hello," the man said to them. "I am Hamid. Welcome." The man shook Atal's hand with his left hand over his heart. He smiled at Hila. "Please, come."

They followed Hamid to his home back up the road. He introduced them to his wife and proudly showed off his six month old son in his cradle. Then he led Hila and Atal to their rooms at the back of the small house. "Welcome to our home," the man said, and then withdrew to let them clean up for the evening meal.

Over the Indian Ocean/Quantum Indeterminate State

Arthur and Sam watched as Gabriel carefully closed the door to the aircraft behind them. "There," he said, turning back to them with a smile, "that's better."

They looked about. They were standing outside the aircraft. It was dark—not completely dark, their surroundings a featureless soft gloom. Light spilled from the plane's windows, but fell on nothing. They seemed to be standing on a soft floor of some type, but it was lost in the same gloom that surrounded them. Above them, only gloom. No stars, no moon.

"Pretty gloomy," Gabriel said, shrugging.

Arthur tried to reason with Gabriel. "Gabe, aren't we supposed to be going at, I don't know, about 600 miles per hour or something? At something like 32,000 feet, I think the pilot said?" Arthur thought it should at least be windy, even if it wasn't a hundred degrees below zero with no oxygen to breathe. There was no wind at all. Just a general gloom.

"Yeah, weird, isn't it?" was Gabriel's jaunty reply. "Follow me guys."

"Weird? That's all you're going to say about us standing outside a plane flying at 32,000 feet?" Samantha asked in a voice tinged with a frisson of hysteria.

Gabriel shrugged and led them away from the plane. The gloom deepened for a bit as they walked, then grew brighter as they seemed to turn an invisible corner of some kind. A few yards ahead, light spilled from an open door. As they approached, they saw that the door led to a brightly lit room. They stepped inside and stood, looking around. It was a sort of parlor or hotel sitting room, the furniture in Louis XIV style but obviously not originals. Poor copies, at best. White light suffused from both the ceiling and the floor.

"Hold it," Sam said. "What the fuck, Gabe? What is this, Gabriel, a sick joke?"

"What do you mean, Sam?" Gabe asked, taking a seat at the small table and indicating that the others should do the same. Arthur sat, still looking about.

Sam remained standing, arms crossed. "This place, Gabe. I'm not an idiot. I've seen '2001' like a dozen times, you know."

Gabriel grinned at her sheepishly.

"You have?" her husband asked.

"I have."

"Sit down, Sam," Gabe said. "Sorry, I didn't think you'd ever seen it. Arthur hates sci-fi, even classic sci-fi."

"Yeah, well, I was actually alive for quite a while before I married him, as a matter of fact."

"Yeah, of course you were. It's just that, well, it's one of my favorite movies, you know. Seemed fitting, that's all."

"Why is a scene from '2001' fitting, Gabe?" Arthur asked.

"Because we're dead," Samantha said.

"No," Gabriel said. "You're not dead, guys."

"You're dead," Sam said.

"True. Technically, I was dead. Not as dead at the moment," Gabriel said. They both stared at him.

"We are so fucked." Samantha sat down. "Start talking, Gabe."

Gabriel took a deep breath and drummed his fingertips on the white plastic table top before him. "Right. So how much do you guys know about quantum mechanics?"

Arthur said, "Oh, you know, Gabriel, the usual. Not a damn thing. What the hell are you talking about?"

"Yeah, I was afraid of that," Gabriel said. "Not my particular area of expertise, either, of course. But I've done some reading, and I'll try to explain—"

"You're going to tell us that we're in some sort of indeterminate state, is that it?" Sam asked.

Arthur gaped at her.

"Exactly, Sam," Gabriel said with relief. "You know something about—"

"Yeah, yeah. I'm not just pretty, you know. I do know a bit about a few things. Like quantum mechanics, for instance," Sam said.

"How?" Arthur asked.

"I read, dear. While you're watching football, you may have noticed me holding a book now and then." Arthur still looked flabbergasted. Sam rolled her eyes at him. "Or maybe not." She turned to Gabriel. "We're in a Schrödinger box of some sort, is that it?" Gabriel nodded. "Was it the device? The one my stupid husband pushed the button on, even though I told him not to?"

"You don't know that," Arthur said defensively.

Gabriel nodded. "Exactly, Sam. The conditions were perfect. You're in an airplane over the Indian Ocean, in the dark, thousands of miles from anywhere. Not even within radar coverage. When Arthur activated the EMP device, it fried—"

"EMP?" Arthur asked.

"Electromagnetic pulse," Sam answered. "Quit interrupting, hon."

"The device fried the plane's transponders, its radios, everyone's cellphones."

"Complete isolation from outside observers," Sam said.

"Complete and total isolation from the outside world," Gabriel agreed.

"A perfect Schrödinger box," Sam said, amazed. "With us inside."

"With you inside."

"Whatch-a-ma-jigger box are you two talking about?" Arthur asked.

"A Schrödinger box, dear," Sam explained, not entirely patiently. "In quantum theory, unobserved particles, like photons, can exist in two distinct states simultaneously. It's called quantum indeterminism. Schrödinger was a mathematician who came up with the basic formula for quantum mathematics, the Schrödinger wave equation."

"He's on your plane, by the way," Gabriel said, interrupting. "And Gödel." They both looked at Gabriel for a moment, then Sam continued.

"Anyways, Schrödinger proposed a thought experiment. Consider a box, with a cat inside. There's a mechanism attached to a light sensor. If a certain polarity of light hits the sensor, the mechanism trips a poison gas dispenser and the cat dies. But light of the opposite polarity doesn't activate the mechanism, so the cat lives."

"So?" Arthur said. "Dead cat experiment. Not impressed."

"The quantum part is this: Until an outside observer looks into the box, the cat's state is indeterminate. As long as there is no outside interference, the cat is both dead and not dead."

"You mean, alive?" Arthur asked. Samantha shook her head. Gabriel nodded. Arthur looked between them, confused. "You mean, the cat is both dead and alive at the same time?"

"Exactly. Quantum indeterminism. Dual state paradox," Gabriel said.

"So we're not dead, because we're in this guy's box," Arthur said, dubiously.

"Yeah, hon. But we're not exactly alive anymore, either," Samantha added.

I WILL NOW EXPLAIN WHY BAD THINGS HAPPEN TO GOOD PEOPLE. READY? GOT A PEN AND SOME PAPER? HERE WE GO, THEN:
BECAUSE WHILE YOU'RE LIVING UNDER MY ROOF, YOU'LL LIVE BY MY RULES.
BECAUSE I'LL GIVE YOU SOMETHING TO CRY ABOUT, YOUNG LADY!
BECAUSE I SAID SO, THAT'S WHY.
JUST KIDDING. THAT'S NOT THE REASON.

New York, NY

"Hello, Grace," Pauley said. "Good to see you, child."

Zimmerman stood with Uriel between Grace and Pauley. Parnell came down from the ramp to join them. "Nice garbage bag," Parnell said. Parnell noticed Zimmerman sitting on the bench, slumped against the wall. He looked back at *Zimmerman*. "Weird," Parnell said.

"I believe," Pauley said, "that this is where you say, 'I'm going to kill you, Donovan,' or some such." He spread his arms, waiting. "I am ready to pay for the pain I have caused you, child. I am ready to die at your hand."

Grace looked at him with contempt. "I killed you once, Donovan. Doesn't look like I accomplished much. I doubt a second time will do any better."

Pauley's smile vanished as he dropped his arms to his sides. "It is why you are here, child. No other reason."

"That's why she's gonna leave now," Uriel said. He looked over his shoulder at Grace. "Isn't that what you're going to do now, girl? Just gonna walk away."

Grace stood, arms crossed. "You came back, too, Donovan. For me. To get me excised. Why? Who sent you?"

"'The work of God is this: To believe in the one he has sent,'" Donovan replied.

"You think you're Jesus?" *Zimmerman* asked, reddening.

"I didn't say that," Pauley replied.

"You think you were sent by God?" Grace asked. "For me?"

"I do," Pauley said, reddening. "I believe it was Him who sent me, yes."

"The devil more likely," *Zimmerman* muttered.

"'Who are you to judge someone else's servant? To their own master, servants stand or fall. And they will stand, for the Lord is able to make them stand.'" Zimmerman muttered from where he sat on the bench.

Grace frowned down at Zimmerman, then stared at the old priest. "Everybody thinks they're doing God's work, don't they, Donovan?"

"My faith is sound," Donovan replied. "I serve the Lord."

"I don't believe you," Grace insisted.

"The Bible tells us," Donovan explained. "'He removes some of them and destroys them, and erases the memory of them from the earth.'"

"Actually, girl," Uriel said, "he's probably right. But that doesn't make it okay." Uriel pointed to the banner that hung over the ticket desk. Grace turned to look. It read, "The Fall from Grace: the Art of The Inferno."

Grace's shoulders slumped. "Weirdest fucking museum," she muttered. She straightened and turned on Donovan.

"Why, Donovan? If it was God who sent you to kill me, why?"

"Not kill you, child," Pauley said. "Excision is not killing."

"Why?" Grace asked again. "What makes me so important?"

Pauley shrugged.

"You don't know why you're doing this?" Zimmerman

asked.

"I do not question the wisdom of our Lord, for I am only a tool in his hand," Pauley said.

"Especially when His work restores your hand," Parnell said. "What a tool."

"'He is the rock, his works are perfect, and all his ways are just. A faithful God who does no wrong, upright and just is he,'" Zimmerman said.

"Where'd you find this guy?" Parnell asked, nodding down at Zimmerman, still slumped on the bench.

"Go!" Uriel said again. "Before this sonofabitch tries something. Just go back now, Grace."

"She can't," Pauley said. "That way is closed."

"What?" Zimmerman asked. "The gate—"

"Is closed," Pauley said.

"You're lying," *Zimmerman* said. "Go, Grace. Uriel is right. Go now."

Grace retreated back down the hallway which held the janitor's closet that served as the gateway she had used upon her arrival. She returned minutes later.

"How?" she asked Pauley.

"The Lord is powerful," Pauley said.

"Kill him, Uriel," *Zimmerman* said. "Kill him now."

"The Lord is powerful," Pauley repeated, "and his servants plentiful."

"What are you talking about, Pauley?" *Zimmerman* asked. "What servants?"

"Killing me serves nothing," Pauley said. "The Lord does not lack for servants."

They each looked about them at the hundreds of people still milling about the museum. Many were young men, white shirted missionaries; many, but almost as many were not.

"Oh, shit," Parnell said. "We're fucked."

Uriel twitched, blinked, then shook his head. He turned to Grace. "The gates are all down. Nonexistent. Time for plan B."

"What's plan B?" *Zimmerman* asked.

Grace looked down at Zimmerman, putting a hand on Julius's shoulder. "Whatever it was I did, Donovan," Grace said. "Whatever the trespass, I won't do it anymore. Tell Him. Go tell your God I promise not to do whatever it was I did. I want this all to stop. We want to go home. He needs to go home," she said, nodding down to Julius.

"It doesn't work that way, child," Pauley said. He raised his hand and twirled his only index finger in a circle above his head. From about the museum, men started to move toward them.

"I haven't done anything, Donovan. I won't do anything. I promise. I promise you—and Him. Just let me go back to my family. Let Julius come home. Please."

Pauley shook his head.

Uriel looked about anxiously, seeing the approaching threat, men surging down the circular ramps from all directions like a tide. "Time for a backup plan, Grace! Any plan gonna do."

"Please," Grace said again. Pauley moved forward, reaching for her. A knife, flat black and silver-edged, appeared in Uriel's hand, the tip pricking at Pauley's neck.

"Come on, Father," Uriel said. "Try harder." He looked back at Grace.

Grace slumped, dejected. She shook her head, saying nothing.

"Come on, Grace!" Uriel urged. He looked about at the men closing in from all over the spiral museum. "Don't care if the plan is B or fuck-all, but this place is starting to look like a goddamn roach trap."

Grace looked at Parnell. "It's your time, Chuck," Grace sighed. Parnell looked at her, eyebrows raised.

"You sure?" Parnell asked. Grace shrugged.

"Do something then, Parnell," *Zimmerman* said. "This is quickly turning to shit." He watched a dozen men approaching from the other side of the lobby.

Grace bent and took Zimmerman's face in her hands. "Chicago, Julius. Find me in Chicago, in three days."

Zimmerman looked up at her, eyes glassy. "What?" he asked her.

"Chicago."

"Where in Chicago?" Uriel asked.

"He knows," Grace said, looking down at Zimmerman. Zimmerman looked lost. She sighed. "Or that one," she said, indicating the other *Zimmerman*. "Three days."

The men Pauley had signaled were close now, crossing the lobby.

"In about one minute, it won't matter," *Zimmerman* said. "Parnell, click your heels or something, man. Whatever you're going to do, do it now!"

Parnell climbed up to stand on the short wall behind the bench. He cupped his hands to his mouth and shouted, "OH LORD, MY GOD!" at the top of his lungs. He then raised both arms, bent at right angles at the elbows. Parnell looked like he was imitating a goalpost. He rotated his arms down, then up again, twice. Immediately, white shirted young men from all over the museum broke into a run, rushing to his aid. Parnell jumped down off the wall and grabbed Grace in a bear hug as scores of missionary youth surrounded them, pushing and shoving Pauley and the others aside as more and more of the LDS faithful joined their group. Within minutes, Grace and Parnell were born away through the lobby and out onto the street, surrounded and protected by a human hive of LDS missionaries.

New York, NY

Zimmerman and Uriel watched as Grace and Parnell, engulfed amoeba-like in the throng of missionaries, were propelled out of the museum and onto the street outside.

"Fuck-all," Uriel said, the knife disappearing up his sleeve with a flick of his wrist. "Fuck-*all*."

Zimmerman scowled at Pauley, but Pauley looked back and forth in amazement between the identical men, wondering at Zimmerman still slumped on the bench, eyes closed, his brow covered in sweat.

"How is such a thing possible?" Pauley asked, looking up at the others.

"Not your problem, Pauley," Uriel said. "Just get out."

Zimmerman grabbed Pauley's arm as he turned. "No," *Zimmerman* said. "He stays with us."

"No chance," Uriel said. "I'm sick of him. Just run the asshole out of here."

"So he can trail along behind Grace, try attacking her on the street or wherever that crew is dragging her off to?" *Zimmerman* asked. "Best to keep him with us, I think."

"Simpler just to slit his throat," Uriel said.

Zimmerman looked about the still crowded lobby. "Not very practical, I'm afraid."

"Fuck-all!" Uriel said again. He dropped onto the bench beside Zimmerman. Pauley shrugged. *Zimmerman* gave him a shove and the old priest sat heavily on the bench on the other side of Zimmerman.

"Chicago, then," Pauley said after a bit.

"What?" *Zimmerman* asked.

"If I'm not to be allowed to follow the girl, then we're going to Chicago. You heard her. In three days, she said."

"As if we're taking you along to Chicago," *Zimmerman* chortled.

"As if you three have any way to get to Chicago," Pauley said. "I'm going to Chicago. If you want to keep an eye on me, you can join me. Unless you're planning on stealing a car."

"You're right, Uriel," *Zimmerman* said. "Just kill him."

Uriel raised his eyebrows at that. "Actually, *Julius*," Uriel said, considering the knife that had reappeared in his hand, "Father Fuck-all here has a point. My funding walked out the door with that mob of Mormons. Unless you got a better day job than this *schlub*," Uriel gestured at Zimmerman, "I doubt we have much in the way of resources."

Pauley looked at the other Zimmerman still slumped next to him on the bench. "What happened to your ring?"

"Threw it in the Potomac," Zimmerman answered, eyes still barely open.

Zimmerman looked at his double, considering. "Fine," *Zimmerman* said after a moment's consideration. "You can always kill him later. How are we getting to Chicago, Pauley?"

Pauley stood. "I'll make a call to the diocese. Be right back." He walked away toward the coat room.

New York, NY

Grace and Parnell found themselves on the sidewalk outside the museum, surrounded by dozens of white-shirted missionaries. They seemed to all be talking at once.

"We got her," one enthused loudly, pumping a fist.

"Shut up," another said. This one turned to Parnell. "Who are you? How do you know the distress signal?"

"I am Dr. Charles Parnell, elder of our church and President of the Council of the Seventy. Who are you, child?"

The younger man blanched. "I'm sorry, Elder," the young man said. "I should've realized it was you. We were told to look out for you as well. My name is Simon, Simon Ellicott."

"Well met, Simon. Are you in charge?" Parnell asked.

"Guess so," Simon said, shrugging. "As much as anybody is."

"What is your intention then?" Parnell asked the man. "We can't just stand here blocking the sidewalk."

"Our instructions are to bring the girl to the Temple, Elder. Actually, we were told to escort you to the Temple as well, if we found you."

"Very well, then. Is it far?"

"No, about a twenty minute walk or so. It's just across the park, on the west side, at Sixty-fifth and Columbus."

"I'm not familiar with this city," Parnell said. "You lead on, child."

"The child isn't leading anyone on, *Doctor* Elder Parnell," Grace said. "I'm not walking crosstown to your temple wearing a garbage bag. I'm not wearing any underwear, *Doctor*," she said. Grace flipped up the back of the bag she was wearing to expose her bare buttocks. "See?"

Every one of the missionaries blushed brightly. Parnell hurriedly pulled the hem of the plastic garbage bag down. "Stop that," he stage whispered.

"Thought you liked looking at my ass, Chuck," Grace whispered back, winking at him. Parnell blushed. "We're going shopping," Grace announced to the group.

All eyes turned to Simon, who looked at Parnell.

"Fine," Parnell said. "It would be improper to allow the woman to enter the Temple in such a state. We'll get her some clothes. Then straight to the Temple. Simon, take us to a suitable women's apparel shop. The closest one, please."

Simon hunched, brow furrowed in deep consideration for a minute, then brightened. "This way," he said, turning to lead the group eastward toward Park Avenue. The gaggle of young men strung out as they all marched down the sidewalk, Parnell walking next to Grace.

"I know what you're planning, Helena," Parnell said.

"It's Grace now, Chuck. Always was, actually."

"Whatever," Parnell said. "Told Gabriel a dozen times you weren't anyone you pretended to be. Whatever. But I know what you're up to."

"Great. Glad to hear it."

"I'm telling you, don't. Just don't."

"Whatever," Grace mused as they walked down the sidewalk.

"I'm serious, Hel—Grace. At least you're safe with us. The LDS Church will protect you."

Grace snorted at that.

"I'm not joking. Do you have any idea what Pauley was

about to do to you? Any idea?"

"Yeah, Chuck. A pretty good idea."

Parnell explained the Catholic Church's plan to have her excised, and what exactly was meant by excision. Grace stopped dead in the middle of the sidewalk. Several of the missionaries bumped into each other behind her.

"You have got to be shitting me!" Grace said, turning red with anger as she stared hard at Parnell.

Parnell took her arm and started her walking again. "No, I'm not 'shitting you.' And you think the Church is about to stop just because Pauley missed his chance in the museum? No way. They'll come after you again."

"I can handle that old goat," Grace said, regaining her composure.

"What makes you think he's the only one? There are probably a dozen Father Pauley's out there, maybe a lot more. Look around us, Grace. There's scores of kids here, all looking for you. That's just right here, right at this moment. How many more, do you think?"

Grace shook her head, distraught. "Why the fuck is every damn religious lunatic after my ass?" Grace asked.

"Maybe because you have such a great ass," Parnell said, smiling. "Ow!" Parnell yelled as Grace elbowed him in the ribs. They had arrived in front of a woman's clothing boutique. Simon was in the process of positioning his missionaries strategically about the store's entrance. "I'm not kidding, Grace," Parnell said. "Don't do anything stupid. Just stay with me. I've got influence with the Church. The Church can protect you."

Grace appeared to consider this. "Thanks, Chuck," she said. "That's sweet of you." Grace stepped in front of Simon. "Credit card," she demanded. Simon hesitated. She stared at him, palm out. He took out his wallet and fumbled over a credit card. Grace spun on her bare feet and entered the store. She sought out a young saleswoman.

Once engaged, she informed the saleslady of her sizes

and her need for underwear, jeans, shirts, a pair of dress slacks, socks, shoes. Enough for three complete outfits. And pajamas, something modest.

When Grace and the saleswoman had gathered a suitable pile of choices, they retired together to the dressing room area in the back of the store. Grace put on an outfit with jeans and practical, flat-soled shoes, suitable for running. She stepped out of the dressing room to look at herself in the mirror.

The saleswoman approached, smiling. "Looks great," the saleslady said.

"Yeah, great. Listen, honey, we have to talk," Grace said, pulling the saleslady deeper into the dressing area. "You gotta help me," Grace said softly. She looked plaintively at the other woman.

"What do you mean?" the saleslady asked, confused.

"Those men," Grace said. "They're holding me, against my will. They're keeping me in the basement of some kind of cult church. I'm a prisoner."

"But, ma'am," the woman stammered. "They seem nice enough."

"What is wrong with you?" Grace demanded. "I came in here wearing a garbage bag! I was naked!" Grace gestured to the garbage bag on the floor of the dressing room. "Call the police, please," Grace begged. "Is there another way out of the store?"

The saleslady nodded. "Back door down the hall, there," she said, pointing. "But—"

"Call the police, please. I'll be out back, hiding until the police come. Just pretend I'm still in the dressing room if any of those sick bastards comes looking for me." The woman started to protest. "But be careful. A couple of them are carrying knives, I think. Warn the cops when you call them."

"Are you sure?"

"Yes, please! I'm begging you. They—they hurt me."

The saleslady nodded and gave Grace a reassuring squeeze of her arm. "Okay, sister. I'm going to call the cops. Just hang out in the back. I'll come for you."

"No, I'm afraid they'll hurt you, too. Please," Grace paused, searching for the woman's name.

"Abayisha," the woman said.

"Abayisha," Grace said. "Don't. Just pretend that I'm still in the dressing room. If they find us together outside, they'll take you, too. There's like a dozen of them outside. I couldn't bear it," Grace stammered, beginning to tear up. "It's so good of you to help me. If they did the things to you —"

"Okay, okay. I'm going to call. You just hide until the cops come." She gave Grace a brief hug, then hurried to the front of the store to call the police and whisper to her manager what was going on. Grace gathered all the remaining clothes into the garbage bag and quietly left the store by the back door.

Helmand Province, Afghanistan

Hila and Atal emerged from their rooms to join Hamid and his wife in the main room of the small home. The baby babbled in his bassinet in the corner. On the table, a meal for the four of them was laid out. Both Hila's and Atal's eyes widened at the sight of the food. To them, it seemed a holiday feast.

Atal bowed his head, saying, "This is too much. We are just simple people."

Hamid laughed as he indicated for them to sit. "You are our guests, you are welcome. It is just dinner, though I admit my dearest wife is a very good cook." He nodded to where his wife was preparing to bring more food to the table.

Hamid introduced his wife as Bala Nashta. Once she had joined them at the table, Hila and Atal waited as Hamid made the blessing and began to eat. Each ate in silence, waiting for their host to begin the conversation.

After a polite period of time, Hamid asked, "Have you come very far?"

"Less than a day's walk east of your valley," Atal said. "Not very far at all, but I never heard of this place."

"I would be very surprised if you had," Hamid said, smiling across the table at his wife. She smiled back at him, eyes twinkling. "As you must have experienced, we are somewhat difficult to find."

"What is the name of this place?" Atal asked.

"It has no particular name," Hamid said, gesturing for the others to eat while they listened.

"The man who led us here, the pilgrim—" Atal began, only to be interrupted by a short laugh from Bala Nashta.

Bala Nashta lowered her eyes and smiled. She left to bring the pitcher of water to refill their glasses.

Hamid smiled at his wife. "The man who led you here is hardly a pilgrim, Atal."

"He saved our lives," Hila interjected.

Hamid nodded at that. "He saved the lives of my family as well. He has saved a great many, I think. That is one reason they follow him here. Others come because they have heard of his work."

"What work is that?" Atal asked.

"God's work, Atal," Hamid said. "The pilgrim, as you call him, is the Mahdi."

Atal half-rose from his chair, face reddening. "You speak blasphemy!"

Hamid only shrugged and gestured casually for Atal to sit back down. "Calm yourself, brother. Do not take offense. I withdraw my words, if they offend you. But they are no less true."

"You claim the man to be the Messiah?" Atal spluttered. "He is, he is—a Westerner! An apostate."

Hamid smiled, shaking his head. "Appearances deceive, Atal. He is a man of God. You will see this in time, I am sure."

"He has not said a word to us since we met him," Hila said, trying to soothe the tone of the conversation.

"No, the Mahdi does not speak," Hamid said.

"Quit calling him that!" Atal said.

"As you wish. Your pilgrim—your savior—does not speak."

"Is this his choice?" Hila asked.

"Who knows? I don't think so. I think he is not able. This is what I believe, but one cannot be sure."

"Why do you call him—what it is you said?" Hila asked.

"You will see," Hamid said. "I do not wish to upset your brother any further. With time, you will come to judge for yourself. But you are our guests, and you have travelled hard. Please enjoy the meal, then Bala Nashta will be pleased to show you back to your rooms for the night."

Quantum Indeterminate State

Arthur and Samantha stared at Gabriel as they sat at the table quietly for a bit, thinking about this.

"I probably shouldn't ask this," Arthur said slowly, "but what happens when someone opens this What's-his-name box—our cat litter box? If we're observed by an outside observer, as it were?"

"The waveform collapses," Samantha said. "The quantum superposition resolves to either of the two possibilities."

"So, we could end up alive or dead?" Arthur said.

"I'm thinking that we're gonna end up dead, hon," Sam said.

Gabriel was forced to agree.

I AM OMNIPOTENT. THAT'S JUST A FACT. OMNIPOTENCE IS PART OF THE ORIGINAL DEFINITION, THE SINGULARITY, THE GREAT OM. STEP ONE: "GOD IS GREAT." EXACTLY.

BUT:

THERE SHOULD NOT BE A "BUT," I KNOW.
YOU'RE THINKING, OMNIPOTENCE HAS NO "BUT."

I AM OMNIPOTENT, BUT I AM
NOT OMNIPOTENTLY OMNIPOTENT.
THAT'S ALSO JUST A FACT.

OMNIPOTENT OMNIPOTENCE IS A NON-STARTER. LITERALLY. START HERE: I AM OMNIPOTENT. THEN: I CREATE SOMETHING, ANYTHING. LIKE THE EARTH, OR THE UNIVERSE, OR A UNIVERSE INSIDE AN EARTHLY COW, INHABITED BY SENTIENT, SELF-AWARE BOVINE BACTERIA THAT BUILD BEAUTI-FUL SHRINES TO ME OUT OF SEMI DIGESTED HAY— DON'T FOCUS ON THAT TOO CLOSELY, IT'S JUST A METAPHOR. IT DOESN'T MATTER. ONCE I ACT, ONCE I CREATE—I CREATE THE 'BUT.' I MAY BE OM-NIPOTENT, BUT I HAVE NOW CREATED LIMITS ON MY OWN OMNIPOTENCE, GET IT? I AM CONSTRAINED, NO LONGER OMNIPOTENTLY OMNIPOTENT. I CAN ONLY BE OMNIPOTENTLY OMNIPOTENT IF I DON'T ACT. WHICH, I GOTTA TELL YOU, IS TEMPTING SOME-TIMES.

Quantum Indeterminate State

Arthur grew angry at this point as the situation began to sink in. "This is how you treat your friends? You set us up, you asshole! We were doing just fine and you trap us into get-ting aboard a plane doomed to crash into the middle of the

Pacific Ocean. What the fuck, Gabe?" At this point he sputtered out, looking helplessly to Sam to continue his point.

"I assume," Sam said, much more calmly, "that you had a damn good reason for all this, Gabriel."

"Um, yeah. Damn good, you bet."

"Good enough to get your two best friends killed? That good?" Arthur spluttered again.

"Yeah, Arthur. That good," Gabriel replied.

"Can't wait to hear it," Arthur said.

CHAPTER 4

New York, NY

Grace found herself in a short alley behind the store. She trotted up the alleyway to East 91st, bag full of clothes in one hand and clutching Simon the Mormon missionary's credit card in the other. She scanned up and down the busy street quickly. She didn't have much time.

Grace looked down at the card. It was a bank card, the kind that could be used as either credit or debit. She would need cash, because very soon the credit card would be either useless or a liability; she thought she had at least thirty or forty minutes before Simon got over his panic at losing her enough to report the card stolen. Grace walked quickly until she saw a bank ATM across the street.

Crossing quickly, she considered. Trying to use the card to access the ATM was a risk. If she pushed too hard, the card would be lost and she'd have no way to buy her train ticket to Chicago. She thought, though, that it was safe enough to try two attempts at the guy's PIN. If it didn't fly, she should be able to cancel and get the card back.

As Grace approached the ATM, she kept her face turned away, then covered the little camera with her finger as she stepped in front. She considered for a few seconds, then smiled, remembering back to her childhood indoctrination at the Catholic orphanage. John was the fourth gospel—worth a shot, she believed. She keyed in 4,3,16 and waited, thinking about her second guess if this one was—no need; bingo! She quickly withdrew the maximum, $500, thinking her Catholic education had finally payed off. Grace pocketed the money, reclaimed the card, and quickly flagged down a taxi.

Grace ran down the escalator into Penn Station and found the kiosks for AMTRAK tickets. She purchased tickets to Chicago by way of a dozen different intermediate cities. They knew she was headed for Chicago, they knew she would be there in three days—but she didn't think they could cover every route, not on such short notice. Grace looked up at the big overhead board displaying the departing schedule as tickets poured from the machine. The train to Buffalo was leaving in three minutes. Grace sorted through the pile of tickets, found the right ones, and went running across the station to the track for the Enterprise Limited. She stopped as she came upon a man sleeping rough against the wall at the top of the stairs to the track's gate.

"Hey, friend," Grace said to the man, stooping momentarily to hand him the rest of the tickets and the credit card. "Here, get out of town, brother. Gonna be cold soon. And that card's only good for about another ten minutes." Then she descended the steps two at a time and jumped aboard the train just as the whistle started to sound.

New York, NY

Pauley returned a few minutes later to the bench where the other three still sat.

"Come, gentlemen," Pauley said.

The three stood, Uriel helping Zimmerman to his feet.

"Where are we going?" Zimmerman asked.

Pauley led them out onto the street. "There's a rental car agency three blocks east." He led them down the street.

"We're driving to Chicago?" *Zimmerman* asked. "Why?"

"Because the archdiocese can't tell how many people are in a rental car, that's why. Because the Cardinal appreciates my frugality. Because I wasn't about to ask his Eminence to cover airfare for each of you. Besides, we have three days. Who's up for a road trip?"

"We'll need alcohol," Uriel answered.

"No doubt," Pauley agreed.

An hour later, they were crossing the George Washington Bridge, Pauley driving with *Zimmerman* riding in the passenger seat. Pauley glanced up at his other passengers in the rear view mirror as he heard Uriel crack open a can of beer.

"Little early, don't you think?" Pauley asked, smiling in the mirror.

"That's pretty funny, coming from you, Pauley," Uriel said from the back seat.

"At least pass one up here, then," Pauley said, his smile evaporating.

"Don't think so, Pauley," Uriel said. "You're driving."

Pauley cursed under his breath and looked ahead to the road, heading west on I-80.

Zimmerman turned in his seat to talk to Uriel. "Do you think she'll be able to get away from those guys?"

Uriel shrugged and took a swig of beer. "You tell me. You know her better'n me."

"There were an awful lot of them," *Zimmerman* said.

"She'll get away," Zimmerman said from the back seat.

"What about Parnell?" Pauley asked.

Uriel looked appraisingly at Zimmerman, who had his head slumped against the back seat. "How're you feeling, champ?"

"Better," Zimmerman answered. "Still need about a week's worth of sleep." He turned to address his *doppelgänger* sitting in the front seat, saying, "Parnell's a bit of a wild card. Not sure whose side he's on in all this."

"Doesn't matter," *Zimmerman* said. "Grace'll ditch him. She doesn't trust him."

"How does she get to Chicago, then?" Pauley asked. "Not like she has any help back there. Or any pockets full of cash in that garbage bag she's wearing."

Zimmerman eyed him suspiciously. "She'll get there. Not your problem, Peter."

New Jersey

The four men stopped at a diner just east of the Delaware Water Gap for lunch. Zimmerman had his head down on the table as the others ate.

Pauley gestured at him with a french fry. "What happened to him?"

"He's tired," Uriel answered irritably. "Leave him alone."

"Who is he?" *Zimmerman* asked. "I mean, he's kinda me, I know, but how can we both—?"

"He's not you," Uriel corrected. He sucked at his chocolate malt.

"Yes he is," *Zimmerman* insisted.

"No, he's not," Uriel replied. "I know who he is, and he's not you."

"What do you mean?" *Zimmerman* asked.

"He's completely different," Uriel said. "He shouldn't even be here, so leave him alone."

"Damn right," Zimmerman said, opening one eye. "Shouldn't even be here."

"So why is he here, then?" Pauley asked, hamburger in hand.

"Because he got fucked," Uriel said. "Like every asshole that's ever done a *mitzvah*, he got fucked for it."

"What's a *mitzvah*?" Pauley asked.

"Wasn't even entirely your fault, Pauley," Uriel continued. "For a second there, looked like maybe you were having second thoughts about excising the girl. She just got you as you were backing away, sent you both sailing off the top of that ramp. You should thank this guy, Peter," Uriel said, pointing with his chocolate malt at Zimmerman again. "You were splattered on the floor of the lobby, dead as toast. Father Zimmerman here saved your ass, too."

"I didn't need saving," Pauley said.

"Oh, that's right," Uriel smiled. "You were in good shape. Girl was excised, so's you had your nice, innocent soul back." He shook his head at that.

"How come you know all this?" *Zimmerman* asked, "and the rest of us feel like it's the first time—I mean, the only time."

"Because it is the only time for all of you. Except him," Uriel said, indicating Zimmerman.

"And you," Pauley said. "Why?"

"Because I'm not like you," Uriel said.

"So what are you?" Pauley asked. "Some kind of god?"

" 'Ray, when someone asks you if you're a god, you say 'Yes!' " Uriel said, smiling.

"Thank you, Dr. Venkman," *Zimmerman* said.

"It wasn't Venkman," Zimmerman muttered, unsticking his face from the tabletop and trying to focus on Uriel. "So how was I fucked, Earle?"

"Can't say exactly," Uriel said. "When you went back, when I sent you back—"

"When you stabbed me in the heart, you mean," Zimmerman said.

"Yeah, exactly. When you looped back to save your girlfriend..."

"You're right," *Zimmerman* said. "I remember now. It was Winston Zeddmore, not Venkman. Wait, why did you call Grace his girlfriend?"

"While you were in the loop, saving Grace," Uriel continued, ignoring *Zimmerman*, "something got switched. You shouldn't have continued on. You shoulda been this one," he said, stabbing a french fry he had stolen from Pauley's plate at *Zimmerman*, "and he should be the only Zimmerman this time around."

"So why am I here?" Zimmerman asked. He let his head fall back against the booth with a soft clop.

"Like I said," Uriel repeated. "Somebody flipped a switch, something changed at just the wrong moment."

"What changed?" *Zimmerman* asked. Uriel shrugged as he resumed eating.

"That's pretty obvious," Pauley interjected. The others turned to look at him. "I mean, can't be a coincidence that something like that happens at that precise moment. It was an intervention."

"Who intervened?" *Zimmerman* asked.

"Same one who wants the girl excised, obviously—God," Pauley answered. He looked around at the others. "Are we getting dessert?"

New Jersey

They filled up with gas and got back on the expressway, heading east across Pennsylvania. *Zimmerman* was driving now, with Pauley in the front passenger seat. Zimmerman was asleep again, face pressed against the window. Uriel watched the undulating countryside pass by outside as Zimmerman's saliva slowly oozed down the glass.

"Why do people live here?" Uriel asked no one in particular. He got no particular response.

Zimmerman awoke with a start, snapping upright with a shout and kicking the back of the driver's seat. *Zimmerman* swerved across the lane, swearing. "Shit, man," he said to the other Zimmerman in the rear view mirror, "what the hell was that?"

"Sorry," Zimmerman said. Uriel stared at him. "What?" Zimmerman asked, staring back at the old man. Uriel said nothing and went back to staring out the window. Zimmerman looked at *Zimmerman* in the mirror. "Where's Jack?" he asked.

"Jack?" *Zimmerman* asked.

"Yeah, Jack. You remember Jack, about this high, drools a lot. My dog."

"Yeah, I remember. My dog." *Zimmerman* considered for a moment. "Left him on the boat."

"You left Jack on the boat?" Zimmerman asked, face reddening.

"Grace drugged me. Probably drugged Jack, too, knowing her. When I came to, she was gone and Jack was licking my face. I panicked, I guess, and went tearing after Grace." He saw how angry Zimmerman was in the mirror. "Settle down, Julius," *Zimmerman* continued. "I called Steve before we left the rental car place. You were asleep. He's going to get him. Steve's a good guy, he'll take care of him."

Zimmerman's color drained back to normal. "Jack always liked him better, anyway," Zimmerman said. "Steve eats a lot of pizza. Probably better off."

Zimmerman smiled from the front seat. "Probably." A thought occurred to *Zimmerman* and he turned to Pauley. "Hey, Peter," he said. "Check your magic book. Maybe it'll tell us what's going on with Grace."

Pauley shook his head, pulling the book from his coat pocket. He tossed it back to Zimmerman in the back seat. "Not magic any more," Pauley said. "Not since the title changed."

Zimmerman looked at the cover, reading aloud. "The Problem *with* God? What gives?"

Pauley shrugged. "Title changed back in the Guggenheim, nothing's changed since. Just a book now." Zimmerman reached out to hand it back up to Pauley. "Not magic any more. You keep it," Pauley said, pushing it back.

Zimmerman lowered the window and tossed it out.

"Why'd you do that?" *Zimmerman* asked.

"Never liked that book," Zimmerman said. He let the wind blow on his face for a bit, then raised the window again. "Everyone dies in the end."

" 'All true stories…' " Uriel said. There was silence in the car.

Zimmerman eventually said, "Grace said something like that, on the boat."

"About Hemingway?" Uriel asked.

"No," Zimmerman said, before *Zimmerman* had a chance to

answer. "About 'The Problem of God.' Said it was a stupid title. She said—"

"It shouldn't be The Problem *of* God," *Zimmerman* interjected. "She said it was a problem *with* God."

"Oh, yeah?" Pauley asked, amused. "What did she say was the problem *with* God?"

Zimmerman answered this time, saying, "The problem with God, Grace said, was that he didn't give a fuck."

Uriel laughed.

"She got that wrong," Pauley said, not smiling. "She should've figured that out by now."

LET'S TAKE A MOMENT—I SENSE THAT MY REVELATION (SEE WHAT I DID THERE?) REGARDING MY OMNIPOTENCE HAS STRUCK YOU—WELL, LET'S JUST GO WITH THE INTENDED DOUBLE ENTENDRE AND SAY IT—DUMB. AM I RIGHT? OF COURSE I AM. AFTER ALL, I MAY NOT BE OMNIPOTENTLY OMNIPOTENT, BUT I'M STILL, YOU KNOW—GOD.

I BELIEVE A MORE PEDESTRIAN ANALOGY WILL HELP YOU UNDERSTAND THIS. ATTEND TO MY PARABLE:

THE WRITER OF A NOVEL IS A KIND OF GOD, IS HE NOT? IN A FASHION, I MEAN. REMEMBER, THIS IS AN ANALOGY, NOT A THEOSOPHICAL TRACT. AN AUTHOR, WRITING HIS NOVEL, A COMPLETE WORK OF FICTION, A WORK CONSTRAINED ONLY BY THE BREADTH OF THE AUTHOR'S OWN IMAGINATION, IS OMNIPOTENT IN HIS ABILITY TO CREATE. THE PAGE IS BLANK, AND THE AUTHOR IS ALL-POWERFUL AS HE

PUTS PEN TO PAGE.

AH, BUT WHAT OF THE VERY NEXT MOMENT? AT THE MOMENT IMMEDIATELY FOLLOWING THAT FIRST SCRATCH OF THE PEN'S NIB, BEFORE THE INK HAS EVEN FULLY SOAKED INTO THE VIRGINAL PULP, OUR GOD-LIKE AUTHOR IS CONSTRAINED. NOW THAT HE HAS BEGUN, AVENUES BEGIN TO CLOSE. POINT-OF-VIEW, SETTING, TONE, AND COUNTLESS OTHER LITERARY FACETS INSTANTLY ARE EXPOSED, AS THE JEWELER WHO MAKES HIS FIRST STRIKE UPON A RAW DIAMOND. POSSIBILITIES ARE NO LONGER WITHOUT LIMIT. CHOICES MUST BE MADE—AND ONCE CHOSEN, THE AUTHOR PROCEEDS DOWN AN EVER NARROWING ALLEYWAY.

NOT TO BELABOR THE ANALOGY, THERE IS AN EVEN GREATER LESSON TO BE GLEANED. BECAUSE, LIKE ME, THE AUTHOR FINDS A FURTHER FRUSTRA-TION AS HE PROGRESSES IN HIS CREATIVE LABORS. CHARACTERS, LIKE MEN, CANNOT BE PUSHED ABOUT LIKE PIECES ON A CHECKER BOARD. MANY AUTHORS WILL TELL YOU THAT THEIR BEST CHARACTERS DE-VELOP A WILL OF THEIR OWN, OFTEN OBSTINATELY REFUSING TO FOLLOW THE AUTHOR'S INTENDED PLOT, SEIZING THE STORY BY ITS EAR AND TUGGING IT IN NEW, UNEXPECTED DIRECTIONS. AND THIS IM-PERTINENCE FROM A CONSTRUCT WITH NO TRUE FREE WILL, YOU SEE? JUST A TWO-DIMENSIONAL SCRIBBLE,

BUT ALREADY SUCH TROUBLE.

PERHAPS THEN, I MAKE MYSELF A BIT MORE CLEAR: OMNIPOTENT, SURE. BUT NOT OMNIPOTENTLY OMNIPOTENT. AND THAT'S A CHALLENGE, EVEN FOR GOD.

Upstate, New York

Grace sat on the train. She was alone in the first class car. Somehow, she must have accidentally punched the button for first class tickets in her haste at Penn Station. She sat in the very front seat, facing backward so she could watch the entire empty car. Nobody first-class wants to go to Buffalo today, she thought to herself.

Grace watched the landscape pass outside, telephone wires gracefully rising and diving just outside the window as she rhythmically clacked along.

" 'The fear of the Lord is the beginning of wisdom,' " Grace muttered to herself, the phrase coming unbidden from memory. Pauley had said that it was God that wanted her excised. She considered this possibility. Pauley was hardly a trusted source. He was so full of shit, he would say anything if it suited his need. He had sounded sincere, however; like the very idea of excising her was bigger than him. She shook her head.

Grace tried to think of another explanation, tried to consider someone else who might wish her—eliminated. Not just dead. Dead she could understand; more than a few individuals in her past had expressed that desire, some on more than one occasion. Excised, though? That seemed a bit over the top. Biblical, even. It seemed, as she further considered, something that God would do. She couldn't think of anyone else who might.

Why, though? She considered, letting her head rest against

the seat back, her eyes closing. God never gave a fuck about her before, of that she was sure. It seemed to Grace that her entire childhood had been a testament to just how little God cared about her. Orphaned with her twin sister on their sixth birthday, raised in a series of Irish Catholic orphanages where she and her sister were subjected to every type of abuse, finally fighting back against Donovan's assaults until that led to her beloved sister's twelve-year-old body lying broken on the paving stones outside the chapel. Where was God then? she wondered. Where were his angels to catch her sister as she fell? Where was God when Grace spent the next six years of her life committed to the St. Brigid's Mental Hospital; drugged, left naked in isolation for days on end, restrained, beaten—subjected to electroshock therapy every Friday at ten am? God wasn't paying much heed to her then, was He? So what changed? What got His attention? How'd she piss Him off so bad that He wants His universe remade so that Grace never was? Grace sighed.

She had killed a man, of course. This fact didn't bother her much. Grace's only regret was that she hadn't killed Donovan sooner, before he had murdered her sister. She certainly had no remorse for stabbing the priest in the heart as he lay on her. If that was why God wanted her excised, then fuck Him, too.

But Grace didn't really believe that murdering a child-raping priest was the reason. Maybe that buys you a ticket to Hell, she thought. A few spins in Purgatory. Not this excision crap. Excision seemed—bigger. Old Testament. Special. Something the Lord Himself would resort to only for the exceptional case. Was she a special case? What had Grace done to earn such treatment? Why excise her, completely and permanently, from the universe? What do you have to do to deserve that shit? She fell asleep wondering, rocking to the train's rhythm beneath her. 'The fear of the Lord is the beginning of wisdom,' she thought to herself. What a strange, terrible thing to say to a child...

Pennsylvania

"From where I'm sitting," Zimmerman said from the back seat, "I think she's wrong."

"She's not wrong," Pauley said.

"There is no God," Zimmerman insisted.

"Oh, there is," Uriel said. "That's the whole goddamn problem. There's God, and there's gods. Too many goddamn gods, goddamn 'em all."

"*Old man starting to lose it back there?*" *Zimmerman* asked of the rearview mirror from the driver's seat.

"How are you so sure, Earl?" Zimmerman asked.

"'Cause I'm like you, Julius," Uriel said. "Only it happened a helluva long time ago. And when it happened, I had a lot farther to fall."

"So what do you know about God?" Pauley asked.

"Enough."

"Who is He?"

"Depends on who you're talking about," Uriel said. "Like I said, lots of folks calling themselves god, or acting like god. Not sure which one you're referring to."

"Making no sense," *Zimmerman* said.

"You'll see when you're dead," Uriel said.

"Not sure I want to wait that long," *Zimmerman* said.

"Might not be all that long," Pauley said.

"What do you—"

"He's just fucking with you, *Julius*," Uriel said. "He don't know shit."

"Well, I have been dead," Zimmerman said. "And I still don't know what the hell you're talking about, Earl. So how about you enlighten us."

"Like I said, I'm not sure what you want to know. If you had spent a little longer being dead, you'd know what it's like. Nicer. So much nicer, almost no one ever look back."

"But some do, I take it."

"Yeah, some do. Like you did, Julius. You had a reason,

son, so yeah, you went back. He came back," Uriel said, pointing at Pauley in the front seat. "But most folk don't give this world another thought. A few, however, take an interest."

"Why?"

"Power, of course."

"Power?" Zimmerman asked. "I'm not feeling particularly powerful."

"That's not why you went back, Julius. Others, though, use their passing to their advantage. People from that level of existence get to influence all they want in the past. Look at your Greek gods, that's a good example."

"Greek mythology? What about it?"

Uriel shook his head. "Nothing mythological about them. Damn real, every one of 'em. From what I hear, bunch of folks who died back in the mid-Fifties. Not sure how it got organized, but they decided to go back to fuck with the Greeks, *circa* sixth century BC. When you know twentieth century stuff—you know, wireless radio, flashlights, electric cattle prods, who knows what-all—wasn't hard to put together a pretty fair show, play gods for a few hundred years."

'So the Greek gods, Zeus and Athena and Hercules and all, were real? But they were just dead men and women from the mid-twentieth century, fucking with the ancient Greeks?

"Yeah."

"Hercules wasn't a god," *Zimmerman* corrected.

Uriel said, "You see, that's what I'm saying. When you ask, 'Is there a God?' I gotta ask exactly what you mean."

"So all those affairs, the stories of the Greek gods having sex with mortals, tossing lightning bolts from the sky—"

"Ancient history, brother," Uriel said.

"And they did this because..."

Uriel shrugged. "Because they could, that's why. Some people see power as a way to help folks. Not most, in my experience. Most see they could fuck with folks, bottom line. Nothing new there."

"Some must have better reasons?"

"Some. As many as there are people, man. Like I said, almost all folk just move on. Let the last life go, good riddance. Others though, have some sort of reason to pay attention. Make something right that they royally screwed up, maybe help someone they care about who is still behind, if they can, that sort of thing."

"Yeah, but that's not God," Zimmerman' said. "Sounds more like 'guardian angel,' or something like that."

"Point of view. Like I said, lots of motivations. Most for power, some for other reasons. The usual venal sins, of course. Look at Krushchev. He felt terrible about nuking New York, went back and made it right."

"What are you talking about, Earl? New York was never nuked by Krushchev."

"Yeah, it was. Nikita completely fumbled the whole Cuban missile crisis thing, spun out of control on him. Like a million dead, smoking hole where Manhattan used to be. Felt so bad, he shot himself at his desk in the Kremlin. Never got over it. So later, he returned and touched that up, got it right."

"You're saying that Krushchev is God?"

"No, not God, asshole," Uriel corrected. "Again, it's definitions. Nikita played god, you could say, for a couple minutes there. But he moved on."

"So he's not God anymore?" *Zimmerman* asked.

"Never was," Pauley said with a sigh.

"So is there a God or not?" Zimmerman asked.

"You mean, capital G kinda god? Old man with a long white beard and listens to everybody's prayers all over the world, dominion over the moon and the stars, that kinda God?"

Zimmerman nodded.

"One old guy, completely omniscient, completely omnipotent, running the whole show from his seat in heaven, that kind of God? Is that what you're asking?"

Zimmerman said, "Yeah, that's what I'm asking. Not these people coming back to play little 'g' god in the past when they can intimidate the peasants with their magic shop hand buzzers. Is there 'A God?'"

Uriel shrugged. "Never met the guy."

Upstate NY

Grace opened her eyes. A young woman, maybe early twenties, was sitting across from her, staring. The girl smiled.

"Hi," she said.

Grace looked away. She glanced out the window briefly, trying to get her bearings. On the train to Buffalo, she recalled. It was twilight outside. She must've slept.

"Hi," the girl repeated, still smiling. "My name's Anna."

"Do I know you?" Grace asked the girl.

"What do you mean?"

"Have we met before?"

The girl shrugged. "Why do you ask?"

"Because," Grace said with a cold tang, "there's a whole train full of empty seats."

"Yeah."

"But you're sitting there."

"Yeah." The girl was still smiling. Grace felt like punching her, but thought better of it. For now. The girl leaned forward to offer a handshake. Grace stared at the girl. Peasant dress, pony tail, no bra. Maybe she got on at Woodstock. She didn't look like a priest, Grace thought. Though she could easily be Catholic. It was hard to tell.

"Are you a nun?" Grace asked. This elicited a bubbly laugh from the girl.

"You're funny!"

"Yeah," Grace agreed. "I'm a real card. What do you want? Money?"

The girl shrugged and finally stopped smiling. "Just being

nice, that's all. You look lonely."

"Do I?" The girl nodded. The endearing smile had returned. Grace again considered punching the little imp. "You mean, because I'm sitting here alone?" The girl nodded again. "You are the perceptive one, Anna." Grace dug in her pocket and pulled a twenty from the cash she had acquired from the ATM. "Here, Anna. Have a good life."

Anna reached across and took the money, not noticing how carefully Grace avoided touching her hand. "Thanks. You, too." The girl made no move to leave.

"Is there anything else, Anna?"

"What do you mean?"

"Anything else I can do for you, before you go?"

"Nope. Don't think so."

"Okay, then."

"Are you going to Buffalo?" the girl asked.

"This train is going to Buffalo, Anna. We're on it. So yes, I'd say we're both going to Buffalo."

"Are you leaving something, or are you going to something?" the girl asked, her eyes inquisitive.

"Not sure what you're asking," Grace answered slowly. "It's a train. Seems like both."

"Well, yeah, I see what you mean. But you got on because of one or the other, right? To get away from something, or to get to something. Are you going to meet your husband in Buffalo, say? Or are you leaving behind a bad affair?" She wore an expression of intense interest.

"I see. Kind of a personal question, seeing as we just met." This answer did nothing to resolve the young woman's expression. Grace sighed. "But to answer your question, mostly leaving a bad affair." Anna nodded knowingly. "How about you, Anna?"

"I'm just on the train."

"Yeah, I can see that. But going or coming?"

"I'm just here on the train, that's all."

"Uh, huh." Grace was wondering if she should change seats

or if the girl would just move with her. Probably.

"Do you think he'll follow you to Buffalo?"

"Who?" Grace asked, looking past the girl and seeing the rest of the car was still empty.

"The bad affair. Will he follow you?"

"I'm sure he will, Anna. You may be too young to realize this, but the bad ones almost always follow you."

Anna nodded at this. "So you'll keep going then, right? So the bad affair doesn't catch up?" Grace nodded. "Where will you go then? Once you get to Buffalo? Another train?"

"Maybe. I don't think it's really your busi—"

"But the bad affair, will he stop following in Buffalo?"

"Let me ask you a question, Anna," Grace said softly. "Are you on medication?"

This elicited another bubbly laugh, and then the smile again, but this time it was quickly replaced by a look of concern. "What if the bad affair doesn't stop in Buffalo?" Anna asked.

Grace looked back at the young girl with sympathy. "I don't think you should worry about me, Anna. Will somebody be meeting you at the station? Do you have family there?"

Anna shook her head. "I'm just on the train. If the bad affair is following you, why would it stop in Buffalo? Why would it ever stop?"

Grace decided she needed to find the restroom. Or a drink. "Excuse me," Grace said. The girl smiled at her as Grace left. Grace headed for the club car.

Pennsylvania

"You may never have met Him, Earl," Pauley said, "but that doesn't mean He doesn't exist."

"True," Uriel replied. "Never met Santa Claus, either. Might be up there, too, living right next door to Him. Give it about the same odds, Pauley."

"There is a God," Pauley said with conviction. "A real God."

"I'm not arguing against that," Uriel said. "Just arguing definitions, that's all."

"Sounds like you are, Earl," Zimmerman said.

"Look, all these religions didn't just spring up out of nowhere, okay? They all have some basis in fact, in history," Uriel said.

"All religions? Not every religion can be true."

"True? Hell, man, none of 'em are true. What's true about religion? True enough to suit the faithful, that's all the truth they need. They all got a story, and every story got a storyteller. Some of them better story than others, that's all. Some more convincing, some with more aggressive PR folk, better funding."

"But the world's religions are mostly monotheistic, Earl. Just the One God."

"If it was just one God, be damn sure He'd do a better job of keeping the narrative straight. Don't see it that way. Too much is inconsistent, too many conflicts."

"Oh? So what do you think happened?"

"Much more likely, some guy from the distant future trundled back to play Old Testament God to the Jews. Got his five books and then some, had a pretty straight-forward narrative. Old Testament God has a pretty good thing going for quite a while, but the world moves on. Maybe the Old Man loses his mojo or just loses interest. Don't know. Someone new decides to take on the deity duty, from the farther, more future future, figures He can do better, you see? Decides to address Old Testament Guy's basic problem."

"Yeah?" Zimmerman said. "What basic problem was that?"

"OT God asked for a lot of loyalty, but hardly gave enough in return to keep the peasants interested. Not hopeful. Low juice to squeeze. People still dying all the time down here. Famine, pestilence, infant mortality. It was depressing. No clear path forward after dying to make it feel worth the effort. Wasn't really catching on with the masses."

"So the New Testament God comes on the scene with a better deal, is that how you see it?"

"Exactly. New Guy sees the people need something more positive, to see there's a way forward besides just doing the right thing for fuck's sake, followed by what? Not a whole helluva lot. So He gives the people what they need to really buy in—a Savior, forgiveness, and everybody that *really* believes gets the big reward after death. A promise for a way better deal, but only for the guys who truly, really believe. And just the promise of the Hereafter. He can't really let them see behind the curtain."

"Why not?"

Uriel shook his head. "No way. Whole gig falls apart if the common folk know God's really just one of them from a place where they have way cooler toys. Mormon guy almost gave the game away when he said the quiet part out loud."

Zimmerman nodded. "'As man now is, god once was. As god now is, man will be.'"

"Lorenzo Snow," *Zimmerman* said.

"Yeah, that wasn't gonna fly. Nobody building churches to that revelation. So New Testament Guy takes up the challenge. Re-energizes the narrative, throws his boy onstage to show the masses how it's done."

"So Jesus was the Son of God? You're okay with that part, huh?"

"Why not?"

"And you're going with Jesus returning from the dead, too?" Zimmerman asked.

"Sure, Father. You know it happens, did it yourself. A lot harder back then, of course, before Frank Lloyd's transcendental Prairie-style portals. Those olden days, there were only the natural channels, probably damn few and those a well-kept secret. That's probably why the whole story unfolds in the middle of the friggin' desert, you know? Gateway in the back of a cave, not some bath house in downtown Rome. Real life Son of New Testament God walks around preaching, performing miracles using far future technology back in ancient Egypt, heals some lepers with antibiotics, that sort of thing. Maybe things don't go quite as He plans, manages to get His son crucified—I mean, Jesus does seem a bit put out there at the end. But he shows the people that something better will be waiting for them if they just believe. But only if they keep the faith. That's the hook. There, happier now?"

"And Moslems?"

"Same deal, different Dude. 'No god but God,' you know. '*Allah ahkbar.*' That tells you something right there, doesn't it? That whole Sunni/Shia thing. You can fill in the blanks yourself. Name a religion, they all got a play, so they all gotta have a playwright. Hell, the Buddhists, the Scientologists, the Zoro-my-ass-terians—same story all over the world, throughout history—just different folks in the leading role."

"How do you know all this?"

Uriel shrugged. "Been there, done that, got lots of tee shirts to prove it. I'm damn old."

"But, no matter how old you are, Earl, Pauley might still be right. You're arguing a negative. Maybe there's a real God —you just haven't met him. Even if you did see some minor god-wanna-be's along the way. Doesn't rule out the One and Only. Beyond even your vast experience, could be the One God, the Creator overseeing it all," *Zimmerman* said.

"I'm not arguing, negative or positive. I understand, Padre, you got a dog in this fight. You want to believe there's an all-loving Creator who looks like Grandpa and spends his time deciding which prayers to green-light, thinks it funny to give your Dad a cardiac arrest while he's *shtupping* a lady who's not Mom, be my guest. Just telling you what I've seen, so far. Haven't met the guy whose picture is on the ceiling in the Sistine Chapel. And even if I did, doesn't prove he's any more the One God than the gods I met already. Just got a better portrait painter than most."

"You're wrong, Earl," Pauley said. "What you're saying

makes no sense. It's a contradiction to think that a man, any man—even a man from the farthest future—is God. No such being could be the Creator. It's not possible to create oneself, no matter how far back in time one goes."

"Exactly," Uriel said. "Anyone tell you He's the Creator, keep walking and check your wallet, son. This universe just is."

Ohio

They finally crossed the border into Ohio.

"About damn time," Uriel said. "They should change the name from Pennsylvania to Purgatory."

"Not much farther now," Pauley assured them. *Zimmerman* was still driving. Uriel and Zimmerman were each polishing off the last of the beers in the back seat.

"What are you going to do, Peter?" *Zimmerman* asked.

"Do about what?" Pauley asked.

"I mean, when you see Grace again. What are you going to do? Are you still trying to kill her?"

Pauley shook his head. "Not trying to kill anyone."

"Oh, right," *Zimmerman* said. "Excise her."

"I'm not sure," Pauley said. "I'm not even sure if I'm still able to—still supposed to."

"Yeah? What made you so sure before, asshole?" Uriel said.

"I was given the task," Pauley explained. "Tried to call it off. I went all the way up to the Cardinal."

"Big fucking whoop," Uriel said.

"You tried to get the Cardinal to cancel the excision?" *Zimmerman* asked.

Pauley nodded. "Said it couldn't be stopped. Said it wasn't his call, wasn't even the Pope's call."

"Then whose call was it?" Zimmerman asked.

"I told you," Pauley said. "It comes from God."

"What makes you so sure?" *Zimmerman* asked.

Pauley said, "Cardinal said as much. Told me it was an authority that didn't take input from the Church at all. Said it wasn't that kind of thing. Above the authority of the Church."

"You believe whatever you want, Pauley," Uriel said. "Doesn't matter in the least. Take the next exit, Julius."

Julius looked at Uriel in the mirror. "Elyria?" he asked, reading the exit sign. Uriel nodded. "I still got over half a tank."

"Take the exit."

Zimmerman took the exit. He drove along a series of increasingly rural roads at Uriel's direction. It was getting on to twilight as Uriel directed him to pull over to the side of a two lane gravel road along a field of stubbled cornstalks.

"Gotta take a piss?" Pauley asked Uriel.

"Gotta take a dump," Uriel corrected. "Get out of the car, Pauley." Pauley looked at Uriel, not understanding. A knife appeared in Uriel's hand. "Told you to get out, asshole," Uriel repeated.

Pauley looked at the other two. Each shrugged in turn.

"This is, like, the middle of nowhere," Pauley protested. Uriel said nothing. "I can just report the car stolen, you know. They'll pull you over in less than an hour."

"Take his phone, Julius," Uriel instructed. Pauley clamped his hand over his coat pocket. "Or I could just cut you and dump your bleeding, sorry ass in the ditch. Your call, Pauley." Pauley handed his phone to *Zimmerman*. With a shake of his head, he opened the door and got out.

Uriel turned to *Zimmerman* as he raised the window. "Drive. Back the way we came." Pauley raised his hand, was saying something—but he couldn't be heard through the window. *Zimmerman* watched in the mirror as the old priest sat down heavily on the side of the road as they drove away.

They were quiet in the car for a bit. *Zimmerman* finally said, "Gee, I don't feel good about that."

"Really?" Zimmerman asked. "Because I was going to get

out of the car and punch him in the face."

"Should've just killed him and left his body in the ditch," Uriel mused.

"What is wrong with you guys?" *Zimmerman* asked, merging back onto the highway. "Pauley wasn't that bad. He was just an old priest."

"Oh, yeah? That all he was?" Uriel asked. "Let me tell you about your old priest. Julius, tell your *doppelgänger* there the old priest's history with Grace." Zimmerman related the priest's previous life in Ireland, including his abuse of Grace and his role in her sister's death, about how the priest had lost his finger. Both Zimmermans were flush with anger by the end of his story.

"I should've punched him in the face," Zimmerman repeated.

"You should've killed him, Earl," *Zimmerman* said. "Almost worth going back. Do you think we're done with him, at least?"

Uriel shrugged. "Wouldn't count on it. That kind of evil has a way of coming back on you. But killing him wouldn't make much difference."

"Still wish I'd punched him in the face."

"Was he right, though? About who wants Grace excised?" *Zimmerman* asked.

"Yeah," Uriel said. " 'fraid so."

Buffalo, NY

After a brief layover, Grace changed trains in Buffalo. She was careful to watch for Anna or anyone else that seemed to be interested in her, but no one gave her a second look as Grace moved through the station and stepped onto the Lake Shore Limited, looking for her seat. She couldn't find it.

"Can I help you, young lady?" an ancient conductor asked her as she tried to decipher the ticket in her hand.

Grace handed over the ticket for the conductor's inspection.

"Right this way," he said. He led her through the doors between cars until he stood outside a cabin. He held the door open.

"Really?" Grace asked, wary.

"That's a first class ticket," the conductor said, nodding. "Sure beats sleeping in a chair all the way to Chicago." He let Grace into the little cabin.

"Thank you," Grace said, handing the man a twenty. "When do we arrive in Chicago?"

"Should arrive before ten in the morning, God willing," he said, pocketing the tip with an appreciative nod. "You need a wake-up?" Grace shook her head. "Well, when you're ready to have the bed turned-down, just push the button there. My name's Micheal."

"Like the angel," Grace said with a smile.

"Not so much. Call if you need anything. Dining car is two cars forward, dinner is six to nine. Enjoy your travels, ma'am." He touched the brim of his cap and left, clicking the door shut behind.

Grace enjoyed a late dinner alone, staring out the window as dark city streets went snickering by. The dining car was otherwise empty. Grace had expected Anna to plop down across from her during the meal, but it seemed the young girl really was a creature of the train to Buffalo, not from Buffalo, after all.

Grace returned to her cabin and locked the door. She changed into her new pajamas, stretched, and climbed into the clean, little cocoon of a bunk Micheal had made up earlier, sighing deeply. Grace clicked off the light. Outside her window it was grey-black, rain softening the eerily glowing lights that flashed by, flashed by, flashed…

Grace knew she was falling, though she was surrounded by a featureless fog in every direc-

tion. *The wind rushed up past her, her eyes watering, her red hair a pendant streaming behind, and somewhere ahead, from the direction of the wind, she knew the ground was waiting for her.*

"I'm so sorry, sister," Grace said, her words lost in the wind. As she spoke, her hand was taken by another's. Grace looked to see her sister beside her, smiling. Her sister shook her head slowly.

"Dear Grace," Fiona said as they fell together, "always so sad and serious, you were."

Grace nodded at that and they fell together, the sound of rushing wind in their ears.

"I prayed for an angel," Grace said. "To catch you up. I prayed so very, very hard."

They saw the ground rushing up through the fog.

Fiona squeezed her sister's hand tightly. "And here you be," she said.

CHAPTER 5

Upstate, NY

"Are you okay, hon?"

Grace opened her eyes to see Gabriel sitting on the edge of the small bed. She looked at him, confused.

"Are you okay?" Gabriel asked again, rubbing her shoulder. "You screamed just now."

Grace sat up, holding the blanket to her chest. She eyed Gabriel warily. "Where am I?" Grace asked. "Who are you?"

"Are you kidding?" he asked. She eyed him with that cut-glass stare, green eyes reflecting flashes of light from the window. It was a look he knew well. She wasn't kidding. "It's me, hon. Really." He reached for her and she stiffened as he tried to embrace his wife. After a moment, she relaxed into him, her head finally dropping onto his shoulder. "Just like the trip to San Francisco, remember? Right after we got married." He gently touched her hair as he held her.

Grace nodded against his neck. "Seems like another life."

"I guess it was."

"How, Gabe? The gates are closed."

"I found another way, Grace. Couldn't let anything keep me away from my wife, could I?"

"What other way?" she asked, straightening to look at him.

"I'll tell you later," he said, leaning forward to kiss her. "I've missed you, hon."

"Tell me now," Grace said, pushing him away.

"You really don't believe it's me?" Gabe asked.

"Tell me," she insisted.

Gabriel sighed in the near darkness. "How much do you know about quantum mechanics?" Gabriel explained the quantum bubble he had created with their friends Arthur and Samantha in the plane over the Indian Ocean.

"That's nuts, Gabe. Besides the fact, it sounds like you basically fucked up our friends," Grace said after Gabe had finished.

"Had to be done," he said.

"Did it?" He nodded. "How many people are getting fucked over to try and save my sorry ass, Gabriel? Maybe they don't feel quite the same way we do, you know?" Grace pulled away, looking at him.

"You can ask them yourself, in Chicago," Gabriel said, reaching for her again.

"Quantum indeterminacy state, huh?" she asked. He nodded, holding her. She caressed him through the sheets. "Seem pretty determinate to me."

IN THE BEGINNING, GOD CREATED THE HEAVEN AND THE EARTH.

THEY MAKE IT SOUND SO EASY.

IT'S NOT EXACTLY EASY, THE CREATIVE PROCESS. IT'S WORK. MORE IMPORTANTLY, IT INVOLVES CHOICES. I MAKE CHOICES. I'M OMNIPOTENT, AND I MAKE THE CHOICES. THE CHOICES, THOUGH, ARE HARD CHOICES. MY CHOICES REQUIRE ME TO SET CONSTANTS. PARAMETERS DEVELOP AS A RESULT OF THOSE CONSTANTS. THE UNIVERSE BECOMES— AND IT BECOMES AS A CONSEQUENCE OF THOSE

CONSTANTS. CONSTANTS BEGET DEPENDENCIES, DE-PENDENCIES RESULT IN DERIVATIVES AND REFLECT-IVE CO-DEPENDENT PARAMUTUAL INTERACTIONS, WHICH INITIATES A WHOLE NEW SET OF CONSE-QUENCES. COSMOGENY BEGETS ONTOLOGY, WHICH RECAPITULATES PHYLOGENY. CREATO, ERGO SUM. ARE YOU GETTING MY DRIFT HERE?

Gary, Indiana

They got off the expressway in Gary, Indiana. *Zimmerman* wanted to drive through to Chicago, but Uriel objected.

"No sense in it," Uriel explained. "Girl said three days. That's tomorrow. They know we're going to Chicago. Best not to show up until the last moment, give 'em less chance of catching us up."

"Who?" *Zimmerman* asked.

"Them, that's who," Uriel explained.

"Whoever, they are," *Zimmerman* continued, "how are they going to find us? Do they know where we're meeting Grace?"

"You tell me," Uriel said. "Do you know where we're meeting Grace?"

Zimmerman looked conspiratorially at Zimmerman. "Yeah," *Zimmerman* said. "We think so."

"Where?" Uriel asked. *Zimmerman* said nothing, just kept looking out the windshield as he drove the streets of Gary looking for a motel. Uriel looked at Zimmerman.

"Fuck you guys," Uriel said. "You think it makes any damn difference not to tell me? If you two know, pretty sure a lot of other folk already figured it out."

Zimmerman sighed. "Restaurant downtown." *Zimmerman* gave him a sideways glance.

"How do you know?" Uriel asked. "You know which restaurant?"

"Yeah," Zimmerman said, ignoring the other man's look. "Pretty sure. Don't think she meant my Mom and Dad's house. That would be pretty weird. What do you think?" Zimmerman asked the other *Zimmerman*.

Zimmerman nodded.

Zimmerman pulled the car into a motel. They booked two rooms, using Pauley's cash.

"You guys can bunk together," Uriel announced, taking up one of the keys. "Sure you got a lot in common." He disappeared up the hallway.

The two Zimmermans each lay on their respective beds, arms crossed behind their heads, staring up at the ceiling in the dark.

"Did she ever say how she knew the guy?" *Zimmerman* asked.

"Who?" Zimmerman asked.

"The restaurant mogul. The rich hispanic guy on the cover of Fortune 500. De la Corazon. That's who she was talking about, right? That's where we're meeting her."

Zimmerman shook his head in the dark. "Don't think she said. She got kinda upset at that point, ran to the bathroom. When she came back, I think she changed the subject."

"Yeah. I think so, too. Probably an old boyfriend who dumped her."

"Don't see her as the one getting dumped. Probably felt bad cause she stole his car or stabbed him on the way out the door or something."

There was silence for a few minutes. "Are you okay?" *Zimmerman* asked the other man.

"Yeah. Just tired, is all."

"What happened to you? Did she drug you, too?" *Zimmerman* asked.

"No," Zimmerman answered. "That's not how it happened. Not for me." Zimmerman told the other man about the chase across Central Park, the fight in the museum, about Grace killing Pauley and being excised in the process, finally about Uriel sending him back to save Grace; about how he pushed Grace off the bridge.

Zimmerman whistled softly in the dark. "And then you waited for her to come back again? How long were you down there, waiting?"

"Not sure. Long time."

"That's some crazy shit. I couldn't do that," he admitted.

"Not as crazy as some of the other shit we've done, Julius," Zimmerman said.

"Yeah? Like what other shit? I've never done that stuff."

"You were never in the Navy?"

"Hell, no," *Zimmerman* said. "Are you kidding? That was Eli's thing, straight out of Stanford. No way Mom and Dad would let me go into the service, not once Eli was killed."

"Eli? Eli—was killed?"

"Yeah, Julius. Just out of SEAL training. Not two months after he was sent to Afghanistan, he—"

"Stop. I don't want to hear it," Zimmerman said in the dark. "Shit."

"Why? Is Elijah still alive in your world? He's the priest and you're a SEAL, is that it?" *Zimmerman* asked.

"No, that's not it," Zimmerman said, exasperated. "Eli died of cancer, senior year in high school. Never made it to Stanford. We buried him with his letter of acceptance in his pocket."

"Shit." There was a pause. "The world is pretty fucked up, isn't it?"

"Seems that way."

"Hold it," *Zimmerman* said, turning in the dark to look at the other man. "I saw you, I think. On the bridge. When I was rowing with Grace that morning. That was you, wasn't it?" The other Zimmerman nodded in the dark.

"Did you sleep with her?" *Zimmerman* asked.

"You didn't?"

Zimmerman shrugged. "I'm a priest."

"Yeah. So was I."

AND GOD SAID, "LET THE WATERS UNDER THE HEAVENS BE GATHERED TOGETHER INTO ONE PLACE, AND LET THE DRY LAND APPEAR."

YEAH, YOU GOT THAT RIGHT. I LET THE DRY LAND APPEAR. I DID NOT HAVE TO DO THAT. ONCE I GOT IT ALL GOING, ONCE I GOT ALL THE MATH TO WORK AND YOUR BIG BANG TO GO BOOM AND THE MATTER TO FORM AND THE SUNS TO LIGHT UP AND FORM THE ELEMENTS AND MAKE THE PLANETS AND DO YOUR LITTLE EARTH—ONCE I GOT THAT ALL DONE JUST PERFECT—I DIDN'T HAVE TO DO YOU, DID I? NO, I DID NOT. I COULD'VE LEFT THE WHOLE PLACE ONE BIG SEA, COULD'VE JUST HAD THE WHALES SINGING MY PRAISES FOR ALL ETERNITY. WOULD'VE BEEN A LOT LESS TROUBLE, I AM TELLING YOU. THOSE WHALES—MIGHT'VE BEEN MY BEST WORK. PROBABLY SHOULD'VE JUST STOPPED THERE. MAN, I LOVE THOSE WHALES.

I CHOSE TO LET THE DRY LAND APPEAR. I CHOSE TO LET YOU BE.

I BELIEVE THAT THIS IS A VERY IMPORTANT POINT.

Chicago, Illinois

Grace walked into Mariangela's Restaurant on State Street, Gabriel following behind. She approached the *maitrè de* and was about to ask to see the manager when she saw her friends sitting at the bar. She took Gabriel's hand. "Come on, hon," she said. "Let me introduce you to a few friends."

"Grace!" *Zimmerman* shouted as he saw her approach. He waved at her. "She lives!" Cheers and perfunctory applause greeted her as Grace smiled at the group at the bar. She embraced each and introduced Gabriel.

"The dead husband we've heard so much about," *Zimmerman* enthused. Zimmerman was more circumspect in his greeting, offering Gabriel little more than a nod and a tip of his beer.

"Back from the dead as well, I see," Uriel said. Uriel was the only one speaking without a slur—it was apparent that they had been waiting for her for quite a while.

"Where's Parnell?" *Zimmerman* asked.

"Dumped him back in New York," Grace said.

"Told you!" *Zimmerman* enthused, raising his own glass in salute.

"Madre de Dios!"

Jesus de la Corazon pushed Gabriel aside to stand before Grace. He fell to his knees and took her hands in his. "*Es un milagro verdad. Dios mio!*" Grace pulled her friend to his feet and enfolded him in a tight hug. "Mariangela, you are a vision, an angel. These men told me that they were your friends, so I have to let them drink at my bar all day. I did not really believe them when they said that you would return to see my restaurant. You have come back—to see me!" Tears flowed freely down both his cheeks.

When Grace let go to look at her friend, she was crying a bit as well. "*Jesus, mi querido.* Good to see you again, *mi amigo.* Long time." She gestured around the bar. "You have done well with my little investment it seems." She introduced Gabriel.

"We've met," Gabriel said, shaking the other man's hand.

"It is good of you to remember, sir," Jesus said. "It was a difficult time for all of us."

"Yeah, difficult," Gabriel agreed. He looked around the restaurant with concern. "I believe, Jesus, that your private room has been reserved for us."

"For you? The room has been reserved, it is true, but the name that was given was an Irish name, I believe," Jesus said, confused. "I can ask my manager—"

"Yes. I made the reservation in the name of Finn McCumhail. That was me." Grace shook her head, smiling at her husband. "Can we go there, Jesus?"

"Of course," Jesus replied. "I will show you, please."

The group gathered their drinks and followed Jesus.

"Funny, he doesn't look Irish. Hope they don't both start up with that damned war cry," Zimmerman said.

Chicago, Illinois

The group followed Jesus to the private dining room in the back of the restaurant, a dark space with a large, rough hewn table that sat a dozen comfortably in deep leather chairs. Two of the chairs were already occupied as they entered.

Sam sprang from her seat with a scream and raced to wrap Grace in a hug. Arthur waved from his chair sarcastically.

"Don't mind me," Arthur said, "I'm not sure I'm really here."

Grace dragged him upright to give him a kiss and a hug. "Are you sure now, Arthur?" she asked him.

"Not convinced. Maybe try again with more feeling," he said, smiling until Sam knocked him back into his chair. They all took seats, Gabriel taking the chair at the head of the table.

Jesus stood behind Gabriel, surveying the group. "Everybody's hungry, no? And wine? I'll be right back, then."

Jesus returned a few minutes later and took the seat at the end of the table opposite Gabriel. Several waiters and waitresses followed a few minutes later, placing platters of appetizers down the middle of the table and filling the wine glasses.

"Are all of you dead, then?" Jesus asked, smiling.

"Not yet," *Zimmerman* said.

Arthur looked at his wife. "Probably," Sam said.

"Hard to say," Zimmerman said.

"So why so many ghosts in my little restaurant?" Jesus said. "And it's not even the Day of the Dead."

"I'm in trouble," Grace said.

"Why am I not surprised?" Jesus asked, laughing. "You threaten to cut off the wrong guy's balls this time, Mariangela?"

"Something like that," Grace said, putting her chin in her hands.

"Whose *cajones* this time?" Jesus asked, still smiling.

"That would be *los cajones de Dios*," Gabriel said.

Jesus laughed briefly, then noticed nobody else was laughing. Jesus stopped smiling. "Maybe we should eat first," Jesus suggested.

There ensued a period of fervent conversation while they all ate and drank and caught up. Sam explained what she and Arthur had been doing the past few years that Grace and Gabriel had been dead. Jesus told the Zimmermans about how he had parlayed Grace's investment into a chain of high end restaurants. Jesus and Zimmerman both did a good job of trying not to look at Grace, though it wasn't long before they each realized what the other was doing.

Jesus stopped in mid-sentence. He nodded in Grace's direction. "She's in real trouble this time?" Jesus asked.

Zimmerman nodded.

"She is in trouble a lot, I think," Jesus said, trying to smile.

"Seems so," Zimmerman said, "This trouble is bigger, Jesus."

"I have to help her," Jesus said.

"Yeah. Join the club."

"She save your life, like she saved mine?" Jesus asked.

"No, not really," Zimmerman said. "Mine didn't need saving."

"So what she do for you?"

"Pretty much just fucked us up," *Zimmerman* weighed in.

"Oh." Jesus pretended to understand for a bit. "You guys twins, huh?"

"Um, not really," *Zimmerman* said.

"No?" Jesus looked surprised. "I mean, you look a lot alike. Identical, even."

"Yeah, we get that a lot," Zimmerman said, sighing.

"Did she really try to cut off the balls of *Jesus Christo*?"

"To be honest, Jesus," Zimmerman said, "I never did figure out exactly what she did to piss Him off. But He is pretty pissed, I can tell you that much."

It was during dessert and coffee that the conversation around the table began to wane, with each of the diners shooting more frequent glances toward Grace. Finally, Gabriel rapped his knuckles on the wooden table top. The sparse remaining talk dwindled into silence as they all looked to Gabriel.

"That was great, Jesus, thank you," Gabriel said.

"For my friends, it is my honor," Jesus said, tipping his wineglass towards Grace. "*Salúd.*"

"We may need more than a good dinner from you, Jesus," Gabriel said.

"What exactly is going on?" Samantha asked.

"Yeah. And it better be pretty fucking awful, Helena," Arthur said. "Because we got pretty screwed getting here, you know."

"Quiet, hon," Sam said. "This isn't about you this time."

"This time? Are you kidding? It's always about her, every time. Even after she's dead, it's still about her."

Sam shrugged apologetically to the group. "Artie's just a little upset about being almost dead, that's all. We thought we were going on vacation. To China."

"Yeah. China." Arthur said petulantly.

"You guys don't look 'almost dead,' " Jesus said.

"They're not really 'almost dead,' " Gabriel corrected. "They're in an indeterminate superposition state."

"Which means what?" Zimmerman asked.

"They're both dead and alive," Gabriel explained.

"That makes no sense," Uriel said.

"It's a quantum duality thing," Gabriel said, trying to sound reasonable. "It's a supercritical state."

"Yeah, supercritical is right. What he means is, we live in a really shitty hotel on the other side of that wall," Arthur said, "in a parallel existence. You should stop by. Oh, that's right, you better not. Because if anybody discovers our quantum-teriffic super-really-fragile-istic semisolid state, our Wee Willie Wonkish wave function collapses and we die instantly. Or, if we're lucky, find ourselves flying again across the Indian Ocean like none of this ever happened. Got that?"

They all looked between Arthur and Gabriel for explanation.

"Exactly," Gabriel assured them. Everybody looked very confused. "The details aren't really important right now."

"Seems pretty important to me," Arthur said.

"Let's move on," Samantha suggested.

"I'm in some trouble," Grace said. "And Arthur, I'm sorry that you and Sam got pulled into this. I don't know how that happened."

"I did that," Gabriel said.

"Oh. Well, I'm sure Gabe had a great reason to get you and Sam killed. Or whatever. Oh, and my name's not really Helena. It's Grace."

"You said you're in trouble," Sam said, pre-empting her husband who had opened his mouth to speak. "What kind of trouble, Grace?"

"That's part of the problem. I'm not really sure," Grace said. "I just know that someone, or something, has been trying very hard to have me removed from the universe."

"You mean, someone's trying to kill you?" Jesus asked, face reddening.

"No. That would be fine, I've been dead before. It would be nice to be dead again, actually. But whatever is going on, it won't let me go back to being dead, either. It just wants me— gone."

"Gone?"

"Gone, like she never was. As in 'never having existed,'" Uriel explained.

"How is that possible? Who can do such a thing?" Jesus asked, visibly upset.

"I'm—I'm not entirely sure. But it seems that it might be God. At least, that's what some people are saying."

"God would not do such a thing. Such a thing is surely the work of the Devil, no?" Jesus said.

Uriel laughed and they all looked at him. "No such person," Uriel said.

"You are wrong, sir," Jesus said. "The Devil is real. You should know this. The Devil's greatest trick—"

" '—was to make people believe he didn't exist.' Bullshit. God's greatest trick was convincing us He did," Uriel said.

"God would not do such a thing," Jesus insisted.

"How the hell would you know?" Uriel asked him. "You ever meet the guy?" Jesus stared at Uriel liked he was looking at a crazy man. "Don't go all googly-eyes on me, *amigo*. Who do you think we're talking about here? Your strikingly handsome but mildly perforated Hispanic appearing namesake, gazing down at what's happening here on Earth? Grow up, come on."

"He's not like that?" Jesus asked, subdued but still obviously confused.

"Um—no."

"I don't understand," Jesus muttered. He looked away from Uriel.

"I must say, Earle," *Zimmerman* added, "that you got me a little confused as well."

"Listen," Uriel said in a modestly calmer tone, "you all gotta grow up here. If we're going to do anything about this situation, you have to drop the childish malarkey and get a grip. You can't walk into this with all the sophistication of a Sunday school class. All your organized religious nonsense is smoke and mirrors. It's an act, a long-running play with lots and lots of actors paid to feed you lines."

"Which religion are you referring to?" Arthur asked.

"All of them, Jew-boy," Uriel said. "Yours, his, theirs—all of them. A couple of different guys playing God and pulling strings, writing the various scripts. Every one of them calling himself 'God Almighty.' "

"But the Bible—"

"Bunch of crazy stories written, and rewritten, a dozen times by guys working for the guy playing God. And nobody doing any damn editing, ever."

"Hold it," Jesus said, holding up his hands. "Let me stop you there. You're saying there is no God."

"No, that's not what I'm saying. Are you not hearing me? Too many damned gods, Jesus."

"No, that's not what he means," *Zimmerman* continued. "He means the real God. You know, 'The God.' Not a lot of pretend—"

"There you go again, Zimmerman," Uriel said. "What are you talking about, 'a real God' or pretend? These folks I'm talking about is as real as it gets. Always been that way, the Real God pretending to be God. Right now, there's some God-awful asshat that's screwing with us and trying to screw Grace out of existence. Some guy looking down and screwing with us. Just the same way that God's been screwing with mankind since the beginning of time."

"Who is this man, again?" Jesus asked Zimmerman.

Chicago, IL

"Okay, then, Earle," Jesus said, leaning back into the conversation. "Let us entertain your theory that there is some-one playing at God. You say this someone is dead?"

"Yes, Jesus," Uriel explained. "Dead. Existing in the after-life, with all the special abilities and perspective that that brings. And almost certainly someone from well up in the future. Way, way up."

"Why is that?" Arthur asked.

"Because He would have the resources necessary to be God. That's a given."

"What kind of resources?"

"Advanced technology. Advanced enough to be miracu-lous. And perspective. By dying deeply in the future, He'd have access to a much longer vantage to work back on, to leverage in screwing with us."

"Not sure I'm getting this," Samantha said.

"I'm sure I'm not getting this," Arthur said.

"Even if what you're saying is true, Earle," Zimmerman interjected, "it doesn't explain why Grace is being excised."

"True," Uriel admitted.

"That sounds like an important point," Jesus said. "What did you do, *mamacita*, to get this future dead God Guy so pissed at you, eh?"

Grace shrugged. "I don't know. I thought it had to do with the stunt I pulled with Gabe, breaking down the barrier be-tween this life and the afterlife. That's what I thought."

"Sounds like a good reason," *Zimmerman* agreed.

"No, it can't be that," Grace said. "I fixed that. I—we," she continued, "went to a lot of trouble to make that right. Pauley said it didn't get me off the hook. And now I learn that there's been all sorts of direct travel between the worlds. What I did was nothing compared to what Wright did to break down the barrier, and obviously he was never excised."

"But the barriers are up again," Gabe said. "Wright gates don't exist anymore."

"None of them?" Grace asked.

"None of them," Gabriel assured her. "In one swell foop, like they never existed."

"Because they never did," Uriel said.

"Yes, they did," Grace said. "I've been through them, a couple of times. So has Gabe." Gabe nodded.

"That was different," Uriel said. "Before this time around. Now somebody changed it up, maybe changed it so that Borthwick never taught Wright the magic trick. The gates never came into existence, so they don't work anymore."

"Who could change that?" Zimmerman asked.

Uriel shrugged. "God. Probably not that hard—must be a thousand inflection points that would prevent Wright from designing that little architectural trick. Maybe Borthwick was excised."

"I don't know who the Borthwick is that you are referring to," Jesus said, "but you're not explaining why my friend Grace is the subject of God's holy wrath, you know? We should try to understand that, I think."

"You're probably right, Jesus," Grace agreed. "I just don't think it has anything to do with the discovery that Gabe and I made. It doesn't make sense."

"Maybe it is because you killed a priest," *Zimmerman* suggested.

"You killed a priest?" Jesus said.

"Once. A long time ago," Grace admitted. "And I don't think that's it, either."

"No, that's not it," Uriel assured her. "Asshole deserved to die. Nobody in this universe could hold that against you."

"So it's not because you created a way to talk to the dead, and it's not because you killed Pauley, and it's probably not because you killed yourself, either," Gabriel said. "Which still leaves the question of why you deserve to be excised."

"I don't deserve to be excised," Grace said indignantly.

"Of course not, hon," Gabe said.

Uriel said, "Just as likely it's something Grace hasn't done. Could be something she does in the future. Like I was saying, the God trying to excise her has a long view ahead, might be He knows something she's going to do that He doesn't want to happen. That could be the reason."

"But I promised I wouldn't do anything," Grace said.

"Might be something you can't not do," Uriel said.

"Like what?" Arthur asked.

Uriel shrugged. "Can't say."

"Well, that just sucks, don't it? We need more information," Arthur said. "We need to know why Grace is being targeted."

"We're not going to get that information," Uriel said. "Not like we have any friends from that far in the future, you know? Just not metaphysically possible."

"Then we just have to deal with the situation," Gabriel said. "For whatever reason, God is trying to excise Grace. We deal with that."

"Yeah," Grace said. "Let's deal with that." She looked around the table at her friends. "How, exactly, do we deal with that?"

Chicago, IL

"I'm thinking maybe it doesn't matter," Zimmerman said.

"Maybe what doesn't matter?" *Zimmerman* asked.

"Why, or who, or how someone is trying to excise Grace."

"Of course it matters," Arthur said.

"Not if we just get Grace back," Zimmerman said. "That's why they're trying to trap her on this side, so they can get to her."

Uriel nodded slowly. "Yeah, I see what you're saying, Padre."

"But the gates no longer work," Grace said. "I can't get back."

"I don't understand," Sam said. "Why can't you just die again, Grace? I mean, you did it once already. Not trying to be insensitive or anything."

"No," Uriel said. "It's not that simple. Just dying again, or getting killed, or committing suicide, would really get her screwed."

"Well, she wouldn't be excised, Earl," *Zimmerman* said.

"No, but she wouldn't be back to her afterlife, either. She'd be lost," Uriel explained.

"Lost?" Grace said.

"Yeah."

"That sounds—bad," Zimmerman said.

"It is. No chance Grace would end up where she was. Not with her family, or anywhere she belongs. For eternity. That's why you need a gateway. Dying keeps you from being excised, but it leads to something a helluva lot worse."

"Well, fuck me sideways," Grace said, softly.

"Maybe we can get them turned back on," Arthur said. "The gates, I mean."

"Not in this life," Uriel said. "We don't know how they were uninvented. Even if we did, God could just find a different way of turning 'em off again, stay one step ahead of us, round and round like that."

"Then I'm stuck here?" Grace asked. "Forever, until He finally gets me excised? Or I die, and then I'm even more screwed?"

"There's another way," Uriel said. "There are other gateways, natural gates. Parnell talked about a natural gateway he used a lot. Before the Wright gates. Like the one used by Jesus, that kind of gate. Can't be turned off, part of the structure of Creation."

"You're one weird dude, Earle," Jesus said. "What do you mean, 'like the one Jesus used?'"

"Not important right now," Uriel said.

"Where is this natural gate?" Gabriel asked.

"One in Ukraine, Parnell said," Uriel said.

"Oh, great." Grace threw up her hands. "What are the chances of me staying alive long enough to get to Ukraine?"

"There are probably others," Uriel said.

"How do we find one?"

"No idea," Uriel admitted.

Arthur said, "We could check out some likely sites, though. You know, like that Vortex in Sedona. Stonehenge. Ayer's Rock. That sort of thing."

"Great," Grace said. "So fucked."

They were all quiet for a time while more wine arrived.

Jesus broke the silence, saying, "So if you're not sure who is trying to do this to Grace, and you don't know why he's trying to to do this to her, maybe it not really going to happen."

"Oh, she's going to be excised, Jesus," Uriel assured him. "It's happened before. We're just a little ahead of Him so far on this go-round."

"So you're sure, then?" Arthur asked. Uriel, Grace, and the Zimmermans nodded. "And you really believe that God is the one behind this?"

"Yeah," Uriel said. "Pauley checked it with administration. Besides, no one else can make this kind of play."

"Well, Grace," Arthur said, "Sounds to me like you're pretty much fucked."

"Thanks, Arthur. That helps a lot," Grace said.

"I am afraid I am forced to agree with Arthur," Jesus said. "One cannot defy the will of God."

"Yes, one can. I can," Grace said heatedly, her face reddening.

Jesus shook his head. "How?"

"I don't know how, Jesus," Grace said. "But I've—we've—been doing it so far, haven't we? I mean, Julius was able to save me. So there's that." Zimmerman smiled weakly.

"Yeah, how is that, Earl?" *Zimmerman* asked. "I mean, if it really is God who wants Grace excised, and He's all-powerful and all-knowing and all, how is it that we're even here talking about this? Why isn't Grace already excised, and we're going on about our lives, none the wiser?"

Grace brightened. "Yeah, why is that?" she asked Uriel.

"Because there are limits, that's why," Uriel said.

"Limits? What kind of limits? For God?" *Zimmerman*

asked.

"Yeah, even for God," Uriel replied. "God is powerful, of course. If this is the guy I think we're going against, like I said, He's relatively all-powerful."

"What does that mean, 'relatively all-powerful'? That's an oxymoron," Arthur said.

"I said relatively, moron," Uriel said. "Like I was telling you before, the God you call God, the God who's probably in play here, is almost for sure The One. One from the deep future, The One who is so powerful that He's been able to prevent other players from playing god since he came on the scene, you know what I mean?"

"Got it. Monotheism," *Zimmerman* said.

"Yeah. One Guy who decided it was time He was The One. No God but God, you got it? That's when the deal changed, right there. It's just a giant interdimensional game of Risk, you see? But God isn't all-powerful, like He can't just snap His fingers and make things on Earth happen from where He's at. It's not magic. He needs agents, mechanisms. That's why He sent His Son in the flesh, you see? He can use His advanced technology and insight and shit, but He has to have agency in this world to make it happen. Can't free the Jews without a Moses."

"That's why He can't just snap His fingers and make me disappear?" Grace said hopefully. "That's why Pauley had to do it?"

Uriel nodded. "Exactly. He's got players, of course, lots of 'em. He got the Catholic Church this time to make the play against you. That crazy book Pauley was using, that was a tool the Church dropped on him to make the job easier. That sort of thing."

"That 'crazy book' didn't help him much," Zimmerman said. "Seems some of the time it was working against Pauley, almost leading him just enough wrong to let us survive."

Uriel nodded. "Yeah, that was weird. Like someone on the other side was messing with it, it seemed. Haven't quite figured that out myself."

"But why Pauley?" Zimmerman asked. "Of all the people God could use, that's one helluva asshole to pick as His agent for this."

Uriel almost answered, but Grace preempted him.

"Who cares?" she said. Grace stood up and started to pace, excited. "But this is good. Well, not good, I'm still pretty fucked and all, but—" She paused, took a deep breath, thinking. "Even if it is God that wants me excised, it's not me against God. It's me against some agent of God, some way that God is trying to get to me down here." Uriel nodded, watching her resume her pacing circles around the table. "Not me against God, then." She stopped behind her husband's chair and put her hands on Gabriel's shoulders. "It's me—it's us—against God's plan."

"Tell you the truth, hon," Gabriel said, "I'm not sure I see the difference."

"And that explains why He has to keep me here, on this side," Grace continued, ignoring her husband. "He needs his minions to get to me here. No minions in the hereafter."

Uriel nodded. "Yeah, I think that part's right. Doesn't make your situation a whole lot better, though."

Grace stared hard at Uriel. "Yeah, it does, Earl. It changes everything. It gives us a play."

JUST A BRIEF WORD HERE ABOUT OMNISCIENCE. I KNOW THAT THE REALIZATION THAT I'M NOT OMNIPOTENTLY OMNIPOTENT WAS A BIT OF A SHOCK. I TRUST THAT YOU UNDERSTAND THE SUBTLETY OF MY EXPLANATION, THAT YOU REALIZE THAT YOUR GOD CHOOSES NOT TO BE OMNIPOTENT. PLEASE, KEEP THAT IN MIND.

AND DON'T GET ANY IDEAS ABOUT

MY OMNISCIENCE. I AM OMNISCIENT. NO RESTRICTIONS. I KNOW EVERYTHING. EVERYWHERE. ALL THE TIME. "ALL KNOWING."

YES, I AM ALL-KNOWING. JUST NOT ALL-CARING.

LOTS AND LOTS OF STUFF GOING ON ALL THE TIME, AND I KNOW ABOUT ALL OF IT. DOESN'T MEAN, THOUGH, THAT I REALLY GIVE A TINKER'S DAM ABOUT A LOT OF IT. ACTUALLY, MOST OF IT. THAT'S JUST THE WAY IT IS. KNOWLEDGE IS INFINITE —CARING, NOT SO MUCH.

NO, I DON'T CARE IN THE LEAST IF YOUR FOOT-BALL TEAM WINS THE DAMN GAME, EVEN IF YOU DID BET THE FARM ON THE GAME SO THAT YOU CAN BUY THAT BONE MARROW TRANSPLANT FOR YOUR PRETTY LITTLE GIRL. JEEZ—GIVE ME A BREAK. I KNOW FOR A FACT THAT YOUR SISTER IS A PERFECT GENETIC MATCH AND SHE'S LOADED UP THE GAZOO EVER SINCE SHE DIVORCED THAT PLASTIC SURGEON, BUT SHE'S JUST BEING THE MANIPULATIVE SHREW THAT YOUR PARENTS CREATED BECAUSE THEY NEVER KNEW HOW TO SAY 'NO.' OMNISCIENCE, REMEMBER? WHY DON'T YOU JUST GIVE HER A CALL INSTEAD OF BUSTING MY CHOPS EVERY SUNDAY?

OH, BUT PLEASE, KEEP THOSE CARDS AND PRAYERS COMING, FOLKS. UNFORTUNATELY, DUE TO THE HIGH VOLUME, OUR STAFF IS UNABLE TO RE-

SPOND TO EVERY PRAYER PERSONALLY. OR EVEN, YOU KNOW, ACTUALLY GIVE A DAMN. BUT PLEASE KNOW THAT WE VALUE YOUR WORSHIP.

Chicago, IL

"God wants me excised," Grace said, standing in the corner of the room now, no longer pacing. "Maybe, He *needs* me excised. We can use that. Use it as motivation."

"Motivation for what?" Gabriel asked.

Grace smiled wickedly. "A game," she said.

"Game? What kind of game?" Arthur asked.

"He needs to have me excised. But I'm not excised. He's been trying over and over again. I'm still here. Maybe God's getting a wee frustrated with this whole deal. Maybe even a little desperate."

"God, desperate? What are you talking about?" Jesus asked, looking over his shoulder to where Grace stood.

"So we give Him what He's looking for, a way forward. A better way than the one He's been trying. A way that we control."

"Oh, that kind of game. You're talkin' about a con, girl," Uriel said.

"A con?" Samantha asked.

Grace smiled, and nodded.

"You're talking about running a con game—with God as the mark?" Arthur asked.

"You're crazy, Grace," *Zimmerman* said.

"That is not possible," Jesus said. "God is all-knowing, God is all-powerful. God cannot be the mark in your con game."

"That's exactly why He's a perfect mark," Grace said, beginning to pace around the table again, pointing at Jesus. "That's why it'll work. He knows He knows everything, so He won't see it coming. And He has to go for it, too, because He can't not be all-powerful. It's perfect."

"It's crazy enough," Uriel nodded. "I give you that. But

what kinda con do you play on God?"

"Yeah, what kind of con, Grace?" Arthur asked. "Every con leverages greed. Don't think God needs more money, do you?"

"Not money, Arthur," Grace said. "Power." Grace started pacing again. "God has to protect His power. He has to have all the power. He can't turn away from even the possibility that He doesn't have it all, you see?"

Uriel was nodding again. "Yeah, yeah. I like your thinking here. Only the Jewish guy is right, you know. Usual con not going to work. Not a wire job, not any kind of insider game. God's got all the insider info He needs, more than we'll ever have. What game are you thinking of running?"

Grace shook her head, thinking and pacing. "No, not a wire. But a big game, it's gotta be. If it's just a small con, He'll squash me like a bug. Just have me excised before we even have a chance to set up a play. No, it has to be something big, give Him a target that's better than me—so big, I don't matter anymore by comparison." She stopped pacing. "A fiddle game, Earl. Gotta be." She touched the side of her nose, smiling, at Uriel.

"I don't know if God even plays the fiddle," Samantha said.

"No, I'm pretty sure that's the Devil," Arthur said.

"One and the same, I told you," Uriel said. "But I don't care if you're danglin' a damn Stradivarius, it's not going to fly. I don't see it, Grace."

"Not literally, come on. A shuffle of the fiddle game."

"But you can't do this, real fiddle or fake fiddle or no fiddle," Jesus said. "He is God! He is not your mark. He knows all. He is all-powerful. He cannot be conned."

"Yeah. Jesus has a point, you know," Sam said.

"But He's not all-powerful here, we've proven that. He has to act through agents, He has to play by certain rules, if only because He made the rules. So we use those rules—his rules — against Him. He may be all-powerful, but we know how things work down here."

"Unless he pulls a miracle on you," Zimmerman said.

"Then why hasn't He pulled a miracle on me already?" Grace asked.

Zimmerman shrugged.

"Yeah, maybe you're right about that part," *Zimmerman* said. "But that still doesn't overcome the fact that He's omniscient. He probably even knows what we're talking about right now." They all looked around. "Shit, He could be moving his agents in this direction right now."

"Should I lock the door?" Jesus asked.

"No, it can't be that easy for Him," Grace said. "He may have more information than we do, maybe some futuristic surveillance and all kinds of super spy shit, but he can't know everything, everywhere, all the time. He can't see every possibility that's coming. If He did, Julius wouldn't have been able to save me. God would've just had Pauley or someone take him out before he could get to me. Had someone jump him or something. It's not that straightforward."

Zimmerman nodded. "You must be right, Grace. He has knowledge, sure, but He can't anticipate every eventuality, every possibility. We're the variables—we must be. Our actions, what other folks do, might change on a whim, can't be counted on even by a God who's seen the future."

"Quantum indeterminancies," Samantha added. They all looked at her for a moment.

"Whatever," Julius continued. "We've got free will, don't we? We make choices, sometimes crazy choices. Why would Pauley have to depend on that book to direct him, if God had perfect intelligence on you? That book sucked, but it was like an all-knowing surveillance tool, kind of. But only of stuff that already happened. Every time Pauley tried to look ahead, it screwed up. It was nonsense."

"Yeah, yeah. I knew it," Grace said. "Not sure what you're talking about, Julius, but you're right. I'm right." She looked at her husband. "You're being awful quiet, Gabe. Say something." Gabriel wore a strange expression, looking at his wife.

"Shit, hon," he said slowly. "You're right."

"I am?"

He nodded. "It's why Arthur and Sam are here."

"It is?" Sam asked.

"It's why I set up the Schrödinger box, why I gave these guys the plane tickets, the instructions for the pulse thing-a-ma-jig. I just didn't see it before—not from this perspective," Gabriel said. He looked with amazement around the table, his gaze finally coming back to rest on his wife. "Listen. Before I came back to get you, to get you and Julius from the basement, I was back in Dublin."

"Dublin? Why, hon?"

"To see my math friend at Trinity College. The guy who helped me figure out your formula, when I was alive."

"I told you, Gabe, it wasn't my formula," Grace said, coming back to the table and sitting down again in her seat next to her husband. She took his hand. "You figured that out. I just left a few bread crumbs, remember?"

"Yeah, right. Whatever. But I didn't come back intending to get you and Julius out of that car dealership. I came back to Trinity College, to get my ring."

"Your ring?" Zimmerman asked, embarrassed. "But I—"

"You threw my ring off the bridge," Gabriel said.

Zimmerman nodded. "I'm sorry. I didn't want it anymore. I didn't think it was right to keep it, not with Grace starting over, so I threw it in the river."

"Right. Threw it in the river, you say?" Gabriel asked. Zimmerman nodded. "You see it splash? Actually go into the river, I mean?"

"Well, no, I didn't actually watch it all the way down. I didn't have to, Gabriel, I threw the thing off a bridge. Not like it was going anywhere else."

"But it did go somewhere else, Julius. It landed back at Trinity College. In Dublin. Right where it was, before my wife stole it."

"No, that's not right, Gabe," Arthur said. "I have your ring. Look." He held up his right hand, showing where the Claddagh ring sat on his finger. "I've worn it every day since you died, buddy."

"It's true, Gabe," Sam said. "As a tribute, you know. Parnell wanted it, but Artie said no."

"But Parnell did have it, in his bag," Zimmerman protested. "And Grace gave it to me to wear, because she felt it was important, remember?" he said, turning to Grace.

"That's right, Julius," Grace assured him. "And it was important. The ring helped you find me. I'm sure of it."

"No, no, you're both right," Gabriel enthused. "That's it exactly, hon. Julius needed the ring to follow you back. I died, the ring ended up with Parnell, eventually you gave it to Julius. But not this time. This time you're here, and Arthur has my ring."

"I wouldn't let Parnell take it," Arthur said.

"Right," Gabriel said, nodding. "When Grace was excised, it was a damn thunderclap where I was sitting. Like I said, would've killed me, I'm sure, if I wasn't already dead. A bolt of lightning, straight into my chest. I had to come back, didn't know what happened. So I backtracked, I went back to Trinity to see my friend. I didn't have the ring, of course—because Arthur had it. But he couldn't have it, because Grace had never stolen it. Grace had been excised, never existed."

"So it was still at Trinity College?" Grace asked.

"That's what I thought—but it wasn't. It had been stolen—but not by Grace. Took me a while to track down the story. Turns out the ring went on the museum tour in the States, same as before. But instead of getting stolen by Grace in Boston, it gets stolen later in the tour, in Chicago."

"So who stole it this time?" *Zimmerman* asked.

"You should know, *Julius*," Gabriel said. "I tracked down the police report. They had an ID on the guy who stole it, by his fingerprints. It was Zimmerman."

"Who, me?" Zimmerman asked. "I never stole it."

"Different Zimmerman," Gabriel said, looking at *Zimmerman*.

"I never stole the ring, either," *Zimmerman* said, reddening.

"No, not either of you," Gabriel said. "It was somebody named Elijah Zimmerman."

"My brother?" both Zimmermans said.

"Yeah," Gabriel said. "That Zimmerman."

"The dead one?" Grace asked.

Zimmerman ignored this. "So what happened to the ring?" he asked. "If they knew he stole it, what happened?"

Gabriel shook his head. "They never recovered it, Julius. By the time they identified Zimmerman as the thief, he was overseas."

"Overseas, where?" Grace asked.

"Elijah shipped out to Afghanistan. That's how they must've known it was him. Matched his fingerprints in the Navy database," *Zimmerman* said.

"Your brother was in the Navy? He didn't die in high school?" Grace asked *Zimmerman*. *Zimmerman* nodded.

"He took the ring with him to Afghanistan," Gabriel confirmed.

"So, did they arrest him? Get it back?" Grace asked.

"No. They never found it. It wasn't with his possessions when..."

"Eli was killed six weeks after he got to Afghanistan," *Zimmerman* said. "Must've done something with it, or lost it before...before he..."

"What the fuck?" Grace exclaimed, looking between the two Zimmermans. "He didn't die as a teenager from cancer, but lived just long enough to die as a Navy Seal in Afghanistan?"

"Yeah," *Zimmerman* said. "Pretty much."

"Man," Grace said, looking over at Julius. "Talk about 'history doesn't repeat itself, but it sure does rhyme.'"

"Doesn't rhyme, either," Uriel corrected. "It just is. So the ring was lost in Afghanistan this time around."

"How can there be two?" Arthur asked.

"Same reason there's two of them," Uriel said, pointing at the Zimmermans.

"I've been wondering about that," Jesus said. "They're not twins, you know."

"No, they're not twins, Jesus," Uriel said. "It shouldn't have happened, but it did."

"What do you mean, it shouldn't have happened, Earl?" Zimmerman asked.

"What should've happened is the same thing that happened to all of them and the rest of creation. Once you pushed Grace off that bridge, he was you. Not supposed to be two of you from that moment on. Except God stepped in to fuck it up. In the time between me killing you, and you catching up to Grace to push her, God made some change that shifted things enough so that you got screwed. Some key point in the past was changed, changed this reality just enough to trap you as you are."

"What do you mean, trapped?" Zimmerman asked.

"Sorry, son. Just like it sounds. You're stuck on this side, just like me. We go round and round, but not to the other side."

"Still don't get how the ring ended up in Ireland," Jesus said.

"Because it never hit the water, that's why," Uriel said.

"Earl's right," Gabriel said. "Just like Julius here. Grace was excised, so it was like she never existed, so she never stole the ring to give it to me. It was just a little burp in the universe, and Grace was back in existence in the new reality. But by then, the split had happened. So two rings."

"And two Zimmermans," *Julius* said.

"Yeah, that too," Uriel added.

"I remember you always telling me, Grace, that it wasn't a fucking ring. You remember that?" Gabriel asked. Grace nodded. "When you were here and suddenly, not here, when you—when Pauley excised you, I felt you disappear. Even from the other side, I felt it like half my heart was torn away. I had to come back, to follow you through the gate you had taken."

"Were you walking around in the rain in a bathrobe?" Zimmerman asked.

Gabriel looked over at him sharply. "How did you know that?" Zimmerman shook his head. "Anyway," he continued, "I flew over to Dublin and saw my friend the professor at the college. Told me about the ring. Once I was back in the States, I was planning on going back to Baltimore, to go back through the same Wright gate and then I don't know what, but—"

"Gate was bricked up," Grace said.

"It was? I never knew. But I didn't have to, I was able to just take a cab from JFK to the Guggenheim and get home. And by then I could feel you again, could see what you were up to, and I went to get you from the basement of that car dealership."

"Cute story," Arthur said. "But it doesn't explain why you had to lock Sam and I up in a box."

"It's entangled," Samantha said.

"What?" Arthur asked. "What's tangled?"

"Not tangled, dear. Entangled. It's a quantum thing, just like us. The two rings are quantum entangled. Einstein called it 'spooky forces at a distance,' because he didn't really understand it. Wouldn't believe in it, actually, because it allows for faster-than-light interactions. Screwed up General Relativity, so Einstein couldn't deal with it."

Gabriel nodded. "Makes sense," he said.

Arthur rolled his eyes. "I can't believe you even said that," Arthur said. "And you," he said, turning back to his wife, "I don't even know who you are. Crazy quantum malarkey, where are you coming up with this stuff?"

Sam shrugged. "Lifetime subscription to Scientific American."

"Don't even know you," Arthur said again, shaking his

head.

"That's what got me on to the Schrödinger setup," Gabriel said. "The ring. Then, even before I knew you were alive again, the setup to get together a group of shills."

"Shills?" Jesus asked, not following.

"Talent. Extras. Players in a con game," Uriel explained.

Gabriel nodded. "I was still so shaken by losing you, I didn't really know what was up. I got together people to put in the box—I mean, to get onto the plane. But this all happened before you made it to the car dealership. How could I have known that we'd be here, and you'd come up with the idea of running a con?"

Arthur turned back to his wife. "Sam?"

"Quantum tunneling," Sam said, matter-of-factly. "Known phenomenon, though it's only been observed at the subatomic scale. Reversal of cause and effect, tunneling through space-time so events or particles are replaced, future into the past."

Arthur rolled his eyes. "Scientific American?"

She nodded. "Couple of months ago. Who'd you get to be on the plane with us, Gabe?"

"About thirty others, hand-picked. Strange group, mostly. Some you'd recognize, probably."

"Like who?"

"Nikola Tesla, for one."

"He's dead, Gabe."

"Yeah, most of the folks I put on your plane were dead."

"Tesla? Who else?"

"Like I said, strange group. Buckminster Fuller. About a dozen engineers, programmers. Some former CIA. A couple military intel guys. Humphrey Bogart and Lauren Bacall."

"What?"

"You heard me. Nice couple, but had a hard time explaining why they couldn't smoke anywhere. They really wanted to smoke. And screw."

"Yeah, I know that feeling," Grace said absently. When

she realized she had said that aloud, she blushed brightly. "Smoking. I meant smoking."

"You never smoked," Samantha said, smiling.

"A few former NASA staffers from the sixties and seventies, some physicists, and a few really old mathematicians," Gabe continued, pretending not to see Zimmerman also reddening at the end of the table.

Arthur asked, "Where are these people, Gabe?"

"On your plane. Or maybe by now, walking around your interdimensional hotel. You know, behind the wall there," Gabriel said, pointing behind Arthur.

"I'm at a loss," Arthur said.

"So we have a crew," Grace said, back to her normal alabaster complexion, clapping her hands together. "And the crew is in this quantum state like you did for Artie and Sam, right?" Gabriel nodded. "So there's your answer, Jesus. They're not alive or dead, so maybe God can't see them. We've got a crew, and we've got a blind."

"Still need a plan, girl," Uriel said.

"Yeah. I'm working on that."

Chicago, IL

They took a break to stand and stretch their legs. Most left the room.

"Hey, Gabe," Arthur said, stopping Gabriel before he left the room with his wife. "How about Sam and I? Is it okay if we walk outside, too, or will our existence come to a sudden end?"

Gabriel shrugged. "Ask Sam. I don't think it's a problem, Arthur. I think you guys can go anywhere you want. Probably can go anywhere on this side or the other, the way I see it. Just don't invite any guests back to the other side with you."

"What do you think, Sam?" Arthur asked.

"Go crazy, hon," Sam said.

Grace and Gabriel stood in front of the restaurant, enjoying the sunshine of the afternoon. Scores of people passed up and down the sidewalk in front of them. Grace huddled at her husband's side, holding tightly to his arm as she looked anxiously up and down State Street.

"Feels like I'm in a bubble, floating. A bubble that may pop at any moment. Nice to know you had my back the whole time," Grace said.

"What, you thought I was just basking in the ethereal sunshine while you were down here busting your ass?" Gabriel asked, squeezing his wife's shoulder tightly.

"Too busy trying to stay in existence to think about it, tell you the truth. But it's good to know that there's a place we can step into that's safe. I'm tired of running, Gabe."

He looked down on her, hugging her to his side. "I know, hon. You've been through a lot. But I'm afraid that it's not a safe house. Not for you."

Grace pulled away to look at him. "What do you mean? You just said to Arthur—"

"It is a safe house for Arthur, and Sam. Anybody on the plane when Arthur pushed that button and created the box. But it only works for people who were on the plane when the duality was created."

"Like you, you mean?"

"Uh, yeah. Technically."

"So you can go back there, where it's safe? Technically?" Grace asked, looking up at her husband. He nodded. "But not me?"

"No," he said, shaking his head. "Not you. Sorry."

"Well, thanks for that, Gabriel. Then I'm screwed, Gabe," Grace said. "This isn't nearly over. And it isn't going to end well. I can't keep running forever. I can't."

"I know, hon. We'll fix this, don't—" But Grace had already turned away and was headed back into the restaurant.

The group regathered around the big table in the back room. Uriel was already seated, speaking earnestly to Zimmerman. They both looked up when Grace returned, followed by Gabriel.

"I got a thought about how to play your fiddle game," Uriel said as they all sat down.

"Do you?" Grace asked. "That's great. Because I have no idea what I was talking about."

Uriel nodded. "Yeah, you do. Stall off the debt by getting the mark interested in a bigger prize. Then get out with the prize just when the mark thinks he's hit the jackpot. Just like the fiddle game."

Grace nodded. "Yeah, that's what I was thinking. And my existence is the prize. That's the easy part, the concept. Doesn't do much for us."

"Here's how I see it," Uriel said. "You been dangling there in front of God for a good while, but He hasn't been able to collect. So you stay in play, just out of reach, but we give Him a bigger target. Something juicier to grab his attention. Something so much better than you, He has to have it."

"Yeah, Earl. Except, that makes me the fiddle in this game. Staying in play and just out of reach is not where I want to be. Since it turns out that the Gabe's safe house hotel works for about everyone except me, that's a scary prospect." She shook her head sadly as she sat with elbows on the table, chin in hand. "And we need a damn big payoff, something that changes the game as a result and gets me off the board. I can't run from God forever."

Uriel nodded. "I know that, girl. I know the situation. Give me a chance here. I'm just starting."

"Okay," Grace said, watching the waiters re-enter the room with new bottles of wine.

"Julius and I were talking while you were out, discussing past events and all. The other forces involved."

"What other forces?" Gabriel asked.

"The Mormons, Parnell, the Catholic Church—others we may not even know about," Zimmerman said, watching one of the waiters pour wine, working his way down the far side of the table.

"Pretty much past tense, aren't they?" *Zimmerman* asked, acknowledging the waiter as he refilled his wine glass.

"No, not at all," Uriel said. "That's the point. Listen, this is a bit more complex than just Grace against God. It's dangerous to oversimplify our situation."

Zimmerman watched as the waiter moved past Gabriel's chair, not attempting to refill his glass. Zimmerman leaned forward across the table, tensing. The waiter had a white towel draped over his forearm, was now leaning towards Grace. But Grace's wine glass was full.

Zimmerman jumped up, knocking his chair over backward. In a second he had jumped up on the table.

"Hey," Zimmerman shouted.

The waiter withdrew a long, thin knife from his draped forearm. No one else moved.

"Knife!" Zimmerman yelled. No one looked up.

"The Messiah comes!" the waiter yelled, dropping the wine bottle and reaching for Grace's head with his free hand, his knife poised before her neck.

Grace screamed. Zimmerman covered the distance across the table top in one step, kicking the man's arm violently. The knife went flying into the air. Zimmerman stepped onto a plate and lost his balance, crashing hard onto the side of the table. The man looked shocked as he looked down on Zimmerman, stunned for an instant. Grace reached behind and seized the man's hair, pulling hard, her chair tilting backward until her knees locked against the table, then she was able to pull the man over, the waiter's forehead striking the corner of the table. With a grunt, the man fell limply to the floor, partly landing on Zimmerman. Julius flailed to get up as the man sagged on top of him. Grace sprung from her chair and fled to other side of the room. Uriel was moving now, out of his chair, and coming forward as the waiter started to recover, the man pushing himself onto his hands and knees. Uriel grabbed up the wine bottle from the floor and smashed it over the waiter's head. The waiter fell prone, unconscious. Zimmerman struggled shakily to his feet.

"Shit!" Zimmerman said. By this time everyone in the room was standing, shaken.

"What the fuck?" Arthur stammered.

Uriel dropped the broken wine bottle. "Yeah, exactly. Glad you saw him, Zimmerman. Close."

"Shit," Zimmerman repeated, shaking.

Jesus was up and moving quickly. He instructed his manager to call 911 and an ambulance. Uriel checked that the man was still alive.

"Doubt he comes around anytime soon" Uriel said. "But just in case, you might want to lock him up in the walk-in or something."

"You think so?" Jesus asked. "But the police, what will they say?"

"Tell them the asshole tried to kill you," Uriel said. "Show them the knife. You know this guy, Jesus?"

"I am ashamed to say I do not. I do not know all the employees any more, you see. I am so sorry," he said, turning to Grace who was still cowering in the corner of the room behind her husband. "I am so sorry." Jesus left and came back with several strong employees. They picked up the waiter and carted him out of the room.

They all drifted back to their seats. Grace was last to return to the table, sitting as she held hands with Gabriel.

"Why?" *Zimmerman* finally asked.

"What do you mean?" Arthur asked, still pale and sweating. He took a deep drink of his wine. "The wine's okay, right?"

"That's not excision," *Zimmerman* said. "That was an assassination attempt."

"Yeah," Gabriel said. Grace was nervously drumming her fingers against the table until Gabriel squeezed her hand.

"Thanks, Julius. That was brilliant." Grace nodded at him but didn't meet his eyes.

Uriel said, "You're right. I don't understand it. Dead is not the same as excised. Why the change?"

"I'm just as fucked if I'm killed," Grace said, still looking down at the table. "More, even."

"True," Uriel said. "But it doesn't accomplish the same thing."

"I don't care what it doesn't accomplish," Grace said hotly. "I'm fucked. It's a lot easier to kill me. I won't last two hours out there."

Jesus returned and took his seat.

"It's not hard to understand," *Zimmerman* said. "There's another player in this. Must be. He yelled something about the Messiah, whatever that means. You were right, Earl. The situation is more dangerous than we thought. More complicated."

"Didn't think things got any more dangerous than being targeted by God," Zimmerman said.

Zimmerman considered. "Getting excised was one thing. But now we're not just running from Pauley, or a group of twenty-something year old missionaries. The threat is anyone that wants to kill Grace, and we don't know who or how many that may be."

"We've got to run," Gabriel said. "We can't just sit here and wait for another attack."

"I have secured the restaurant, Gabriel," Jesus said. "No one will get in this room without my say-so."

"They could drop a fuckin' bomb on our heads," Arthur said.

"No, let's not start talking nonsense," *Zimmerman* said. "We're still sitting in the middle of Chicago. It's not like there's an army after her."

"True," Uriel said. "But *Zimmerman*'s right. Something else is in play. God, the Catholics, want Grace excised. The Mormons are trying to keep her alive, on this side. But somebody just wants her dead. Maybe more than one somebody."

"Actually, when you think about it, we're not even sure why the Mormons are interested. Why they're working to keep Grace on this side," Gabriel said.

"True," Uriel said. "Maybe for the same reason the others want her dead."

"He didn't see me," Zimmerman said, to no one in particular. "Did you see that?"

Uriel nodded.

"Saw what?" Gabriel asked.

"You saw that, right?" Zimmerman asked of Uriel. "I was right in front of him, but he acted like I wasn't even there." Uriel nodded again, but said nothing. "Why was that, Earl? It happened before, I think. At the car dealership, I was…"

He trailed off, shaking his head. Zimmerman flexed his fingers where his knuckles had struck the side of the table as he fell.

"He didn't see you," Uriel said. "Just be thankful he didn't, Julius."

"But why?" *Zimmerman* asked.

"It happens," Uriel explained. "It's because of our—situation. Sometimes, we get thin. Sometimes."

"Thin? What are you talking about?" *Zimmerman* asked.

Uriel shook his head. "This isn't the time. The game has changed. God wants Grace excised. But others are involved —others who think killing Grace is good enough."

"We're completely on the defensive here," *Zimmerman* said. "We won't survive—Grace won't survive—if we keep sitting and talking."

Grace nodded.

"And we need to split up," Gabriel said. Grace looked up sharply.

"He's right," Uriel said. "Too big a group."

"Julius," Grace said, "You need to stay with me."

Zimmerman nodded.

"Grace, Julius, and I will make a run," Gabriel said. "Arthur, Sam—you guys get back to your hotel. I'll get back to you. Organize your crew."

"Organize them for what? I don't know the plan." Arthur

said.

"I'll let you know as soon as we have one," Gabriel said. "Earl, you and the other Julius here are on your own. See what you can find out about our situation. We need information more than anything. I'm not sure how we'll get in touch, but we'll figure something out."

Uriel nodded.

"What about me?" Jesus asked. "I know I almost let Grace get killed in my restaurant, but I want to help."

"If it wasn't for you and your restaurant, Jesus," Gabriel said, "I don't think Grace would still be alive. But we do need your help. We'll need cash."

"I can do that, Gabriel. But where will you go? I can find a place, maybe."

Grace shook her head. "Just the money, Jesus. That will be great."

"Okay," Jesus said. He stood. "I'll start working on that." He started to walk to the door, then stopped and turned around. "Maybe a gun?" he asked Julius. "I'm sure one of my employees could come up with one. This is Chicago."

Julius shook his head. "Thanks, anyway, Jesus."

Jesus shrugged and left.

So GOD CREATED MAN IN HIS OWN IMAGE, IN THE IMAGE OF GOD HE CREATED HIM; MALE AND FEMALE HE CREATED THEM. AND GOD BLESSED THEM, AND GOD SAID TO THEM, "BE FRUITFUL AND MULTIPLY, AND FILL THE EARTH AND SUBDUE IT..."

SOME MAY FIND THIS A BIT OVERGENEROUS ON MY PART. THE WHALES, FOR INSTANCE, WERE NOT THRILLED WITH THIS DEVELOPMENT. NO ONE CAN CLAIM THAT THOSE WHALES AREN'T SMART—THEY

SAW WHAT WAS COMING. IF I HAD ANY REGRETS (WHICH, OF COURSE, I DO NOT) IT'S THAT I PRETTY MUCH SET UP THOSE WHALES, BIG TIME. AND THOSE WHALES ARE GREAT, THEY DON'T DESERVE THE WAY YOU GUYS TREAT THEM. I WILL SAY, THOUGH, THAT I AM PRETTY DAMN SICK OF THOSE WHALES BEACHING THEMSELVES ALL OVER THE PLACE, JUST TO RUB MY NOSE IN IT. HAD TO BE DONE, WHALES! DEAL WITH IT.

OBVIOUSLY, MANKIND IS NOT UNIQUE IN MOST WAYS. IN MOST EVERY WAY, ACTUALLY, I DID BETTER WITH A LOT OF OTHER CREATURES. LOTS OF THEM HAVE SKILLS, LOTS HAVE PRETTY GOOD INTELLECTUAL CAPACITY (I'M LOOKING AT YOU, DOLPHINS! FLIPPER-HIGH FIVE!), EVERY ONE OF 'EM HAVE A NICE FEELING OF SELF-AWARENESS. LOTS AND LOTS OF GREAT CREATURES. SO WHY DO YOU? IT PAINS ME TO TELL YOU (METAPHORICALLY), BUT THE UNIVERSE NEEDS YOU.

I HAD TO CREATE MAN, AND GIVE YOU DOMINION, BECAUSE THE UNIVERSE NEEDS A CREATURE WITH AGENCY. UNFORTUNATELY, IT'S TRUE. THE UNIVERSE ONLY WORKS IF IT IS INHABITED BY A FORCE WITH THE CAPACITY TO INFLUENCE ITS EXISTENCE. WHALES ARE COOL, AND SMART, AND NICE —BUT THEY DON'T HAVE AGENCY. THEY CANNOT EFFECT THE UNIVERSE. THEY SWIM AROUND, THEY

THINK GREAT THOUGHTS, SING THE BEST DAMN SLAM POETRY YOU'LL EVER KNOW—BUT WHALES CAN'T ACT UPON THE UNIVERSE. FLIPPERS AIN'T OP-POSABLE THUMBS, YOU SEE. NOBODY BUT YOU FOLKS CAN DO THAT.

WHY DOES THE UNIVERSE NEED A FORCE FOR AGENCY? BECAUSE IF I CREATED A UNIVERSE WITH-OUT YOU, WITHOUT YOUR CUTE LITTLE CAPACITY TO ACT, THEN THE WHOLE THING JUST FREEZES UP. WITHOUT YOUR FRISSON OF FABULOUSNESS, YOUR JE NE SAIS QUOI, THE UNIVERSE—THE UNI-VERSE I CREATED—IS JUST A REALLY INTRICATE CLOCKWORK. LAPLACE'S DÆMON, RIGHT? EVERY-THING THAT HAPPENED LEADS TO EVERYTHING THAT WILL HAPPEN. WELL, IT'S TRUE; OR IT WOULD BE TRUE, IF I DIDN'T CREATE YOU GUYS. YOU GUYS TAKE THE WORK OUT OF THE CLOCKWORK, YOU SEE? YOUR QUANTUM MECHANISTIC BRAINS MAKE POSSIBLE THAT CRAZY FREE WILL OF YOURS—AND THAT'S WHAT MAKES THE WHOLE UNIVERSE HUM. WITHOUT MANKIND AND THE CRAZY THINGS THAT YOU DO, I MIGHT AS WELL HAVE JUST PAINTED A PRETTY MOVING PICTURE AND HUNG IT ON MY COS-MIC WALL.

Chicago, Illinois

They all started to get up from their chairs. Uriel re-mained seated, rapping his knuckles on the table until he had their attention.

"Sit your asses back down," Uriel commanded.

"What?" Gabriel said. "You heard the plan. What's the problem, Earl?"

"That wasn't a plan. That's just running. Just a good way to get folks killed, more than likely."

Gabriel dropped back in his chair. The others did the same. "Not sure it's such a great idea to sit here, Earl."

"You don't have any idea, great or otherwise," Uriel said. "Because we don't know what in hell is happening. But going out there and running around like a bunch of blind chickens isn't going to save anyone's ass. Least of all, hers," he said, nodding at Grace. "We sit for a bit and come up with a real plan. Then we split up."

"Okay," Grace said, trying to look relaxed as she put her feet up on the table, ankles crossed and hands behind her head. "Arthur, you and Sam go through the people on your plane, or in your hotel. Whatever. Inventory your assets. See what skill sets you got. Get control of your earthly assets, too. Command and control, communications. Finances. That sort of thing."

"No idea what you're talking about," Arthur said.

"We got this, hon," Samantha assured him. Grace nodded at her.

"Good. Like Gabriel said: Earl, you and less-morose *Julius* there need to figure out what's going on. Get us some information to act on, find out who wants what. Who wants me excised, who wants me dead. What's up with the Mormons, too. What's their angle in wanting to kidnap me? We're too much in the dark here."

Uriel nodded.

"What about you three?" *Julius* asked, nodding at Grace, Julius, and Gabriel.

"We're going to try to stay alive," Julius said.

"No," Gabriel said. "That's not good enough. Earl's right. We need a plan to go on the offensive.

"Okay, here's the plan," Grace said, pulling her feet off the table and letting her chair rock forward onto all four legs. "We create a target, somebody so big and so important that God, or whoever's playing God, has no choice but to notice him, to take him on instead of me. Get God to buy the big fuckin' fiddle. Somebody who makes me not worth His trouble anymore."

"Yeah, like who, exactly?" Arthur asked.

"Gotta be the Devil himself," *Zimmerman* said.

Uriel shook his head. "No such being, I told you."

"So you say, Earl," *Zimmerman* said. "How about you, then. A misfit Archangel, or whatever you are."

"I'm just a tired old black man," Uriel said, shaking his head.

"Yeah, like hell," *Zimmerman* said.

"If there's no devil, maybe we can create one," Samantha suggested.

"Just what I was thinking," Gabriel said. "Or if not the devil, then maybe a messiah."

Grace nodded at her husband. "That works," she said. "A distinction without a difference: Either way, it works."

"Second Coming. The Rapture," Zimmerman said. "That would get His attention."

"Hell, plenty of momentum working in that direction already. If we could just push the right buttons, we could build momentum on this pretty quickly," Arthur said.

"Except there is no Messiah," *Zimmerman* said. "Same problem as no Devil."

Uriel looked thoughtful, drumming his fingers on the tabletop. "So we make one, like Grace said. There is a candidate."

All turned to look at Uriel. "What? Who?" Gabriel asked.

"Don't know his name, exactly," Uriel said. "Just know he exists. In Afghanistan."

"Afghanistan? What are you talking about, Earl?" *Zimmerman* asked.

"You know who I'm talking about," Uriel said, looking at Zimmerman.

Zimmerman looked back at him with a pained expression, shaking his head.

"How would Julius know?" Grace asked. She looked back and forth between the two men. "You mean, the people he killed when he was in the service?" Zimmerman blanched at her statement, his hands balling into fists on the table before him. Grace leaned over and laid a hand on his arm. "Sorry, Julius, that's not what I meant. I mean, the family you were involved with. Who all died—Operation Salome, right?"

Julius swallowed audibly and looked away from her, addressing Uriel. "That guy's dead, Earl," he said softly. "Dead and gone."

Uriel shook his head. "Not this time, Julius. You were never in the service, remember," he said, pointing at the other *Julius*. "Never were in the service, were you, boy?" *Julius* shook his head. "So I'm thinking that the otherwise dead guy is not so dead this time around."

"What makes you say this Afghani guy is the Messiah?" Arthur asked.

Uriel shrugged. "He isn't. He's a tool. We get some folk to think he might be. And that's all we need, right?"

"That's all we need," Grace agreed, nodding back at him. "For a start."

CHAPTER 6

Chicago, Illinois

The discussion around the table was interrupted by the sound of sirens pulling up to the front of the restaurant.

"Must finally be the cops coming for your attacker, Grace," Arthur opined. Which seemed reasonable until the sound of shouts and orders being given in loud but unintelligible voices started coming through the door to their private dining room.

"That's interesting," Arthur said, looking at the others.

"Does anyone smell smoke?" Samantha asked. The others shook their head.

"Getting back to this Messiah con—" Grace began, until she was interrupted by Jesus opening the door and sticking his head in.

"Kitchen fire," Jesus announced. Now that the door was open, they could all smell smoke. Behind him the others could see firefighters moving through the main room of the restaurant. "They want everyone out."

"No way," Grace said. "Come on, Jesus. A stupid little kitchen fire? You must have one of those a week."

"Yeah, no. Not like this," Jesus said, stepping into the room and closing the door behind him. He dropped two large carry-out bags on the table. "There's ten grand in hundreds and twenties. It's all I could come up with so fast."

"No problem, Jesus. That's more than enough, I'm sure," Gabriel said.

"Good," Jesus said. "Because now you all have to go. It's a

pretty big fire."

"No way, Jesus," Grace said, shaking her head. "This is no coincidence. It's just another way to get at me."

"Agreed," Uriel said. "But staying here and getting burned alive doesn't sound like a better choice."

"I'm not leaving, not yet. We have to make our plan. Then we go," Grace insisted.

"Suit yourself," Jesus said, shrugging. "I gotta go see how the firemen are doing. If it gets bad, I suggest going out the bar entrance. It's away from the kitchen, so you might not die." He gave Grace a quick hug. "*Buena suerte, mi amiga. Vaya con*—oh, maybe not. Bye, *mamacita*." He left, closing the door behind himself as a small cloud of dirty smoke puffed into the room.

"Is this what it's always like with you, since you died?" Arthur asked Grace.

"No," Grace said.

"Yes," Julius said. "Pretty much all the time."

"A plan?" *Julius* said.

"Okay, then," Grace said, focusing. "Fiddle game, with the big prize being the Second Coming of the Messiah. Sam and Arthur, start running the store. Once we get our store stood up, we get the mark to—"

"You mean God, right?" Arthur asked.

"Yeah, God," Grace agreed. "We get God to believe that the Messiah has just appeared behind His back. Apocalypse, now. That'll get His attention."

"Are you even listening to what this sounds like?" *Julius* asked. "How do we get God to believe—"

"Doesn't matter," Uriel said, cutting him off. "That part's for later. What's the hook?"

"I'll take care of that," Grace said.

"Yeah? How are we going to take care of that?" Julius asked. "I mean, since the three of us are a team, here."

"We'll kick the hornet's nest. But you guys," she said, turning to *Julius* and Uriel, "are going to have to find a way to push the 'Go' button on the Rapture."

"Oh. Sure, no problem. Great plan," *Julius* agreed.

"Okay, that'll work," Uriel said, nodding.

"You're serious?" *Julius* asked the other man.

"Yeah," Uriel said. "Shouldn't be hard. We need to find your friend, Parnell. That spring is already wound up pretty tight."

"True," Grace said. "Though it's hard to believe that idiot is going to be able to do anything to help us."

"You underestimate the man," Uriel said.

At this point, they all noticed the smoke rolling in under the door.

"Seems like the fire isn't going out," Samantha said. This was accompanied by the sounds of more shouted orders outside the room, along with what sounded like a fire axe splitting something wooden.

"We need to go, Grace," Gabriel suggested.

"Fine, fine," Grace said. "So we have a plan. Me, Gabe, and Julius will work the hook. Earl, you and Father *Julius* there work up some intel. Tap Parnell, find him in Salt Lake, probably. We'll meet you there. Arthur, Sam—assets for running a damn big game—the Apocalypse. Got it?"

"Sure, Grace—the Apocalypse. No problem," Arthur said. "Sarcasm."

Grace started to take packs of money out of the carryout bags and pocketed half a dozen, then tossed a few packs to each of the others around the table.

"But how do we get back in touch?" *Julius* asked. "The mark is omniscient, remember?"

"Through Arthur and Sam," Gabriel said. "Everything goes through them."

"Fine, fine," Grace said, impatient. "Let's go, then."

Chicago, Illinois

Grace led Gabriel and Julius down the hall towards the bar. The patrons and staff had all been evacuated but firemen were still hurrying in every direction. There was an impressive amount of smoke everywhere.

"Doesn't look that bad," Julius said. "Maybe we just hole up in the bar for a while."

"It's tempting," Gabriel agreed. "Not going to be drinking much in Salt Lake City."

"We're not going to Salt Lake," Grace said, still walking quickly towards the exit. "Come on." She hit the door onto State Street and kept going.

"Not going to Utah? Then where are we going?" Julius asked.

"Church," Grace said, as the other two caught up to her. She led them down the block. Just ahead of them, a cathedral's serrated silhouette loomed on the shadowed side of State Street. Grace walked purposefully up to the Holy Name Catholic Church: "Where Chicago Goes To Pray." Or so said the sign in front of the imposing edifice. She swung open the large wooden door and strode in.

"I don't see this as a good idea," Julius said.

"Have to agree, hon," Gabriel said, looking about the huge vaulted church. He wasn't exactly sure what kind of threats he was looking for, but looked about nervously nonetheless.

Grace ignored them as she strode up the center aisle, passing under the giant suspended wooden crucifix without a glance upwards. Julius and Gabriel looked up, both picturing the device crashing down onto Grace as she continued forward towards the altar. It didn't fall, however. As the three of them approached the front of the sanctuary, an elderly woman stopped in her efforts to straighten the linens covering the altar, turning to watch them approach.

"Hey, you," Grace called as she approached, getting the attention of the already attentive woman.

"Can I help you, child?" the woman said, stepping down off the altar to greet them.

"Where's the priest?" Grace asked.

"The priest? What do you mean?"

"I mean the priest who runs this church, lady. Not a tough question."

"Yes, of course, but there are several—"

"The priest in charge, the boss priest."

"I'm not sure I know exactly who—" the woman stammered.

"Oh, Jesus, Mary, and Joseph," Grace said, striding past her onto the altar.

"You can't go that way," the woman said, turning to Gabriel and Julius. "She can't go—" but Gabriel and Julius had now passed her as they followed Grace across the altar and through the door to the offices behind.

Grace stormed down the dark paneled hallway, glancing at the doors on either side. At the end of the hall, she came to a door marked "Archbishop." With barely a pause, she pushed open the door and marched inside.

The gray-haired man sitting at the desk, white shirt-sleeves and black collar, looked up from his work. Grace stood in front of his desk, glaring at the man.

"Can I help you?" he asked, laying aside his pen.

"Do you know who I am?"

"Should I?" the man asked, smiling kindly.

"Don't fuck with me, Your Eminence," Grace said. "Just answer the question."

"Yes, child. I know you. Of course I know you."

Grace heard the door close behind her.

Chicago, Illinois

Gabriel and Julius reached the door just as it closed. Julius tried the knob.

"Locked."

"What the hell?" Gabriel asked. Gabriel pounded on the door.

"I don't believe the Archbishop wishes to be disturbed."

Gabriel turned to see Pauley standing behind them.

"Chicago, you said," Pauley continued, approaching. "But

I didn't think that you'd come to find me. Almost too much to hope for."

"Hope is the weak sister of faith, Peter," Julius said. "You won't have her today."

"We'll see."

Grace glared at the Archbishop. "Why?" she demanded.

The Archbishop shook his head, his smile evaporating. "It's not for you to know, child."

"You don't know, do you?"

"It is enough to obey. Even more to obey without question, to obey with the faith that we do the Lord's bidding."

"Well, bid this, asshole," Grace said. "Someone's trying to kill me."

"The world is a dangerous place for one such as yourself, it seems."

"You can spare me the sanctimonious platitudes, Father. If I die, if I'm killed, you know what happens. No excision. Whatever holy plan you're faithfully fulfilling goes up in white smoke, right? I get it in the neck, your Lord's gonna be shit outta luck. The world just goes on and on like I always was, forever and ever."

"Just as well, then, that you saw fit to present yourself at our door, dear child."

"I came here to tell you, so that you can call your boss," Grace said, "Tell Him that there are other forces abroad. That those forces better be dealt with, or His holy plans are *kaput*. You, your Boss, your people—they need to deal with it. Deal with it or I die. And if I'm dead, I don't get excised. He loses."

"I believe that we can deal with this right now," the Archbishop said, rising from his seat. He stepped around his desk. Grace backed away towards the door. She glanced over her shoulder and saw a young priest standing behind her, holding the key to the locked door.

"Open it," she demanded. The priest didn't move. A knife

slid into Grace's hand as the Archbishop came up to her.

"Please don't be afraid, child," the Archbishop said softly. "There is no sadness in your passing. You won't be missed. It will be as if you never were, that's all."

Grace raised the knife so that both the priest and the Archbishop could see its wicked gleam as it caught the light from the stained glass window beside them.

The Archbishop smiled. "I don't think that will accomplish anything, young lady," he said. "It only requires a touch, you see. Once touched, you'll never have been, and any wound that you manage to inflict, even if you stab me in the heart, will be undone in a moment."

"It's not your heart I mean to stab," Grace said, raising the knife to her neck. The Archbishop's smile disappeared.

"You cannot be serious, child," the Archbishop said. "You would be lost, you know. For all eternity."

"You call me 'child' one more time, I will stab you in the heart, asshole," Grace said. "Now tell him to unlock the door. I'm leaving."

Gabriel turned as the door swung open. He didn't see Pauley step forward towards where Grace stood, back to the door, until the old priest was already past. "Behind you, Grace," Gabriel managed to yell.

Grace started to turn, but Julius was already in the room, appearing between her and Pauley. Julius pushed the old man roughly into the room, past where Grace stood with her knife to her own throat. He pushed the younger priest aside. Grace backed away from the Archbishop.

"Tell your boss," Grace commanded, pointing the tip of the knife at the Archbishop. The three of them backed down the hall and left the Holy Name Catholic Church.

Chicago, IL

"What the hell was that?" Gabriel demanded as they ran down the steps of the church, into the sunshine outside.

"What was what?" Grace asked. She was walking rapidly

up the sidewalk now, with Gabriel and Julius on either side of her, each looking about warily.

"Grace," Gabriel said, "you were a hair's breadth from being excised in there. That was even worse than what happened in the Guggenheim."

"Had to be done," Grace said.

"Why?"

"That's called 'the hook,'" she explained. "Damn, Gabe. Didn't we ever watch 'The Sting' together?"

Julius was on the street side, watching everything, occasionally twisting to look behind.

"Great movie," Julius said. "Love ragtime."

"Yeah? So who am I, Redford or Newman? Because I feel like I must be that lovable old guy who gets knifed in the street," Gabriel said.

"Completely different con," Grace said. "But you'll always be my Paul Newman, honey, just without the blue eyes and —"

"Look out!" Julius yelled, shoving Grace and Gabriel farther up onto the sidewalk. He jumped after them as a taxi careened over the curb and crashed onto the walkway just behind them. Its horn blared as people screamed.

Julius picked himself up off the sidewalk and grabbed Grace's arm. "Let's go!" he commanded, leading her quickly across the street to the opposite sidewalk. "Come on, Gabriel," he called over his shoulder.

Gabriel caught up as they stepped onto the sidewalk on the opposite side of the street. "Shit!" Gabriel said, out of breath.

"Yeah. Shit," Julius agreed, dropping Grace's arm. They kept walking, now at a slower pace. "We keep walking, you're going to get us all killed," Julius added.

"We have to get off the street," Gabriel agreed. "Where are we going, hon?"

"Time for you to get our assets in gear, Gabe," Grace said. "Can you get in touch with Arthur?"

"Yeah, of course," Gabriel said.

"Of course. Then do it," Grace said. "Tell him we need a plane, like that time in California. Julius and I will get to Midway, tell him to have it waiting there."

"To fly where, Grace?" Gabriel asked.

"Someplace safe," Grace said.

"Might be a good idea to have some security types on board, too," Julius added.

Grace smiled at him. "I got you, don't I?"

"Good idea, Julius," Gabriel said. "I'll get to Arthur. Not sure how fast he can put this together, though."

"Use some quantum trickery," Grace said, giving her husband a quick kiss. "Make it happen yesterday. We'll see you at Midway."

Gabriel nodded to Julius. "Keep her safe." Gabriel turned and disappeared down a narrow alley.

Julius pointed to the elevated train station farther up the street. "Let's go," he said to Grace.

Chicago, IL

Uriel and *Julius* stood outside the door of the Mormon Temple. Uriel knocked hard.

"You keep the matron busy," Uriel said.

"What? Why? What are you going to do?" *Julius* asked.

The door swung open before Uriel answered. "The Temple does not admit visitors," the elderly lady standing in the door said, before *Julius* even had the opportunity to say hello.

"Of course not, madam," *Julius* said, astounded as he watched Uriel walk right past the woman and into the Temple without a word. "I am Father Julius Zimmerman. I'm sorry to trouble you..."

Uriel made his way to the first unoccupied office he could find. He closed the door behind and sat at the desk. He picked up the phone and dialed for the operator. "New York

Temple, please," Uriel said when the operator had answered.

"Whom in particular would like to speak to?" she asked.

"Dr. Charles Parnell," Uriel informed her.

Chicago, IL

Julius sat behind Grace on the elevated train, scanning the other passengers. He was uncomfortable, as the end seats were occupied, forcing them to sit somewhat forward in the car. Julius looked past Grace's shoulder and noticed a man staring back at him; a small, elderly, rotund man, wearing a *yarmulke*. He smiled at Julius. Julius looked away, continuing to survey the train car as it rattled along above State Street. They would have to change trains at Lake to get to Midway. He glanced back at the old man. The old man was still smiling at him. He winked at Julius, then pointedly looked to Julius's left. Julius followed his gaze and saw a young man two rows ahead staring fixedly at Grace. The man appeared nervous, his knee bouncing as he leaned forward, still staring at Grace. Julius glanced back at the old Jew, who was still looking at him, though not smiling now. The old man nodded slightly.

There was a squeal as the train braked for the station, but not Lake Street yet, and Julius saw the young man to his left start to stand, but the man was looking at Grace, not at the door. Julius watched, tensed, saw the young man's hand come out of his pocket with a knife.

Julius sprang to his feet, yelling into Grace's ear, "Grace, knife!" He moved forward but the young man was quicker, Julius wasn't going to make it around the seat, the man's hand was already raised to strike. Grace turned to see the man but there was no time to move away, she was already blocked by the man in front of her, already moving to strike.

The old man struck the emergency stop button above him. The squeal of the brakes jumped several octaves as the train suddenly lurched just short of the station, the young attacker thrown sideways off his feet, landing hard on the floor alongside the old man, the knife clattering loose. The old man nonchalantly kicked the knife down the aisle towards Julius, who was staring in disbelief as he held onto the pole alongside Grace's seat. The young man scrambled to his feet and ran away along the length of the train car, pushing through the door to the car beyond. The old man winked at Julius, smiling once again. Julius bent to pick up the knife, a cheap switchblade which he folded shut and pocketed.

"What the hell just happened?" Grace asked, looking up at Julius.

"Not sure," Julius said, sitting down next to Grace as the train lurched back into motion, slowly closing the remaining yards to the station. The train heaved to a stop with a sigh as the doors opened. "Not our stop." He looked up to see the old man get up and shuffle off the train without another glance.

Chicago, IL

Uriel returned to find *Julius* engaged in a heated argument with the Temple Matron, claiming that he had been specifically invited to visit today in order to interview a church dignitary, a man named Charles Parnell. As Uriel walked out, again passing the matron without her giving him a glance, *Julius* raised his hands in surrender.

"Fine, fine, your Matronliness, whatever," *Julius* said with mock formality. "I give up. Have a blessed day." The woman stepped back into the Temple and slammed the door. *Julius* turned and caught up to Uriel. "Well, that was fun. Where are we going to visit now, the zoo?"

"We got some time to kill before Parnell comes to pick us up. Thought we'd go see if they got that fire put out, get us some more free drinks."

Quantum Indeterminate State

Gabriel stepped into the first class cabin of the airliner. It was empty. He walked back to the galley, which was also empty. The door was open to the darkness outside. He stepped through. In the distance he could see the glow of the rooms he had arranged. They looked different—bigger, brighter. He walked toward them.

Gabriel arrived much more quickly than seemed right for the apparent distance. Nothing was as it had been. The room, for one, had changed completely. It no longer appeared to be a *faux* Louis XIV hotel room. Now he was in something more very like the lobby of the Fairmont in San Francisco, as near as he could tell. Scores of people, smiling, talking, laughing, moved about. He walked over to the main desk and was greeted by a young woman in a flight attendant's uniform.

"May I help you?" the woman asked.

"I'm looking for Arthur Schlessel," Gabriel said, still looking about.

"Mr. and Mrs. Schlessel reside in room 1309. But I believe they are currently in a meeting in the conference center. The River Styx Room, I believe."

"The conference center?"

"Yes, straight down the hall and past the elevators. You can't miss it." She smiled.

Gabriel opened the door labelled "River Styx Conference Room." About thirty people sat around a large oval table. Samantha stood at the front of the room next to an electronic white board with a roughly drawn table of organization. She stopped talking in mid sentence as she saw Gabriel.

Arthur swiveled in his seat at the far side of the table. "Gabriel, hey! So you finally found us, buddy." Gabriel stood, mouth agape, as everyone turned to look at him. "Everybody, let's take a break. Twenty minutes." He looked at his watch, then chuckled. "I keep doing that. Such an idiot. Anyway, everybody go away for a while and then come back. Not too long, though." Arthur and Samantha came over as the rest of the people streamed past Gabriel.

"Conference room?" Gabriel asked, looking about the large conference room. "River Styx?" He dropped into one of the chairs and swiveled about, hands on the polished mahogany table top. Sam and Arthur sat with him.

"Well, we couldn't very well live on the plane, could we, Gabe?" Arthur asked.

"And that *schlock* Kubrick knock-off you gave us wasn't going to cut it, either," Samantha added.

"I love what you've done with the place," Gabriel said.

Arthur said, "Well, shit, Gabe, there's almost three hundred of us, you know. We had to come up with someplace to live—maybe not live, exactly, but to do whatever it is we're all doing here. Thanks to you."

Sam put a hand on her husband's arm. "There, there, Artie. We've moved past that, hon."

"I haven't," Arthur said.

"Well, it's nice to see that you haven't wasted any time in getting organized," Gabriel said, gesturing towards the white board. "Just like old times, Arthur. You always liked the start-up part the best, remember?"

"Yeah, just like old times, Gabe," Arthur said. "Except in the old times, Sam and I weren't dead."

"We're not dead, hon."

"Not yet, anyway," Arthur said, squeezing his wife's hand. "What brings you to the Purgatory Hotel and Conference Center, buddy?"

Gabriel smiled at the name, then immediately grew more sanguine. "We're in trouble down there, Art. We need your help."

"Not surprised. Been wondering what was taking you so long to get back to us."

"So long? I left you guys at the restaurant—"

"The restaurant that was burning down around our ears, you mean?"

"Yeah, that one. Only left you guys a couple of hours ago."

"No way," Samantha said. "It's been like a week, Gabe."

"Okay, you say so. Does that mean that you guys have had a chance to get things organized?"

"Absolutely. We've got great people, Gabe. The best."

"Well, I tried to get you—"

"Rough going at first, of course. A bit disorienting, you know. Took us a while to get on track, get everyone to come to terms with the reality of the situation. Sam was great, took the lead with the whole orientation, introduction and support sessions, that sort of thing. One woman HR department." Sam smiled humbly, nodding. "But we have total buy-in at this point, great enthusiasm. Pretty much everyone's on board."

Gabriel gestured around. "I take it resources aren't a problem."

"Unlimited, near as we can figure, buddy," Arthur said, smiling. "More money than God, remember?"

So now you know what a special little snowflake you are. The universe needs you, because I need an actor with stage presence, a marquis maven to make this drama move. 'Without you, baby, the stars would fall, baby there'd be no time at all...'

Literally. No time. You get the idea.

So not only did I create you 'in My image,' as it were, but I allowed you something no God in his right mind would grant—I gave you free will. The ability to affect the universe I created.

I thought it was important. And you're welcome, by the way.

Obviously, putting such capacity in your hands was not without risks. Lots of risks. I mean, let's face it—you guys do have a tendency to screw things up. A lot.

But that's okay. I saw this coming. Not my first rodeo, as they say. (Not really certain who 'they' are in this context, but no matter.) I didn't just give you guys the keys to the sports car on day one and wave as you sped off down the bumpy rode of existence. I set down some rules. Put in place some parental restraints to keep you from running straight off into the ditch. I kept the good booze hidden on the top shelf. Kept the really dangerous technological stuff hidden in my magical mystery cellar until you were mature enough to handle it. For the most part, anyway. Laws of thermodynamics, lots of weird-ass genetic code, coronary heart disease, earthquakes, dark matter, quarks—all sorts of stuff to pump the brakes on your ability to wreak havoc with My universe. It's worked pretty well—I mean, you're still here, right? As a species, you haven't extinctified yourselves, haven't completely screwed up the universe for everybody or anything. Not yet, anyway.

SO, CONGRATULATIONS ON THAT.

Chicago, Illinois

Parnell found Uriel and *Julius* sitting at the bar at the back of Jesus's partially burned out restaurant. The restaurant was closed and empty except for a handful of workers assessing the smoking wreckage. Uriel helped himself to a bottle of Jameson from the shelf behind the bar and poured for himself and *Julius*. He looked up as Parnell approached.

"Hey, Chuck!" Uriel said, saluting the man with his drink before downing it in a gulp. "Get you a drink? I'm buying."

"No, thanks, Earl. This places smells like it's still on fire," Parnell said, taking a seat on an adjoining stool. "Is it safe?"

"Drinks are free, Parnell. Safe enough," Uriel said.

"Why did you even call me, Earl?" Parnell asked.

"Because you're the base that nobody's coverin' ," Uriel said.

"That's not why," *Julius* said. "Grace said she and Gabriel were going to Salt Lake. Said it was the safest place."

"She's right," Parnell said.

"She was lying," Uriel said. "Grace isn't going to Salt Lake. She's got no intention of giving herself up to your Mormon friends."

"But Gabriel agreed," *Julius* added.

"He's not calling the shots." Uriel said.

"But she was right," Parnell insisted. "We can protect her, we will protect her. There's no other way."

"Protective custody not that girl's style, Parnell. Thought you'd have that figured out by now, given recent events. And what's this 'we' shit? You and I both know that you're really not a captain on that team anymore."

Parnell looked about the restaurant nervously and made a shushing gesture to Uriel.

"Then why are we going to Salt Lake City, if we're not going to meet Grace?" *Julius* asked, ignoring the pantomime.

"Yeah. Why did you even bother to call me, then?" Chuck asked.

"Because we need to figure out what the hell is going on, that's why. Same thing you've been doing, right, Chuck?"

"Trying," Parnell nodded. "Not easy," he mumbled. "Even harder with you two jokers trailing along, giving me a hard time."

Uriel polished off his second drink and stood up. "Let's get going, gentlemen," he said.

"Get going where?" *Julius* asked.

"Salt Lake City, Father. Keep up, padre," Uriel said.

"Now?" *Julius* asked. He looked at Parnell.

"As good a time as any," Parnell answered with a sigh.

Chicago, Illinois

They took a cab to the Mormon temple just outside of Chicago. Once again, Parnell was stuck paying the fare.

Parnell presented his credentials to the temple matron and the trio was admitted with uncustomary civility. The matron led them deep into the temple interior, finally stopping when they stepped into a room nearly filled by a huge baptismal fount, supported by giant, sculpted gold bulls.

"Do you know the way, Dr. Parnell?" she asked.

"I believe so, matron. Thank you," Parnell answered. The matron left with a nod.

"What are we doing here?" *Julius* asked, looking at the fount skeptically. "What way is she talking about?"

Parnell looked around the room, getting his orientation. "This way, I think." He led them around the circular room twice, then shook his head with a mutter and doubled back half a rotation before pulling up short in front of the door again. "Here we go," he announced.

"What do you mean, 'here we go?'" Uriel asked. "This is where we came in, Bozo."

"'My Father's house has many rooms.' Come on." Parnell led them out of the room and back through the maze of hallways towards the main entrance of the temple. They came upon a woman sitting at the desk in the entry. "Good afternoon, matron," Parnell said, nodding to the woman.

"Good morning to you," she said. "Have a blessed day."

"How many matrons you got working this club, anyway?" Uriel asked, following Parnell across the lobby to the door.

"Just the one," Parnell said.

"What do you mean?" *Julius* asked. "That wasn't the same matron we saw before."

"No, it wasn't," Parnell answered, holding open the door to the outside for the others to exit.

The three stepped outside and stared at the city around them, ringed by snow-capped mountains.

"Toto, I don't think we're in Chicago anymore," *Julius* said.

"Holy shit," Uriel said.

"Yeah, you could say that," Parnell said, smiling. "Let's go gentlemen. My office is in that building, across the square. At least, it was last time I was here." He led off down the walkway. The other two followed, still shaking their heads.

"This is Salt Lake City," *Julius* announced.

"Yes, it is," Parnell confirmed, still walking. "Another beautiful morning in the waiting room of Paradise."

"Thought that was Florida," Uriel muttered as he walked just behind. "'Many rooms,' my ass. Fuckin' witchcraft if you ask me," he said.

"How?" *Julius* asked, looking about at the bustling morning scene around them.

Parnell shrugged, opening the door to the Joseph Smith Memorial building. "Though it has many rooms, there is only one Temple," he explained.

"Makes no damn sense," Uriel said, following *Julius* into the building. "Just fuckin' witchcraft, that's all."

Helmand Province, Afghanistan

"Hila," Atal whispered in the darkness.

Hila sat up and clutched her blanket to her neck. "Atal? What is it? What is wrong?"

Atal sat on the floor next to the bed. Hila could make out her brother shaking his head by the moonlight from the window.

"You shouldn't be in my room," Hila whispered to him. "You insult our hosts like this. It is not right."

"You are my sister. There is nothing wrong with my being here," Atal insisted.

"That is not what I mean, brother. These people have treated us with kindness. They have given us their food and these beds. Yet you were rude to our hosts at dinner. And now, what is it you want?"

"It is not rude to challenge blasphemy, little one. It is our duty to Allah."

Hila rolled her eyes in the darkness. "I am tired, brother. What is it you want? Tell me and leave, so I can get to sleep."

"This is a cursed place, Hila. We must leave." Atal squeezed her arm in emphasis.

"You are an idiot, Atal. Go back to your room and let me sleep," she said, lying back down in the small bed.

Atal leaned over her and tried to take his sister's arm. "Do not speak so to your brother, little one. We must leave this place right away. I command it."

"Command, my ass," Hila replied, twisting out of his grasp and turning away from her brother. "Now go back to bed before I break your other arm."

Atal glared down at his sister in the moonlight. "Fine, Hila. You are tired and so speak disrespectfully to your brother. I will let you sleep, then. We leave in the morning."

"Good plan, brother," Hila said, pulling the blanket about her more tightly. "After breakfast, maybe."

Atal opened his mouth to argue, but thought better of it, yawning instead. He returned to his room.

Chicago, Illinois

Julius and Grace sat nervously in the main departure lounge of Midway Airport. Each constantly looked about.

"This is nuts," Grace said, biting her lower lip.

"Agreed," Julius said.

"We could be waiting here for hours, maybe even days. Who knows how long it'll take for Gabe to come back for us."

Julius shrugged. He watched as a young couple walked in their direction, wondering if the baby strapped to the man's chest was really a bomb. He decided to play it safe, even though he could see two pudgy little legs swaying in the chest carrier. "Let's go," he said, taking Grace's hand.

"We just sat down," Grace protested.

"Sorry, but I don't think it's a good idea to stay in one place very long."

"We just sat down," Grace repeated, standing and looking about. "Really, Julius? You're worried about them?" she asked, nodding at the couple with the baby.

"Let's just walk, okay?"

Grace started to protest but stopped at the sound of the public address speaker: "Father Zimmerman, please check visual paging. Father Zimmerman." Grace and Julius looked at one another, then looked about for a paging kiosk.

Julius pulled Grace down the lobby to stand in front of the monitor. On it, he read "Fr. Zimmerman/Guest—Concourse C, immediately, please." Following the signs, they hurried hand in hand to the concourse.

Concourse C was empty, except for half a dozen Marines in battle fatigues. Each looked about, acting nonchalant without much success. As soon as Julius and Grace stepped into the concourse, a blond-haired Marine the size of a commercial refrigerator approached them. "This way," he said, turning toward the gate.

"Hold it a second, Marine," Julius said, standing his ground with Grace still in hand as the other Marines formed up around them.

The leader turned back, eyeing him. "This way, Father

Zimmerman. If you please, sir." His tone made it clear that he had added that last bit purely as sarcasm.

"Yeah, right," Julius said, looking about at the squad around them. None of the men was less than six inches taller than himself. He smiled at the squad leader, who was looking rather impatient. "It's just that the lady and I have had a pretty rough time of it, Sergeant. No offense, but I need some sort of assurance that you're on our side, you know, before we follow you wherever."

"My instructions, Father, are to get you and the young lady onto the plane," the Marine explained.

"To go where, exactly?" Julius asked.

"I say we go with him, Julius," Grace said, smiling. "He called me 'young lady.' I like him."

Julius held her fast by the hand. "To go where, exactly?" Julius repeated.

"Someplace safe," the Marine explained. He gestured to the gate again.

"Good enough for me," Grace said. She smiled at Julius. "Come on, hon. Let's go someplace safe."

Julius said nothing, but let Grace pull him along in the giant sergeant's wake. Grace stopped cold as she came outside and looked up at the plane.

"What the fuck?" she said, not moving.

Julius stopped beside her. "Sergeant?" They stood looking up at a black 747. There were no markings save a grey tail number. Even the cabin windows were darkly tinted.

"Ma'am, Father," the sergeant insisted, shepherding them toward the air stair that led up to the open cabin door above them. "Not a good place to be stopping." The six other Marines formed up on either side, scanning the tarmac. Each turned and followed as Julius and Grace entered the plane.

Grace stopped as the door was closed behind her. The Marines brushed past on their way to their seats in the rear of the plane so they could reconvene their poker game.

"Hey, gorgeous," Samantha called, walking back from the

front of the cabin.

Grace turned and smiled to her friend. "Hey, yourself."

"I was talking to Julius," Sam said, giving Grace a hug. "But it's good to see you, too. Come on." She led them to the forward cabin, on the way passing Humphrey Bogart and Lauren Bacall who were quietly sitting, holding hands and looking out the window.

Julius pointed as they passed. "Is that?"

"Yeah," Samantha said, laughing. "I'll introduce you later. We gotta grab our seats, we'll be taking off." She showed them to a cluster of deeply cushioned seats arranged on either side of a low table. A flight attendant walked by, reminding them to buckle their seat belts for takeoff.

"Where's Gabriel? Where's Arthur?" Grace asked as the plane began to taxi.

"Gabe's up front talking to the Captain, I think," Sam said. "Artie had to stay back. He's in 'start-up' mode, running between committees and conference rooms. I haven't seen him so happy since we sold off Thought Technologies."

Grace glanced out the window, then lowered the blind. "Where are we going?"

"Someplace safe," Sam said, smiling.

"No, really. Where are we going?" Grace repeated.

"I'm not supposed to tell you, Grace," Sam said. "Sorry. But it is someplace safe, I'm sure."

"What do you mean, you're not supposed to tell me?"

"That's just what Art said. He's not sure how people keep showing up and trying to kill you—"

"Yeah, that has been a bit of a problem," Julius said.

"So, I'm not supposed to say. Need to know, only."

"What do you mean? Arthur thinks that somehow I'm leaking the information? What?"

Sam shrugged. "He doesn't know. But he's worried, that since, you know, we're going up against you-know-who and all, maybe He can read your mind or listens in on your conversations or something. So he's keeping all planning confined to Purgatory."

"Purgatory?" Julius asked.

"It's just what we call where we live now," Sam explained.

"You can't be serious. Arthur thinks he can keep me in the dark, just because—"

"Yeah, exactly," Gabriel said, coming up the aisle and bending down to kiss his wife.

"Because God might be reading my thoughts? Bullshit."

"Why is it bullshit, hon?" Gabriel asked, sitting down in the chair next to his wife and buckling his seatbelt. "It is what we used to do for a living, remember?"

Grace closed her mouth, considering. "You really think?"

"We don't know. But if we could do it, seems a pretty safe bet God might have the same technology. I think Arthur is right to minimize the risk. He's calling the shots, since he's the wizard behind the curtain. At least until we have a better idea of what we're dealing with."

They listened as the engines spooled up and the plane slowly gathered speed for takeoff. Grace let her head fall back against the seat, eyes closed.

"Someplace safe, then," she said.

Airborne, USA

Grace napped while Julius and Gabriel watched her nap.

"Hey, Gabriel," Julius eventually whispered, "is that really Bogart I saw when we came in?"

Gabriel nodded, smiling. "And Bacall," he whispered back.

"Can you introduce me?"

"Sure," he shrugged. Gabriel stood and took a protective glance at his wife still sleeping.

"Probably safe here, don't you think?" Julius said, noticing his concern.

"Yeah, I guess so," Gabriel said, then led Julius back to where the others were sitting. He stopped next to Humphrey Bogart's seat. Lauren Bacall was asleep next to him, holding his hand.

Julius noticed Bacall was asleep and said, "We can come back later, Gabriel."

Bogart looked up and smiled at them. "Not at all—she's not really sleeping, are you, dear?" Bacall shook her head and, opening her eyes, smiled at them.

She sat up and offered her hand to Julius. "I'm Lauren Bacall," she said, smiling at him.

"My pleasure, Ms. Bacall," Julius said, blushing. "Mr. Bogart," he added, shaking the man's hand in turn.

"Please, join us," Bogart said, gesturing to the facing seats. Julius and Gabriel sat. "So are you one of Gabriel's unwitting accomplices, too?" Bogart asked Julius.

Gabriel laughed as Julius just looked confused. "No, Mr. Bogart, Julius is hardly 'unwitting.' This is Father Julius Zimmerman, my particular friend and my wife's protector in my absence."

"Really? Father Zimmerman, huh? That's a confusing juxtaposition, isn't it?" Bogart saw the flight attendant coming from the front of the plane. "Oh, here's our friend, Lauren." He gave a polite wave and the attendant came over.

"Can I get you something, Mr. Bogart?" the attendant asked.

"Dear? What can she get you?" Bogart asked.

"Nothing for me, thanks," Bacall said.

"Whiskey for me," Bogart said.

"How do you like your whiskey, Mr. Bogart?" the attendant asked.

"In a glass," Julius said before Bogart could answer.

Both Bacall and Bogart laughed at that. "Father," Bogart said, "I don't care if you do have an oxymoron for a name. I like you."

Zimmerman beamed. "My roommate and I watched 'The Big Sleep' three times."

"Roommate, huh? Didn't know priests had roommates. What's her name? I'll send her an autographed picture."

Bacall gave Bogart a playful slap on the arm. "Don't be

disrespectful, Bogie. The man's a priest, for god's sakes. Oh, sorry."

"No offense taken, Ms. Bacall. But I wouldn't bother with the picture, Mr. Bogart. Jack—my roommate—is an English bulldog."

"I'm just glad you weren't referring to my wife," Gabriel said. The ensuing awkward silence was relieved by the arrival of the whiskey, in a glass.

Airborne, USA

Samantha walked back to join Gabriel and Julius, who were still sitting with Bacall and Bogart. "Hope everyone's comfy," Sam said as she sat down, smiling.

"Comfy? Are you serious? This is beyond ridiculous, Sam," Julius said, gesturing to the plane around them.

Samantha laughed. "Yeah, crazy isn't it?"

"Arthur's doing," Gabriel explained. "Arthur found it online, used."

"Seems a bit ostentatious," Julius chided.

"That's what I said," Sam agreed.

Gabriel shrugged. "Arthur has his reasons. He's in his glory—he lives for the start-up. It's just like thirty years ago, when we were first putting together Thought Technologies."

"Exactly, Gabe," Samantha agreed. "It's like he's back in his thirties. He's a new man. After you passed, you know, the business took a pretty dark turn—most of it was government spook shit the last couple of years."

Bogart looked confused, trying to follow the conversation.

"I'm sorry, Sam," Bogart said, "since who passed?"

Samantha blushed as Julius and Gabriel exchanged embarrassed glances. "After Lou passed on, one of the original partners," Sam said, recovering. "Just wasn't the same afterwards. Lots of work for the NSA, CIA, that sort of thing. Way too serious. How's the drink, Mr. Bogart?"

"Top notch, Sam. Top notch. Just like everything on this

cruise. Lauren and I appreciate the ride."

"Our pleasure, Mr. Bogart."

"I don't mean to pry," Julius interjected, "but what exactly are you and Mrs. Bacall doing on board?"

"Just hitching a ride to LA," Bogart explained, draining his drink.

Gabriel explained, "Mr. Bogart and Ms. Bacall are going to Hollywood to pitch a movie deal."

Julius's eyebrows lifted. "Seriously?"

"Seriously," Bacall said, holding onto Bogart's arm. "And Humphrey is going to direct it, aren't you, hon?"

"Hope so," Bogart agreed, setting his glass down on the table before them. "If the producers go for it."

Julius turned to Gabriel. "Really? Is this really a good idea?" he asked.

"You don't think my husband can direct?" Bacall asked.

"Well, no, I'm sure Mr. Bogart would be a great director, surely, just that…" Julius stammered, looking between Samantha and Gabriel for help.

"Just what?" Bogart asked.

"Nothing," Julius said.

"Arthur says there won't be a problem," Bacall assured him. "And he owns the studio."

"Oh. Well, if Arthur says there won't be a problem, then best of luck, Mr. Bogart. What's the name of the movie?"

"Don't know yet," Bogart said. "It's a documentary, of sorts. Arthur's got some guys putting together a treatment, said he'll get it to me in two or three days. He seems pretty sure it'll fly, though."

"Something about the Bible, I think," Bacall added. "Arthur said it's very timely."

"Timely. Sure. Biblical is always timely, my opinion," Julius assured them. "I'm going to find that attendant and get myself a drink." He looked at the others. "Anyone else need one?"

"I'll join you," Gabriel volunteered.

LET ME SAY THIS TO YOU PLAINLY: IT IS YOUR STRIVING WHICH IS YOUR UNDOING, YOUR NEED TO "UNDERSTAND." I SEE YOUR SCIENCE, AND IT GALLS ME. YOUR INSISTENCE ON RATIONALITY BEFORE FAITH, YOUR NEED TO FATHOM MY WAYS IN EVERY MATTER, IS AN AFFRONT TO ME. I AM INEFFABLE. WHY DO MY WORKS DESERVE SUCH DERISION? YOUR SCIENCE SEEKS TO MAKE PLAIN THE MIRACULOUS, DISTILLS THE MYSTERY OF MY ACTIONS. YOUR SCIENCE IS FAITHLESS.

I KNOW YOUR HEART. I KNOW YOUR ROLE IN MY WORLD. ONLY I AM YOUR HOPE FOR YOUR SOUL'S SALVATION. YOUR SCIENCE WILL NOT SAVE YOU. YOU CANNOT ENGINEER A FUTURE APART FROM THAT WHICH I HAVE SET FOR YOU. BY YOUR CONSTANT ASPIRATIONS TO SEE BEHIND MY MECHANISMS, TO UNDERSTAND AND MAKE YOUR OWN THE LAWS WHICH I MYSELF HAVE DECREED AT THE CREATION, YOU INSULT ME. YOUR FAITHLESSNESS INSULTS ME. YOUR NEED TO NOT JUST KNOW ME, BUT TO KNOW MY WAYS, IS A CHILDISH INGRATITUDE. FEAR OF THE LORD IS THE GREATEST WISDOM.

PART TWO

CHAPTER 7

Dublin, Ireland

The Taoiseach sat in his wood-paneled office, drumming his fingers against the desk. He looked at his watch.

"Where in hell is she, Ravi?" he asked his Attorney General, who was seated across the desk.

"Delayed, no doubt," the AG answered.

"Yeah, no doubt. Brilliant, Ravi."

An elderly woman appeared in the doorway.

"Her Honor has just arrived, sir," the secretary said. "Should I show her in?"

"Yes, yes, straightaway," the Taoiseach said. He stood and came around the desk to greet his guest.

The retired Magistrate appeared, clad in a macintosh dripping rain onto the carpet. The Taoiseach reached to shake her hand but recoiled at the puddle forming about her.

"I am so sorry," the Magistrate said, taking off her hat. "It's miserable out, miserable. Nowhere to park at all. They took my space, you know, took it a full week before my last day on the bench." She removed her coat, which was still dripping.

"Helen! Please come fetch her Honor's coat," he said. The secretary returned and took the coat. The two men shook the Magistrate's hand warmly and ushered her to the other seat before the Taoiseach's desk.

"Good to see you, Sadhbh. Very good of you to come. You know Ravi, I believe."

"Of course," the Magistrate said. "Been before my bench many times, haven't you, Ravi? Congratulations on your appointment." She turned back to the Taoiseach. "Why am I here, Leo? I'm retired. And very, very wet."

"Yes, I'm truly sorry for that. Should've sent a car," he said. "Good of you to come."

"You left me no choice. That ancient assistant of yours is tenacious, isn't she? Got her teeth in me and wouldn't stop shaking me about until I told her I'd be down. 'Within the week,' she insisted. Left me no choice at all."

Ravi chuckled.

"So what's so important I'm missing my grandson's graduation?" she asked.

The Attorney General handed the Magistrate a folded newspaper from the previous Sunday.

The Magistrate scanned the front page briefly. "Oh, no," she said, shaking her head vigorously and tossing the paper onto the desk. "Get somebody else. Get Ryan to take it up, reinstate his commission. I'm too old for this, Leo."

"I need you, Sadhbh," the Taoiseach said. "Ryan's health is shit. Couldn't ask him to do it, anyway, not after what he's been through. You know what this will be like. This will be bigger than Ryan's report in a way, much more delicate. It's for you, Sadhbh. There's no one else with your credibility, your impeccable reputation."

"Oh, shut up, Leo," the Magistrate said. "I won't do it. Let Ravi do it, he's the AG."

"You know he can't, Sadhbh. They'd take his head off. He's not Catholic." The Taoiseach paused briefly. "You're not Catholic, are you, Ravi?" Ravi shook his head emphatically. "Right. Didn't think so. No, Sadhbh. It has to be you."

"No."

The Taoiseach leaned forward and tapped the newspaper on his desk. "I'm not asking, Sadhbh. I've got eight hundred dead babies in a fuckin' septic tank, Saidhbhín. Don't sit there and give me grief. This is your writ. Period."

"I'm retired, Leo. So, no."

"You can still be retired, since we probably won't be paying you. Budget's tight."

"And no budget? I'd need a staff, Leo. Jesus, Mary, and Joseph, I can't believe you're doing this to me, Leo."

"Hire that busted-down barrister you love so much. Ravi will get you set up, won't you, Ravi?"

Ravi nodded, smiling weakly.

Sadhbh swore again softly. "This is why I didn't vote for you, Leo."

"Should've told your friends, Sadhbh."

"I did."

Airborne, USA

Gabriel and Julius walked forward in search of an airline attendant. They came upon Grace, now curled up in a chair, hugging her knees to her chest. She was staring out the window, gnawing on a thumbnail. The two men looked at each other with concern, then walked over.

"Hey, Grace," Gabriel said. "Everything okay?"

Grace looked at her husband searchingly, eyes narrowed.

"Why, shouldn't it be?"

"Sorry?" Gabriel asked. Grace shook her head and went back to looking out the window. "Julius and I are going to try to hunt down something to drink. Get you something?" Silence. "Okay, then," Gabriel said, turning to go.

"We need to talk," Grace said to the window.

"Sure, hon," Gabriel said, turning back to his wife.

"Not you," Grace said. Gabriel and Julius exchanged a glance. "In private."

Gabriel shrugged. "O-kay," Gabriel intoned. "I'll just go grab a drink." He arched an eyebrow at Julius as he moved off.

Julius sat down next to Grace. Grace took his hand but kept her face to the window.

When she didn't start talking, Julius said, "What the hell was that?"

Grace turned to Julius, brow furrowed. "I can trust you,

right? You're still Julius? The guy who saved my ass all those times, the guy on the boat?"

He squeezed her hand. "Yeah, Grace, that's me. The guy on the boat. That's what we're calling me now? What's the problem?"

"Seriously, you're asking me what's the problem?" She shook her head. He waited. "We've been through some shit. People trying to keep me from going back. Pauley trying to excise me from existence."

"Yeah, Grace. I agree, we've gone through some shit. Still going. So what's on your mind? I've never seen you like this."

"Nobody tried to kill me before."

"That's not true, Grace."

"Not like this," Grace said. "Shit, Julius. You know what I'm talking about. This is bad."

Julius thought about this for a moment. "I guess that's true. I hadn't really thought about it. I mean, complete excision from the universe, having never existed—seems pretty awful. Folks trying to kill you—doesn't seem quite as bad, on the face of it."

"But it's worse, Julius. The one threat, that excision shit, I'm dealing with. I can deal with Pauley. But ever since I stepped back into whatever this is we're in, now complete strangers are coming at me with knives. In the restaurant, on the train—"

"Oh, you saw that, huh?"

"Yeah, Julius, I saw that. Are you nuts? You think I could miss that guy?" She looked at him, eyes moist. "You weren't going to stop him, Julius. You were too late."

Julius reddened.

"I'm not blaming you, Julius. It's not your fault. But something's changed. Why, all of a sudden, is it okay just to kill me off? Why isn't excision required?"

Julius relaxed a little. "Don't see that as much of a difference, frankly."

"But it is, Julius. It's a lot easier to kill me. I don't even know why so many people are trying. And, and—if I'm killed, I'm just as fucked. More, maybe. I won't go back. I won't just be gone. I'll be—somewhere else. Who the hell knows where I end up. Lost. Without you, or my sister, or..." She trailed off, shaking her head.

"Or Gabe," Julius completed. Grace looked at him. "What? You're worried about Gabe?"

Grace nodded. "Nobody ever tried to kill me before," Grace stated flatly. "Gabriel shows up at the dealership, then —then everything changes. You get left behind. People start trying to kill me. Something's different."

"Well, yeah, Grace. Everything's different. I'm not exactly the same as I was, you may have noticed. That other Julius that's now hanging around—there's a development for you."

"Maybe your not the only one that's changed, Julius. Maybe Gabriel isn't himself, either."

"You're not serious," Julius insisted. Grace looked down at her lap and shook her head. "You need to stop this. Just stop, Grace. We're in this too deep to start questioning one another."

"Tell Gabe that. I'm not allowed to even know where we're going. 'Someplace safe, my ass.' How come I'm the weak link, huh?" Grace squeezed his hand. "I trust you, Julius."

Julius pulled his hand away. He looked at her, worried.

"Anyway, Grace, maybe we're not as totally fucked as you think," he said, smiling weakly.

"Yeah? How's that?"

"On the train, the little guy—the old Jew. You see him?" Grace shook her head. "Didn't think so. Little fat guy wearing a *yarmulke*. He's the one who took out the guy with the knife."

"Old fat Jew took out the guy with the knife, huh?"

Julius nodded, smiling. He stood and squeezed her shoulder, kissing the top of Grace's head. "Yeah. So you see, not just more people trying to kill you, Grace. Strange new people on our side, too."

"One old fat Jew," Grace said. "Great."

Dublin, Ireland

"You are aware, Mr. O'Sullivan," the black robed Magistrate asked, leaning forward to stare down from her bench, "that you are under oath?"

"I understand what an oath is, Your Honor," O'Sullivan muttered, looking up but not quite meeting the judge's gaze. O'Sullivan was suddenly blinded by a dozen flashes from the photographers crouching alongside the benches. O'Sullivan blinked.

"If you please!" the Magistrate roared at the photographers. "I will not say it again. Photographs to be taken only as the witness takes their seat at the table or upon leaving once dismissed. Only then! Or I'll have the lot of you removed, do you ken me?" She glared about the packed courtroom. The Magistrate took a deep breath, then continued in a softer tone. "Mr. O'Sullivan," she intoned in her brogue, "please inform the court of your duties during the period in question."

"Pardon me, ma'am?" O'Sullivan asked.

"You worked at the convent in Galway, sir, did you not?" O'Sullivan shrugged. "It is my understanding, Mr. O'Sullivan, that you were employed by the Bon Secours Mother and Baby Home in County Galway. Is this not true, Mr. O'Sullivan?"

"Not exactly. I did some work for the Sisters, that's true, but—"

"Could you please tell the court what work you did for the Sisters, then, Mr. O'Sullivan?"

"Just odds and ends, helping out here and there, was all."

The Magistrate frowned down from her bench in frustration. She sighed and took a sip from her glass of water. "Did your duties, Mr. O'Sullivan, include the particular task of collecting refuse from the convent from time to time?"

O'Sullivan nodded, again looking down at the table. "It will be necessary, Mr. O'Sullivan, to answer verbally."

"Pardon?" O'Sullivan said, looking up.

"Yes or no, please."

O'Sullivan nodded. The Magistrate sighed.

"Yes," O'Sullivan said.

"Thank you. Where did you collect the refuse from, Mr. O'Sullivan?"

"All about the convent, Your Honor."

"Was there a particular refuse location at the south wall of the convent, Mr. O'Sullivan?" O'Sullivan flushed but didn't answer. He stared a hole in the table. "Was there a particular bin, Mr. O'Sullivan," the Magistrate continued, "located on the south wall of the convent? A bin that you were required to unbolt periodically to check for refuse?" The witness said nothing. "Mr. O'Sullivan?" O'Sullivan nodded. "In words, please, Mr. O'Sullivan."

"Yes, there was a bin as you say."

"And what sort of refuse did you collect from this bin?"

"Nothing, usually."

"What do you mean?"

"I mean, most times when I'd undo the latch, there'd be nothing in there."

"And the other times?"

"Other times, something needing to dispose of," the man muttered.

"What type of refuse, Mr. O'Sullivan?" the Magistrate asked, staring. O'Sullivan said nothing. "Mr. O'Sullivan," the Magistrate urged quietly, "I know this is difficult. It is important, sir, that you answer my questions. This is not a trial. We are simply after the truth, not to judge you, sir." O'Sullivan looked up with a pained expression. "If you please."

"Bundles. Bundles, was all. Laundry. Dirty laundry, in bundles. Sometimes. Not usually, though. Usually, when I checked the place, there weren't anything there. Most every day, your Honor, nothing there." He looked down again at the table.

"I understand," the Magistrate said. "When there was a bundle to be disposed of, though, Mr. O'Sullivan," she waited for O'Sullivan to look up from the table, "on those occasions when there was a bundle of laundry to be disposed of, sir, in what manner did you deal with it?"

"I threw it in the septic tank."

"In the septic tank?" O'Sullivan nodded. "Why did you do that?"

"It was contagious, that's why. Infected sheets and all. Dysentery. It needed disposing of in the septic tank, they said."

"Who said?"

"Sisters. The Mother Superior."

"I see."

"The children would get sick; dysentery, and such," O'Sullivan said, "make a real mess of the sheets and bed-clothes and all. Was contagious, that's all there was to it. Nothing more."

The Magistrate stared down at the old man at the witness table. The old man's hands were shaking before him on the table. "Would you care to take a break, Mr. O'Sullivan? Perhaps continue tomorrow?" O'Sullivan looked up at the Magistrate, blinking back tears. He nodded.

The Magistrate looked down at the man with pity and almost caught his gaze. He started as she struck her gavel. "We stand adjourned," the Magistrate intoned.

O'Sullivan remained seated, staring down at the table.

"You are excused, Mr. O'Sullivan," the magistrate said. "We'll continue in the morning, sir, if you please."

The old man looked up at the magistrate. "I am?" he asked. The bailiff helped O'Sullivan from the stand. O'Sullivan shuffled up the aisle, following his flickering shadow as the fusillade of cameras again burst into staccato flashing. He escaped through the ornate double doors but never came home. That evening, he threw himself off the Ha'Penny bridge.

Airborne, USA

Julius walked forward to find Gabriel standing in the galley, nursing a bottle of beer. Gabriel raised the bottle in greeting.

"Any more of those?" Julius asked. Gabriel nodded to the small refrigerator and Julius helped himself.

"She okay?" Gabriel asked.

Julius opened the beer and sucked foam as it rose over the top. He shook his head. "Not so much," Julius said.

"She's had a pretty rough time. Kidnapped in the museum. People trying to stab her to death, burn us up in the restaurant. Pretty stressful," Gabriel said.

"You and I know she's seen worse. And dealt with it."

"True."

"It's more than that. Grace doesn't let other people handle her problems. Grace handles her own problems. But this—she's not right," Julius said.

"You seem to know my wife pretty well," Gabriel said.

Julius flushed. "Don't know why this has her so rattled, all of a sudden."

"Because—all of a sudden—she thinks it's me," Gabriel said, looking at Julius. "Which is pretty fucking ironic, because you're the one who fucked her up."

"Why do you say that?" Julius asked.

"Because I was her husband, Julius."

Julius took a long pull from the beer, eyeing the other man as he lowered the bottle. "Was?"

"Is. Am. Whatever."

"Look, Gabriel," Julius stammered, "I'm sorry about... Grace and I—"

"That you slept with my wife? Shit, Zimmerman, you're just lucky I was dead at the time. That's not the real problem," Gabriel said.

"Really? What's the real problem, then? That you're not dead anymore?"

"The problem, asshole, is that you fucked up everything. We were fine, we were together. She was safe. But she came back, one more time—for you. And that, Julius," Gabriel said, "fucked everything up."

"She didn't have to come back for me," Julius protested.

"No, she didn't," Gabriel agreed. "That's what really pisses me off. We were done with all this shit, finally. But she wouldn't leave you behind like that. She didn't *have* to come back for you. She wanted to."

"But not you?" Julius asked.

"No," Gabriel said, downing the dregs of his own beer and tossing the bottle into the trash. "I didn't."

Gabriel walked aft. His wife was no longer in her seat. He kept walking and found her sitting with Samantha, Bacall and Bogart, listening. She stiffened as he sat down next to her.

"Did you ever find the stewardess?" Bogart asked.

"Flight attendant, dear," Bacall corrected.

"Found a beer, instead," Gabriel said.

"Almost as good," Bogart said.

"Even better," Gabriel said. Julius sat down with them.

"Anybody want to explain this," Julius said, gesturing to the airplane around them.

"Arthur's doing," Gabriel explained. "He's in tight with the DoD, intel community, all that crazy stuff. This used to be an Air Force One, back in the day."

"Hardly inconspicuous," Julius said.

"Arthur wasn't going for inconspicuous," Gabriel agreed. "Didn't think that would matter, given who we're up against. More like a kind of flying refuge. Try to stay ahead of trouble."

"Arthur sounds like a worrier."

"He is that," Samantha said.

"Not sure how he managed to commandeer a full Marine

security detail, though," Julius said. "Never seen that kind of security for a civilian."

"It's not," Gabriel said. "Well, in a way, it is for Grace," he said, nodding to his wife. "But the Senator thinks it's for her."

"Senator?" Grace asked.

"Yeah," Samantha said, "Senator Mallory. Caitlin Mallory. You remember her, don't you, Grace?"

"Nope."

"From California. She ran that little PR firm, the one we hired when we were just starting out. Arthur and I have been supporting her since she first ran for office. Had half a dozen fund raising dinners over the years, at the house. I'm sure you and Gabe were at a couple."

"She's on board?" Grace asked, looking around.

"Yeah," Samantha said. Grace inclined her head towards Bacall and Bogart. "Walked right past," Samantha said, smiling. "When you've been a Senator for as long as Cate, people notice you, not the other way around. She's upstairs, in the VIP suite. Cate thinks this is all for her; the security detail, the plane. Pretty much all of it. Her staff is in the back."

"Why is she on board?" Grace asked.

"For the conference," Gabriel said, smiling.

"Conference?" Grace asked.

"Security conference," Sam explained. "Very top secret. Senator Mallory is the ranking member on Homeland Security. Artie works with her a lot, since Thought Technologies has been so involved with intelligence and that black arts shit. Arthur spun up a conference to brief the Senator on a developing threat in Afghanistan. And the conference is in 'someplace safe.'"

Grace scowled. "The devil, you say."

Julius whistled softly. "Arthur doesn't waste any time, does he?"

"He's a man on a mission," Samantha agreed.

Dublin, Ireland

The day after the janitor jumped from the Ha'Penny bridge, the Magistrate sat behind her desk in chambers. Across the desk sat her friend, Ian Connolly. Connolly had graduated with the Magistrate from King's College and years ago retired from the law himself. Connolly was a widower, and in an effort to restore some normalcy to his life, had come out of retirement to become the Magistrate's investigator.

"Tell me why the old man would jump off a bridge, Ian," the Magistrate said, shaking her head. "It makes no sense at all."

"Makes all too much sense, Sadhbh," the man replied. "He wasn't about to come back for a second day before your bench."

The Magistrate looked at her friend with shock. "You think I was the reason? My questioning?" Connolly nodded. "Why? He was just the janitor, Ian."

"I've no idea, Sadhbh. But in my experience, it isn't so unusual for a janitor to know things hidden from the sight of most others."

"What things, do you suppose?" The man shrugged. "Find out, Ian. Find out the janitor's secret, if he indeed had such a thing. And be quick about it, my friend. I'm running out of witnesses and running out of time. My writ ends in less than two months."

"I know. You'll be pleased to hear I located you another witness to bring before your inquisition, your Honor." He smiled.

"Who?"

"The Mother Superior."

"Really? Damn good work, Ian! I had given her up for dead."

"Nearly. She's ancient, of course. But she's competent, of that I'm sure. Not just competent, Sadhbh. Still holdin' onto the iron rod of God's wrath, my impression. Don't think you'll knock this one off a bridge."

"Well, that's a comfort."

"Comfort is the last thing you'll get from Sister Hildegard, Sadhbh. The last thing."

San Francisco, CA

The plane landed at SFO and was met by a small convoy of armored limousines and black Suburbans. The Senator and her staff rode in the lead limousines. The Marines filled the front Suburbans. Grace, Gabriel, Samantha, and Julius brought up the rear with the support staff.

"What about Bogart and Bacall?" Julius asked as the line of cars set off.

"Staying on the plane for a ride to LA," Gabriel explained. "I'm sure Arthur's got a limo waiting for them there. And an entourage. They'll be fine."

"Anything that Arthur doesn't take care of?" Julius said.

Samantha shook her head. "Arthur's good at this, loves this shit. Especially this gig—a big project with unlimited resources. He's in heaven."

"Literally," Gabriel said.

"Arthur ever run a con before?" Julius asked.

"He's a very successful businessman, Julius," Grace said. "So, yes. By definition."

Half Moon Bay, CA

"This is 'someplace safe?'" Grace asked, as the convoy made the exit into Half Moon Bay. "I hope we're not heading to our old house. Somehow, I don't think we'll all fit in a two bedroom bungalow."

"Nope. My place," Samantha said. "We'll fit. It'll be just like old times, huh guys?"

Grace and Gabriel nodded. "But is it 'someplace safe,' Sam?"

"I'm sure it is, Grace."

Arthur was standing on the broad front porch, waving as they pulled up. He was flanked by two Great Danes, one brindle, one blue, each the height of Arthur's shoulder as they sat. The two dogs had replaced the children who were now grown. Arthur stepped off the porch as the Senator got out of her limo, greeting her. Several men and women came out of the house to take the bags and escort the guests to their rooms. It was a big house. The dogs stayed seated on the porch, tails thumping the deck with excitement.

Arthur was back on the porch waiting for them as Grace and Gabriel came up the steps to each be greeted with a hug. He showed them inside.

The house was crowded with activity. The Marine security detail had joined another half dozen members of the security team that had already established a command center in the third floor loft. A chef was busy supervising his crew in the kitchen.

"You guys get my room," Arthur told Grace and Gabriel, leading them up the stairs to the second floor. "Sam will just have to put up with my snoring for a few nights."

"More likely she puts you out on the balcony," Grace said.

"Probably," Arthur agreed. "At least it'll be a fairly warm night. Hope you don't mind sharing the room with Bran and Sceólang. Here we are."

"The dogs? Both of them?" Gabriel asked.

"Yeah, they insist on sleeping in my room—your room, I mean. Don't worry, at least they don't snore." He showed them where he had stashed clothes for them in the dresser and the closet.

"Thought of everything, Arthur," Grace said, nodding appreciatively.

"Hope so. You guys rest up, then come down for dinner in an hour." He closed the door behind as he left.

When Grace and Gabriel came downstairs, they were shown to their seats at the large dining table. Julius was deep in conversation with Samantha as Grace took the seat on her opposite side, while Gabriel sat beside Arthur.

"How was the flight?" Arthur asked.

"Are you kidding?" Gabe said. "It's a 747, Arthur."

"And I had them get that beer you used to like," Arthur said, smiling.

"Nice touch, Arthur. If you're down to picking the drinks for the plane, I'm assuming you're pretty on top of this whole shit storm."

"You assume correctly, Gabe. We've got a good team up there. First rate."

"Glad to hear it. Anybody missing? You need anything?"

"No, don't think so. Half my team is made up of the smartest people who ever lived. And if there's a really tough problem that absolutely nobody else has a clue how to tackle, I just give it to Bucky Fuller. Guy's a first-class genius in the field of fucking everything."

"Great. We going to light the fuse on this anytime soon?"

"That's really what this is all about, you know," Arthur said.

"I figured. So what's the Senator doing here?"

"She's at the other end of the fuse. You'll see." Arthur stood, wine glass in hand. The table became silent. "Senator, friends, guests," Arthur said with a smile as he surveyed the table. "Sam and I are pleased to welcome you to our home. It was an imposition, I know, to gather you here on relatively short notice, and we thank you for clearing your schedules to join us."

"Things were pretty dead for Gabe and me," Grace said, raising her glass at Arthur. "Thanks for the invitation, Arthur."

"Glad you could make it, Grace," Arthur said. "The real conference will begin in the morning, after breakfast. I'm sure then, Senator, you will appreciate why I asked you to attend this meeting. As you will see, we face an emerging, and significant, threat to our security."

"Which we won't ruin our evening by discussing quite yet, will we, hon?" Samantha said.

THE WISE SILENCE OF GOD

"No, of course not," Arthur said. "But due to the nature of the threat, and in light of the Senator's attendance, I think it best if we do take a moment before our dinner to allow our Chief of Security to speak for a moment. Corporal?"

A large, bald Marine stepped up to the table, accompanied by an older man in a dark suit.

"I am Corporal Bettler. I am commanding the Marine security detail assigned to this event. This is Special Agent Rickson, of the FBI liaison staff. Together, we will be responsible for maintaining the security of this conference." The Corporal pressed a button on a remote control he held and the wide screen panel over the fireplace dissolved from a reproduction of Ansel Adam's "Evening, MacDonald Lake" into an overhead view of the house in which they were seated. "This is a view from a surveillance drone being maintained over our site. It is manned and operated by the Air Force at Pillar Point Air Station just up the coast. They will maintain a constant overwatch of our facility during the duration of this conference." He picked up a box from the sideboard and placed it on the table. "In this box you'll find a locator device with your names on it. It may be worn as a necklace. Please take your device and wear it at all times while you are attending the conference. I mean at all times, people. It is waterproof. Wear it while you shower." He pushed another button and clustered small green dots appeared on the screen in the overhead view of the house. "We will monitor your positions." He pushed a button again and the ghostly heat image of each of them sitting around the table swam into view as the screen zoomed in. "If we identify an individual without an identity tag, we will investigate. In this manner, we mean to maintain the premises free from any unknowns throughout this event. Any questions?"

"What about your security team?" Arthur asked.

"They have their own tags," the Corporal said. He used the remote to briefly reveal a swarm of amber colored dots about the house and the grounds, with additional dots along the road to the house and on the beach at the base of the bluff below the house. Julius noticed two amber dots in the house on the ridge line next door.

"That's a lot of dots," Grace commented *sotto voce*.

"Not to mention the sniper team rooming in with the next door neighbors," Julius whispered. The amber dots disappeared from the map.

"We are taking the security of the Senator and the rest of you all very seriously," the FBI agent said, stepping up beside the Corporal. "In addition to the subject matter, we have added concerns relating to recent intel. Maintaining your safety and security is our highest priority. Please utilize the devices provided to make our jobs that much easier. If you have any questions or concerns, the Corporal and I are at your disposal. Enjoy your dinner."

The guests finished passing the box of devices around the table. Each guest donned their device.

"What's the button for?" Sam asked, looking at the back of her device.

"It's an alert," the agent said. "If you have a security concern, push the button. Somebody from the security detail will contact you directly."

"You mean, over the device?" Sam asked.

"No. I mean that a security officer will immediately contact you in person. Please only employ that alert for security concerns."

"Not if we're out of toilet paper, then," Grace said.

"Exactly. Let me emphasize that individuals located on the grounds by surveillance without an identifying tag will be assumed to be hostile. Your cooperation in this matter will minimize the chance of a false alarm."

"Or getting shot."

"Yes. That, too," the agent said, smiling. "Again, thank you for your cooperation. Good evening."

Half Moon Bay, California

Dinner was a buffet affair, the participants eating and mingling, accompanied by informal conversation. Dessert and coffee were served on the deck, overlooking the Pacific as twilight fell. The Senator was advised to keep indoors.

Grace sat with Julius and Gabriel on Adirondack chairs surrounding the fire pit on the rear patio of the house. They stared out at the ocean below. Behind them, the conversations were dying out as most of the guests moved off to their bedrooms.

"Where do they have you sleeping?" Grace asked Julius.

"Not sure," Julius answered. "The couch, I guess. You?"

"Gabe and I have Arthur's room," Grace answered.

"With the dogs," Gabe answered.

"Nice."

They looked out over the ocean in the deepening twilight.

"It'll come from there, won't it?" Grace asked.

"Probably," Julius said. "If it comes."

"What?" Gabe asked.

"Trouble," Julius said.

"Then maybe we should get to bed, hon," Gabriel said.

Grace nodded. She reached over and squeezed Julius's hand. "Night, Julius. Sleep well."

"Yeah. You too, guys. Good luck with the Danes." Gabriel nodded at the other man and turned to walk his wife back to the house. "Hey, Grace," Julius called after them. They both stopped and turned. "This here is our GODD." He smiled at her.

Grace smiled back. "You say so, Padre. G'night."

Grace and Gabriel walked to the house.

"What was that about?" Gabriel asked. "That thing he said about god?"

Grace shrugged. "It's a Jesuit thing, I think."

The next morning, the guests came into the kitchen to a buffet breakfast. Most ate on the deck as the morning was pleasant and the fog bank stayed out to sea. The Senator ate with her entourage in the dining room. Gabriel gestured with his cup of coffee towards the beach.

"Isn't that Julius?" he asked his wife. Grace squinted in the direction of the coffee cup and saw a man in shorts running, barefoot and shirtless, up the beach in the distance. Definitely Julius, in his boxers. Different ocean, same ass.

"You say so. Pretty far away."

"Priest gets up pretty damn early."

"Must be a Jesuit thing."

Arthur came onto the deck. "We're starting in twenty minutes, guys."

"Sure, Arthur," Gabriel said. "How'd you sleep?"

"Great," Arthur said, smiling. "Sam slept on the balcony, though."

"You don't deserve her, Arthur," Gabriel said.

"True. Don't tell her."

"Don't need to. She figured that out a long time ago," Grace said.

Half an hour later, Arthur stood in front of the stone fireplace in the Great Room, his guests arrayed on couches and chairs in a semicircle in front of him. The Senator had the place of honor, seated in an overstuffed leather chair.

"Senator Mallory, guests," Arthur began. "Thank you for coming. This briefing will consist of two sessions, one this morning and another after lunch. As you know, Thought Technologies has, for several years now, provided a unique surveillance capability for the US government. In that capacity, we have recently become aware of a newly emerging threat in the Middle East. This emerging threat is the subject of our conference."

"Where is the briefing paper?"

Arthur stopped to face the Senator's legislative aide who had spoken. He didn't think the man could be over twenty-five. "There isn't one," Arthur answered, smiling at the man.

"Shit," the man said. He started to pull out his laptop computer.

"Please don't," Arthur said.

"Don't? Don't take notes?" the man asked.

"Just give it a rest and listen for now, Edgar," the Senator admonished.

Arthur smiled at the Senator. He nodded to the large flat screen television above the fireplace. The image of Magritte's "The Human Condition" dissolved into a topo map of Afghanistan.

"Helmand Province," Arthur continued, and the map zoomed in on the southern portion of the country. "Site of the fiercest fighting in each of the modern Afghan conflicts. The map transitioned to a satellite image of the region revealing the mountainous terrain as the point of view swept lower, finally coming to rest over a verdant box canyon. "And here, in this isolated valley, is the base of operations for a newly developing terrorist organization."

"What is the source of your information?" Edgar interrupted.

"Edgar," the Senator said. "Please let the man speak."

Arthur continued, "Intel has documented a significant and increasing in-migration of individuals—mostly Afghani, but some Pakistani and other nationals—to this remote and previously sparsely populated locale. Here is a satellite image of the valley six months ago, and here..." He pushed a button on the controller he held and the image changed, now showing numerous structures where previously there had only been rolling fields, "...an image from two days ago. You can appreciate the significant development that has occurred in the interval between these images." Small details in the picture were highlighted in turn as Arthur continued, "Storehouses, living quarters, communal dining facilities, a large generator. In addition, please note the extensive agriculture which has developed, implying the installation of a new water resource of impressive capacity. And people who need to eat."

"How many people?" the Senator asked.

"We estimate the population to have increased from less than fifty scratch farmers a year ago to now over thirteen hundred, Senator."

"Wow," Edgar said.

"What is more impressive, however, is that the rate of in-migration has continued to increase. This image, also obtained two days ago, shows columns of individuals approaching the valley from several directions. Not scattered individuals, not even groups, but an almost continuous stream of combatants assembling in this location."

"Combatants?" an analyst from CIA asked.

"That is our belief," Arthur said.

"Your assumption," the analyst corrected. "Who are they?"

"We don't know yet," Arthur admitted. "We have suggestions which we will discuss in greater detail this afternoon. At this juncture, let me just introduce this bit of data," Arthur zoomed the image out and the view shifted to an area just outside the ring of mountains. "This is the site of a recent drone strike on a known terrorist cell."

"Ours?" the CIA representative asked.

"Yes, David," Arthur continued. "Five confirmed KIA. Including this man, Ahmad ben Khalid," a bearded man's face appeared on the screen next to the satellite image, "with whom I am sure you are familiar."

"You're not supposed to know that," the CIA man said.

"Was it Kalid's show, then?" the Senator asked.

"No, Senator," Arthur continued. "That does not appear to be the case."

"Whose then? Are they Daesh?"

"That is a matter of some conjecture." A very blurry aerial image of a man leading a mule, dressed in a white robe and topi appeared on screen. "This image is taken from the surveillance drone that monitored the strike. This man was seen exiting the target area less than twelve hours before the strike. We don't have a name yet. But many in the area speak of him. They speak with great reverence."

"Reverence?"

"Indeed. Most call him 'Mahdi.'"

"Well, that can't be good," a voice said from the back of the room. Grace turned in her seat on the couch to see Julius, dressed now in jeans and a tee shirt, leaning against the back wall, hair still damp from his shower.

"What does 'Mahdi' mean?" Edgar asked.

"Messiah," Julius said. Arthur nodded.

Purgatory

Half a dozen people sat in chairs before monitors in a darkened control room. The young man at the central console tapped violently on his keyboard, cursing around a mangled red Tootsie Roll pop.

"I got no sound here. I see them all talking down there, but I got *bupkis* on audio. What the fuck, guys?"

"Workin' on it, Boss," a younger man on the other side of the room said. "Not exactly easy cracking into a mil-spec surveillance system."

"Shit, Kevin, I'm looking at the video. I can see Arthur standing there pontificating like Christ in the fuckin' temple but I can't read lips. Goddamit, man! The audio should be the easy part."

"Well, it ain't," Kevin said. He swore under his breath as his fingers danced across the keyboard.

"Give him a minute, Elliot," one of the others said. "We're making this up as we go along."

"Fuck that, Debbie," Elliot said. "I don't hear what's being said, we're screwed. We're not much help just sitting up here with our thumbs up our asses."

"Suck on your lollipop and shut up for a minute, Elliot," Debbie said.

"Dammit, dammit," Kevin muttered. His face was now two inches from the monitor.

"Hell, Kevin, are you nearsighted or just gonna dive in and hack that shit from the inside?" Debbie said, moving to stand behind his chair.

"Don't make me come over there and do it myself, buddy," Elliot said.

"Five minutes. Dammit."

"Bullshit, five minutes. This thing will be over in *two* minutes, get on it," Elliot intoned, stabbing his bent lollipop at Kevin.

"Jeez, Elliot, spare us the shitty 'Top Gun' dialogue, will you?" Debbie said.

"Got it!" Kevin said, nose almost touching the screen before him.

"Still don't hear anything—"

Debbie walked over to Elliot's console and twisted a knob. Arthur's voice boomed into the control room: "—why I asked you to this meeting. As you will see, we face an emerging, and significant, threat to our security."

"Nice," Elliot said, clapping his hands. "We're in business."

"You're welcome," Kevin said, leaning back in his chair.

Half Moon Bay, California

As there was little firm information to provide the group, the rest of the morning consisted mostly of a survey of various opinions and possibilities. The overall theme, however, was the conviction that something big, bad, and dangerously ambiguous was taking place in that remote valley in Afghanistan. The fact that so little was known made the whole affair much bigger and badder. On that point, there was general agreement. They broke for lunch.

They reconvened over cake and coffee. The Senator was back in the overstuffed leather chair, surrounded by her aides as she held a murmured conversation with the CIA liaison. Arthur waited until the Senator was done and she smiled at him indulgently.

"Questions?" Arthur said. Then he spent the next two hours fielding intensive questioning regarding the morning's discussion, sources, corroborative evidence, and implications. Finally, the Senator asked the only important question.

"Arthur," Senator Mallory said from her chair, "I want to thank you for arranging this and for the very important work that you presented. What's next?"

Arthur sighed deeply before answering. "Thank you, Senator. Judging by the incisiveness of the questioning these past couple of hours, it seems the next step is pretty obvious. We need to get more information. I hope that I have convinced you of the validity of the possible developing security concern. If I have, then you will see the importance of allocating the resources needed to improve our understanding of the nature of the threat which may be building in that valley."

"Quit the bullshit, Art," CIA said. "What do you want?"

"Dedicated satellite overview," Arthur said, watching the Senator's face.

"No fucking way," Edgar said.

"It's the only way," Arthur responded, still watching the Senator, who remained impassive. "We have no other available assets appropriate to the task. Spec Ops can't get anywhere close, not any more."

"Surveillance drones out of Pak," CIA offered.

"Not enough dwell capability, David. SigInt is pretty worthless, they're not generating any chatter. We need visuals over time, to identify players, map movements, characterize energy utilization—you know what we're dealing with here. A dedicated sat is the only answer, Senator. If you think that the threat is significant enough to justify it."

"David?" the Senator asked.

The CIA man shrugged. "Yeah, I see his point. Drone overflights won't give us what we really need, even a series of flights. And we don't like to do a series, anyway. That's a good way to get the little robots shot down. So yeah—Arthur makes a good point. Except you're making a lot of assumptions, Arthur. That valley could just be filling up with a bunch of Hari Krishnas, you know, not jihadis."

"Yeah, David," Edgar said, "because Helmand Province is the new Shangri-La, right?"

The Senator rolled her eyes. "So we're talking about tasking an intel sat for dedicated surveillance. What else, Arthur?"

"More? What more can he possibly want?" Edgar asked.

Arthur said, "Somehow, this guy—this 'Mahdi' or whoever —is getting the word out. He's attracting followers from all over the region, maybe the world. Until we know what he's about, we need to silence his message. Put a bubble over this guy—complete black hole treatment, Senator."

The CIA officer nodded in agreement.

"You're wrong, Arthur. I used to be in PR, remember? Way back in the day, when we both were young," the Senator said. "Worst thing you can do, if you don't want a client to be noticed, is to go silent, you know. We put a curtain around this valley, it won't be too long before it's the most famous place on earth. Journalism abhors a vacuum. The tabloids will have it on the front page as the headquarters of an alien invasion. Area 42. Bad idea, Arthur."

"I disagree, Senator," CIA said. "Maybe from a PR standpoint, you're right, but we're not talking PR. I agree with Arthur. Until we know what's going on in that valley and what this guy is up to, we need to isolate him, get him off the grid. No coded web sites, no YouTube recruitment videos hitting the Web, no 'Mahdi is Great, join the cause' crap going out over the jihadi network."

The Senator rubbed her temples for a minute. "Maybe you're right. I'll take it under advisement." She stood. "You've given me a lot to think about, Arthur. I need a beer."

I GET A LOT OF GRIEF ABOUT THE RECENT LACK OF MIRACLES. I KNOW, I KNOW— DON'T BE EMBARRASSED. I HEAR YOU. LIKE A MILLION TIMES A DAY, I HEAR YOU.

IT'S TRUE, I USED TO DO A LOT OF MIRACLES. I LIKE DOING THE MIRACLES. THEY'RE FUN. AND BACK IN THE DAY, I HAD NO CHOICE, BELIEVE ME. I MEAN, YOU GUYS WERE SCREWING UP EVERY OTHER DECADE, GETTING YOURSELVES CAUGHT UP WITH THE CRAZY DEITIES, GOING OFF THE RAILS WITH HUMAN SACRIFICE AND THAT AWFULNESS, GETTING YOURSELVES ENSLAVED OR DISPERSED ALL OVER CREATION. I MEAN, WHAT AM I GOING TO DO WHEN MY CHOSEN ARE JUST SO ATROCIOUS AT GOVERNING, AND FIGHTING, AND ALWAYS GETTING CONQUERED? LET THEM JUST GET WIPED OUT? NO, THAT WOULDN'T BE RIGHT. I HAD A DEAL WITH THE TRIBE. SO I STEPPED IN HERE AND THERE, TOSSED DOWN THE OCCASIONAL MIRACLE INTO THE MIX. NOT JUST THE JEWS, YOU KNOW—DID IT FOR A LOT OF FOLKS. IT WAS AN EFFECTIVE STRATEGY. A WELL-PLACED PLAGUE EVERY ONCE IN A WHILE GETS A PEOPLE'S ATTENTION. TECTONICALLY SHIFT THE RED SEA FOR AN AFTERNOON SO MY PEOPLE CAN MAKE A RUN FOR IT—GOOD STUFF. WORKED LIKE A CHARM, PRETTY MUCH EACH AND EVERY TIME. DEUS

EX MACHINA, AM I RIGHT?

BUT NOT ANY MORE, MY LITTLE FRIEND. I MAY BE YOUR GOD, I MAY BE OMNIPOTENT, I MAY BE OMNISCIENT, BUT THE MIRACLE THING JUST DOESN'T CUT IT ANYMORE. THOSE DAYS ARE OVER. IF I TRIED ANYTHING MIRACULOUS THIS WEEK, HOW LONG BEFORE THE NETWORKS ARE HAVING THEIR EXPERTS ANALYZE THE SUPER SLO-MO TAPES, HOW LONG BEFORE THEY FIGURE OUT HOW I PULLED IT OFF, HUH? THEY GOT SCIENCE. AND THERE'S ALWAYS SOME GUY WITH A CELLPHONE FILMING EVERYTHING NOW, ISN'T THERE? I MEAN, I DID GET AWAY WITH SETTING THAT PLANE DOWN NICE AND SMOOTH ON THE HUDSON, BUT THAT WAS A ONE-OFF, BELIEVE ME. THE ONLY WAY I GOT AWAY WITH THAT WAS THAT EVERYONE LOVED SULLY, SO FOLKS DIDN'T LOOK TOO CLOSE FOR THE STRINGS. WHICH IS FINE WITH ME, REALLY. BUT I HAD TO BE REAL SUBTLE. BACK IN THE DAY, I COULD'VE USED THE GIANT, LOVING HANDS TO GENTLY SET THAT AIRLINER DOWN IN FULL VIEW OF THE MASSES, WOULD'VE BEEN GREAT FOR MY IMAGE. THE STORY WOULD BE TOLD FOR A COUPLE OF MILLENNIA. CAN'T DO THAT STUFF ANYMORE. EVERYBODY LOOKING FOR THE STRINGS, ALL THE TIME.

I MISS DOING THE MIRACLES.

Half Moon Bay, CA

During dessert that evening, Arthur introduced the dinner speaker, Colonel John Boyd, USAF (ret). A chiseled, square-jawed man, fit and wiry despite advanced age, the Colonel stood in front of the huge unlit fireplace as the guests sipped coffee.

"Good evening, ladies and gentlemen," the Colonel began in a gravelly voice with a plain Midwest accent. "Mr. Schlessel, here, asked me to give you a few words regarding my theories. Didn't say exactly why I should do that or who the hell you all are, but Mr. Schlessel can be very convincing.

"Anyway, I'm here to talk to you about combat. I'm a fighter pilot—well, was a fighter pilot once upon a time, a very long time ago—and I developed these theories with a couple of other fighter pilots back in the day. The theory that I'm going to present to you, I believe, is as relevant today as it was then.

"During the Korean conflict—nobody ever got around to calling it a war—American aviators flew the F-86 Sabre, a jet that was in many ways grossly inferior to the enemy's MIG-15. Despite this fact, American pilots scored seven kills to the MIG's one. They did this because we mastered a technique that I call the OODA loop.

"OODA stands for Observation, Orientation, Decision, and Action. Those four elements are required in any strategic activity, whether you're engaged in air-to-air combat, gettin' a gal's phone number, or trying to defeat your competitor in the business of selling shoes. Observe, orient, decide, and act. It's a basic life process for all us sentient beings, from ants to aardvarks to attorneys.

"When two jets are closing at over a thousand miles per hour, ladies and gentleman, there is precious little time to ponder. First, you observe—you look out your windscreen and see that little contrail way off in the distance and say to yourself, 'shit, John, that looks like a MIG heading our way.'

Next, you orient. What's the closing angle, the relative altitude, is he alone or part of a formation? Based upon this orientation, I gotta decide what I think is the best course of action. And then, once I decide what that best course is, I act. That's the OODA loop at a thousand miles per hour in a life or death encounter.

"I taught our aviators how to process that loop faster and better than the guy flying the other plane. Observational abilities being generally equal—remember, this was in the days before radar, we're talking eyeballs here—I taught our pilots to orient, decide, and act faster than the other motherfucker. First, orient: there are only a limited number of factors which must be determined. It is critical to assess those factors rapidly, accurately, and to the exclusion of all else. Focus on the fight at hand, not what any other motherfucker might be doing or saying on the radio. With the pertinent facts at hand, decide. There are only so many choices in this situation and a skilled pilot will sort them quickly; five possibilities, to be specific. I can either turn right or left, climb or dive, or keep driving straight. Knowing this fact, I act. I will myself turn, climb, or dive. The guy in the other cockpit, of course, is currently doing the same damn thing.

"It doesn't matter which of those choices the enemy makes or which action I choose. What matters, ladies and gentlemen, is that I execute my OODA loop faster than that fucker flying at me. I process my loop and act," here the Colonel slapped his hands together sharply, " before the other guy gets to the end of his loop and acts. I'm inside his loop, see?

"What if I chose wrong, you ask? It doesn't matter. By processing the OODA loop first and thereby acting first, I fuck up the other guy's OODA loop. He sees me breaking in a hard turn—he's now back to the beginning of his loop, back at the first 'O' in his OODA loop, observing my break and he has to restart his thinking process, has to reorient. He's suddenly recycling his OODA loop. Then, before he even gets to the point where he's deciding what to do in response to that, I reverse my break," here the Colonel demonstrated with his hands simulating the flight of the relative aircraft. "I keep processing my loop faster than the other guy, maneuver and response, get to his six and blow that bastard out of the sky." The Colonel looked about the room, as he gestured the left hand plane blowing up. He paused. "Now, I have no fucking clue what you all are up to," he continued, smiling, "but I suggest that whatever it is, you keep your OODA loops tight, fast, and always inside the other guy's. Thank you for listening. Good night."

As the small group applauded politely, the Colonel walked over and shook hands with Arthur. He gave a half wave over his shoulder to the others and left. Arthur sat back down at the table to finish his dessert.

"Very inspiring, Arthur," the Senator said. "That's the shortest damn dinner talk I ever heard."

"Yeah, Boyd's a pretty smart guy," Arthur agreed. "Works out to about five thousand bucks a minute, probably."

"Pretty damn well preserved," Edgar said, shaking his head. "Unless the dude was six years old when he was flying jets over Pyongyang, he's gotta be over a hundred, right? Doesn't look a day over seventy."

Arthur sipped his coffee.

Grace leaned over to whisper into Arthur's ear. "Sounded like the man said we should stop screwing around."

Arthur nodded.

Purgatory

"What the hell?" Elliot said. The three of them were still watching the feed from Arthur's house.

Debbie said, "That little speech sounded like it was meant for us, Elliot."

Elliot pushed his chair back from the monitor, rubbing the back of his neck. "It kinda did, didn't it?"

Kevin was typing rapidly on a laptop alongside the main

monitor. He tapped the screen, saying "Colonel John Boyd, USAF. Born January 23, 1927. Died March 9, 1997. Our dinner speaker is back from the dead. What the fuck is going on down there?"

"What the hell, Elliot? Who are those people? Whose side are they on?" Debbie asked.

"I told you guys, I don't know," Elliot said. "All we can do from here is watch, see what they're up to. Keep following Arthur's lead."

"But what they're up to could be getting Grace excised—or killed," Debbie said.

"Maybe," Kevin said. "But Arthur is the one calling the shots. We gotta assume he's got a plan."

"In the meantime," Elliot said, turning back to the monitors, "we need to push forward on the con Grace laid out. Can't be sure when Arthur's coming back up."

"But we don't really know what she's talking about, Elliot," Debbie said. "Not like we're all practiced grifters up here. She says we're running a shuffle on the fiddle game, doesn't really conjure up a fully crystallized plan for me. You?"

"No, not really. But we know she wants to set up the guy in Afghanistan to take the fall. He's the fiddle in this scenario. It can't be coincidence that this Mahdi dude is the subject of that entire conference down there."

"No, not a coincidence," Debbie agreed. "But it's not obvious how we're supposed to be working the setup."

"Yeah," Kevin said. "Not quite sure how this is all shaking out. The whole 'black hole' thing could be a problem."

Elliot was shaking his head. "Not thinking about that yet. But consider this: remember, we were talking before, about the con, about how we needed to build this guy up."

"Yeah, this little game supposedly has God as the mark," Kevin said. "So we need a damn big fiddle."

"Yeah, Arthur said he wanted us to make this guy in Afghanistan look like the Second Coming," Elliot said.

"It was a figure of speech, Elliot," Debbie said.

"Aim high," Elliot said. "We might need to go that way to get Grace out of this."

"Well, if that's the case," Debbie said, "we should get ourselves a Star of Bethlehem, shine it down on this guy. That would be a great start."

"Geez, Deb," Kevin said, "Can't be done. A star doesn't stay fixed over one spot on Earth. I shouldn't even have to explain this. Even if we could arrange for a goddamn supernova to explode, even if it went off in just the right part of the sky, ignoring the fact that the light from the explosion would arrive a couple of centuries from now—any closer and the thing would sterilize the planet, solve our problem right there, I guess—but even if we got ourselves a supernova, it doesn't stay fixed over one spot—even the Star of Bethlehem wasn't the Star of Bethlehem. Get over it."

"Yeah, I see your point," Debbie said. "Except our boss down there," she continued, pointing to the image on the monitor of Arthur sipping coffee, "just handed us our very own Star of Bethlehem."

"What? How?" the other tech asked.

Debbie sat up straight in her chair. "You think, Elliot?"

"Maybe," Elliot said. "Art did just get the US government to park a spy satellite in geosynchronous orbit right over our fiddle."

"Senator didn't say she'd do it," Kevin corrected.

"Sure as shit she'll do it," Debbie continued. "It's perfect."

"You're right, Deb," Elliot said, "it'll be positioned perfectly. But it's not a star. It's just a satellite. Nobody'll be able to see it's there."

Debbie smiled. "Unless..."

"Unless what?" Kevin asked.

Debbie said, "Our own baby supernova, on cue and smack dab right over our mark. The Star of Kandahar. It has a nice ring to it. Shepherds will see it for a thousand miles around, just like the Charlie Brown Christmas special. Perfect!"

"No way in hell," Elliot said.

Debbie stared at the group breaking up for the evening on the monitor. "Maybe I'll just mention it to Sam, then," she said slowly, "once she gets back. See what she thinks."

"Please don't, Deb," Elliot said.

"Can't stop me. OODA, baby!"

Grace opened her eyes in the night and smiled as she snuggled against Julius's chest. She felt the gentle rocking of the boat beneath them. She hugged him more tightly and sighed. "Storm's coming," Julius said softly.

Half Moon Bay, California

Grace awoke to insistent knocking on the door of the bedroom. She sat up, rubbing her eyes and wondering if she had dreamt the sound. No, there were the two Great Danes, sitting up at alert and staring at the door. Grace turned to awaken her husband, but he wasn't there.

"What the hell?" she said half aloud.

More knocking, louder this time. "Mr. and Mrs. Sheehan?" An official voice, a military tone.

Grace pulled the sheet about her and crossed to the door, opening it. Two members of the Marine security detail, a man and a woman, stood before her. She recognized them from seeing them patrol the house the last two days. But now, she noticed, they were wearing full combat gear, helmets and bullet-proof vests, whereas before they had walked about in shirtsleeves and sunglasses with only a sidearm. Each now had an automatic weapon slung at combat-ready across their chest.

"What's up?" Grace asked.

"Is Mr. Sheehan with you, ma'am?" the woman asked, looking past her.

"Don't think so," Grace said. "Is there a problem?"

"We need you to stay in your room, please," the woman said. "Please lock this door and stay here. We'll locate Mr. Sheehan."

"I was staying in my room, sleeping," Grace said, irritated. "Then you woke me up. What the hell is going on?"

"Overlord has picked up some bogies heading our position," the woman said, now looking up and down the hallway. "Nothing definite, could just be a flock of geese or something. But we'd like you to stay in your room with the door locked, just in case."

Suddenly, there was an explosion from the rear of the house that shook the entire building. Grace stumbled and went down on one knee, the dogs barking. "Those are some big fucking geese," Grace cursed.

The two Marines put their hands to their ears, listening to a sudden burst of chatter in their com sets. The man barked something to the other Marine, then yelled at Grace, "Stay here, lock the door." He slammed the door in Grace's face.

"Shit," Grace said, then turned to find some clothes. She dressed in a pair of black jeans and navy tee shirt, found a dark stocking cap in the back of a drawer of the dresser and tucked her red hair beneath it. The sound of a short burst of automatic weapons fire came from the back of the house. "Shit, shit, shit," she whispered. She looked at the dogs. "You guys staying or coming?" The dogs stood up, looking at her. "Coming then. Let's go." She crouched down and opened the door. The hallway was dark now, whereas the hall lights had been on when the Marines were talking to her. Someone had cut the power. A real assault, then, not just a single bomber. But who was the target, she wondered, her or the Senator? She wasn't sure it much mattered. Security would be moving to protect the Senator, not her—of that she was certain. Grace moved slowly into the dark hallway, listening as she moved along the wall towards the back stairway, the dogs trailing her warily. Another, smaller explosion rocked the house, followed by several shouts and a short burst of gunfire. One of the dogs gave a low, menancing growl. Then si-lence again.

Grace broke into a run, the dogs following closely on her heels as she launched herself down the narrow butler stairs at the end of the hall. A dark mass appeared on the landing of the stairway, a dark silhouette of a man, two eerily glow-ing green dots for eyes and as he started to raise a weapon, Grace crashed down on top of him, knocking him into the wall, followed by both the Danes. One of the dogs bit down on the man's forearm, the short black assault rifle clattering from his grasp to the steps, a guttural cry as the other Dane's muzzle closed on the man's neck, then Grace was up and run-ning in a crouch, ducking behind the island in the kitchen.

Grace looked around the corner of the stone-topped is-land and saw barely visible red lasers playing crazily in the great room beyond. Occasionally, she caught a glimpse of paired green-glowing night vision goggles looking her way, but she couldn't tell if friendly or foe. The dogs silently joined her, each lying flat on either side of her, breath-ing hard. Dark blood matted the fur of Sceólang's muzzle. "Time to get to GODD," she whispered to herself.

Grace could hear occasional shouts, running boots, all seemingly now towards the front of the house. If the assault had come from the rear, the location of the first explosion, the bad guys might be sweeping towards the front and up-stairs by now. She hoped so. She looked around the other corner of the island and saw a gaping hole in the wall where earlier in the day there had been glass French doors to the patio. Broken glass on the kitchen floor reflected the moon-light from outside.

"Fuck it," she whispered, then broke into a run, sneakers sliding over the shards of glass. She jumped through the hole to the outside, listening for gunshots, for shouts, waiting for another explosion—but all she could hear was the panting of the dogs as they paced her, their paws scrabbling on the hard surface. She dove behind the decorative bushes at the back of the patio. Still nothing. Grace moved slowly to the other side of the patio, her eyes adjusting now and seeing better in the pale light of a thin crescent moon. She stood, looked once behind her, then jumped the hedge and sprinted for the fire pit, hoping.

Julius caught her as she flung herself to the ground next to the fire pit. The dogs arrived a split second later, very softly growling as they bared their fangs at Julius.

Grace sat up, extricating herself from Julius. "You better back off a little," Grace said quietly. "They tore the throat outta the last guy that looked at me cross-eyed."

"No problem," Julius whispered back. "Who's with you?" Grace shook her head as the dogs lay down, both still watching Julius keenly, tails stock still. "Gabriel?"

"Not sure where he is," Grace said softly. "He wasn't in my room when this started."

"Hmph," was all Julius said in response. After a moment, he said, "You know we can't go looking for him." Grace nodded. Julius pointed towards the moonlight glinting off the ocean. "That way."

"Yeah," Grace agreed. "But there's a big drop between here and the beach."

"We'll have to jump it," Julius said.

"Last time I did that, I was blind drunk," Grace said, remembering. "Didn't work out well."

"Well, you've had practice then. That's not the big problem, though."

"Oh, great. What's the big problem?"

Julius held up his locator device, then pointed to her own necklace. "They're tracking us."

"So? They're on our side, remember?"

"Are they?" Julius asked. "You sure?"

"What do you mean?" Grace asked, looking about.

"You're the one who said something was fishy, not me. Remember? Now Gabriel's missing, when he should be with you."

"You think this is an inside job? To get me?"

"Or the Senator. I don't know, maybe both of you. But it's too cute. This assault got past the surveillance drone, not to mention the beach patrols, the patrol boat offshore, the whole fucking security system."

"The Marines told me they had picked up the attackers, thought it might be just a false alarm," Grace reasoned.

"Guess they were wrong. I don't think we should assume anybody is on our side, that's all I'm saying."

"You sound as fucking paranoid as me, Julius," Grace said, shaking her head.

"I'll never be as fucking paranoid as you," Julius said. "We gotta move. Now. Ready?"

"But the trackers—maybe we should just ditch them first."

"No," Julius said, shaking his head in the dark. "They got thermal imaging overhead, they can see us anyway. If we're not identified with the trackers, they'll have to assume we're bad guys and light us up."

"But you just said that there might not be any bad guys. Or the good guys are the bad guys," Grace protested.

"I don't know, Grace," Julius whispered back. "Either way, I don't want to give them a reason to shoot us in the back as we make a run down the beach. Because they will see us."

"Well, fuck." Grace thought for a moment, then said, "Give me your tracker."

"I just said--" Julius said.

"I'll give it right back." Julius handed over his tracker and watched as Grace removed her own. "Be right back," she said.

"Where--" Julius started, but Grace had disappeared to the otherside of the firepit. She returned after a minute and handed Julius his tracker.

"What did you do?" Julius asked. But just then Julius turned to the sound of someone shouting to their right. Something metallic clanged against the back of the house.

"Down!" Julius yelled. He grabbed Grace by the back of the shirt and hauled her down behind the fire pit. A flash, then a deafening explosion.

Purgatory

Sounds of occasional gunfire and shouting came through the control room speakers as they watched the monitors.

"What the hell is happening down there?" Elliot asked. He scanned the monitors, confused.

"It sounds like a damn war zone," Debbie said.

"What does?" Gabriel asked, walking into the darkened control room wearing pajamas. He looked at the monitors. Arthur, also in pajamas, walked in behind Gabriel.

Elliot jumped in his seat.

"Elliot," Arthur said. "You haven't fucked up everything while we were down there, did you?"

"Not everything, Boss," Elliot said, swiveling in his chair. "Looks like you two came back just in time. Not much fun right now at your old place."

"Why? What's going on?" Arthur asked. Elliot, Kevin, and Debbie all pointed at the monitors.

"Holy shit," Gabriel whispered.

THE PRAYING: WE MUST TALK ABOUT THE PRAYING. THE CONSTANT, INCESSANT, INTERMINABLE, UNENDING, BLEATING OF MY FLOCK—WHAT SHEPHERD BEFORE ME HAS BEEN FORCED TO ENDURE SUCH A CACOPHONY OF PLAINTIVE PLEADING? DO YOU ALL THINK ME DEAF? OR SO THICK AS TO NEED A REPETITIVE HAMMERING OF THE SIMPLEST REQUEST BEFORE I MAY UNDERSTAND YOUR NEED? AM I SO OBTUSE THAT FIFTY, FIVE HUNDRED, FIVE THOUSAND REPETITIONS ARE NEEDED TO ACHIEVE WHAT I HAVE NOT GRANTED ON YOUR FIRST SUPPLICATION? WHAT

THE HOLY HELL?

I'M SORRY. MY PATIENCE IS, OF COURSE, INFINITE. BUT YOUR LORD IS BEFUDDLED BY THE VERY NATURE OF YOUR PETITIONS. IS IT UNDERSTANDING FOR WHICH YOU PRAY, TO KNOW WHY THE THINGS YOUR LORD HAS SEEN FIT TO VISIT UPON YOU HAVE OCCURRED? IS IT ONLY THAT YOU WISH TO KNOW MY WAYS, SO THAT YOU MAY BE COMFORTED THAT THIS, TOO, SHALL PASS? THAT MY RIGHTEOUS ACTS ARE A WORTHY CHALLENGE FOR YOUR FAITH? OR IS IT THAT YOUR CRIES ARE NOT FOR UNDERSTANDING, BUT FOR YOUR LORD'S INTERCESSION? AM I TO TAKE YOUR PRAYER FOR DELIVERANCE AS A STATEMENT THAT YOU HAVE NO FAITH IN MY WORLD'S WAYS, THAT YOUR CONDITION IS NOT OF MY MAKING OR EVEN DESERVED, BUT RATHER AN INCONVENIENCE OF WHICH I SHOULD OBLIGE YOU WITH REMEDY? WHICH IS IT, CHILD?

IF YOU HAVE NO ANSWER, THEN NEITHER DOES YOUR LORD.

Dublin, Ireland

The Magistrate looked down from her bench as the withered, bent woman was rolled in her wheelchair to the witness box and sworn in. The elderly nun lowered her right hand and stared up icily at the Magistrate.

"Thank you, Reverend Mother," the Magistrate said, "for agreeing to appear before this court. I am sure that your insights will be very helpful." The woman said nothing, so the

Magistrate continued. "Am I correct, Reverend Mother, that you served as Mother Superior of the Bon Secours Home for Mothers and Babies for a period of time?"

"Aye," the woman answered dryly. "For thirty-seven years, I served the Lord in that capacity."

"Would you be so kind, Reverend Mother, to tell the court the nature and purpose of the facility that you led during that time, please."

"In the service of God Almighty, Jesus Christ, and with the guidance of his Eminence, I and the sisters in my charge provided care for mothers and their babies, such as the name of our facility implies, I believe." Her voice was a steely rasp.

"Indeed, Reverend Mother. Were these mothers and babies in general, or was there some particular characteristic to your charges?" the Magistrate asked.

"Bon Secours was charged with the care of the lost and the destitute, of course. As are we all, young lady."

A barrister leaned toward the Mother Superior at the witness table. "Please address the court as 'your Honor,'" he said. The woman glared at him, then at the Magistrate.

The Magistrate continued, "And by the lost and the destitute, Reverend Mother, do you mean to describe unwed mothers?"

"We had a particular charge to care for such, indeed."

"And the offspring of these women, as well?"

"Of course," the wizened nun replied, shifting in her wheelchair. "We took in the offspring as well."

"From Galway?"

"From Galway, yes, but also from much of the south of Ireland."

"From Dublin?"

"Many, many from Dublin, yes."

"Were the mothers trained to be nuns as well, Reverend Mother?"

"No, of course not. These were not women called to service. Quite the opposite. Fallen in spirit and deed. We took them in, in Christ's mercy. They and their offspring."

"It was charity, then?" the Magistrate asked.

"It was our Christian duty," the nun said icily, unblinking.

"Did the mothers work for their charity at all, Reverend Mother?"

"They did what they could to help out, of course."

"In the kitchen, for instance? Or in the fields?"

"Precisely. These were able-bodied young women, you understand. They were eager to help."

"Of course, Reverend Mother. They helped out in the convent, then?"

"Aye."

"Were any required to work at the laundries, as well, Reverend Mother? The laundries that took in work from the area about Galway?" She waited, but the old nun only glared at her. "I believe that the profits from these laundries were used to support the Church, were they not, Reverend Mother? The profits from these women's labors?"

"The Church does not make profits, young lady. The women in our charge did all they could to help defray the expenses associated with their care, as well as the care of their illegitimate offspring. They were more than happy to do so, to have a meaningful way in which to pay penance for their trespasses."

"No doubt," the Magistrate muttered. She shifted some papers on her bench, then stared down at the nun once again. "Tell me about the babies, Reverend Mother."

"I'm not sure I understand you."

"Tell me about the children of these women. The offspring of these unwed women."

"I'm not sure what it is that you want to know," the nun said, shifting again with a creak in her wheelchair.

"If the mothers were working, doing their penance as you put it, who cared for the children?"

"They were cared for in the nursery, obviously. The sisters, for the most part, cared for the little ones."

"During the day, you mean? Until the mothers returned from their duties?"

"The children were cared for in a communal manner. They slept in the nursery as well."

"Then when did the mothers of these children spend time with their babies? Was there a particular time of day or evening that afforded the mothers time with their children?"

"That type of behavior, such as you describe, would not be appropriate."

"Not appropriate? In what way, Reverend Mother, not appropriate?"

"It would be detrimental."

"Detrimental? Detrimental to whom?" the Magistrate asked.

"To the children. These were not normal maternal bonds. These offspring were the product of sin, each and every one. The mothers did not possess the maternal instincts required to provide what was necessary for these children. It would have been detrimental to the well being of the children to pretend otherwise. That is what I mean, your Honor."

"I see. Do you believe the mothers shared your opinion, Reverend Mother?"

"It is not an opinion which I express. I speak the Lord's truth."

The Magistrate looked down at her papers again momentarily. She removed her glasses and pinched the bridge of her nose. "At some point, Reverend Mother, a point in time where the mother had done her penance, as you put it—at that point were the children returned to the care of their mothers?"

There was a pause during which the Magistrate and the nun only stared at one another, before Reverend Mother said, "I believe I made it clear that that was not the case."

"Surely, it was not possible to raise up so many babies and children to young adulthood, Reverend Mother? Did you have the facilities, the resources to care for so many for a prolonged period of time?"

"We did not, no."

"If the children were not returned to the care of their mothers, then, what became of them?"

"The children were frequently adopted."

"Adopted? By whom? By the residents of the environs of Galway proper? Irish families?"

"No, your Honor. The babies were given to good families, I assure you. Mostly American families, though many from England and Canada, as well. Very good families."

"Given, you say?"

The nun hesitated only a moment. "There were fees, of course. To cover the associated expenses."

"Of course there were expenses, Reverend Mother. No doubt."

"If you mean to imply, your Honor, that the practice of the Church was nefarious in any way—"

"Imply, Reverend Mother? I imply no such thing. I believe that you have made it quite clear that these children were taken from their biological mothers without consent, that these mothers were required to work for the privilege of having their babies taken from them, that your activities profited the Church by the systematic, wholesale merchandising of these children to the affluent families that purchased them and then took them overseas, away from their own mothers and their mother country. I meant no implication, Mother."

"I will not sit here, madam, and have you slander the Church and the good practices of my sisters. I will not—"

"Tell me about the Room of Ascension."

Color drained from the old woman's face. She looked away from the Magistrate.

"The Room of Ascension, Reverend Mother. Please tell the court of the—"

"I don't know what you're talking about."

"Tell the court, please, Reverend Mother. About the babies who were sick." The nun looked out the window at the side of the room and said nothing. "It is my understanding that disease was not infrequent in the Bon Secours Home. Many, many children died of dysentery, of influenza, of measles, of other childhood illnesses, did they not?" The witness nodded. "As a matter of inquiry, it has been established that the infant mortality rate at your home for mothers and babies was over thirty percent, Reverend Mother. A rate over three times that of similar Irish institutions. Are you aware of this fact, Reverend Mother?" The woman looked fixedly out the window. "And it was your practice, Reverend Mother, to isolate a particularly sick child from the other children in the nursery?"

"It was necessary, of course."

"To prevent the spread of disease, of course." The woman nodded. "And when a baby became gravely ill—when it became apparent that the child was unlikely to survive, the child was placed in isolation. The baby was placed in a room apart from the other children, yes?"

The nun nodded. "It was necessary, to protect the other children," she said.

"And this isolation room, it was called the Room of Ascension, was it not?"

The elderly woman nodded slightly.

"Please answer aloud," the Magistrate said.

"Some referred to it in that way, I believe," the nun said softly.

"And what happened in that room, Reverend Mother?"

The old woman looked up finally and met the judge's gaze.

"They died, of course."

Purgatory

"Holy shit," Gabriel said again, louder.

"What now?" Arthur asked.

"Are you seeing this?" Gabriel asked, pointing at the monitor. It was dark.

"I don't see anything, Gabe," Arthur said. "I'm trying to figure out if—"

"They're under attack, at your house," Gabe said.

"What? By who?" Sam asked, coming up behind Gabriel as Arthur rolled his chair back to the console.

"I can't tell. Shit, shit, shit. Can we get the feed from the drone?" Gabriel asked.

"Yeah," Elliot said, twisting over a different monitor and typing vigorously on his keyboard. He stared at it. "Here it is. Shit."

"Get us the sound," Arthur said. "The comms from the security feed. Shit, there are a lot of people running around our house. Oh, fuck!"

A white splotch blossomed across the back of the house. "That was some kind of explosion!"

Kevin keyed in more commands and the speakers above the monitors crackled: "—the beach, rear of house, multiple ban—" A series of clicks were heard as throat mikes were keyed in acknowledgment.

A new voice, that of a woman, said, "Package secure, ready to move. Clear for evac?"

"What package?" Samantha asked, straining to make sense of the multiple colored dots moving about in blurry trails onscreen through the floor plan of her house.

"The Senator, I'm sure," Gabriel said.

"Roger, go for evac, clear to move."

"Moving now."

"If they're evacuating the Senator, what about Grace?" Sam asked, looking at Gabriel.

They all strained to find the heat image labelled with the locator tag of Grace on the screen. "There!" Arthur said, stabbing his finger into the monitor, rocking it. "Back of the house."

"Who is she with, I can't make it out," Gabriel asked.

"Julius, and—"

"Great," Gabriel said.

"And the dogs," Arthur added. "Jeez, even our dogs have locators. Ridiculous."

"Not ridiculous," Sam said, leaning in next to her husband to watch the screen. "The dogs are as big as Grace. Without trackers, they'd look like intruders to the surveillance drone."

"Package away," the speaker announced. They watched the thermal image of several cars speed away from the front of the house towards the main road. "Overlord has tactical; Rule change. R-O-E-2, repeat R-O-E-2, now, now, now. I-F-F and weapons free. All units, acknowledge." Again, there were a series of clicks. "Team one, secure main access road, no activity at present. Team two, upper level, clear and secure, be advised multiple friendlies sheltering in place. Team three, clear and secure lower level, be advised multiple bandits your level, west wing. Push to rear of building. Team four, secure rear exterior and cover Team three's north flank, advise friendlies your area. Execute." Again, clicks.

"Shit, Grace and Julius are in the middle of a firefight," Sam said.

"Who the hell are these guys?" Gabriel asked.

"No clue," Arthur added. They all scanned the images on the monitors before them.

The speaker crackled, a man's voice, breathing heavily. "Contact, west wing, multiple bandits, automatic weapons fire. Engaging."

"Copy, Team 3." On screen, a white flash blossomed and faded at the back of the house. An instant later, the fading report of an explosion could be heard on speaker as a mike opened, closed. Then, "Overlord, Team 4. Breaching charge west wing, bandits moving to exterior, rear. Advise."

"Copy, Team 4. Engage and pursue. Team 3, engage in place. Be advised 3, Team 4 to your right flank and on the move, engaging your tangos. Advise, advise: four—no, two friendlies your vicinity.

"Shit, Overlord, is it four or two?"

"Two. Two friendlies rear of house. The other two are the dogs." This was answered with two clicks.

Half Moon Bay, CA

Julius covered Grace with his body as debris from the explosion rained over them. The dogs huddled close on both sides as the four of them crouched in the shelter of the outdoor fireplace. Short bursts of automatic weapons fire, stuttering flashes accompanied by a sharp staccato, appeared to their right. Julius watched as dark shapes, stabbing red lasers and faint smears of green goggles moved stealthily towards them from the site of the explosion.

"Now, now, now!" Julius yelled into Grace's ear, though he knew she probably couldn't hear a thing except the buzzing aftermath of the deafening explosion. He grabbed her around the waist and hauled her into a half crouch. She looked into his eyes, dazed. "Run!" Julius pulled her along as they ran towards the bluff in the dark, heading away from the conflict playing out behind the west wing of the house.

At the brush line, Grace grabbed Julius and pulled him up short. The buzzing in their ears had abated.

"We can't," she said into his ear as they crouched at the edge of the gorse that marked the top of the bluff. "Did it once, almost got killed. Find a way down. This way," she said, pulling him by the hand as she ran in a half-crouch back east along the ridge line, the dogs silently at heel on either side.

"There," Grace said, coming to a halt. She pointed to the top of a ladder sticking up from the brush, the rest disappearing in the darkness down the side of the bluff.

"Careful," Julius said. "Might be rigged."

"Fine, you first then," Grace said. She watched as Julius tested the ladder. He gestured for her to follow.

"Seems okay," he said as she moved to crouch next to him. "I'll go first. There might be someone on the beach. We'll stop about halfway, speed slide the rest. You can do that?" She nodded. "When you hit the sand, run right ten yards and drop on your belly. I'll be going the other way. Okay?"

"Run right and drop. Okay," she said. "Just give me a second to do this."

"Do what?" Julius said in a harsh whisper from the top of the ladder. "We don't have a second, Grace. Let's go!"

Grace rubbed the head of the Danes, lying next to her in the grass. "Thanks, guys. Go!" She clapped her hands and the two dogs took off into the dark. She turned to Julius and nodded.

"That's what you needed to do? Thank the dogs?" Julius said.

"I thought you liked dogs," Grace whispered.

Julius shook his head and moved lower on the ladder. He looked down at the beach, moonlit waves breaking in the surf below.

"Halt! Stand your ground!" Julius and Grace looked back into the darkness from where the shout had come from. "Identify yourself! Halt! On your belly, on the ground! Now!"

That's a lot of orders, Grace thought to herself.

Purgatory

"They're gonna get killed," Sam said, watching the screen. Arthur and Gabriel said nothing. It looked on the screen like she was probably right. The gun battle on the monitors was playing out in apparent slow motion all too close to the little pair of dots that represented their friends.

"They're making a break for the beach," Arthur said, pointing.

"No way they can make it down your fucking cliff, Arthur," Gabriel said. "Grace almost killed herself that time, remember?"

"Not like they have a choice, Gabe," Sam said.

"Team four," the speaker announced, "movement your

six, breaking towards the beach."

"Shit, Overlord, you said two friendlies. What the fuck?"

"And dogs. You said dogs, Overlord."

"Team four, advise you task four-three, four-four, I-F-F and engage. Tags say friendly but they are at your six and moving fast. Get eyes on and engage."

Two mike clicks responded. They watched as two Marines, marked by amber dots on the monitor, split off from the main group and moved towards the dots marking Grace and Julius, now at the cliffside.

"Shit," Sam whispered, watching. The dots on the screen converged.

The speaker crackled as a mike opened. "Halt! Stand your ground! Identify yourselves!"

On the screen, the dots moved tentatively, then, "Halt! On your belly! On the ground! Now!"

They watched as the dots labelled Julius and Grace ran away from the group, back towards the house.

"Bogies not identified, Overlord, advise, advise! Not complying. Two bogies, re-engaging back to the house. Advise!" There was a brief pause, then, "Overlord, do you copy? Bogies are moving to re-engage Team four, back of house. What do you want me to do?"

"Copy four-three. Target and neutralize. Do not let them re-engage."

"Shit, no!" Sam said, clapping her hand to her mouth.

Two clicks.

They watched as the two amber dots of the Marines moved to engage the green dots labelled Grace and Julius, moving back to the house.

"Halt or I will shoot your ass, motherfucker!"

On the monitor, the green dots kept moving.

The three of them watched in stunned silence, waiting.

"Hey! What the fuck?"

"Four-three, say again. Status? Have you engaged targets?"

"Negative, Overlord, negative."

"Say status, four-three."
"You have us chasing the fucking dogs, Overlord."

I'M NOT GOING TO KID YOU: YOU AND I HAVE A PROBLEM.

UP TILL NOW, I'VE BEEN FILLING YOU IN ON THE BASICS, TRYING TO GET YOU UP TO SPEED. BUT NOW I HAVE TO TELL YOU WHERE WE STAND.

WE ARE IN DEEP TROUBLE.

SORRY TO SPRING IT ON YOU. I KNOW YOU WERE HOPING FOR UNICORNS AND RAINBOWS HERE, TO HEAR THAT I GOT IT ALL UNDER CONTROL. NOT SO, AMIGO. THIS IS REALITY WE'RE LIVING IN, SO I'M GOING TO GIVE IT TO YOU STRAIGHT.

MANKIND IS IN TROUBLE. BIG TROUBLE. I'M NOT TELLING YOU ANYTHING THAT YOU DON'T ALREADY KNOW, I'M SURE. GLOBAL WARMING. FOOLS WHO DON'T BELIEVE IN GLOBAL WARMING EVEN THOUGH IT'S OBVIOUS THAT EVERY SINGLE SCIENTIST THAT DISAGREES WITH GLOBAL WARMING IS ON THE TAKE FROM BIG OIL. OVERPOPULATION. RELIGIOUS FANATICISM. TERRORISTS. TIN POT DICTATORS WHO THINK WE'RE STILL LIVING IN THE TWENTIETH CENTURY. NUCLEAR WEAPONS. CRAZY VIRUSES. TALK RADIO. I'M NOT TELLING UNTO YOU ANY GREAT REVELATION, AM I?

HERE IS THE PART THAT'S REALLY UPSETTING: I

CAN'T FIX IT. SORRY. REALLY, I AM. IT'S NOT BE-
CAUSE I DON'T WANT TO, BELIEVE ME. I'VE ALWAYS
BEEN THERE FOR YOU, YOU KNOW THAT. BUT TIMES
HAVE CHANGED. I CAN'T MANIPULATE YOUR UNI-
VERSE LIKE I USED TO. MANKIND HAS PROGRESSED
TOO FAR FOR ME TO STEER. OH, I'VE BEEN ABLE TO
DO A BIT HERE AND THERE, AT THE MARGINS. I'VE
STOPPED A COUPLE OF GUYS FROM GETTING THEIR
HANDS ON A NUKE. STOPPED NEW YORK FROM AP-
PROVING FRACKING—THAT WAS KIND OF A MIRACLE, I
GOTTA TELL YOU. BUT I CAN'T DO THE REAL BIG
MIRACLES LIKE I USED TO. BELIEVE ME, NOTHING
WOULD'VE MADE ME HAPPIER THAN TO JUST GRAB
THOSE PLANES OUT OF THE AIR BEFORE THEY HIT
THE TOWERS AND GIVE THEM A LITTLE SHAKE UNTIL
THOSE ASSHOLES FELL OUT, YOU KNOW? BUT I CAN'T
DO THAT STUFF ANY MORE.

IT'S WORSE THAN NOT BEING ABLE TO DO THE
OCCASIONAL MIRACLE. YOUR GOD IS NO LONGER
DRIVING THE BUS. YOU'RE GOING TOO FAST NOW,
AND YOU'RE WAY FAR DOWN THE ROAD. MANKIND
HAS PROGRESSED TO THE POINT WHERE YOU FOLKS
HAVE SEIZED THE WHEEL. BEFORE TOO LONG,
YOU'LL HAVE ATOMICALLY PRECISE MANUFACTUR-
ING TECHNIQUES. NOT MUCH LATER, YOU'LL FI-
NALLY HAVE THE FUSION THING FIGURED OUT. I
MEAN, I CAN'T KEEP SCREWING UP YOUR EXPERI-

MENTS FOREVER. YOU GOT QUANTUM COMPUTING, ALMOST. THIS IS FUNDAMENTAL STUFF. YOU'RE GETTING CLOSE TO USING MY TOOLS NOW, TO BEING ABLE TO SEE THINGS FROM MY PERSPECTIVE. AT THAT POINT, I'M OUT OF THE GAME. YOU'LL BE ON YOUR OWN.

GOOD LUCK WITH THAT.

Half Moon Bay, CA

Grace looked down from her position on the ladder but couldn't see much in the thin moonlight. She guessed she was about twenty feet above the beach but couldn't be sure. She was sure that Julius was off the ladder, had felt him slide down and drop onto the sand. Grace looked up briefly as she heard shouted commands from above the bluff. Then she took her feet off the rungs and straddled the ladder, sliding the rest of the way onto the beach. She hit the sand and her knees buckled as she rolled. She clambered up and began to run.

She ran straight over Julius, lying prone in the sand. Grace went flying, landing face first. Julius crawled over to where she lay.

"You kicked me in the ribs," he whispered in her ear.

Grace spat sand. "Yeah, well, you tripped me. You said go right."

"Yeah, right. This is left."

"You didn't say if it was right facing the ladder or the beach. It was confusing."

"Look," he said, pointing.

Grace raised her head and looked where Julius was pointing. A boat—a Zodiac, black and pulled up on the beach twenty yards away.

"Is it empty?" Grace asked.

"Probably. If anyone was in it, would've shot us by now with this clown show we're doing."

"So, do we go boating again, partner?" she asked, smiling in the dark through a face caked with sand.

"Safest egress is reverse of the attackers' ingress, or so they taught me a long time ago," Julius said.

"You mean, run like hell in the opposite direction."

"Exactly. After you."

Grace and Julius pushed the boat into the surf before jumping aboard. He started the engine and gunned the throttle. The Zodiac wheeled around and skittered over the waves as they moved through the darkness towards the open ocean.

"Where are we going?" Grace yelled into Julius's ear, holding onto a tie-down as the boat bounced in the surf.

"Away!" He reached over and pulled the dog's tracker from where it hung around Grace's neck. He threw it overboard, then his own.

Dublin, Ireland

The magistrate took a sip of water before continuing with the witness.

"Were other children, defective children, ever—" she stopped, the nun staring at her with an accusing stare. She started again. "The children who were left to die in this room, were they—"

"They were ill. They were sick to death, and suffering. They were being called by God to come home and be comforted. We did all we could, every day. Some children get sick. Most recovered with care and nourishment, but not all. Not all. When God called them home, we made their journey as comfortable as was possible. That was what we did, your Honor."

"These children, these babies, were ill, you say."

"Yes."

"Were any of the children dying of other causes?"

"I'm not sure what you mean to say, your Honor."

"Is it possible that some children, some of these babies, died, not of disease, but rather of malnutrition, for instance? Or dehydration?"

"There were some that were not capable of sustaining themselves, if that is what you mean."

"Because they were defective in some way?"

"Precisely."

"What form did these defects take, sister?"

"All forms."

"Could you be more specific, Reverend Mother?"

The aged nun sighed deeply. "There were a variety of defects that the children suffered from. These babies, these children, were the product of an ill-conception, often traumatized at birth."

"Specifics, please."

The nun shifted again in her chair. "I am not a doctor, your Honor."

"Were some of these infants mentally deficient?" The nun nodded. "Please answer aloud, Sister Hildegard, for the benefit of the record. Mentally deficient?"

"Yes."

"Physically deformed?"

"Yes."

"Lame? Missing or deformed limbs?"

"Yes."

"Blind?"

"Yes."

"Deaf? Mute?"

"Yes."

"And if these 'products of ill-conception' as you called them, if these infants and babies could not thrive in your communal nursery, they found themselves in the Room of Ascension. Is that accurate?"

"You are twisting my meaning, young lady—your Honor. You have no right to accuse me of such things. No right."

"But the healthy babies, the pretty babies, these were sold to the wealthy Americans. Even though ill-conceived, they managed to make it to rich homes abroad. I believe that is your testimony, Reverend Mother, is it not?"

"I believe that I am finished here, your Honor."

The magistrate leaned forward on her bench, glowering down on the witness beneath her. Softly, she asked, "How, Reverend Mother, did there come to be 796 corpses of babies in the septic tank behind the Bon Secours Home for Mothers and Babies? The Home which you ran for nearly forty years."

The old nun looked up at the magistrate aghast.

"Nearly eight hundred babies, Reverend Mother! None given a Christian burial, not even a marker or the basic dignity of a grave! Eight hundred children disposed of like so much fetid waste. Was that where the babies that you had placed in the Room of Ascension ended up, Reverend Mother?"

"You dare, madam! You dare too much. I am quit of you!" The Mother Superior shook her bony finger at the judge.

"The court has more questions, Reverend Mother."

"I will not answer any more of the court's questions. I wish to be excused."

"That, Reverend Mother, is not within my power." The Magistrate struck her gavel. "We stand adjourned."

CHAPTER 8

Helmand Province, Afghanistan

The next morning, Hila and Atal breakfasted on goat cheese and eggs with their hosts. The baby slept in his mother's lap as she ate. After breakfast, they all walked outside, the baby still asleep in his mother's arms. They were joined by many others as they walked towards the center of the small village.

They came to a central clearing already filled with people sitting in a wide semicircle. Facing the crowd, the pilgrim that had led them was seated on a raised dais of rough hewn wood. He sat, smiling and acknowledging those gathering before him.

"What is this?" Atal asked his host as they reached the edge of the crowd. "Morning prayers?"

"Something like that."

They followed Hamid as he found an open spot for all of them to sit. Bala Nashta arranged her shawl to keep the sun off her baby.

"Who will lead the prayers?" Hila asked, sitting cross-legged on the ground.

"The Mahdi," Bala Nashta answered.

"But I thought he cannot—" Hila began.

Bala Nashta put her finger to her lips. "Just listen, little one," she said, smiling.

They listened.

"Your Mahdi makes a sound like the bleating of goats," Atal said, but Hamid only shook his head in reply. On the little stage, the pilgrim closed his eyes and raised his hands in greeting.

"Good morning, brothers and sisters."

Atal and Hila looked at one another, shocked, checking to see if the other had heard.

"It is a fine morning to be together, to be alive, to breathe the cool air, is it not?"

Atal was wide-eyed and pressed his hands over his ears, but he heard the man's voice no less clearly.

"It is a fine morning to share the company of our new brothers and sisters..."

Purgatory

"Oh no," Sam said, "the dogs are being washed out into the ocean," pointing. "They must've shot them after all."

"Don't think so, Sam," Gabriel said. "I don't think that's the dogs."

"It says it the dogs, on the monitor," Arthur said.

"I think Grace and Julius switched tags with the dogs," Gabriel said. "And now they're leaving. Must've found a boat."

"Oh. Well, good for them."

"Hope so."

"Where will they go?" Sam asked.

"No clue," Gabriel said.

"Well, we gotta help them," Sam insisted.

"Help them how?" Arthur asked.

"I don't know—we just have to, that's all," Sam said. "That's why you put us in this damned Purgatory, right? That's why you set us up here, Gabe. What do we do?"

Gabriel sat, deep in thought.

"We have to find out what they're doing," Arthur said, tired of waiting for Gabriel to say something. "Somehow. Then we can help them."

"How do we do that?" Sam asked, turning to Gabriel.

Gabriel shook his head. "We can't."

"So what, then? We do nothing?" Arthur asked.

"No, we have to do something. We have to help them!" Sam said.

"We have to tell them what to do," Gabriel said. "That's the only way. We tell them."

"Okay, sounds good," Arthur said. "How do we do that, exactly?"

"I don't know," Gabriel said. "That's why you have a whole plane-full of geniuses, Arthur. Go do that thing you do and get your people to give us a way to talk to Grace."

"My people? Do my thing?" Arthur rolled his eyes. "Sure, Gabe. I'm on it. Just give me a minute. Be right back." He walked out the door and down the hall. Gabriel and Samantha exchanged a look. They both turned back to the screen, watching the small green dots move out to sea.

Arthur returned two minutes later, bringing along an elderly gentleman dressed in a dark, rumpled suit and wrinkled white shirt, a black bowtie askew at his neck. The man stood before the monitors and blinked behind thick, tortoise shell eyeglasses.

"Tell them, Bucky," Arthur said, gesturing to Sam and Gabriel. Sam and Gabriel looked at the man, waiting, but the man said nothing. "Bucky," Arthur encouraged. "This is Buckminster Fuller," Arthur explained to Sam and Gabriel. "He has a way to help, I think. He thinks."

Fuller pointed at the monitor. "We need to see them," he said, leaning closer to the screen. "This won't do. Won't do at all."

Elliot shrugged and tapped keys on the keyboard. The monitor changed to a visual feed from the drone, showing an overview of the house and the beach in the dark.

"Better," Fuller said, straightening up. "Find the man and woman. The people we need to talk to, show me."

Elliot wheeled a small joystick about until he caught sight of the Zodiac speeding across the ocean, heading away from the beach. It was dark, and the boat was black, but its wake showed as a phosphorescent vee in the moonlight. He zoomed in and the monitor filled with an overhead view of Julius and Grace, holding on tightly as the boat jounced over the waves.

"No, this is no good," Fuller said, agitated. "This won't work at all. They need to be stationary. This is no good, this careening along like this, this is no good at all. Make them stop and I can contact them." He looked at Sam, arms folded. He nodded to the monitor. "Make them stop," he repeated.

Elliot stared at the man, nonplussed. "How am I supposed to do that?" he asked.

"It's no good," Fuller said, throwing up his hands. He spun on his heels and walked back out of the control room. The three watched his back as he left.

"Well," Samantha said, "he wasn't much help."

Arthur smacked his forehead. "Genius. Fucking genius." He held up his hand to keep Gabriel from saying anything. "I'll be back." He left the way Fuller had gone.

Pacific Ocean

Julius cut the throttle and the rubber boat settled into the ocean swell. Silence and darkness surrounded them.

"Why did you stop?" Grace asked.

"Because we're here," Julius said, sagging against the inflatable's sponson, the adrenaline that had been juicing through him as they ran now spent.

"Here? Where are we?"

"Away, Grace. We got away." He smiled weakly at her.

"Yeah, okay. Great, we got away. Shouldn't we be going someplace, though? Someplace, I don't know, farther away?"

"Sure, Grace. Where do you think we should go?" She stared at Julius, then collapsed back against the sponson alongside him. "Yeah. Exactly," Julius said. They stared up at the stars and listened to the waves slap at the boat as they bobbed softly.

"Do you think it's safe? I mean, to just sit here like this," Grace asked, still looking up at the dark sky.

"Safe? We're in the middle of the ocean, in a little black dingy, in the middle of the night. I'd say if this isn't safe, then we are well and truly fucked, Grace."

"We might be well and truly fucked, Julius," she answered, taking his hand.

"We might be," he agreed.

They were quiet for a time.

"I wish I knew what the hell was going on," Grace said softly. "Do you know what the hell is going on?" she asked, turning to look at Julius in profile against the sparkle of the darkened waves.

"I do not," he replied, head back against the inflatable and staring at the sky. He blew out a deep sigh. "Not a fucking clue."

Grace let her head fall back as well. She blew a ringlet of hair off her forehead. "Well," Grace sighed, "at least it's a nice enough night."

"Nice enough."

"Thanks for saving my ass, by the way."

Julius shrugged. "Just followed you. Didn't do much saving."

"Bullshit. You knew. You gave me the GODD thing." Grace looked at Julius again in the dark. "How'd you know?"

"Didn't know," Julius said.

"Just a feeling, huh?"

"Yeah, Grace. Around you, I get that feeling a lot."

"I should've told Gabriel."

"About what? Us?"

"No. He asked what you meant about GODD."

"And you didn't tell him, did you?"

Grace shook her head. "And now he's gone."

"No, Grace. You know why you didn't tell him."

"What do you mean?"

"You know what I mean. You told me yourself, on the

plane. You had a bad feeling. You didn't trust him."

"I was just being paranoid, you said."

"Yeah, that's what I said. But something's not right. He wasn't going to meet us, even if you trusted him enough to tell him. He was already gone."

"You think so? You're not just saying that?"

"Why would I say that? To make you feel better? That he's okay somewhere and coming to our rescue?"

"Not to make me feel better, Julius. Because you don't want him here."

"Really? Is that what you think?" Grace let go of his hand and looked at the sky. "You're an idiot, you know that? We just ran through a damn firefight, nearly got our heads blown off back there, and where the fuck is your husband, huh? Where was he, back there when he was supposed to be lying next to you in bed when this whole shitstorm started?"

"I don't know."

"Yeah, neither do I. None too helpful, your husband."

"That's not Gabriel, Julius," Grace said, looking at him again. "That's not how he works."

"Oh, well. Let me know when he starts working. You know, to save your ass. When he shows up again."

"Thanks, Julius. I feel so much better now."

"Feel free to cry on my shoulder," he said, pulling her closer. Grace put her head on his shoulder.

Purgatory

The monitor still showed a zoomed-in night-vision enhanced image of the boat, now floating motionless, Grace with her head on Julius's shoulder. Samantha stole a glance at Gabriel before Elliot zoomed the image out, the boat becoming a dot bobbing on the ocean.

"She's safe, at least," Samantha said.

"Yeah, she's in good hands," Gabriel said.

Arthur walked back into the room. "He's working on it," Arthur said.

"Who's working on what?" Samantha asked, thankful for the distraction.

"Fuller," Arthur said, falling into a chair. "Trying to find a way to get an idea down to Grace. Says it's tough—but he thinks he can rig some kind of targeted antenna. Maybe. Sounds pretty hit or miss." He looked up at the monitor. "Is that them? They stop moving?"

"Yeah," Gabriel said, deadpan. "Looks like they're planning a sleepover."

"Really?" Arthur beamed. "That's great. Fantastic."

"Yeah. Fantastic," Gabriel said.

"What's your problem?" Arthur asked. "Fuller said no way this is gonna work unless they've stopped moving. And they've stopped, so that's great."

"What do you mean 'get an idea to Grace?'" Sam asked. "Like some kind of signal?"

"Yeah, hon, an idea. A thought signal," Arthur said. "Like we used to do, only reverse."

"You mean, Thought Technologies? My old stuff?" Gabriel asked.

"*Our* old stuff, you mean. Yeah, of course. But broadcasted. Like Chuck had going with the DoD, there at the end. And sending, not just receiving," Arthur said.

"I didn't know we could do that," Gabriel said.

"What, you thought the world stopped spinning when you died, buddy? That technology just stopped advancing? You've been gone a while, Gabe," Arthur said. "All the stuff you were worried about? Done. And lots of shit we never even thought to worry about."

"Great. Good to know my life's work has fucked up the world since I died," Gabriel said.

"Hey, everything's a double-edged sword, right?" Arthur said. "Our stuff's more good than bad, so far."

"It's really helping, Gabriel," Samantha said. "Big strides in treating mental illness. You and Grace should be proud."

"Hmmph," Gabriel said.

"Well, be thankful the shit works, Gabe," Arthur added. "Our little con would already be over if it didn't. We picked a real winner to be our fiddle, you know."

"No, what?" Gabriel asked. "You started setting up the Mahdi already? While I was still down below with Grace?"

"Yeah," Arthur said. "You said to get moving, so we got moving. You think that presentation I just gave was bullshit? That's all real, Gabriel. That valley is ours. 'The Store,' I think the cons call it."

"That's our store?" Gabriel asked.

"Yeah, all of it, right down to the plumbing. Biggest problem was that stupid shill you guys picked to be the fiddle for Grace. Some messiah you guys gave me to work with."

"Why? What's the problem with the shill?" Gabriel asked.

"He can't speak, Gabe," Samantha said.

"What do you mean?" Gabriel asked.

"Just what Sam said," Arthur said. "The dude who's supposed to be the new messiah? He's a mute."

"A mute? You mean he can't talk? At all? Why not?"

Arthur shrugged. "Who knows. Guy doesn't speak."

"How can he be the Messiah if he doesn't speak?" Gabriel asked, incredulous.

"Yeah, that was a challenge," Samantha said.

"It all worked out," Arthur explained. "Better this way. More messianic, I think."

"What is?" Gabriel said.

"We had to rig it so that Mahdi beams his thoughts directly to his followers. Gotta admit, it's been damn effective."

"I bet it is," Gabriel said.

I'M SORRY TO BE SUCH A DOWNER DEITY. IT'S NOT LIKE ME, YOU KNOW THAT. I WANT MANKIND TO BE HAPPY. TO BE SUCCESSFUL. "BE FRUITFUL AND MULTIPLY," REMEMBER? WHAT'S MORE FUN THAN

THAT, RIGHT? ONLY, IT DOESN'T LOOK LIKE THAT'S ON THE AGENDA.

THE FUTURE IS NOT IMMANENT. YES, I AM OMNISCIENT AND OMNIPOTENT, BUT REMEMBER, I GAVE MANKIND AGENCY. I MADE MY CHOICE WAY BACK IN THE DAY, SO MAN'S FREE WILL IS THE INCALCULABLE ELEMENT IN ALL THIS. LAPLACE'S DÆMON DOESN'T EXIST. IF IT DID, I'D BE HIM, AND I COULD TELL YOU WHERE THIS IS ALL HEADING. BUT THAT'S NOT THE UNIVERSE YOU LIVE IN. THAT'S NOT THE UNIVERSE I MADE FOR YOU.

MAYBE IT WON'T BE SO BAD, YOU'RE THINKING. GOD'S JUST COMPLAINING BECAUSE WE WON'T LET THE OLD MAN DRIVE THE SHINY NEW SPORTS CAR. YEAH, YOU'RE WRONG. I'VE RUN THE NUMBERS. IT'S NOT A MATTER OF 'IF'—JUST 'WHEN.' IF EVERYTHING BREAKS JUST RIGHT, I GIVE YOU FOLKS ABOUT ANOTHER CENTURY, MAYBE—PROBABLY NOT, BUT JUST MAYBE—TWO. I MIGHT BE ABLE TO BUY YOU A THIRD IF I KEEP WORKING THE MINI-MIRACLES AROUND THE MARGINS AND WE'RE REALLY, REALLY LUCKY, BUT I'M NOT HOLDING MY BREATH. IT'S ALL GOING TO GO TITS UP, AND I WON'T BE ABLE TO BRING YOU BACK. SORRY.

IT'S NOT WHAT I WANT FOR YOU. I WANT YOU TO DO GREAT THINGS. COLONIZE DISTANT WORLDS. SHAKE HANDS WITH YOUR SIZZLING ALIEN NEIGH-

BORS. *INVENT GREAT STUFF. CURE SUFFERING. CRE-*
ATE ART AND MUSIC AND REALLY LOVELY STORIES
THAT MAKE ME CRY AND LAUGH OR JUST SMILE
WHEN I WATCH WHAT YOU'RE UP TO. LOTS AND
LOTS OF GREAT-GREAT-GREAT GRANDKIDS. THAT'S
WHAT I WANT FOR US.

I'M GOING TO MAKE THAT FUTURE POSSIBLE.

I'M TAKING BACK THE WHEEL, PEOPLE. YOU'RE
DRIVING TOO FAST, YOU'VE BEEN DRINKING ALL
MY GOOD SCOTCH, YOU'RE ABOUT TO PUT IT ALL
IN THE DITCH—SO I'M TAKING BACK CONTROL.

I HAVE TO. IT'S FOR YOUR
OWN GOOD, BELIEVE ME.

Pacific Ocean

"This isn't helping, you know," Julius said.

Grace straightened up and wiped her eyes. "It was helping me, asshole," Grace said. She looked at Julius in the moonlit gloom until he met her gaze. "Do you think Pauley was telling the truth? About it being God who wants me excised?"

"I'm sure he thinks so. It's the way we think."

"What do you mean?"

"Proverbs 1:7, Grace: 'The fear of the Lord is the beginning of wisdom.' God is great, so you should not piss Him off."

"But how can that be, Julius? I mean, if it is God that wants me out of the picture, I mean, He's omnipotent, why hasn't He just done it, for fuck's sake? Why doesn't His wrathful hand just reach down right now and smite the shit out of me?"

"Don't tempt Him, Grace."

"Really, I mean it."

"That's not how He works. He isn't omnipotent, not when it comes to mankind. We know that."

"We do?"

"Of course we do. That's the great paradox, the burden of original sin. If He's omnipotent, why did He let Eve eat the apple in the first place, huh? How'd she get that past Him?"

"So if God isn't truly omnipotent—"

"He has to work in mysterious ways."

"This has certainly been mysterious, I'll give you that."

"Mysterious as fuck, that's for sure. This whole time, since we met up in that basement..." Julius said.

Grace nodded next to him. "We've been running. Like rats, we've been running."

"From the moment Gabriel found us—"

"—and you didn't follow us," Grace said.

"I didn't follow you because I couldn't," Julius said. "You and your husband dumped me in that closet with no where to run."

"It's like we've been running a damn maze," Grace said. "The dealership, the museum, Chicago—every time, it's a crisis, there's no chance to choose a direction or figure out what's going on. Now this—it's like He doesn't want to give us a chance to take the initiative, making us stay on the defensive so that we can be maneuvered or something. It's that OODA shit, but we're the ones being screwed."

"We've been taken for a ride, that much is obvious. But who's driving? What's the point?"

"To have me excised. That's the point."

"I thought so, too. But that doesn't make much sense anymore."

"Because we don't know why I have to be excised," Grace said.

"Well, yeah, that's true. But even without knowing why, this whole thing doesn't fit—it's bigger than having you excised now. It's not like the last time around, at the museum. That wasn't a bunch of Mormon kids running around with assault weapons back there," Julius said, jerking a thumb over his head. "And that wasn't Pauley or anything to do with the Catholic Church."

"Wasn't Mormons," Grace agreed. "The Mormons were protecting me, kind of. Kidnapped me, taking me to Salt Lake City against my will, of course, but not trying to kill me or excise me."

"But somebody's trying to kill you. That guy on the subway, with the knife."

"A bunch of somebodies. That waiter in Chicago. These guys, at the house. I got the feeling they were pretty serious, too."

"Gave that impression."

"So what do we do now?" Grace asked.

"Sleep."

Galway, Ireland

Ian Connolly sat in an old pub a few blocks from the wharf, reading about his friend's interrogation of the Mother Superior in the newspaper. He shook his head and gave a low whistle under his breath. "Sidhbh, my friend, you are going to hell," he said softly.

An elderly woman on the stool next to his smiled and winked at him. "She'll be in good company," the woman said. She nodded at the article that he had been reading. "That old nun ran a regular death camp, it sounds."

"Did you know the place?" Ian asked, folding the paper.

"Of course. Lived here in Galway all m'life."

"But that must not be much more than forty-odd years," Ian said. He nodded to the barman to bring a fresh round for both of them.

"Oh, aren't you the flatterer," the woman said, blushing. "I'm seventy-six years old, young man."

"You are not!"

The woman giggled and raised the newly filled glass to him. "*Sláinte!*"

"*Sláinte,*" Ian echoed, raising his glass to hers. "Tell me, then," Ian said after they had each drank. "Did you know the old man who was the janitor, the caretaker of the place. A man named Padraig O'Sullivan?"

"Aye, I know 'im. And his wife, Ida. Ida and I were school chums, back in the day."

"Did you hear what happened, then?" Ian asked her. The woman shook her head. "Old Mr. O'Sullivan jumped off the Ha'Penny bridge, I'm sorry to say."

"Oh, my! I am sorry to hear it. Oh!" She crossed herself and took another drink.

Ian raised his glass in toast. "God bless the dead," he muttered and took a sip. He gazed at the woman but said nothing more.

The woman shook her head. "Poor Paddy. He deserved a better end, I'll tell you. He was a good man."

"Was he?"

"Yes, a good man. I knew them well, good people both."

"Why would he do such a thing, do you suppose?" Ian asked conversationally. He gestured to the bartender who nodded back.

The woman raised her drink. She seemed to consider for a bit, then finished her drink before asking Ian, "Do you believe in fate?"

"Not sure," Ian said. "Do you?"

"I'm starting to," the woman said, nodding to the barkeep appreciatively as her new drink was poured. "There's a price to be paid for everything, isn't there?"

"A price for what, do you mean, ma'am?"

"For a baby, for instance."

Pacific Ocean

"Dawn breaks, and earth's vain shadows flee," Julius said. Grace stirred from where she lay sleeping on his chest. She opened her eyes and stretched.

"What the hell?" she asked, sitting up.

"Fog," Julius explained.

Grace looked about. In every direction, the only thing to be seen beyond the boat was a suffused white light. Even the sound of the waves was muffled.

"It's like being in a bowl of milk," Grace said.

"Or heaven," Julius smiled.

"No, it isn't. I've been there—it's nothing like this. I don't like it. Let's get out of here."

"Get out of here? No way, Grace."

"What do you mean, no way? I don't like it, Julius. Start up the damn motor and let's go."

"Which way do you want to go?"

"I told you, I don't care. I can't stay here, Julius. Start the motor, dammit."

"We can't, Grace. Settle down. In this fog, there's no way we can move. We could head straight out into the Pacific, or be going in circles for that matter, until we run out of gas."

"Don't tell me to settle down, Padre. Just pick a direction and get us there. We can't stay in here!"

"What do you mean—in where? You're shaking. What's wrong, Grace? Why are you so—oh shit—Grace!"

Grace opened her eyes to see only darkness. She shivered, naked beneath the sheet, alone. A cold, fine rain came down from the darkness.

Grace remembered having fallen asleep in Julius's arms, but now he was gone. She sat up, staring about in the dark, her bare feet sliding on the slick deck as she tried to stand. The world pitched about her and she reached out to steady herself, but found nothing to hold onto. She screamed.

Purgatory

"It's just a prototype at this point," Fuller explained.

Samantha and Gabriel sat across from the man at a table in one of the smaller conference rooms. Arthur paced about the room, running his hand through his hair.

"We get that, Bucky," Arthur said. "But does it work?"

"Of course it works. Will you please sit down, Arthur? You make me anxious, with all your pacing. You are inhibiting the free exchange of information." Arthur sat down, reluctantly.

"You were saying," Samantha prompted.

"Oh, yes. Of course it works, the principle is your own. The work of that Think Techniques company of yours. So the principle is sound. But the implementation requires more work. I'm applying my principles of Tensegrity, you know, a free-floating structure to focus and project the mimetic information, a projector with geodesic properties—"

"Yes, yes, Bucky, we get it. Brilliant," Arthur said. "So what's the hold-up?"

"The hold-up? This is research, Art," Fuller protested. "Prototyping, development, iteration. There's a process. The process must be respected."

"Technologies," Samantha corrected.

"Yes, a process of technology," Fuller agreed.

"Our company. It's called Thought Technologies," Samantha explained.

Fuller looked at her, confused.

"Bucky—can I call you Bucky?" Gabriel asked. Fuller nodded. "I appreciate your concerns. We realize that what you're doing is a challenge. But, right now we're in a bit of a jam, you see. My wife, and her friend, are in danger. We must have a way to communicate with them, Bucky. Now. We must talk to them now. Can you do it?"

Fuller shook his head. "The prototype is rudimentary at best. Not under the conditions I just witnessed, it is not possible. I am sorry that your wife will die, or be harmed, or whatever, but what you ask is not possible."

Gabriel hung his head.

Samantha reached across the table and took Fuller's hand. The old man grimaced. "Can you try, Bucky? Can you try your prototype?" Sam asked.

Fuller swallowed audibly and looked between Sam and the other two. "If you say I must, I will try. Sure, I will try it to save them. But there are limits to what I can do with this device. You must understand that."

"What limits?" Gabe asked, raising his head and looking at the man.

"Well, they must be stationary for one thing. None of that buzzing about in the little boat. Stationary, to give me time to achieve focus. It is a prototype, you understand."

"Yes, a prototype. We understand. You said so about twenty times. What else?" Gabriel said.

"Even if I can achieve focality, I can project a meaningful communication for a very limited time with this rudimentary device. Very limited time, because—"

"—It's a prototype. Yeah, we get it. How limited?"

"Fifteen or twenty seconds."

"What?"

"Fifteen seconds? Are you kidding?"

"Perhaps as much as twenty, no more with this prototype. It will lose focality, you see, as soon as the transmission is initiated. There is a feedforward problem. Standing wave formation. I'm not sure where it's coming from. I'm not even sure the subjects will be sufficiently—"

"It'll have to do," Gabriel said, slapping the table. "Twenty seconds." He looked at Arthur. "What can we tell them in twenty seconds?"

"Tell Grace you love her, just before she dies," Arthur said.

"Not helpful, Arthur," Gabriel said. "And not a bit funny, either."

"We tell them where to go," Samantha answered for her

husband.

"Okay," Gabriel agreed. "That makes sense. Where do we want them to go?"

"Los Angeles," Arthur said. "The plane is still at LAX. Get them back on board, we can figure out where to send them later. For now, get them airborne."

"Right," Gabriel said.

"No, not right," Samantha said. "We can't tell them to go to LA. Don't be ridiculous. They're in a little rubber dingy thing. They can't make it all the way down the coast to LA."

"Well, they can't just go back to Half Moon Bay, hon," Arthur said. "They'll walk right back into a shitstorm."

"San Francisco? That's pretty close," Gabriel said.

"No, that doesn't do them any good. They don't have any resources, just the clothes on their backs. San Francisco is a dead end." Samantha stood up and pulled up a map of the California coast on the electronic whiteboard on the wall of the conference room. She stared at it, then stabbed her finger on a spot just south of Half Moon Bay. "There. Monterey. We send them there. Artie, you arrange to pick them up in Monterey, take them to LAX and your 747."

"I can try," Arthur agreed. "Bucky, fire up your telepathic telegraph. We got a one word message to deliver. 'Monterey.'"

"It might not work, it's only a—" Fuller protested.

"Prototype," Arthur and Samantha said.

Fuller nodded.

Pacific Ocean

Grace sat up and looked about, dazed. The fog had burned away, leaving a hot, blue sky.

"Monterey," Grace said.

"Are you okay?" Julius asked, grabbing her by the shoulders, staring into her eyes.

"I'm okay. Why?"

"Why? Because you had a seizure or something, that's

why. You were completely out, like 'in a coma' out. You scared the living shit out of me, that's why."

"Monterey."

"You heard it, too?" Julius asked.

Grace shook her head. "I don't know. Didn't hear it, exactly, it was—"

"—in your head. Yeah, me too. What was that? Was that something you did? Something you did while you were in your trance?"

"Me? No, I didn't do it."

"Then what the hell happened to you?"

Grace shrugged. "It happens sometimes. I don't know what it is."

"You never told me."

"You could write a book about the stuff I haven't told you, Julius. It hasn't happened since I died. I used to hear things, too. But you heard it, too? You heard 'Monterey?' "

"No, not heard. Like you said, it wasn't a sound. It was in my head. One word, then nothing. What do you think it means?"

"Means? It means Monterey. Saddle up, partner. Let's go."

"Go where?"

"Monterey. The spooky magic voice in our heads said we go to Monterey."

"Which is where, exactly?"

"South. Not far, it's like two hours' drive from Half Moon Bay."

"You say so. That we can do, Grace. What happens when we get there?"

"I don't know, the little voice in my head didn't say. Did yours?"

Julius shook his head as he clambered back to start the motor. "Just let me know if you get any more signals, or whatever. And don't pull that catatonic shit again, okay?"

"Sure, Padre. No more catatonic shit."

Atlantic Ocean, West Coast of Ireland

Ian vomited over the side of the ferry to Inishmore.

"We're hardly swayin' at all," a crewman admonished him. "Calmest seas in a month, and you're heaving your guts. Ha!"

Ian wiped his mouth with the back of his hand. A ferry ride the morning after matching the old woman in the bar drink for drink was hardly his best idea ever. He tried to smile at the old sailor but was overcome with nausea once again. The other man laughed and made his way forward.

Twenty minutes later, Ian stumbled onto the dock of the small island. The short ferry ride from Galway could have been worse, he supposed. He looked about and spotted the road leading up to town. He began to walk.

After asking directions, Ian found the small inn he was looking for. The door was open. Ian knocked anyway.

"It's open," a woman called from inside.

Ian stepped into a handsome living room. A woman, white-haired and humming softly, sat before a large stone fireplace. She was knitting as she rocked, seated in an ornately carved chair, a woolen blanket covering her lap.

"A man!" she exclaimed, looking up from her knitting. "Well, it is my lucky day, isn't it?" Ian smiled back at her and removed his cap. "Wanting a room?"

"Perhaps, ma'am. But first, I'm looking for Mrs. O'Sullivan. Are you she?"

"I am. Who might you be?"

"My name is Ian Connoly, ma'am. He moved forward and shook her hand. "May I sit?" She nodded. "I am sorry to bring you bad news, Mrs. O'Sullivan, but—"

"You mean about my Paddy? I already know, Mr. Connoly. I hope you didn't make a special trip all the way out here to tell me."

"I'm very sorry for your loss, Mrs. O'Sullivan." Ian sat in an upholstered chair across from hers. "I know it was sudden."

"Sudden, was it? I suppose. If you say so."

"What do you mean, ma'am? Had your husband been ill?"

"Don't think so. We've been separated for many years, Mr. Connoly."

"Please, call me Ian."

"Ian, then. Paddy left the island near twenty years ago. I haven't seen him since." She took up her knitting. "I'm surprised it took him so long to finally jump, to tell you the truth."

"He was depressed, then? Is that what you mean?"

"He was broken, Ian. Broken and guilt-ridden."

"Because of the work."

The woman stopped knitting and eyed him keenly. "Who are you, Mr. Connoly?"

"I'm an investigator, Mrs. O'Sullivan. I am assigned to the Magesterial Court, from Dublin."

"And why would an investigator come all the way to Inishmore to talk to an old woman, Mr. Connoly?"

"You used to live in Galway I believe?" The woman nodded. "And your husband was employed as caretaker at the Bon Secours Home, was he not?"

"Oh, I see. I should ask you to leave, I think, Ian." She stared at him appraisingly.

"I come only for information, Mrs. O'Sullivan. You are in no trouble, I assure you. It's not that type of investigation."

"It isn't? I dare say, it should be."

"Your husband testified before the court, before he died."

"Did he?"

"Yes, he did. He described his duties at the home. How he disposed of the linens from the home, in the septic tank. Because they were contaminated." The woman stared past Ian out the window and said nothing. "The evening after he testified about these matters, your husband jumped to his death, Mrs. O'Sullivan. Do you know why he would do such a thing?" He paused, but the elderly woman offered no response. "It is odd, it seems to me, that a man charged with such a simple task would have cause to take his own life." He watched the woman as she shook her head slightly.

"Do you want to tell me about it, Mrs. O'Sullivan?" The woman shook her head more emphatically. Ian saw a glint of light from the window reflect from a new moistness in the woman's eyes. "There was more than just linens, wasn't there, Ida?"

The old woman turned to face Ian, wiping away tears with both hands. "He didn't know," she said softly. "He was a good man. He didn't know what they had him doing."

"Of course, Ida. When did he—how did Paddy come to find out?"

"You don't know, then?" She clapped her hands to her mouth. "You're not here because—"

And then she passed out.

Pacific Ocean, California

Julius piloted the small rubber boat along the coastline south, past the surfers and the beaches at Santa Cruz, until Grace pointed out the Monterey Aquarium in the distance. Julius brought the Zodiac in on the crest of the breaking waves, slowing at the last minute with a series of swooping S-turns until he found the seaway that led between the breakwaters to fisherman's wharf. He tied up at the commercial pier and helped Grace clamber onto the dock before the dock master had closed to hailing distance.

"This way," Grace said, taking Julius by the hand and leading him away from the water.

"Where are we going?" Julius asked, ignoring the calls of the dock master.

"Following a hunch." They walked quickly along the streets of downtown Monterey, hot in the bright sunshine of late morning. "This way." Grace pulled Julius along until they stood in front of a plain, two-story white building.

"The French Hotel," Julius read off the peeling sign affixed to the front of the building. "Some hunch. I think we can do better, Grace."

"It's not really a hotel, silly. This is the Robert Louis Stevenson house. He stayed here."

"And we're not?"

"No. We're not."

"So why are we here? Looking for a signed copy of *Treasure Island*?"

"No. Looking for my Dr. Jekyll—or Mr. Hyde."

"*And* Mr. Hyde, you mean," Julius corrected.

"Perhaps," Grace said. "There," she said, pointing to a car parked in the lot next to the building. Julius looked over and saw Gabriel leaning against the hood of the car, smiling. Gabriel waved to them.

"What the devil?" Julius began.

"Might be," Grace said, and headed over to the car. Julius followed.

Grace's pace quickened as she approached the car. Gabriel stood up, smiling and reaching out for an embrace. Grace shoved him in the chest and he stumbled back hard against the car. His smile disappeared.

"What the fuck, Gabe?" Grace demanded, bright red and hands on hips as she stood before him.

"I know, I know, Grace," Gabriel said, straightening up.

"You don't know jack-shit, asshole," Grace said, trembling with anger. "I was nearly killed six ways from Sunday at Arthur's house. There was shooting, and explosions, and Arthur's fucking attack poodles—"

"Hey," Arthur said, getting out from the passenger side of the car. "Those were not poodles. Bran and Sceólang saved your ass back there."

Grace wheeled on him. "Oh, yeah? How the hell would you know, asshole? I didn't see you, either, running around in the dark, dodging bullets with the rest of us, Arthur."

Arthur raised his hands and began to say something but Gabriel interrupted.

"Listen, Grace," Gabriel said, looking nervously past her to the approach road. "I know you're pissed, but we have to go. We have to go now."

"Yeah, right," Grace said, "as if we're following you two yokels anywhere."

"He's right," Arthur said, looking at his watch, "we have to move. Now. In another minute or two—"

Gabriel was looking up the road at an approaching van. "We've got to go *right now!*" Gabriel said, reaching for Grace's elbow. Julius followed his gaze and saw the approaching van.

"Why?" Julius asked. "What happens in two minutes?"

"Yeah, Gabe," Grace echoed, jerking her arm from her husband's grasp, "what happens in two minutes? You two pricks disappear again? Actually, I'm thinking I punch you in the mouth in about thirty seconds."

"In ninety seconds," Arthur continued, "we're gonna get killed, Grace. So get in the fucking car. Now!"

"How would you—" she began, but Julius had the back door open and was pushing Grace into the seat.

"Give 'em the benefit of the doubt," Julius said. "I got a bad feeling."

"Damn right," Gabriel said, getting in the driver's seat and slamming the door closed. "Bad feeling." He started the car as Arthur and Julius got in on the passenger side, then floored the accelerator, spewing rocks from the parking lot as he swerved onto the road. "Hold on!" Gabriel yelled as he neared the approaching van. The van swerved into their lane as they approached but Gabriel anticipated this and swerved into the opposite lane, passing the van and accelerating away.

"Damn, Gabe, that was sweet," Grace said. "I didn't know you could drive like that, honey."

"Yeah, usually he can't," Arthur said. "Most of the time he just hits people head-on."

"What do you mean, most of the time?" Julius asked, twisting around to look behind. "They're turning around."

"Yeah, I know," Gabriel said. "They can't catch us now. We're okay for a while. I think."

"Oh, really, Gabe? You think we're okay now?" Grace asked from behind her husband. "Maybe then this would be a good time to choke the life out of you?" She reached around and put her hands around her husband's throat.

"Hey!" Julius said, pulling her back. "The man's driving."

"Well, you better start talking *and* driving. Both of you," Grace said. "What the fuck is going on?"

"Not a good time," Gabriel said.

Grace opened her door. "I think it's a good time, dear. Otherwise, I'm getting out."

"Close the door, Grace," Julius said.

Gabriel looked at his wife in the rear view mirror and nodded. He looked over at Arthur, saying, "You tell her, Arthur."

"Me? Why me? She was your wife."

"Exactly."

"What is this 'was' shit?" Grace asked. Grace closed the door.

Purgatory

Elliot sat next to Debbie and Samantha in the control room.

He threw up his hands, saying, "Guys, guys, guys! I'm in the dark here!"

"Settle down, Colonel Slade," Debbie said, pushing Elliot away from the monitors. "Give me some space."

Samantha watched as Debbie worked to get them an image.

"Where are they?" Elliot asked, looking between monitors, which now showed an overhead view of Monterey. "There's the boat, at the wharf. But they're not there."

"Yeah, Elliot, we can see that," Samantha said. "Any ideas, Deb?"

Debbie's fingers flew over her keyboard. "Yeah, I'm pulling up the security cams from fisherman's wharf."

"But they're not there," Elliot protested.

"I know that, Elliot," Debbie said, "but we can run the

cams back until we see them arrive. Deep breaths there, partner."

Debbie scrolled backwards through the security feed until they saw Grace and Julius arrive in the Zodiac.

"There!" Samantha said.

"Yeah, we can see, Sam Let's see where they go," Elliot said. They watched Grace and Julius leave the wharf.

"Follow them, Deb. Where'd they go?"

"I can't follow them. I've got to find another camera, give me a second."

By patching between camera feeds, Debbie was able to track the two to the Robert Louis Stevenson house.

"Hey, I know this place," Sam said. "Grace and I stopped there when we were driving down the coast, I think."

"Girls weekend, huh?" Elliot said. "Nineteenth century bed and breakfast on your wild road trip. You two sound like a regular 'Thelma and Louise.' No wonder the girl killed herself."

"Hey," Samantha protested.

Elliot held his hands up in apology. "Sorry, maybe a bit over the line, gotta admit."

"Look," Debbie interrupted, "There they are. And there's Artie and Gabe."

They watched their friends get in the car and careen from view as it sped from the parking lot.

"Lost 'em," Elliot said.

"Yeah, no shit," Debbie said, working her keyboard again. "Try this."

They watched an overhead view appear, following the car as it swerved out of the parking lot.

"I took over a remote traffic feed," Debbie announced. "Not sure how long we'll have it, though."

They watched as the car with Grace and Julius swerved to avoid a head-on collision with an oncoming van.

"Holy shit!" Samantha said, "Did you guys—"

"Yeah, Sam," Elliot said. "We saw that. We're losing them."

"I know, I know," Debbie said. "I'm out of tricks, here. Sorry." They watched the car disappear into the distance.

"You can't follow them?" Elliot asked, dropping back into his chair.

Debbie swiveled to face the other two. "Sorry, guys. Unless you got a spy satellite on line that I can tap into, we're blind again."

"Sam?" Elliot asked.

"You mean, an extra spy satellite? Arthur was only able to arrange for one spy satellite, and that one is being tasked to oversee our shill--in Afghanistan, remember?"

"No other tricks up your sleeve?" Elliot asked.

"Not at the moment, guys. Sorry," Debbie said, shaking her head.

"I think that van tried to hit them. That's what I think," Elliot said.

"Looked like it," Sam agreed.

"We have to figure out what's going on," Elliot said, rubbing his temples. "Why is everyone always trying to kill that girl?"

"Good question. Well, at least they were heading south," Sam said.

"They were? You're sure?" Elliot asked.

"Yeah, I'm sure. They headed for US-1, south. Hopefully they're to going to LA," Sam said.

"Hopefully they won't get killed on the way," Elliot said.

"Yeah. Hopefully," Samantha agreed.

Inishmore, Ireland

Ian sat in a chair next to the woman's bed. The nurse practitioner had left after assuring Ian that Mrs. O'Sullivan was "far too ornery to die anytime soon." She had 'taken a swoon,' was all. She left him with instructions to ply her with tea when she came around.

Ida's eyes fluttered open. When they focused on Ian, the woman smiled. "Still here?"

"You fainted," Ian said.

"Did I? It's been so long since a young man has come courting, you see. I am all aflutter."

"I'm going to make you a cuppa."

Ian returned with a steaming cup of tea. Ida propped herself up on her pillows. She took the cup and saucer from him and he sat back down in the chair beside the bed.

"Thank you. Milk, no sugar," she said after taking a sip. "Perfect."

"There was milk, but no sugar. Wasn't hard."

"You are quite the Sherlock Holmes, Ian." They sat in silence while Ida sipped her tea. "They can't hurt us now, I suppose," she said wistfully. "And it's been so awfully long." She set the cup on the bedside table. "I'll tell you a story, Mr. Connolly, since you've come so far. If you've a mind to listen."

He smiled and nodded.

"Paddy and I were married then for just over twelve years. We lived in Galway, and Paddy was the caretaker—well, you know that part already, I suppose. I could'na have a baby, Ian. We tried, we wanted children, but my pregnancies never took. It made Paddy sad, of course. Both of us, but Paddy the more so. He did so want to be a Da', you see.

"You'll know of the work they had him doing at the Home. He didn't know a thing about—well, you know. Honestly, I'm sure he didn't. My Paddy was a good, decent man. If he'd 'ave known what the sisters were bundling in those linens, he would've lit the building afire, I tell you. He didn't know. No one did, Ian.

"One day, my Paddy runs home to me in the middle of the day, crying and yelling, completely out of sorts. I never saw him in such a state. He couldn't even tell me what was wrong, why he was so distraught. Just dragged me back to the Home, running and pulling my arm the whole way. He pulls me along to behind the Home and shows me a bundle of linen on the ground. 'Well, what of it?' I asked him, but he's shaking and crying and can't do anything but point at it. And as I stare at the thing, I seen it move, just the littlest bit. 'Dear sweet Jesus,' I said and scooped it up without even a second's thought. I ran and ran with that bundle all the way back to our home, left my Paddy just standin' there in such a state.

"He was the most perfect, beautiful baby boy you ever saw, Ian. The most perfect. Green eyes, full head o' red hair. Beautiful. And so strong. So strong, my little boy.

"Paddy said we had to give him back. Ha! Told him if he ever said such a thing again I'd stab him in the heart! I wasn't kidding, and he knew it. Never said such nonsense again, you can be sure. 'But they'll know,' he says. And he was right about that, of course. Old Ida and Paddy, childless all their dozen years, suddenly with a beautiful baby boy! What will people say? What will they think? We found him in the garden!" She laughed and took a sip of her tea, then dabbed at her tears with a corner of her sleeve.

"My boy knew what was, too, you know. Quiet as a church mouse. Never made a peep, so's we could keep him secret until Paddy could get us away. In a week's time he'd quit his job, in two more he'd sold our belongin's and bundled us up for the ferry to Inishmore, goodbye and good riddance to fair Galway forever.

"Made ourselves a good, simple life here on this little island. After scratchin' for a couple o' years, we were able to buy this inn and cozy enough it's been since then. A fine home for our little family. A right good place to raise our boy up. No one to know that Ida was barren, but now with child, you see. Like another world. Another life. A fair good life."

"What happened?" Ian asked when she had stopped and didn't seem to be interested in continuing.

"Hm?"

"To your boy? What happened to him, Ida?"

"Why, he grew up, Ian. That's what little boys do, you

know."

"Is he still on the island, then?"

She smiled at him. "Oh, I'm sure I couldn't say," she said.

"Of course he's not," Ian said. "A young man with no birth record, no real parents—"

"He had real parents! He had me and my Paddy! We did just fine by him." She glared at Ian indignantly.

"Of course you did," Ian soothed. "I meant only that the boy would be without any sort of official records." Ida nodded at this. "You sent him away?"

"Had to. Paddy was against it. Oh, we almost came to blows more than a few times. But Paddy knew it had to be. He just wasn't strong enough to give him up, was all. The boy was his penance, you see, for all the other babies that he'd—well, that he didn't save, I guess. It broke him. When the boy was sixteen, and asking questions that we had no answers for, we had to send him away. Osian understood, even if my Paddy never did. My boy knew up from down. He had the sense of it."

"Where did he go?"

"Took ship from the port of Galway. He was big and strong, and smart. A fine looking lad, too. No trouble finding a berth as an able seaman. And just like that, my boy was gone, Ian. Gone to the sea."

"Do you hear from him, Ida?"

"Wouldn't you like to know," Ida said smiling, but it was a sad, wistful smile. "Wouldn't you just like to know."

Purgatory

They met in the conference room. There was no reason to stay in the control center, since they had no incoming feed.

"Okay, group," Elliot began, rapping his knuckles on the oval table. Most of the twenty-odd people seated around the table came to attention. Fuller, however, continued his heated argument with Nikola Tesla at the other end of the table. Samantha waited, staring at them in exasperation.

"Guys!" Samantha finally said, interrupting the two long-dead scientists. "Shut up or take it outside. Either one." The two stopped arguing and Fuller smiled sheepishly.

"Thank you," Samantha continued. "As Elliot here keeps muttering, we're working in the blind at present. We've been lucky so far, but we need intel, preferably real time visuals at least, of what's going on with Grace and Julius. Audio would be nice as well. How do we do that?" There was silence as almost everyone studied the tabletop or their fingernails.

"Come on. Anybody," Elliot implored.

"What are you asking for, buddy?" a man in a black turtleneck, leaning against the wall in the corner of the room, asked. "Bird's eye view, tracking intel? Or do you need something up close and personal?"

"Both, actually. And the ability to switch between. I'm sorry—who are you, again?"

The man in the turtleneck stood up straighter, hands jammed deeply in his pockets. "Jobs. I think I might have something for you, I was working on it just before—well, before, anyway. It's a differential VR setup. Might suit. I'll need a team, it's still pretty much a concept."

"Differential VR?" Fuller asked. "What does the VR stand for?"

"Virtual Reality," Jobs answered.

"That is an oxymoron," Fuller said. "Is it reality, or is it virtual? It makes no sense, what you're saying."

Jobs rolled his eyes and addressed Elliot. "Engineers. Do we have engineers? Software guys, sensor specialists, guys that can set up real time high fidelity image analysis, that sort of thing? Spatial audio dynamic imaging?"

"No idea what you're saying there, Jobs, but I'm sure we got people," Elliot said. "I'll get you a team right after the meeting. Big team of engineers."

"Fine. Next problem," Jobs said. Fuller scowled.

"Communication," Elliot continued, nodding to the

group. "Bucky got us a one word message delivered when we needed it in a pinch, but we've got to do better. We can't just be spectators up here, we have to be able to communicate with our players on the ground. Bucky, where do we stand?"

"Well," Fuller began, standing. "Of course, we are still in early stages, but my new friend Nicky, here," he gestured to Tesla seated next to him, who nodded, "has employed the work of Dr. Sheehan involving thought processing to conceive of a projector, you see. Now, by applying Dymaxion principles, we have been able to develop a prototype that achieves a reliable transmission of telepathic informatics with selectivity of focus and quite accurate target acquisition, I believe. The prototype utilizes a Tensegrity structural analog that—"

Arthur held up his hand. "Bucky! Can we talk to people on the ground? Yes or no?"

"Talk? No, I don't think so. But we can project thoughts into their minds. I'd hoped that might suffice."

Everyone around the table stared at Fuller, Tesla bobbing his head enthusiastically.

After a moment, Elliot recovered himself. "Yeah, Bucky. That'll do just fine, I'm sure."

CHAPTER 9

DON'T FREAK OUT ON ME HERE. I KNOW THAT 'TAKING BACK CONTROL' SOUNDS A LITTLE OMINOUS TO YOUR GROWN-UP EARS. YOU THINK THAT YOU'RE PAST THAT, THAT IF I JUST CUT YOU A LITTLE MORE SLACK, GIVE YOU ANOTHER CHANCE, THAT YOU'LL FIGURE IT OUT AND MANKIND WILL BE ALL RIGHT.

I WISH IT WERE TRUE. NOT GOING TO HAPPEN, PARDNER. IT'S TIME FOR AN INTERVENTION.

DON'T WORRY, I'M TALKING SUBTLETIES HERE. HEY! GIVE ME A SECOND TO LAY IT OUT FOR YOU. DEEP, CALMING BREATHS. GOOD. BREATHE INTO THE BAG FOR A LITTLE BIT WHILE I TELL YOU HOW WE'RE GOING TO FIX THIS.

STEP ONE: I'M GOING TO FINE TUNE THE 'FREE WILL' THING. STOP—JUST BREATHE, OKAY? USE THE BAG. GOOD. I'M STILL COMMITTED TO MANKIND HAVING FREE WILL. REALLY. I KNOW WHAT I JUST SAID, JUST GIVE ME A MOMENT, OKAY? GO BACK TO THE PART WHERE I TOLD YOU WHY 'THE WHOLE

UNIVERSE ONLY WORKS IF MANKIND HAS FREE WILL.' REMEMBER THAT? IT'S STILL TRUE. YOU GUYS STILL NEED TO HAVE YOUR HANDS ON THE WHEEL. I'M NOT MESSING WITH THAT.

BUT I HAVE TO KNOW WHERE YOU'RE GOING. I NEED TO ANTICIPATE YOUR ACTIONS SO THAT I CAN BE BETTER AT THE SUBTLE MANIPULATION THING I DO TO KEEP YOU ALIVE. DON'T START YELLING AT ME, THIS IS JUST HOW IT HAS TO BE. YOU KEEP THE KEYS, YOU CAN DRIVE ANYWHERE IN THE UNIVERSE YOU WANT TO, BUT I GET TO KNOW WHERE YOU'RE GOING.

HOW? IT'S SUBTLE. BELIEVE ME, YOU WON'T EVEN NOTICE A CHANGE. I WOULDN'T EVEN HAVE THOUGHT OF IT EXCEPT A COUPLE OF YOUR PEOPLE CAME UP WITH THIS LITTLE DISCOVERY ABOUT THE BRAIN. LIKE I SAID BEFORE, THIS IS THE KIND OF STUFF THAT MAKES ME PROUD THAT I DECIDED TO GIVE YOU GUYS AGENCY. YOU COME UP WITH ALL SORTS OF STUFF THAT I NEVER WOULD HAVE THOUGHT OF. IT'S A QUANTUM BRAIN THING. I'M SURE THEY DON'T EVEN UNDERSTAND IT THEM-SELVES. I DON'T THINK THE WOMAN EVEN KNEW WHAT SHE WAS PLAYING AT, HONESTLY. AND I'M NOT PLEASED THAT SHE WENT ON TO SCREW WITH SOME PRETTY FOUNDATIONAL ELEMENTS THAT I SPENT A LOT OF TIME CONSTRUCTING. I MEAN, THE

GIRL REALLY OVERSTEPPED, WHICH I'LL HAVE TO
DEAL WITH DIRECTLY. BUT THE REDHEAD GAVE ME
THE INSIGHT THAT THE QUANTUM THOUGHT IM-
PULSES IN YOUR MIND CAN BE READ EN MASSE, COL-
LECTIVELY AND INDIVIDUALLY, AS NEEDED. THINK
OF IT AS GOD REALLY LISTENING TO ALL YOUR
PRAYERS, ALL THE TIME. SOUNDS GREAT WHEN I
EXPLAIN LIKE THAT, AM I RIGHT? AND EVEN MORE
WILD, I CAN FRONT-RUN YOUR MIND. YEAH, I CAN
KNOW WHAT YOU'RE THINKING EVEN BEFORE YOU
DO! HOW WILD IS THAT, HUH? NOT A WHOLE LOT
SOONER, OF COURSE, JUST A FEW FENTO-SECONDS.
BUT IT WORKS. THAT'S ALL I NEED. YOUR GOD IS
REALLY GOOD WORKING WITH TIME; JUST GIVE ME
A LITTLE, I'LL MAKE IT WORTH THE WHILE. WORKS
LIKE A CHARM.

FRONT-RUNNING IS THE TOOL I NEED TO GET
BACK IN THE GAME, PEOPLE. I'LL BE AHEAD OF MAN-
KIND AGAIN. NO MATTER HOW SCIENTIFICALLY AND
TECHNOLOGICALLY SUCCESSFUL YOU BECOME, NO
MATTER HOW FAST YOU START DISCOVERING STUFF,
I'LL ALWAYS BE ONE STEP AHEAD. AS YOUR GOD
SHOULD BE, RIGHT? I'LL BE AHEAD OF YOU, TO MAKE
SURE THAT YOU'RE NOT GOING TO DRIVE MANKIND
TO THE SEEDY SIDE OF VEGAS, OR DO OTHER STU-
PID STUFF. LIKE BLOW YOURSELVES UP, OR DESTROY
THE PLANET, OR BLASTING THAT STUPID SONAR AT

MY WHALES ALL THE TIME. BECAUSE YOU'RE REALLY PISSING OFF MY WHALES, PEOPLE!

FRONT-RUNNING MANKIND'S FREE WILL. THAT'S MY TOOL. EVEN BETTER THAN MIRACLES, BECAUSE I CAN INTERVENE BEFORE ANYONE NOTICES. THAT'S STEP ONE. SEE? I TOLD YOU IT WASN'T TOO BAD. YOU WON'T EVEN KNOW I'M HERE. HAVE FAITH—JUST LIKE BEFORE. YOU WON'T EVEN FEEL ANYTHING CHANGE.

TRUST ME.

Southern California

Gabriel pulled off at the Del Monte shopping center and cruised the parking lot, while everyone else looked about for things threatening.

"What do you guys feel like?" Gabriel asked. "Pizza, burgers? My treat."

"Someplace we can get a beer," Grace said.

"I second that," Julius said.

"Hmm, I'm thinking pizza, kids," Gabriel said, swinging into a parking space. "You two wash up and Arthur and I will get us a table."

"And some beer," Grace added, heading through the revolving door on her way to the restrooms in the back.

"And some beer," Gabriel agreed.

When Julius and Grace joined the others in the booth, two pitchers of beer were already waiting.

"Where's the menus?" Grace asked. "I'm starving."

"Already ordered," Arthur said, "we're in a hurry."

"You don't know what I want," Grace protested.

"You wanted beer," Arthur said, pouring. "I got you beer."

Grace was thinking of complaining some more but was

stopped by the arrival of appetizers. She decided to eat instead.

"Things are actually going great," Arthur said. "Got the whole team running like a well-oiled machine up there. They're working hard to set up your fiddle player, Grace."

"He's not a fiddle player," Grace corrected. "The play is the fiddle."

"Yeah, whatever. I don't quite get that part, tell you the truth. What I do know, is they're making progress. But they can't handle the other threats, not from where they are right now."

"Yeah, let's talk about those other threats," Julius said. "Who in hell keeps trying to kill us?"

"Not you, Julius," Gabriel corrected. "Nobody's trying to kill you."

"You could've fooled me," Julius said.

"Yeah, well, get used to being beside the point. It's Grace they're after. Always has been. Nobody gives a shit about you in all of this," Gabriel said.

"Well, that's a relief, Gabriel," Julius said. "I'll just hide behind your wife, then."

"Settle, you two," Grace said. She leaned across the table to Gabriel and Arthur. "I'm getting a little tired of having a target on my back, so why don't you tell us who's trying to put me down. I'm guessing—I'm hoping—that the Big Guy hasn't decided that it's too much work to have me excised, decided to just take me out the easy way."

Gabriel shook his head. "No, no chance of that," he whispered back. "Sources monitoring Pauley's team say He still needs you excised, not dead. But a lot of other folk want you just plain dead."

"Who? Why?" Grace asked.

"Almost everyone, Grace," Arthur said, leaning in. "A dozen different religious zealots, not any one group. Christian fundamentalists, Sunni militiamen, militant Baptists, Shiite jihadists—every day it's another new faction. Every religion that expects a Messiah. Which, it turns out, is almost all of them. Rastafarians. Buddhists! Can you believe that? Always thought Buddhists were pacifists. Well, that's not true! It's probably the first cause all these guys have had in common in two thousand years. Congratulations."

"Why? Why do they all want me dead?" Grace asked.

"Because," Gabriel explained, "if you're dead, you can't be excised. It's as simple as that. Pretty much every religious fanatic in the world does not want you excised, Grace. So that's a good thing, right?"

"Is it?" Julius asked. "Why? What's in it for all of them if Grace dies instead of being excised?"

"Not entirely sure," Arthur said, looking for the waitress.

"Well, give me your best guess. Dammit, Arthur, quit playing games here," Grace said around a slice of pizza.

"We're trying to nail it down, Grace," Gabriel said. "So far, the only thing we got is that all these religious crazies believe in the coming of a Messiah—rumors are that he's close, that the end-times are nigh."

"They always think that, Gabriel," Julius said.

"Yeah, but these are the folks that are motivated to kill Grace. Somehow they think Grace is linked to the Messiah's coming."

"I *am* linked to the Messiah's coming," Grace said, taking another slice. "That's the con we're running."

"Well, then it's going great," Gabriel said. "'Cause these folks aren't treating it like a con."

"But it is a con," Julius said. "So why the enthusiasm to kill Grace?"

"Not sure exactly why it's working so well, to be honest," Arthur said.

"Maybe you're really good at what you do, Arthur," Julius said.

"Maybe," Gabriel said. "Problem is, there's a widely held belief among the wildly crazy folk that Grace's death leads to the End."

"Huh," Grace said. "That makes sense."

"It does?" Julius said.

"Kinda," Grace said. "If I'm excised, I never was, the con never happened, no Messiah."

"And if you're killed, you can't be excised," Gabriel said.

"But it's a con," Julius said. "He's not the Messiah."

Arthur spotted the waitress. "Check, please!"

"No dessert?" Grace asked.

"No time," Gabriel said.

"Might be my last chance," Grace said. "Hate to go out without at least a slice of cheesecake."

Southern California

The four of them left the pizza restaurant and got back in the car, again heading south on US-1. Arthur drove, with Gabriel constantly looking around for whoever might be trying to kill them next.

"I should be driving," Grace announced.

"Yeah, right," Gabriel scoffed. "Why wait until someone else tries to kill us, when we can just go careening off the cliff into the Pacific."

Grace started to protest but was cut off by Julius asking, "Where are we going, anyway?"

"Can't tell you that," Arthur said, looking in the mirror.

"Why, you'd have to kill us?" Grace asked.

"No, someone else will take care of that," Arthur said.

"This is nuts," Grace asked.

Grace watched the ocean waves crashing on the rocky coast below them as they drove south. "'In this refulgent summer it has been a luxury to draw the breath of life,'" she recited, softly. "I wish I were dead, though," Grace added.

"You were. You came back, remember?" Julius said, softly enough so that the men in front couldn't hear.

Grace shook her head, still looking out the window. She found Julius's hand and squeezed it. "What do you SEALs say, about not leaving a man behind?" Grace whispered to the window.

"We say, 'Keep running and don't look back,'" Julius answered.

"Too late."

Southern California

"Someone's coming," Gabriel announced from the passenger seat, staring hard into the rearview mirror.

"What do you mean?" Arthur asked, glancing at his own mirror as he drove. "I don't see anything."

"What is it?" Grace asked, turning to look out the back window at the cars behind.

"A van, coming up pretty fast. I just watched him pass two cars," Gabriel said.

"Not the same van as before," Arthur said. "Couldn't be."

"Not sure," Gabriel agreed. "But he's coming pretty hard. I don't like it."

Arthur sped up and passed a slow moving truck, moving back into his lane. "I'll try to stay ahead," he announced.

"Still coming," Gabriel said.

"I see him," Grace said. She watched out the rear window. "There he is. Look," she said, elbowing Julius.

Julius twisted around and stared where Grace was pointing. He nodded. "Just the driver in front. It'll be from the side, I think."

Grace leaned forward to talk to Arthur. "Listen, Arthur," she said. "This is what you're going to have to do."

"Maybe I should pull over, let you drive, Grace," Arthur said, stealing a worried glance at the rearview mirror. "Shit."

"Move it, Arthur," Gabriel said. "He's only about six cars back now."

"I see that," Arthur said.

"Listen," Grace said, leaning farther forward between the front seats to speak directly to Arthur. "This is going to happen fast, so listen. You keep speeding up, passing everybody you can—"

"It's just a rental, Grace."

"Rental's always the fastest car on the road, Art. Listen, this is what you're going to do. You keep speeding up, make him work for it. They got a guy sitting in the back. It'll come from the side door. They'll try to come abreast before they take the shot."

"How do you know that?" Gabriel asked, still staring in the mirror.

"They'll want to kill the driver," Julius explained.

"Oh, great," Arthur said. He went faster, passing another car on the inside as he swerved around a bend.

"Nice, Artie," Grace soothed. "Keep it up."

"But he's still gaining, Grace," Arthur said.

"Yeah, he's going to catch us," Grace said. "That's why you have to be moving as fast as you can when he does."

"I don't get it," Arthur said, scattering rocks from the shoulder as he slid wide around another turn. "Shit, this thing handles like a garbage truck."

"Yeah, just listen," Grace continued. "Doesn't matter. This is a problem in related rates. Remember related rates, in school?"

"No. Accounting, not calculus."

"Come on, Arthur, listen." She glanced back out the rear window. "Pretty soon now. Get up to speed and keep it there. He'll be coming up behind in a couple of minutes. When he's right behind, floor it. As he makes his move to come alongside, that's when you really go. Got it?"

"I don't think I can outrun him in this heap," Arthur said.

"No, you're not going to. Related rates, Arthur. When I tell you, you jump on the brakes, both feet. Got that?"

"Yeah, got it. Doesn't seem like much of a plan," Arthur said.

"That's not the whole of it. You ever watch stock car? You ever a Dale Earnhardt fan?"

"Old Number 3? Sure," Arthur said.

"Yeah, him. A tenth of a second after you jump the brakes, you swerve left. Got it? You have to hit him just behind the rear axle. Can you do that? Not broadside, we'll just bounce off—just behind the rear wheels. Clip his rear fender, hard."

Arthur turned to look at her. "Pretty sure that's the move that put Dale into the wall. What if I don't hit him?"

"Then we end up getting shot. Or at the bottom of that cliff," Grace said, gesturing. "Probably both."

Southern California

"Shit, shit, shit," Arthur said, staring up into the rearview mirror. "Here he comes."

"Don't look at him," Grace said. "Just drive. Faster, Arthur."

Grace reached forward and twisted the rearview mirror so she could see the van coming up. "Italian rule of racing, Arthur," Grace said. "What's behind you don't count."

"One car left," Julius said. "Showtime."

"Hit it, Arthur," Grace said, leaning in next to his ear. "Just drive. I'll tell you when."

"Pulling out, making his pass," Julius said. They could see the driver clearly. There was no one in the passenger seat. "It'll be from the side, like you said. Nobody in shotgun."

They all watched as the white van started to come alongside.

"Faster, Arthur! Right now, faster!" Grace urged.

"Door's opening," Julius said. Arthur turned to look as the side door started to slide open.

"Don't look, just drive," Grace yelled in his ear. "Faster, Arthur."

"I've got it floored, Grace!"

"Gun," Julius said, matter-of-factly. "Automatic weapon, side door."

"Shit, Grace. Now?"

"No!"

"Coming up now," Julius said.

"Not yet, Arthur. Keep it to the floor!"

"Aiming," Julius said.

"NOW, Arthur! Now! Brakes!" Arthur stomped the brakes with both feet. As everybody jerked forward, Grace yelled in his ear, "Left!" Arthur twisted the wheel and watched a flash from the end of the gun as his left front fender just caught the van's rear bumper. In apparent slow-motion, they careened into the left lane as the van arced across the front of their car. It rolled drunkenly as the driver tried to correct, then swerved more severely and struck the outside guardrail. As their own car came alongside, still slowing, they could see the van's driver clawing at the steering wheel as the van rolled over the railing and disappeared over the cliff.

"Holy shit!" Arthur said, struggling to straighten the car.

"Look out!" Gabriel yelled as an oncoming car appeared ahead from around a bend. Arthur steered back into his lane as the oncoming car swerved up onto the embankment, narrowly missing them. In the mirror, Gabriel watched as the other car struck hard on an outcropping of rock halfway up the embankment and rolled onto its roof, bursting into flames.

Arthur regained control of the car and kept slowing, starting to pull onto the shoulder.

"Don't stop! Go, go, go," Grace yelled, still looking back.

"But we should see if they're okay," Arthur said.

"They're not okay," Gabriel said.

"Drive, Arthur. Go!" Grace repeated.

"But—"

"Go!"

Arthur started to accelerate, swerving back onto the highway.

"But the van went over, I saw—"

"They might have a backup, Arthur," Julius explained. "Keep driving, buddy."

"But that other car..." Arthur protested, looking at the others. Gabriel shook his head.

"What?" Arthur asked.

"They didn't make it," Gabriel said.

Arthur swerved off the road and skidded to a stop.

"What the hell, Arthur?" Grace said, shaking his shoulder.

"You need to—" Gabriel began.

"I can't!" Arthur said. He pounded the top of the steering wheel. "Shit, shit, shit! Are you fucking kidding me, Gabe? I just killed somebody back there?" His face had gone ashen, eyes wide in fear. Gabriel nodded.

"Arthur, come on," Grace said.

"Come on?" Arthur yelled at her, twisting in his seat to face her. "Come on? You just had me fucking kill somebody back there, maybe a whole car full of somebodies. God damn it, Grace! God damn you!" He smacked the steering wheel again and then put his head down, forehead on the wheel. "God damn you," he said again, softly.

Grace got out of the car and opened the driver's door. "Come on, Arthur," she said soothingly. "I'll drive."

He looked up at her. "Too fucking late, Grace." He wiped his eyes with the back of his hand and got into the back seat. "Too fucking late," he repeated from behind her. Grace drove the car back onto the highway, heading south.

"Where in hell are we going?" she asked.

"Got that right," Arthur said.

Southern California

"Los Angeles," Gabriel announced from the passenger seat, looking at his wife as she drove.

Grace nodded, adjusting and checking her mirrors. "Why LA?"

"Actually, LAX, hon. Executive terminal," Gabriel said.

"Really?" Grace asked. "Where we flying to?"

"I can't say," Gabriel answered.

"What do you mean, 'you can't say?' Is it like, a really big word?" Grace asked.

"You know what we're up against, hon," Gabriel shrugged.

"Just go with it."

Grace shook her head, muttering.

"Works for me," Julius said.

"Yeah? So where do you and Arthur go?" Grace asked.

"Tagging along for a bit," Gabriel said.

"Not me, Gabe. I'm done," Arthur said.

"I'm sorry, Arthur," Grace said.

I WON'T SUGAR-COAT THIS NEXT BIT: STEP TWO IS A BIT HARSH.

I NEED TO HIT THE RESET BUTTON. AGAIN. I KNOW, I KNOW, I PROMISED NEVER TO DO IT TO YOU AGAIN, BUT I HAVE TO. SORRY.

STOP GIVING ME THAT LOOK. IT'S NOT GOING TO BE LIKE THE LAST TIME. NOT LIKE THE FLOOD. YOU CAN KEEP YOUR RAINBOWS, OKAY? I PROMISED NEVER TO WIPE IT ALL OUT AGAIN, AND I WON'T. BUT I HAVE TO KNOCK YOU BACK A LITTLE.

HOW LITTLE? ABOUT A HUNDRED YEARS, I FIGURE, GIVE OR TAKE.

SHOULD WE GET THE PAPER BAG AGAIN? DO WE NEED TO TAKE A LITTLE BREAK HERE? FINE. LET'S NOT BE CHILDREN. THOUGH, TECHNICALLY, YOU ARE KIND OF LIKE MY CHILDREN. SORT OF. I JUST HAVE TO THINK OF YOU THAT WAY, OKAY? CAN YOU INDULGE YOUR OLD MAN THIS LITTLE THING? THANK YOU.

I NEED SOME SPACE TO WORK, TO GET THIS BUS BACK ON THE ROAD AND GOING STRAIGHT DOWN

*THE HIGHWAY. NEED TO PUMP THE BRAKES A LIT-
TLE, TO KEEP UP THE METAPHOR. I'M NOT TALKING
ABOUT A MASS EXTINCTION EVENT HERE. NO ASTER-
OID STRIKE LIKE I HAD TO DO TO GET THE DINOSAURS
OUT OF THE WAY. HEY, I DID THAT FOR YOU, OKAY?
QUIT JUDGING ME. THEY HAD PEAS FOR BRAINS—
NEVER KNEW WHAT HIT THEM.*

*GO READ A HISTORY BOOK OR SOMETHING:
THE 1920's WERE A SPECIAL TIME FOR HUMAN-
ITY. EVERYBODY WAS IN A GREAT MOOD, ALL THE
TIME. WATCH "THE STING." EVEN THE MUSIC
WAS GREAT. AND WE CAN DO IT EVEN BETTER THIS
TIME AROUND. JUST BECAUSE WE'RE GOING BACK
TO THE 1920's TECHNOLOGICALLY, DOESN'T MEAN
WE CAN'T STAY IN THE TWENTY-FIRST CENTURY SO-
CIALLY. NO NEED TO GO BACK TO JIM CROW OR ANY
OF THAT. YOU CAN HAVE GAY MARRIAGE, A WOMAN
PRESIDENT, WHATEVER YOU WANT. JUST NO QUAN-
TUM COMPUTERS. NO INTERNETS. YOU EVER READ
STEAMPUNK? LIKE THAT. EVERYBODY LOVES STEAM-
PUNK, YOU KNOW. WHO WOULDN'T WANT TO GO
ACROSS THE OCEAN IN A DIRIGIBLE? A SLOWER,
MORE RELAXED LIFESTYLE. YOU'D LOOK GREAT
WITH A MONOCLE, BELIEVE ME. SOPHISTICATED.*

*NO, I'M NOT SURE HOW IT HAPPENS YET. I'M
STILL WORKING ON THAT. IT'S TRICKY. I'M GOING
TO HAVE TO REDUCE THE PLANET'S POPULATION BY A*

PRETTY SIGNIFICANT AMOUNT, I WON'T KID YOU. IF WE'RE GOING BACK TO THE FOOD TECHNOLOGY OF 1920, NO WAY WE CAN FEED SIX BILLION MOUTHS. POPULATION REDUCTION IS A PRETTY UGLY BUSINESS, ANY WAY YOU CUT IT. PLAGUE OR PANDEMIC IS PRETTY QUICK, BUT IT'S INDISCRIMINATE; FAIRLY HARROWING, ACTUALLY. WAR MIGHT BE BETTER, MORE FOCUSED. SOME FOLKS KNOW THEY'RE GOING TO GET IT IN THE NECK, THE REST OF THE WORLD JUST WATCHES ON THE TV AND THANKS ME OVER AND OVER AGAIN THAT IT'S NOT HAPPENING IN THEIR NEIGHBORHOOD. EASIER ON ALL OF US.

PROBLEM IS IN KEEPING IT LIMITED. A STEP BACK OF THIS MAGNITUDE CAN EASILY ESCALATE, YOU REALIZE. INSTEAD OF A REGIONAL CONFLICT TAKING DOWN THE POPULATION ABOUT 25%, SOMEBODY DOES SOMETHING STUPID AND BEFORE YOU KNOW IT, WE'VE GOT WORLD WAR THREE AND THE EARTH LOOKS LIKE THE HIND END OF A BABOON. NO, I DON'T WANT THAT, EITHER; THAT'S MY POINT. THAT'S THE PROBLEM WITH THE CONFLICT SCENARIO. DISEASE I KNOW HOW TO HANDLE, IT'S ALL IN THE GENES, JUST A PERCENTAGE THING. THE EXECUTION IS PRETTY STRAIGHTFORWARD. NO, I WASN'T TRYING TO MAKE A JOKE. WHAT DO YOU MEAN?

ANYWAY, I JUST WANTED TO LET YOU IN ON MY THINKING HERE. DON'T WORRY ABOUT THE DE-

TAILS JUST YET, THAT'S MY DEPARTMENT. I JUST FELT THAT IT WOULD BE UNFAIR NOT TO GIVE YOU A HEAD'S UP ABOUT ALL THIS. I DID IT FOR NOAH, I'D DO IT FOR YOU, YOU KNOW THAT. THIS IS EVEN HARDER ON ME THAN IT IS ON YOU, BELIEVE ME. JUST KNOW HOW MUCH I LOVE ALL OF YOU AND THAT I'M DOING THIS FOR US.

Southern California

Eventually, they made it to the airport without any more assassination attempts.

"Executive terminal," Gabriel instructed his wife.

Grace followed the signs and pulled up in front of the business terminal. They left the car at the curb and went in.

"Déjà vu," Grace said, looking about the empty terminal.

"Déjà vécu," Julius said, pointing. At the back of the terminal, a group of people sat in front of large windows overlooking the tarmac. Outside the window, they could see their black 747 at the gate. They walked over.

"Are we expected?" Grace asked Gabriel.

"One way to find out," Gabriel said. He gestured towards the gate. "After you." Grace led Julius and Gabriel to the doorway. Gabriel stopped before entering and turned around. "Are you coming, Arthur?"

Arthur stood in the now empty gate, arms crossed and shook his head. "I'm done, Gabriel."

"What do mean, you're done? Done with what?"

"Done with her," Arthur said, waving dismissively at the door to the gate. "Go on, Gabe. She's your wife. But I can't..." He shook his head. "I just won't, that's all."

Gabriel walked back to his oldest friend and took him by the shoulder. "I'm sorry, Arthur. It was an accident. It wasn't your—"

"Yeah, whatever. Save it, Gabe. It's too much. She's too much—trouble."

"What will you do, Art?"

"Going back to Purgatory. Go on, Gabriel. I'll catch up."

"Make sure you do, Arthur." Gabriel embraced his friend and slapped him on the back. Then he turned and walked to the gate.

"Hey," Arthur called. Gabriel stopped and turned. "This is yours." Arthur twisted the Claddagh ring from his finger and tossed it to his friend.

Purgatory

Arthur walked into the conference room and looked about. Over a dozen people sat in chairs about the table. Several nodded hello's. He saw his wife at the other end of the conference table. Arthur walked over and sat down. "Sam, where do we stand with our spy satellite?"

Samantha looked up from her notes. "Hey, hon. Welcome back." She gave him a kiss on the cheek. "We're getting there, Art." She pointed at a bespectacled guy slumped in a chair at the back of the room. "Yo, Elliot," Sam said, "tell Arthur what's going on with the satellite."

"Oh, hi boss," Elliot said, yawning and stretching. "Didn't know you were back." He sat up straighter. "Give you the update: We have solid to-and-fro with the bird. I have control but I'm not letting on just yet, since the Senator signed off on moving it for us, anyway. Once it's in position, we should have complete coverage of the valley, continuous and full spectrum."

"That's good, Elliot. Good work. What about Debbie's idea, the *Star of Bethlehem* gambit? Sam told me you guys were working on it," Arthur said.

Elliot shook his head, no longer trying to smile. "You're joking, right? I assumed she was kidding about that."

"What?" Sam said, leaning onto the table. "Why would

you assume that? I wasn't kidding."

"No," Arthur said, "she wasn't kidding, Elliot. Once the sat is over the valley, we need to light it up. Can you do that?"

"What do you mean, 'light it up?'" Elliot asked.

"Just that. You know, glow in the dark, really bright. Like a nova, Elliot. What, you never watched 'The Charlie Brown Christmas Special' when you were a kid? Sam was thinking that you can plus up the plutonium generator—"

"Yeah, she mentioned something about that," Elliot interrupted. "That's insane."

"It's not insane," Sam said. "I didn't say blow it up, nerd-boy, just kick it up into incandescence."

"Insane," Elliot insisted.

Arthur looked at his wife, head tilted and raising one eyebrow. "You'll work on it, hon?"

Sam shot an invidious look at the engineer, then scribbled something on a yellow pad as she nodded at her husband.

"Okay, then. Good progress, team," Arthur said. "Media relations, we'll put off your report until next meeting. Let the Senator do our work for us with her whole 'black hole' *schtick*. No better publicity than a complete absence of publicity, I always say. Class dismissed. You know what to work on. Let's meet here again at some point, for an update."

The room cleared, accompanied by the sounds of laptops snapping shut and lunch plans being made. Only Arthur and Samantha remained seated in the conference room. Arthur started to stand, sighing as he did so, until Sam laid a hand on his arm.

"What?" Arthur asked, dropping back into the chair.

"I saw what happened down there," Samantha said. "You were driving, weren't you?" Arthur nodded. "It was an accident, Artie. Shit happens. Car accidents happen. It wasn't your fault."

"We both know better." Arthur shook his head. "Damn that girl, Sam. She's like a fuckin' tornado, a disaster that you can't get away from," Arthur said. "That's not going to change no matter what we're doing up here."

"Yeah? So?" Samantha said.

"Not sure she's worth it," Arthur said.

Helmand Province, Afghanistan

The Pilgrim, the Mahdi, the One—they called him many names. He sat on his rustic platform and surveyed the crowd of people gathered in the square before him. Every day, there were many, many more. As he looked out over the expectant faces raised to him, it seemed there must be hundreds more than last week. Where were they coming from? What drew them to this place? He didn't know.

He looked about, smiling. *"It is a fine morning,"* he said again. So many new faces, and they all were able to hear him, though he wasn't at all sure how this was accomplished, either. He only knew that within this valley, his thoughts were perceived by all who cared to attend. He smiled and closed his eyes, beginning his lesson.

"I read a book a long time ago—a storybook, not a true book, not a holy book. The story concerns a young man, born into wealth —the son of a high priest, raised in luxury and educated so as to follow in his father's path. But the young man rebels, as young men will, and instead forsakes his faith and his family. This young man has many adventures. At one point, he follows the path of a pilgrim, eschewing all his previous wealth and privilege to become a beggar and an ascetic. When this fails to bring him enlightenment, he becomes a follower of a wise and revered holy man, but again he realizes that the man's teachings, though worthy, will not make him wise. He goes on to try the way of sensuality and worldly things, becoming a wealthy merchant and taking a beautiful lover, he fathers a son—but still finds no fulfillment. Finally, stripping off his fine robes, he comes to a river. He befriends the ferryman who tends the river's crossing. He becomes a disciple of the river, becoming an apprentice to the old ferryman, spending his days contemplating the river. In this way

he finally attains his goal of spiritual enlightenment. Oh, and his son rejoins him as well. It is a nice story."

The man they called Mahdi, the One, paused to survey his audience. They appeared enraptured, every one. He closed his eyes, feeling the warmth of the sun on his face.

"*Why the river?*" he continued. "*Why, when meditation, and deprivation, and study, and earnest striving, and love of family—all these things failed to bring him to enlightenment—the river was his path to ultimate wisdom? The river speaks to our hero, teaches him, laughs at his paltry worries, shows him what is truly important. There are many such stories, are there not? In every culture, ours and in the West, and in the Orient, this is a common teaching. The answer to the great mystery lies not within us, but in who and what surrounds us. We, it seems, are but a part of a greater whole. We may only find meaning in our place in the world. We must find our place in the greater whole.*

"*What is this whole? In the book of which I speak, the river signifies the whole. The river, constantly flowing, yet always present. Does the river suggest the greater whole? Always flowing, moving, arriving, leaving, existing—never ceasing. We could do worse for a teacher, I believe.*"

The One stood and took a few steps about the small stage.

"*But the river is not the whole. The river is of a part with all the waters of our existence. It has a headwater, in the mountains perhaps, where it arises imperceptibly from the snows and the ice that are of a part of the great body of water. Is this not true? And the river is of a part with its delta, where it blends seamlessly with the sea, again of a part with the whole. It appears to us to be moving, to be flowing, because it is we who are at a standstill, standing in its depths and feeling the current press against us. But the whole of the river is already everywhere. The pressure we feel against our shins as we stand on its muddy bottom, this is not the river leaving us, but rather our resistance to its force. The river is a force against our presence only because we press back against it. If we let go, if we choose to allow ourselves to become one with the river and surrender to its flow, then the pressure re-*

lents, and it is no more."

The man they called the Mahdi sat back down on the little pallet in the middle of the stage. He sighed.

"Time is like this, my friends. We think of time as a river, do we not? Always flowing past, carrying us downstream, our actions and events roiling in the surf that is our lives as we strive to stay afloat, to keep our noses above the water. But time is not really like this, any more than the river is. Time, like the river, is of a whole. We perceive it to flow, but time is all one, and we only feel the pressure of time against our skin as we struggle to stand against its current.

"Time, it is like the river. It is one, and we may be as one with time. In the oneness that is time, is the whole, the universe of our being.

"Thank you for listening. Peace to you."

Helmand Province, Afghanistan

"What a crock of shit," Atal said, standing and smacking the dust from the seat of his pants.

Hila looked at him aghast. "Are you serious, brother?"

"Yeah, I'm serious. You believe that crap?"

Hila could only look at him. "But he speaks—directly," she said, in amazement.

"Yeah, I don't get that, either."

Hila looked up at her brother quizzically. "What do you mean, you don't get that?" she asked him.

"The trick. How he did that," Atal asked, waving at the stage dismissively.

"Trick? It is no trick, brother," Hila said. "He is Mahdi."

Atal slapped his sister, hard, across her cheek. "Do not speak in that way, little sister," Atal admonished. "It is blasphemy."

Hila put her hand to her cheek and lowered her gaze. "It is not blasphemy, my brother," she said softly, "if it is the truth."

Atal raised his hand to strike her again. *"Stop,"* Atal heard loudly, seeming to come from a point between his eyes, painfully forceful. He looked about and saw no one, but lowered his hand. Instead, he spat on the ground in front of his sister. With a grunt, he turned and walked away from the village square.

Hila braced for the expected blow, and when it didn't come, looked up. The Mahdi stood before her, smiling benevolently. Hila knelt down in the dirt before him.

"You are Mahdi," Hila said, eyes lowered.

The tall man touched the top of her head. *"Perhaps,"* she heard softly in her mind. He touched her reddening cheek. *"Are you hurt, child?"*

Hila shook her head, embarrassed. She felt in the folds of her skirts for the object she had been carrying ever since she left her parent's home. She produced the heavy ring from her pocket and offered it up to the Mahdi.

The man took the ring from her and looked at it closely. Finally, he touched her on the shoulder and gestured for Hila to stand.

"Why now do you give me this?" Hila heard.

"I don't know, Mahdi," Hila answered, eyes still lowered. "But I think it is for you to have."

The Mahdi inclined his head, considering. *"Perhaps you are right, child,"* Hila heard. The man slipped the ring on his finger. *"Thank you for bringing it to me."* He turned and started to walk away. *"Tell your brother,"* Hila heard in her head as the Mahdi left, *"to come see me."*

Purgatory

Arthur stood in the front of the big conference room, the room they had begun referring to as "The War Room." He addressed the group seated around the large conference table.

"Okay, people," Arthur said. "Let's go around the table, Mission Control style." He turned to Elliot sitting to his right.

"What, me?" Elliot asked.

"Yes, you," Arthur said, rolling his eyes. "Come on, Elliot, you never saw 'Apollo Thirteen?'"

Elliot shrugged. "The bird's in position. Full intel, across the spectrum, twenty-four/seven. Don't know why we're spying on a valley full of peasants in the middle-of-nowhere, Afghanistan, but we can count the number of hairs in the beard of one of their goats if we want to. But please don't ask me to do that."

"Is it lit up?" Arthur said. Elliot said nothing, instead intently studying his fingernails. Arthur turned to his wife at the end of the table. "Sam?"

"Tell him, Elliot," Sam said across the table. "It's your bird."

Elliot flushed redly, still staring at his hands. "Yeah, lit up like a Christmas ornament," he said. Sam smiled wickedly.

"Any problems with overheating?" Arthur asked the man.

"Not yet," Elliot muttered.

"Okay, then," Arthur continued. "Communications, Bucky?" He looked at Fuller, asleep in the chair next to Elliot. "Bucky?"

Debbie reached over and shook the elderly bearded man next to her. Fuller woke up with a snort. "I'm awake," he announced.

"How are we doing with communications, Bucky?" Arthur asked again.

"Fine, fine," Fuller answered, scrubbing at his white beard. "All set. We worked off the material from that aborted government project, the one that proposed to use the antenna arrays to monitor public thought waves. What sick bastard almost got that up and running?" he asked.

"You don't want to know," Arthur said. "So we can monitor what's going on down there? And project comms in their direction when we need to?"

"Absolutely," Fuller enthused. "Direct telepathy. Not just from up here, either. We got that other project up and running, too."

"What other project?" Elliot asked from his seat across the table, next to Sam.

"Show him, Sam," Arthur said.

Samantha brought the screen on the sidewall online with a few keystrokes from the controls in front of her. An overhead image of the valley in Afghanistan swam into focus. With a flurry of tapping, a small white dot zoomed into view. It enlarged as the view zoomed in with dizzying rapidity, becoming a large geodesic dome apparently just below the other side of the mountain ridge.

Fuller pointed. "The dome houses the local array and electronics," he explained. "Our new Messiah has complete telepathic projection capability over the valley. That should make his job a bit easier," Fuller continued. "More messianic."

"Hold on," Elliot said, concerned. "How the hell did you get that down there? We don't have people on the ground—"

"People? Who needs people?" Fuller answered. "Self-assembly."

Elliot looked at the man nonplussed. He found his voice, saying "Yeah, but, okay, self-assembly. But how did you even get it there?"

Fuller shrugged. Elliot looked at Arthur.

Arthur turned to the other side of the table and looked at a man that didn't appear older than twenty-three or twenty-four. "Peter?"

"What, you don't what to call me 'Logistics' or some such shit?" the young man asked. Arthur waited. Peter addressed Elliot at the end of the conference table. "APMU's. Got 'em scattered all over the valley." He went back to drawing intricate mazes on the yellow pad in front of him.

"What's an 'ap-muse?'" Elliot asked.

Peter looked up, annoyed. "A-P-M-U's," he spelled. "Atomically Precise Manufacturing Units." Elliot still was obviously at a loss. "Maker bots? Remember them? 3-D printers? Come on, old man, I can't break it down any more than that, can I?"

"Try," Elliot encouraged. "And by the way, I'm 36, okay?
Don't be giving me any 'old man' shit, buddy."

Peter rolled his eyes. "Unit starts out as a nanoscale auto-
assembling manufacturing device with a basic supply of
substrate elements, then builds itself up into a macroscale
factory, utilizing atomically precise fabrication techniques
to build whatever you want, atom by atom. Just add water,
some carbon, a couple other elements, give it some code—
it'll make whatever we tell it to make. Make you a car or
an antenna array, make you manna from heaven if you want.
Or a double cheeseburger with mustard and relish. Don't
matter, it'll make anything, man. Just send down the schematics. Poof!"

"Poof? Really?" Elliot asked, amazed.

"Really," Peter said, obviously bored. "Next question,
Pablo."

"Wow," Elliot muttered. "Does our guy down there know
about this?"

"No," Arthur said. "Course not. He just has to think he's
some kind of god." Elliot nodded.

Helmand Province, Afghanistan

Atal entered the hut without knocking. The Mahdi sat on
a cushion. A low fire was burning in the grate. He gestured to
Atal to sit with him.

Atal remained standing, arms crossed and chin held high.
He stared down at the other man. Finally, Atal said, "I should
kill you." The other man inclined his head, questioning. "It
is the will of Allah, to destroy the blasphemer," Atal continued. "You may control the mind of a weak little girl, but
not a man such as myself. It would be His bidding to kill
you." The Mahdi shrugged and gestured to the seat beside
the fire again. Atal shook his head. "You will not control my
mind, like you do the weak. I know you to be The Devil, the

One Who Claims Righteousness. I saw how you entered the minds of those people. But not me. I am strong, a soldier of Allah."

"*Are you?*" Atal heard softly at the front of his mind. Involuntarily his hands flew to his ears, to block the sound, but the voice continued clearly, "*What do I do to anger you, Righteous Soldier?*"

Atal forced his hands down to his sides but took a small step back warily.

"You claim to be Mahdi," Atal stated.

"*I have made no such claim.*"

"Everyone in this valley gives you this name," Atal said. "You do not deny it."

The man shrugged again.

"You do not deny it," Atal insisted, "and for that you are a blasphemer. I should kill you."

"*But what if they are right, Atal? Who then has done God's will, and who is the usurper?*"

"You are not Mahdi," Atal said.

"*Perhaps you are right, little Soldier of God,*" the voice in his head said. "*Perhaps you are right. Time will show us the truth, as it always does. Until it does, please sit and drink tea with me, Atal.*" He gestured to the seat again and waited.

Atal looked confused. "You do not claim to be Mahdi?" Atal asked.

"*I claim only to make a good cup of tea,*" the man who might be Mahdi conveyed. "*Let us sit together and drink.*" The man stood, turned and stooped to take the kettle from the fire. He poured and made tea in two plain clay cups, then presented one to his visitor. With a nod, he took a sip of his own. As the silence stretched out, eventually Atal took a sip of his. It was good tea, Atal noted, but he said nothing. "*I need you to do something for me, Atal.*"

"I do not serve a blasphemer," Atal said, indignant and starting to put down his cup.

"*I do not ask for your service, Atal,*" the man said. "*Drink your tea. *It is good tea. I ask only that you leave this valley. That is what you wish, is it not?*" Atal nodded, sipping his tea reluctantly. "*Then it is what you should do.*"

"I will not keep quiet about what is happening here, Devil," Atal said. "I will not keep your secret."

"*I do not ask you to. Nor do I ask you to proclaim that which you do not believe. But listen to this, Atal: Soon, a bright light—a star—will appear in the sky above my valley.*"

Atal looked at the man and smiled slightly. "You are crazy."

The man sipped and shook his head. "*You may think so, but it is true, nonetheless. You will see. As you travel from here, you will see that this new star, the star that marks this place, will appear. As you travel, Atal, look back to this place, and if people ask, you may tell them who it is that lives beneath the star. You can tell them that you were here, and that you met the man who sits beneath that star. If people ask.*" He smiled at Atal and drank his tea.

"You are crazy. The Taliban will find this place. When I tell the brethren of your blasphemy, they will come for you."

"*Perhaps you are right, Atal. With time, we'll see.*" He gestured to Atal's cast. "*How is your arm, brother?*"

Atal flexed his fingers and nodded. "It is good, I think." Atal swallowed and muttered, "Thank you."

The man stood and waited for Atal to put down his cup and stand as well. "*You may go in the morning. A donkey, with some supplies, will be ready for you then.*" He gestured to the door of his hut.

"We will leave in the morning," Atal said.

"*I don't think she will go,*" the Mahdi conveyed, shaking his head. "*But if she wishes to join you, of course you may take her.*"

"It is not a choice for her. She is just a little girl."

"*Little or no, just or not,*" the man said in his head, "*she will make up her own mind, Atal. You have made up yours, and so you shall leave in the morning. Go with God and with my blessing, Little Soldier of God,*" the man said.

Atal returned to his hut. Inside, he found Hila sitting with Bala Nashta and playing with her baby.

"Sister," he declared, "I have met with your Devil and he has surrendered to my demands. We leave in the morning."

Hila stared at him. "I am going nowhere, brother," Hila said.

Atal grabbed her by the arm and pulled her upright. "I am your guardian, little sister. Our father is dead. Our family is dead. You will come with me. We will go in the morning." He released her with a shake and stared defiantly at the two women, then stomped to his room.

That night, a pure white light appeared in the sky, directly above the valley; no bigger than a star, but even brighter than the moon. When Hila called her brother outside to stand with the others, all staring up in wonder at this miracle, he refused to come look. Sweating with fear, he stayed in bed and prayed. He held up his hand and stared at the shadow cast by the new star's light streaming in through the window.

At dawn, he left alone.

Salt Lake City, Utah

Three steps into the building, Parnell was confronted by an elderly, white-haired man flanked by half a dozen younger men on either side.

"Charles!" the elderly man said, advancing to embrace Parnell in a bear hug.

"Prophet," Parnell said, straightening from the man's greeting. "How did you—"

"Your Father's house has many rooms, all right. And many security cameras, asshole," Uriel murmured from behind Parnell.

"Welcome home, Charles, welcome home," the First President of the LDS Church enthused, taking Parnell by the arm. You and Father Zimmerman are most welcome," he added, ignoring Uriel completely. He led them through the lobby to the bank of elevators, with Uriel trailing the group. As they entered the elevators, Uriel allowed the doors to close in front of him, remaining behind. He turned from the elevators, shaking his head, and stopped short. Sitting on a couch in the sunlight drenched lobby was an old friend.

Uriel crossed the space to stand before the old man, whose eyes were closed as he appeared to bask in the warmth of the sunshine streaming in through the large windows. Uriel smiled down at the man.

"Dear friend," Uriel said, touching the old man's shoulder.

The rotund, balding man in a *yarmulke* smiled back in greeting. "My dearest friend, Uriel," the little man said, eyes opening and twinkling in the sunlight. "So good to see you, old friend." He patted the couch next to him.

Uriel sat, shook the other's hand with both of his. "Dear Azrael, it is good to see you as well. After so long, I admit you have surprised me, friend. How is it that you're here?"

The old Jew shrugged. "A man wanders, you know. Wander long enough, a man finds himself just about everywhere at some point."

"Yeah, I get it. How'd you really get here?"

"Same way you did, Uriel. Did you know about that 'One Temple' business?" Uriel shook his head. "Neither did I, until I followed you guys out the door and stepped into Salt Lake City. Cute."

"You may call it cute," Uriel scowled, "Scares the crap out of me. These guys have a few tricks, it seems. Don't like it."

"Indeed, indeed. More tricks than you know. 'These guys,' as you call them, are not to be taken lightly, Uriel. They have a deep understanding, and it gives them a great deal of power."

"Doesn't seem like they mind using it, either," Uriel said.

"Quite true." Azrael leaned heavily on his gnarled cane as he stood, grimacing with the effort. He straightened his skullcap on his head. "We need to talk, old friend."

"What about?"

"These guys, and their tricks. But not here," Azrael said. "Let's grab a taxi."

"Where to?"

"Feldman's. Decent enough deli, for where we are. I mean, you'll have to close your eyes to the decor, it's an abomination. But the pastrami's not completely inedible. Come."

Los Angeles International Airport

Gabriel stepped onto the plane and looked about, amazed. Unlike the last time, there was a buzz of activity as scores of people moved about. The seats in the rear of the aircraft were now filled. He looked about for Grace, but couldn't see her for the crowd of people milling about.

The plane's steward, dressed in uniform, emerged to greet him.

"Dr. Sheehan," the steward said, taking his elbow. "Right this way, please." Gabriel followed the man to the front of the plane where they stopped at the foot of a circular staircase. "Your party is upstairs, sir."

"Thanks," Gabriel said and mounted the narrow stairs. As he climbed, he left the noise of a hundred conversations behind and emerged into the quiet of a large seating area, with a small bar at the far end of the room.

A woman in a uniform similar to the steward's smiled at him as he stepped up. "Right this way, Dr. Sheehan." She led him back to the sitting area just foreword of the bar, where Grace and Julius were seated with Bogart and Bacall around a low table.

"Here he is," Grace said. She reached up and pulled Gabriel into the seat beside hers. They all exchanged greetings as the attendant stood by.

"I'm fine, thanks," Gabriel said to her, settling into the chair.

"In that case," the attendant said, smiling, "please fasten your seat belts. We should be taking off shortly. Please let me know if you need anything." She left.

They heard the engines spool up and the plane slowly moved away from the terminal.

"Where's Arthur?" Grace asked.

"He's not coming," Gabriel said.

"Not coming?" Grace asked. "Where's he going?"

"Said he was heading back to the office."

"The office?" Julius asked.

"Yeah. Lots of work to do, he said," Gabriel said. "Said he'd catch up later."

"What's later?" Grace asked.

"He wasn't specific," Gabriel said. "Maybe in Hawaii."

"Hawaii?" Grace asked. "Why in hell would we—"

"Only as a first stop," Gabriel said. "For refueling."

They fastened their seatbelts as the plane began to accelerate down the runway.

"Oh? Where are we going after that?" Julius asked.

"Afghanistan," Gabriel said.

The plane tilted as the color drained from Zimmerman's face.

"The hell you say," Julius muttered, staring out the window as the ground fell away.

Dublin, Ireland

Ian dropped his report on the Magistrate's desk and sat down. "It's all in there, Sidhbh," the investigator said. "Should add a spark of humanity to your report, I think."

The Magistrate nodded as she thumbed through the report. "I'm sorry to have ever called upon the old man as a witness. Perhaps he'd still be alive today."

"Perhaps, Sidhbh, perhaps. You tore the scab from a deep, festering wound, that's for sure."

"It's a foul business, Ian," the Magistrate replied. "Any idea what became of the lad?" She said, looking up from the report.

"An idea, aye," Ian said. "But I can't see how it pertains to your writ, Sidhbh."

"Oh, you can't, can't you?" the Magistrate said, tossing the report back on her desk. "Maybe you should let me be the judge of that, Ian. Seeing, you know, as I am the judge in this matter. I know you too well, my friend. I'm sure you pulled a little harder on that thread before you let it go."

"I might've, Sidhbh. You know how I love a mystery."

"I do. That's why I hired you, you old sot. So, what of the boy?"

"Records were thin, to be honest. For as far as I could follow, though, he took employment on a freighter bound for Dubai."

"Dubai?" she said. "And after that?" the Magistrate asked, intrigued.

Ian shook his head. "No clue. Never returned to Europe, by all I could tell. Disappeared somewhere in the Middle East."

"Just as well, perhaps."

"Just as well."

Over the Pacific Ocean

"I'm thinking, I get off in Honolulu," Zimmerman said.

"Not sure that's possible," Bacall said. "Isn't it just a refueling thing?"

"Why do you want to get off?" Bogart asked.

"I've been to Afghanistan," Julius explained. "Not keen on going back."

"That bad?" Bogart asked.

"Worse," Zimmerman said. "Wouldn't recommend it, to be honest."

"No choice, Father," Bogart explained. "That's where our subject is."

"Subject?" Grace asked.

"Of our film," Bogart said. "That crew," he continued, gesturing to the deck below, "is for our documentary."

"Documentary?" Grace asked. "About what?"

"A guy they are calling the New Messiah," Bogart said.

"No shit," Grace said. She looked at her husband, reddening. "What happened to getting me to Kiev? The gate is in Kiev. Is this Arthur's idea?"

Gabriel shrugged.

"If by Arthur, you mean Mr. Schlessel," Bacall interjected, "it's my understanding that it was, indeed, his idea. Certainly not what we had in mind when we came to town."

"Let me guess: Yours was a remake of *The Big Sleep*?" Julius asked.

"We floated it as a possibility," Bacall said, smiling. "Thought we were getting some traction, too. But when the owner of the studio asks you to take on a project, well..."

"Arthur owns a movie studio?" Grace asked. She looked at her husband again, who shrugged again.

"So you're shooting a movie about this guy in Afghanistan?" Julius asked. Bogart and Bacall nodded. "What are you doing about security?"

"All taken care of, Father," Bogart assured him. "My understanding is that there's a military unit of some kind assigned to us. Navy SEALs, I think."

"Oh, great," Julius said.

Grace turned on her husband again. "So that's why we're on this plane, Gabe?" she asked. "To gin up our fiddle, up close and personal?"

"What fiddle?" Bacall asked. "The messiah plays violin?"

"Gabriel?" Grace said, ignoring Bacall's question.

"Don't know, hon," Gabriel answered. "On the way to Kiev, I guess. Maybe we can just wait on the plane."

"On the way to Kiev?" Grace said, rising halfway out of her seat. "Kiev is that way," she said, pointing to the right. "Afghanistan is that way," she added, pointing left.

"What's in Kiev?" Bacall asked.

"Sightseeing," Gabriel said. "A thousand year old cave monastery. Supposed to be magnificent."

"Cave monastery?" said Bacall. "Sounds damp."

"Magnificent," Gabriel assured her.

"On the way, my ass!" Grace said, fuming.

CHAPTER 10

Honolulu, Hawaii

The black 747 touched down just after midnight at Honolulu airport and taxied to the executive terminal. Most of
the passengers remained asleep in their seats. Bogart and
Bacall slept in the VIP cabin. The flight attendants kept the
lights low so as not to disturb the sleeping passengers.

As the plane took on fuel, a new passenger came quietly
aboard. Gabriel looked out the window at the stars as Grace
lay sleeping in the seat beside him, her head resting on his
shoulder. The stars were the thing he missed most while he
was dead. The stars, and sourdough bread. And Twizzlers.

> *Time and Discomfort,*
> *Hunger and Regret:*
> *These are the things*
> *the Dead may forget.*

He didn't recall where the little rhyme had come from,
only that he'd heard it sometime after he died. Now that he
was back in the world, however, seeing the stars outside and
feeling the weight of his wife's head on his shoulder, Gabriel realized two truths of which he was previously unaware:
Without hunger, there was no satisfaction. And regret is the
price one pays for caring.

Gabriel twisted the ring on his finger and hoped Arthur
was okay. He missed his friend. And wondered if they had
Twizzlers in Afghanistan.

Grace shivered uncontrollably, her eyes

clenched tight shut. She struggled beneath the sheet but couldn't move, her arms bound fast by her sides. She opened her mouth to scream but a block of leather was immediately pushed hard between her teeth.

"There now, little one," a voice said. It was an Irish voice. "Now, now," the voice soothed in Gaelic, "not like it's the first time, is it? Hush now, it'll be done in a bit."

Grace opened her eyes to the sad smile of the starched white nurse standing over her. Suddenly, flashbulbs popped off behind her eyes, she smelled something burning, and the world went sizzling white.

Honolulu, Hawaii

"Hey, buddy," Arthur said, standing in the plane's aisle and looking down on Gabriel. "She asleep?"

Gabriel nodded, smiling at his friend. "Decided to join us after all, huh?"

"Not joining. Just here."

"How'd you get to Hawaii?" Gabriel asked.

"Floo powder," Arthur said, smiling. "Listen, Gabe," Arthur continued, his smile fading. "We need to talk." Gabriel inclined his head toward Grace. Arthur shook his head and said, "I'll be upstairs. Drinking." Gabriel nodded.

Gabriel found Arthur in the lounge, drinking as promised. He sat down at the otherwise empty little bar.

"I'll have what he's having," Gabriel told the bartender.

"You got some catching up to do," Arthur said.

Gabriel made a face as he took a sip from the drink produced by the bartender.

"Wow, you must be depressed," Gabriel said, putting down the glass.

"You could say that," Arthur said.

"So?" Gabriel asked, turning on his barstool to face his friend. "I thought you were staying above the circus."

Arthur finished his drink and signaled for another. "Stopped by to get some things straight, since Sam and I are pretty much trapped in this clown show of yours."

"What things?"

"Like what the fuck is going on with your wife, if you're asking. I mean, since she managed to have me kill a carful of nice people, I was a little curious about what the hell I've gotten myself into."

"You don't know that, Art," Gabriel said, laying a hand on his friend's shoulder.

Arthur pushed Gabriel's hand away. "I do know that, Gabe. That was the first thing I checked. Mom and Dad and three kids, coming back from Disneyland. You want to know their names?"

Arthur shook his head. "I'm sorry, Arthur—"

"Bull-shit, Gabe. You're not any sorrier than your wife. Just roadkill in her personal nightmare."

Gabriel decided not to argue the point.

"Bill and Gloria Sullivan, from Lodi, and their three lovely children: Susie, age 7, Bill junior, age 4, and the baby, Sharon. Not yet 2 years old. I say 'lovely' because I saw their last Christmas card, posted two months back. And yes, they all died in the crash. So did those two jokers in the van. Didn't get their names, though." He started on his new drink.

"Why'd you come back, Art? So I could feel guilty, too?"

"Don't think you two feel guilty about much of anything anymore," Arthur said.

"So why are you here, then?"

"Because I don't think either one of you has a clue as to what's going on. I was so pissed off about what happened, I decided to do some checking. Try to find out how we got to this point, old friend. How you got me to this point." He sarcastically toasted his friend.

"How much checking did you get done in a day, all the while making your way to Hawaii?"

"A day? Maybe for you, Gabriel. I had plenty of time, believe me."

Gabriel shook his head and took another sip of his scotch.

"Do you even know why you're on this plane, Gabriel?"

"I think so," Gabriel said evenly. "We're heading to Ukraine, to a gateway back. A natural gateway, not one of the Wright gates that got shut down. Or uninvented, or whatever."

Arthur nodded. "Or whatever." Another swig. "Ukraine by way of Afghanistan."

"I think it's on the way," Gabriel smiled and Arthur snorted derisively at that.

There were several beats of silence while both of them looked out the window at the night sky. The plane had started moving again.

"Did you know, Gabriel, that almost every religion and culture, no matter how isolated or primitive, has a mythology about a great, killing flood? Did you know that?"

"I think I might've heard that once, yeah."

"Even nomadic tribes in the middle of the Sahara, people who have never seen so much as a big puddle, have an oral tradition of a great flood, sent by a wrathful god to wipe out everything. Weird, huh?" Arthur asked. Gabriel said nothing, waiting for Arthur to make his point. "Seems everybody's god is a dick," Arthur muttered into his drink. "And how many of the world's great religions do you think have a prophesy of a world-saving Messiah coming to rescue the true believers at some point in the future? What percentage?"

Gabriel thought about this for a bit. He shrugged.

"What percentage? Islam, Mormons, Jews, Zoroastrians?

How many different religions are waiting to be saved?"

"I'm thinking—"

"All of them," Arthur interjected.

"Really?"

"Yeah, really," Arthur assured him. "All of them."

"Fascinating, Art. So what does that have to do with Grace?"

"You don't see a fascinating tension between those two facts, huh? Don't see the implication? Believe in Me, I'm coming to save the ones I choose—the rest of you are all going to die. No matter. Here's the thing: It turns out, good buddy, that most every religious sect *currently* shares the opinion that your wife," and here Arthur gestured with his glass toward the lower level of the plane, "is the only thing standing between our current lousy little world and the coming of that saving Messiah."

"I'm sorry, what?"

"Grace is the key. Something to do with the appearance of the Messiah on earth. Every denomination of Christianity, every denomination of Islam—"

"Moslems believe in the Messiah?"

Arthur nodded. "You heard Zimmerman. The Mahdi."

Gabriel sucked at the dregs of his scotch. The bartender brought another. "How is Grace supposed to bring forth the Messiah, or the Apocalypse, or whatever."

"She doesn't 'bring forth' the Messiah. Not exactly."

"Then what, exactly?"

"There is a widely held belief," Arthur explained slowly, "that the Apocalypse is nigh."

"Yeah, I've heard. Nothing new there."

"True. But this is a little different. This time—major, mainstream religions, and at the highest levels. And Grace doesn't bring the Messiah. Other way around, I'm afraid."

"What does that mean?"

"While Grace is alive, there is no Messiah. Or there's a risk that the Messiah won't come, more accurately. But if she's dead..."

"Grace has to die for the Messiah to arrive? Who the hell came up with that one?"

"Um, just about everyone. It's a little more subtle than that, partner. While Grace is alive, there is a risk that the Messiah doesn't come, or the Apocalypse fizzles out, or something like that."

Gabriel laughed.

"Laugh. Except almost every major religion in the Western world, and a few others, are trying to kill your wife."

Gabriel stopped laughing and looked at his friend. "But that's ridiculous."

"It's their religion. Tell them."

They both finished their drinks.

"See you in a bit, Art," Gabriel said, standing and turning to the stairway. "Gonna check on my wife while I can still get down those stairs."

"Yeah, Gabe, you do that. She needs checking on."

Over the Pacific Ocean

Gabriel found his wife in the small galley at the front of the plane.

"What?" Grace asked him. "What is this 'thousand year old cave monastery' shit? Where the hell are we going—really?"

"It's true. It's called Pechersk something or other. It's in Kiev. That's where we're going. Arthur is working on getting us there."

"That's our way back?"

"It's a way back. Maybe the only way back, since we lost the Wright gates, hon."

"And this gate—it's in a monastery? In a cave?"

Gabriel nodded. "So I understand."

"Is it a Catholic monastery? Are we trying to tiptoe past the exact people we've been running from?"

"Maybe, I don't know. Hopefully it's Orthodox or something. You'd rather try the Vatican? That seems a little risky."

"You think?"

"Arthur was working on something in Arizona, up by Sedona. Seems there might be some kind of natural gate in the area, but he couldn't pin it down."

"So we're flying to Kiev—by way of fucking Afghanistan—instead of Arizona? Shit, Gabe."

Gabriel shrugged. "Arizona wasn't panning out. Kiev looks like our best shot."

Grace slumped against the bulkhead. "Are you sure we're the ones running this clusterfuck?"

"Just running, Grace. We just go with this."

"We could go to Hell with this, Gabe."

"I know, hon. But unless you have a better idea, I say we ride this plane to Kiev."

"By way of Afghanistan," Grace said, shaking her head.

"Have to. It's part of the game," Gabriel explained. Grace looked at him skeptically. "Don't give me the look. It was your idea, remember? Let's go upstairs. Arthur dropped by to see you."

Over the Pacific Ocean

Grace and Gabriel found Arthur still drinking at the bar, though now more slowly as the night, and the plane, droned on.

"There you are," Grace said, sitting the stool next to Arthur.

"Can't argue with that," Arthur said.

"Arthur," she said, taking his hand. "I'm sorry for what happened."

"You are?" Arthur asked her, looking down at her hand on his. Grace nodded. Arthur looked into her eyes and held her hand tight. "It was a whole family, Grace. Both parents and three kids. One was a little girl, less than two years old."

"I'm sorry, Arthur, truly I am. Were they hurt badly?"

"They're all dead, hon," Gabriel said.

"Oh," Grace said, retrieving her hand. "Well, shit."

"Yeah," Arthur said, taking another gulp from his glass. "Shit."

"Well," she said, "at least they're all together."

"Seriously?" Arthur said, staring at her.

"Well, yeah, Art," she said, giving the bartender an appreciative nod as he served her a drink. She took a deep swallow. "Thanks." She turned back to Arthur, saying, "Come on, Arthur. Everybody dies. It's not the worst thing that happens."

"The baby wasn't even two," Arthur said.

"Not the first dead baby, Art, come on."

"Probably not a good time to start with the dead baby jokes, hon," Gabriel advised.

Grace shrugged. "If you say so. Still…"

"Don't," Arthur cautioned.

"It was an accident, Arthur," Grace said after a pause.

"Was it?" Arthur asked.

"Was it what?" Grace asked.

"Arthur's been explaining his conspiracy theories to me for the past half hour," Gabriel said.

"Maybe I should've just let that joker shoot you a few times, Grace," Arthur said. "I mean, you'd only be dead, right? No big deal."

"It's not the same, Arthur," Gabriel said, "and you know it."

"Dead is dead," Arthur said petulantly.

"No it isn't," Grace said. "Not for me."

"You're special," Arthur said. "None of the rest of this matters, nobody else matters, as long as you make it back. Why? What makes you so damn important?"

They were silent until Arthur repeated his question.

"I'm not trying to be special, Arthur," Grace explained. "I'm not trying to get anyone killed. I just want to get back to where I belong. I'm important because somebody is making me important. And I'm pretty damn tired of it. I'm tired of being chased around, of being hunted for god only knows why. I'm tired of feeling the blood whispering through these dead veins, of feeling my skin tightening to where I can barely breathe, because I shouldn't be here breathing." She polished off her drink and set the glass onto the bar. Grace rubbed her temples. "I just want to get home. That's not too much to ask, is it, Artie?"

"It might be, Grace," Arthur said. He turned to Gabriel. "You and I have to get back to the office. We've got work to do."

Purgatory

Arthur and Gabriel walked into the darkened control room.

"Something's happened," Arthur said. "What's happened, Sam? Something's not right." He scanned the room.

Sam was seated in the darkened room, shaking her head at the images.

"This is crazy," Sam said to no one as they walked in.

"What's crazy?" Gabriel asked, taking a chair in front of the console beside Sam. He scanned the monitors and squinted in confusion. "How? What is this? These aren't overheads."

"No, they're not," Sam agreed.

"How could the surveillance satellite show—"

"It's not the satellite feed," Samantha explained. "That's up there," she said, gesturing to a monitor higher up on the wall beside them. "This is something—different."

Gabriel scanned the monitors surrounding the front three sides of the small room. Each monitor showed a ground level view of the village, as if they were actually there.

"How is this possible?" Gabriel asked.

"Wait," Sam said. "Listen to this." She twisted a knob on the console and the room filled with the sounds of the village. They could clearly hear people talking, children laughing, water splashing. Arthur and Samantha looked at

Gabriel.

Gabriel reached forward and twisted the knob, lowering the sound. "Surveillance satellites don't pick up sound, guys. What is this?"

"We're not sure," Elliot said, coming into the room. "But Sam has some kind of crazy theory about quantum breath mints or something."

"Quantum entanglement," Sam corrected. "We talked about the possibility, remember? At the restaurant? It's not a theory. Look at this." She fiddled with her console, saying, "Look at the center monitor. This is an image from 2 hours ago. It's the first thing that came up on this feed, or whatever it is. Look." She rocked back in her chair and pointed to the middle monitor. It showed an image of a man's hands, a large ring on his right ring finger. He was twisting the ring, inspecting it.

"That's my ring!" Arthur explained. He looked at Arthur, incredulous.

"No," Gabriel said, "this is my ring." He held up his right hand where he wore the large Claddagh. "You gave it back, remember?"

"There's really two of them?"

"Not really two," Sam interjected. "They're the same ring, the same way that there are two Zimmermans. It split, somehow, the same way that Julius was split when he went back. He was wearing your ring when he went back. Anyway, somebody down in that village is wearing it now."

"I still don't understand how this is happening," Gabe said.

"The two rings are entangled. They're both in indeterminate states, just like we are. And we're linked, until one of the states collapses."

"Quantum entanglement," Gabriel said. "Weird."

"Pret-ty, pret-ty weird," Sam agreed.

Arthur put his head down on the console. "This is giving me a headache."

Gabriel tapped at his chin as he studied the monitors

again. "If we're really entangled with what's going on down there…" Gabriel said.

"There may be implications," Sam said.

"What implications?" Arthur asked, raising his head.

"It's all just theory, Sam," Gabriel said.

"It's theory because nobody ever experienced it before, Gabe," Samantha said. She pointed to the screen in front of them. "It's not theory anymore. And since we're looking at an entanglement phenomenon, everything that implies has to follow. Not theory."

"What everything? What's implied?" Arthur asked, looking between his wife and Gabriel.

"A faster than light connection. Simultaneity. Just a complete contradiction of the fundamental tenet of General Relativity."

"Is that bad?" Arthur asked.

"Well, maybe," Sam said. "For one thing, it leads to anomalous time."

"An omelette time?" Arthur asked. "What's bad about that?"

"No, dear. Time anomalies. A breakdown between cause and effect."

"Oh. That sounds bad."

OKAY, I CAN SEE MY LAST BIT OF DIVINE MESSAGING HAS CAUSED A BIT OF CONSTERNATION. SO MUCH WAILING AND LAMENTATION! ENOUGH, ALREADY. LET'S BE ADULTS ABOUT THIS, PLEASE.

WEREN'T YOU LISTENING WHEN FERMI ASKED, "WHERE IS EVERYONE?" COME ON, PEOPLE—LOOK UP! THE NIGHT SKY IS PRETTY DAMN DARK, ISN'T IT? IF EVERY WORLD JUST WENT ON AND ON AND ON, GETTING BIGGER AND SMARTER SINCE THE DAWN

OF CREATION—WHERE IS EVERYONE? LIFE EXPANDS TO FILL EVERY NICHE, RIGHT? IF THIS ALL HAS BEEN GOING ON SINCE WAY BACK WHEN, WHEN I LET THERE BE LIGHT, THEN BY NOW EVERY WORLD AROUND EVERY SUN IN EVERY GALAXY SHOULD BE LIT UP LIKE TIMES SQUARE AT CHRISTMAS, RIGHT? THE LIGHT FROM A BILLION CIVILIZATIONS SHOULD MAKE THE NIGHT SKY SHINE.

PRETTY DARK UP THERE, AIN'T IT, BUBBA? SURE IS.

I'M NOT DEALING YOU ANY CARDS THAT EVERY OTHER ADVANCED CIVILIZATION GETS DEALT. HAS TO BE. YOU GET TO THIS POINT, LADIES AND GENTLEMEN, YOU GET TO EXPERIENCE THE GREAT FILTER. HAPPENS TO EVERYONE. THINK OF IT LIKE YOUR COMING OF AGE RITE, YOUR BAR MITZVAH, AS IT WERE. MAZEL TOV. LIFE, CIVILIZATION, THE ASCENT OF MAN—IT'S NOT AN EXPONENTIAL CLIMB, BRONOWSKI. COMES A POINT WE GOTTA TAKE YOU DOWN A NOTCH. FOR THE SAFETY OF YOU, ME, EVERYONE IN CREATION, ACROSS THIS UNIVERSE WE ALL CALL HOME. IT'S UP TO GOD, YOU SEE, TO KEEP YOU IN CHECK, SO YOU DON'T BLOW US ALL TO KINGDOM COME. BECAUSE KINGDOM COME IS NOT THE PLACE WE ALL WANT TO GO. NOT EVEN ME. ESPECIALLY NOT ME.

Salt Lake City, Utah

The First President of the Church of Jesus Christ of Latter-day Saints sat behind his desk and smiled at his two guests. Both Julius and Chuck looked distinctly uncomfortable, each taking turns staring out the window to the Temple Square below.

"I must say, Charles," the President began, leaning forward, elbows on his desk and smile broadening, "we had hoped that you would bring the girl back with you. It is a disappointment."

Parnell tried to smile back. "The girl?"

"Yes, the girl. Grace. You appeared, for a bit there, to be well on your way to escorting her here. Disappointing."

"Yes, disappointing, Prophet. She's not an easy person to deal with, you know," Parnell said.

"So I gather. But surely she understands her situation, the extreme danger that she's in. Why would she go to such lengths to avoid our protection?" the President asked, steepling his fingers and assuming a look of deep concern.

"Oh, she knows she's in danger," Parnell assured him, then silence.

"But she doesn't trust you, is that it?" the President encouraged.

Parnell nodded and returned to looking uncomfortable. "We have a complicated relationship."

"I might be stating the obvious here," *Julius* interjected, "but maybe Grace ran away from your people because she doesn't understand your role in all this, Mr. President. I mean, no offense, but I'm sure I don't understand your motivations in wanting to—well, in wanting to abduct her." *Julius* looked over at Parnell, who was grimacing and looking out the window again.

"Not abduct the young lady, Father, not at all. Protect her. Our motivations, Father Zimmerman?" the President asked. "Why, there should be no doubt in your mind, none at all.

Our motivations, our role, is to serve the Lord."

"Yes, of course," *Julius* said, leaning into the conversation. He shot a look at Parnell and didn't understand why the other man looked so pained. This was, after all, his church. "That may be the concern, right there," *Julius* added.

"Why would our service to the Lord be a concern, Father?"

"Not to me, of course," Zimmerman said, "but to Grace. From what I gather, Grace is concerned that the Lord may not be exactly in her corner right now."

The President looked astonished. "Does she believe that the Lord has forsaken her? The poor child—"

"Not forsaken, exactly," *Julius* continued, not picking up Parnell's subtle efforts to get him to stop talking by shaking his head vigorously and making a subtle slashing motion at his throat. "Grace believes that God is actually behind the plot to excise her."

The President looked confused. "Excise her? I don't understand."

"She believes that God is intent on removing her very existence. Father Pauley told her as much. He seems to have an understanding of the matter, seeing as he was the one most involved in the efforts to have her excised," *Zimmerman* explained.

"The Devil you say!" the President said. "Oh, the poor child. To think that she believed that snake! To actually believe that she is the victim of a plot by the Lord Almighty —oh, it is almost too much to believe, even from that evil man." He sat, slowly shaking his head.

"So you don't believe it to be true, then?" *Julius* asked.

The President looked up at him. "True? How could such an outrageous statement be true? It's not true, is it Charles?"

Parnell turned back to the President with a weak smile. "Of course not, Prophet. Of course not."

Purgatory

Arthur sat at the head of the conference table. He opened

his mouth to speak several times, each time shaking his head and reconsidering. Gabriel and Samantha sat on one side of the table. Elliot sat across from them, looking annoyed. Kurt Gödel, the mathematician, sat beside him, looking confused.

"What?" Elliot asked. "What now? Want my bird to shoot death rays at the nice people in that valley? Send down rainbow colored bubbles filled with unicorn plush toys? Just give the word, boss."

Arthur started to speak again but was pre-empted by his wife. Samantha ignored the impudent engineer and addressed the mathematician. "You've had a chance to work up the problem, Kurt?"

The German mathematician spread his hands before him on the table and gave a slight nod.

"And?" Samantha asked.

"You are asking questions that I cannot answer," the man said in a thick accent, not looking up from his hands.

"It's not a question, *herr* Professor," Gabriel interjected, again jumping ahead of Arthur who had opened his mouth to speak. "It's a project, sort of. Did you look at it?"

The man nodded again.

"Good," Gabriel said, his smile reassuring. "That's good, Kurt. This is Elliot," he indicated the man sitting next to him. "Say hello, Elliot." Elliot looked at the other man and waved at him. "Elliot is going to work with you on the project. He's going to help."

"Help with what?" Elliot said. "I've got plenty to do already, you know."

"Actually, you don't, Elliot," Sam said. "We're not using the satellite for surveillance anymore."

"You're not?"

"No," Arthur said. "We're using—something else. That's what we want you to help Kurt with."

"What are you using?" Elliot said. "I went to a lot of trouble to get that bird in place, you know."

"We know, Elliot," Sam said, soothingly. "Now we're using a different technology."

"Quantum entanglement surveillance," Gödel explained. "Much more robust."

"That's just a concept," Elliot said, scoffing. "Never really happen."

"Um, really happened, Elliot. I mean, it's up and running, right now," Arthur said.

Elliot looked at each of the others in turn, astonished and interested despite himself. He was, after all, in the business of surveillance. Before. Gödel looked at him and nodded significantly.

"Wow," Elliot said. "Can I see?" He was used to being compartmentalized in this business, often not allowed to see the results of his own work.

"Sure, sure, Elliot," Gabriel assured him. "Only, there's something we need to do first."

"Do what first? You just said it was working," Elliot said.

"Yeah, it is," Arthur said. "Only—well, it's complicated."

"Very complicated," Gödel agreed.

"Okay," Elliot said. "Explain it to me."

Arthur and Gabriel looked at Samantha. Sam took a deep breath. "Sure, Elliot. It's like this—Kurt, just jump in here if I get this wrong—we have surveillance of the valley, quantum surveillance, by means of entanglement. You know about quantum entanglement, right?" Elliot nodded dubiously. "Good. So we have entanglement established between our location and the valley by means of a token, an entangled token co-located in—"

"What token?" Elliot asked.

"My ring," Gabriel said. He held up his hand.

Sam said, "The entangled token is this ring. We know that there's an identical ring being worn by someone down there. That's the point of entanglement."

"Cool," Elliot said. "How did you get a quantum entangled ring down there? I mean, that's a statistical impossibility, right? Entanglement at the macro level, like that? Can't be stable."

"Uh, yeah. That's the problem." Sam explained.

"What do you mean?" Elliot asked.

"We didn't put the ring there." Sam looked at Kurt, but the man was studying his hands again.

"So how did it get there?" Elliot asked.

"We're not entirely sure," Sam said slowly. "But we've been able get some—insight—sort of. It became entangled during a CTC event."

"A what?" Elliot interrupted.

"A closed timelike curve," Gödel explained.

"No idea what you're talking about," Elliot said.

"He is no help, no help at all," Gödel said. "How am I—"

"Just a second, Kurt," Samantha said. "There was an event, where a man wearing this ring went back in time—"

Elliot snorted.

"Just listen for a second," Samantha continued.

"No help at all," Gödel repeated.

"And a split occurred," Samantha went on. "That's why the ring's entangled. The ring was colocated at the time of the split. And now there are two identical rings, which are entangled. One here, and one down there."

"Let's say what you're saying is somehow true," Elliot said. "Just gonna give you the benefit of the doubt with this CTC time travel bullshit—"

"It is no bullshit," Gödel said.

"Whatever, Kurt. Whatever you say. You're contradicting yourself. You said it occurred in a time event split or some such bullshit. So the entangled ring should be in the past. Not in the here and now."

"Exactly," Sam said, smiling at Gödel. "I told you he could help."

Gödel nodded.

Elliot stood to leave.

"One more thing, Elliot," Samantha said.

"What?"

"We want you to kick up the reactor on the satellite."

"What? Why? No way, Sam."

"It needs to be brighter. Much brighter. Bright enough so that it can be seen in the daytime, not just at night."

"That's crazy and you know it. It's a satellite, Sam, not a fucking lighthouse. You'll toast the electronics."

Samantha shrugged. "So toast 'em, Elliot. We don't need it for surveillance. We need it to light up. Like a fucking lighthouse."

"Yeah? How about when your magic ring of Sauron goes 'poof?' How about then? You'd rather be blind than have my bird still working?"

"You and Kurt won't let that happen, right?"

Elliot looked down at the older man. "Yeah. No problem. Eh, *herr* Professor?"

Kandahar Province, Afghanistan

They had to land at the military airport at Bagram. They were supposed to land in the capitol, Kabul, so that Bogart and Bacall and the whole film crew could be greeted by the President and provide some much needed positive PR for the Afghani government. A suicide bomber on the front steps of the Central Parliament Building, the location of the planned PR event, suggested to the director and the associate producer that it might be prudent to skip the niceties and head straight to the shooting location. Maybe the PR could wait for the return flight, assuming the government was still standing.

Many on board the plane were not excited at the change of plans. None were more perturbed at the prospect, however, than Julius. As soon as he learned of their destination, he inveighed against getting off the plane to everyone within earshot.

Julius planted himself at the top of the little spiral stairway that led off the upper deck of the plane, effectively blocking the others from leaving. Grace had never seen him like this, pale and agitated, his gaze darting between each of his friends standing before him.

"You don't understand, Grace," Julius said, his voice a half-octave higher than usual. He swallowed hard. "I've been here before, you haven't. None of you have been here before."

"War's over now, Julius," Grace soothed. "It's not the same, hon." She moved toward him but Julius shook his head in agitation.

"The war's never over in this place, Grace. Not since Genghis Khan passed through. We're not getting off the plane, period. We'll wait for the film crew to get off and then we'll get out of here."

"Well, then, Father," Bogart said, stepping forward, "you'll have to let Ms. Bacall and I pass, won't you?" He held his wife's elbow as they stepped forward. Julius stared at them, apparently confused as to what to do next.

Grace stepped over and took Julius's hand. "Let's just sit for a bit, Julius," she said softly. He looked at her and passed a hand over his face. Nodding, he let her lead him over to the couch. Bacall and Bogart headed down the steps. Grace spoke softly to Julius, holding both his hands, leaning in. Julius stopped shaking his head, sighed deeply and lay back, closing his eyes. He opened them again and nodded slightly. Grace smiled at him and gave his hands a reassuring squeeze.

The entire film crew loaded into a convoy of white trucks left over from the UN mission. Two armored Humvee's led off the convoy as they moved off the tarmac in the baking sun, a third trailing behind. Grace sat next to Julius in the lead truck. The driver glanced over at Julius as he drove, noticing that his eyes were tightly shut and that he squeezed Grace's hand so tight her fingers were purple.

"Nothin' to be scared of, sir," the driver offered in an amiable drawl. "No *mujahadin* in these parts for the last six months. Nobody about but us chickens," he gave a gap-toothed smile to the others alongside. Grace smiled back but Julius was sweaty and stone-faced. Despite the Texan's continued efforts, little in the way of conversation passed between the group for the four hour journey to the Forward Operating Base where they would be housed during their stay.

Julius opened his eyes when the truck squealed to a stop. He took one look out the window and whispered, "Fuck." Then he let his head drop back and closed his eyes again. Gabriel and Arthur emerged from one of the buildings, waving.

"Here we are, guys and gals," the driver announced. "Welcome to F.O.B. Fiddler's Green," he enthused, his gesture including the wide expanse of flat brown dirt dotted with buildings. "HQ—I mean the Visitor's Hospitality Center—is that building straight ahead. Why don't you all say hi to our C.O. while I see about getting this truck unloaded."

"You go ahead," Julius said softly, not opening his eyes. "I think I'll wait here for a while." Grace got out to greet her husband.

The next morning they had breakfast in the mess and re-assembled at the line of trucks. It was already stifling hot. They had all been issued desert fatigues, supplied by the film studio. Somehow, Julius had been provided chaplain's bars which he wore on his collar. They stood in the dust, waiting for Bogart as he approached with several uniformed men. Bogart wore his fatigues like he was a career officer, carrying himself with the bearing of being the man in charge. He pulled the group of SEALs over and introduced them to. Arthur wore a pair of sunglasses, the same as worn by the SEALs and the other special ops personnel.

"My team will be escorting you to the valley," the SEAL Captain explained, cleaning his sunglasses carefully with a handkerchief he produced from one of his pockets.

"What are we going to find?" Bogart asked.

"Not a clue," the Captain answered. "We've been pretty close, but never really entered the valley itself."

"What about recon?" Julius asked.

The Captain squinted at him, eyeing the chaplain's bars. He replaced his glasses on his nose and shook his head. "We've been all along the ridge this side of the valley. Popped a drone over the ridge line yesterday but couldn't get anything."

"What does that mean?" Julius asked.

"Just that, Father," the Captain answered irritably. "Lost the drone. Those suckers ain't cheap, so let's leave it at that. Techies think it might have something to do with radiation from the star."

"Star?" Grace asked.

"Didn't see it last night, ma'am?" the Captain smiled.

"Went to bed early, Captain," Gabriel answered. "Didn't take the midnight stroll around the grounds."

"Don't blame you. You'll see it tonight, though, seeing as you'll be sleeping right under it," the Captain explained. "Brand new star, damndest thing I ever saw. Nobody has a clue how it got there. Appeared three nights ago, like flicking on a light switch."

"A star that gives off radiation?" Arthur asked skeptically.

"Nothing dangerous, sir," the Captain assured them. "More like electromagnetic interference. That's what they tell me, at least."

"What do you mean, we'll be right under it?" Grace asked.

The Captain pointed to the northwest. "Because it sits right there, right over where we're going. Damndest thing."

"Damndest thing," Julius echoed.

The Captain stared at him hard, glancing again at his chaplaincy bars.

"Everthing okay, Father?" the Captain asked.

"No, everything is not okay, Captain," Julius said, looking down at the man with a cold stare.

"What's the problem, Father?"

Grace tried to interject but Julius stepped in front of her to stand toe to toe with the Captain. "I'll tell you what the problem is, Billy. I'm not too pleased to be going in-country in a ragtop truck, for one thing. That's one big problem right there, Billy-boy." Julius stared down at the shorter man.

The Captain's jaw set and he straightened, hands on hips. "I don't remember telling you my first name, Father," the Captain said slowly, unblinking. "I'd appreciate it if you referred to me as 'Captain Ahern' or just Captain. And I don't appreciate being told how to do my job by a priest."

"Just as well I didn't use your real name then, Wilbur," Julius said with a sardonic smile. The other man reddened. " Since I'm assuming that it's your job to keep our asses from getting fragged out there, I'm thinking that an APC might be more appropriate. Captain, sir."

The other four members of the SEAL team snickered behind their Captain's back.

"I assure you, Father, my squad will keep your asses safe and sound," the Captain said. "Like I said, Father," the Captain added in a dangerous undertone, "I really don't like being told how to do my job."

"Shit, Billy," Julius said, wiping sweat from his forehead, "I'm just trying to keep all these nice people alive."

"Let me worry about that," the Captain said, clasping Zimmerman on the shoulder a bit more firmly than what one would consider friendly. He stared hard at Zimmerman's name printed on his camo blouse. "Zimmerman's a funny name for a priest," the Captain said. "Had a good sailor in my command with that name. Hey, Reg," the Captain said, turning to one of the men behind him. "What was Zimmerman's first name?"

"Eli," Zimmerman said before the other man could answer. The Captain turned back to Julius. "He was my brother."

The Captain nodded. "Don't see the resemblance," he said.

Zimmerman opened his mouth but Grace stepped up and pointed to the front of the convoy where Bacall was waving.

"Time to go, guys," she said.

The Captain nodded and moved off. Julius called to the tallest of the other SEALs as he left. "Reggie," Julius said and the man turned, looking back at Julius with a puzzled expression. He came back a step and Julius approached him. Grace tried to tug him back but Julius stepped up to the other man and said, "Reg, I've got a bad feeling. This is gonna be a shit-show, I'm sure of it." The SEAL said nothing, inclining his head in confusion. Julius continued softly, "Any chance of getting a sidearm, at least?"

The SEAL looked at Julius and said, "I have no idea who you are or how you know who I am, Father, but no, there is zero chance of me providing you with a weapon. Hell, no." He blushed, and added apologetically, "Sorry, Father, didn't mean to swear at you or anything. Sorry about your brother. Eli was a good sailor—wicked smart. But it's gonna be okay, really. This is a pretty safe place, all things being equal." He smiled reassuringly and moved off to follow the other members of his squad to the front of the convoy.

Grace stepped up to Julius as the other man left.

"What the hell is wrong with you, Julius?" she demanded. "Are you having a fucking flashback or something? Knock it off! This is not your war, Zimmerman. This is a freaking documentary film shoot! Just shut the fuck up and ride along, okay, Julius?" Julius nodded. "Good. Now get in the damn truck."

Kandahar Province, Afghanistan

The truck convoy slowly navigated the rock-strewn track across western Helmand Province. Julius had insisted that they ride in one of the trucks to the rear of the convoy, where now he sat next to Grace, constantly scanning the rugged countryside. Grace could feel him trembling next to her. He jumped as she put a hand on his thigh.

"It's okay, Julius," she assured him.

He turned from the window to stare at her briefly, his eyes wide. "No, Grace. It is not okay," he said emphatically, then returned to his surveillance out the window. She could feel the muscles of his thigh through the fatigues, hard as a rock as he turned to look behind, then to the front, then to scan the low mountains out the side window. "Not okay at all. This is the exact same road, Grace. I'm sure of it. The exact same." He turned to look at her briefly to emphasize just how not okay he was with everything that was happening.

"The exact same as what, Julius?"

"As the 'Salome' op, that's what. Exactly the same. The valley we're going to? The same as where the village was that I—that I was at. I'm sure of it."

"You can't know that, Julius." He looked at her and shook his head disparagingly. "Fine, Julius, even if it is. It's not the same thing, Julius. It's a different world, completely."

"Just one helluva coincidence, huh?"

"Not a coincidence, I didn't mean that."

"And the fact that every member of my old SEAL team is here, too? How's that for a coincidence? It's the same fucking story, Grace. We're about to have our asses blown to shit."

"It's not the same, Julius. Your old team might be here, but you're not."

"I'm not? Then where the fuck are we, Grace? I'm right back in it. That's no coincidence. There!" He pointed to a ridge line ahead, his finger trembling.

"What?" the driver asked.

"That's the spot, just over that ridge, I'm sure of it," Julius said, his voice rising. "We've got to stop the convoy. It happens right *there*!" He was dead white, beads of sweat appearing on his forehead.

"No, Julius, please," Grace soothed, trying to put her arm around his shoulder.

"Tell them!" Julius yelled at the driver. "Tell the lead to stop, now, I'm telling you."

"Why? What's up there?" the driver said, looking around.

"A fucking ambush, that's what. IED in the middle of the road, with bandits on both sides of the ridgeline, *right up there!*"

The driver reached for his comms unit but looked at Grace before he keyed the mike. Grace shook her head slightly.

"Don't listen to *her*," Julius said. "She doesn't know shit. *Tell them now!*"

The driver looked between the two of them as he drove, still holding the mike in his lap. He shook his head. "Too late anyway, buddy," he said, nodding ahead. "Lead Humvee's already crested the ridge."

"Oh, fuck," Julius said, taking the mike from the driver's lap and twisting the knob on the comm unit to full gain. "Lead, state your status."

There was a crackling silence for a moment, then, "Lead is clear." A pause, then, "Who the hell's asking?"

"Billy," Julius said, holding the mike in both hands, "stay sharp. IED half a click past the crest, bad guys with automatic weapons and RPG's both sides of the road."

A crackle again, then a loud curse. "Is this that fucking priest? What is he doing on my goddam ops channel?"

The driver leaned across Grace and tried to take the mike from Julius but Julius held it fast. The driver clicked off the power on the comms unit.

"Don't!" Julius protested, wild-eyed.

"Buddy," the driver said, "I don't know what your problem is, but you're pissing off the C.O. Give me back that mike or I'm gonna have to put your head through my windshield." He reached for the mike. Grace pried the mike from Julius and handed it to the driver. Julius reached over and turned the comms unit back on.

"Anything, Reggie?" the Captain's voice crackled over the speaker.

"Negative, Cap'n."

"Location?"

"Two almost three clicks past the crest. Nothing to report."

"Somebody tell that fuckin' priest that I want his ass in front of my Humvee two seconds after we make waypoint. You got that?"

"Roger that, Cap'n," the driver said into the mike.

The driver gave Julius a sideways look. Julius looked out the window. Tears streamed silently down his cheeks as Grace tried to rub his shoulder, but he twisted away.

Salt Lake City, Utah

Uriel sat across from his friend and sipped at his coffee. "Seriously hoping these guys make a better pastrami on rye than they do a cup of coffee. Dishwater—we might as well be in London."

"Told you not to order the coffee. And quit looking around, you'll just get more depressed," Azrael said. "Of course," he continued, yo-yoing his teabag in a cup of lukewarm water, "they can't make tea, either. London, they know how to make a cup of tea." He sighed.

"Tell me again why we came here?" Uriel asked, squinting at the faux animal heads on the wall.

"Mostly because we don't know how to use that Temple transporter thing to get our asses back to Manhattan for a decent cup of regular coffee, mostly. So since we aren't sitting at Stage Deli, just suck it up and relax for once." Uriel grunted and tried to drink his coffee, almost touching the mug to his lips before losing his nerve. Azrael continued, "You've been spending a lot of time with Mr. Parnell, Uriel. Must've learned some modicum of tolerance, seeing as you haven't put one of your knives in his spleen yet."

Uriel gave a short, guttural chuckle. "Came close a few dozen times, Azrael. Damn close."

"So what stopped you this time? As I remember, you put

the man down a couple times in the past without a moment's hesitation."

"Different circumstances," Uriel explained. "I'm hoping he's still got a part to play in this. On our side, whatever that means."

"Maybe. But even if he does, Uriel, you and I know there's a better than even chance he'll fuck it up."

"True. That's why I've kept him close. It's a work in progress." He managed to get the mug to his lips and took a drink. He shook his head. "Damn. Anyways, you know why I'm here, obviously. Why are you here? Just to buy me lunch?"

"Who said anything about me buying?" Azrael said. The sandwiches arrived.

"No mustard," Uriel commented. "At least in London, they have mustard."

"Yeah, but they don't have pastrami," Azrael said. "I'll get us some mustard." He flagged down the waiter. Eventually, mustard was delivered.

"Sandwich's cold now, Azrael," Uriel said, finally biting into his.

"I may have to borrow one of your knives unless you quit *kvetching* about my restaurant," Azrael said. "We're in Salt Lake City, Uriel. Keep that in mind." He ate. "You know, Uriel," he said, putting down his sandwich. "I had to keep the redheaded lady from getting her neck slashed a couple of days back."

"You did?" Uriel said.

"Indeed I did," Azrael said. "And that priest was with her, her bodyguard. Not this one, the tough one," he said, gesturing towards Temple Square with his french fry.

"The fucked up one, you mean," Uriel said.

"You're no one to judge, now," Azrael said. "We're all victims, you know. Seems to me, Father Julius has done a damn fine job of keeping the lady in existence. Particularly, given the number of forces arrayed against her."

"You're right, Azrael, as usual," Uriel said. "I should give the good Father his due. Had to put a blade in him, you know." Azrael nodded. "He's done well, no denying the man's mettle. Never whines, that one. Though Lord knows he's got good reason to."

"Is he recovered from—from whatever it was that happened to him?"

"Recovered? Don't think he'll ever recover. I never did."

"Not the same thing, Uriel," Azrael said. "You had much longer to fall."

"True," Uriel said, nodding. He ate. "Bad piece of luck, though. Bad enough I had to send him back to save Grace, but then to not move on…he got a raw deal, ending up like that. Raw deal." He looked up at his friend. "Not sure exactly how that happened."

"I can tell you," Azrael said, leaning in conspiratorially "It's important that you know, because it shows just what we're up against in our current situation."

"What do you mean?"

"He," at this Azrael covered his head with his hand as he continued, "did it personally."

"Personally?" Uriel asked, leaning in as well.

Azrael nodded. "And the timing could not have been a coincidence, either. He must've gamed the whole thing, the window was that damn tight. At the exact moment your priest was resetting things for your Grace lady, He interceded with the priest. Had to be some kind of watershed moment in Julius's past, a 'one stroke' kind of deal. Masterful, to be honest. Never seen anything quite like it."

"'One stroke,' eh?" Uriel said. "Couldn't do that on the spur of the moment. Not even Him. Had to be researched, premeditated."

"Exactly," Azrael agreed.

"Damn," Uriel said. "That seals it then. No way anyone else could pull that off—"

"Except Him. Exactly. Nobody else would know the chain

of consequence like that, know the exact intercession.

"No way, not without perspective. It was chaos in that museum, couldn't even get off a throw." Azrael nodded in sympathy. "Damn," Uriel swore. "I was hoping that the ass-hole was just blowing smoke."

"Which asshole?"

"Pauley, Donovan—whatever you want to call him. He said as much in the museum, after the reset. Said he was working for God, that it was God Himself wants Grace excised. Damn."

"He wasn't lying, I'm afraid," Azrael sympathized. "It fits my information, my friend."

"Well, we're pretty much fucked, then, it seems."

"Not necessarily, Uriel. She's not excised yet. Not even dead."

"Yeah, about that." Uriel polished off his old dill and pointed at the spear on the other man's plate. "You gonna eat that?"

"Are you kidding? It would kill me," Azrael said, handing over the pickle. "Be my guest."

"Thanks," Uriel said, taking the pickle from the other man's plate. "If God really wants the girl excised—and we'll get back to that, we need to talk about why that is—can't be He wants her dead, too. Makes no sense."

"No, He doesn't want her dead, Uriel. If He did, she'd be dead. Period."

"'Course. But somebody wants her dead, that's for certain. Besides the attempt you stopped, must have been three or four other pretty good tries at killing the lady just in the last few days."

"Been at least two more attempts since you left her company," Azrael added. "One was an all-out assault on the house she was staying in. Looked like something out of a Clancy novel, I'll tell you."

"Who's trying so hard, then? As far as I know, the poor girl hasn't done much to piss off anyone in a very long time. Except for this afterlife revelation shit—which she went to a great deal of trouble to make right—she's been a good soul. Good enough, anyway."

"You mean, except for murdering a priest, running a dozen cons since she was seventeen, practicing burglary on two continents—"

"Donovan needed to be killed, no points off for that, Azrael—"

"Rigging a few high-stakes motorcycle races, framing those brothers for prison...I'm sure I'm missing something here, give me a minute." Azrael smiled.

Uriel said, "All that doesn't explain what's going on now, none of it."

"No, you're right," Azrael admitted. "I'd hoped when I came into this whole thing that that's all it was, but you're right."

"So who is it then?"

Azrael put his elbows on the table and cradled his chin, looking very weary. "Better to ask who it isn't, Uriel. It isn't anyone or anything from the girl's past. It's everyone else, though."

"What do you mean? Who is everyone else?"

"Not any one person or faction. It's every faction, Uriel. I've been keeping tabs, running down who's behind each of these assaults. Hardly the same group twice."

"Who?"

"Zealots, religious fanatics, splinter groups, lone wolves. It's insane, I tell you. Unprecedented. That guy on the train? Shiite. A pair of militants from a splinter Mormon group in Texas, polygamy sect, just made a go at her on the highway yesterday. Sunni sleeper cell did the attack on the restaurant in Chicago."

"No shit? How does Shia and Sunni both try to kill her? They never move in the same direction, doesn't make sense."

"You wouldn't think so, would you? I mean, what could

they both want to accomplish, right?"

"Right, exactly. And the assault on the house? That sounds like an organization of some kind, not just a lone wolf."

Azrael nodded. "You're right about that. It was a professional assault, ex-military. If your friend Arthur hadn't had the place protected by a squad of Marines, Grace would be dead as a doorknob. No doubt."

"So who could come with something like that?" Uriel asked, polishing off his coffee and signaling the waiter for a refill.

"Militant Baptist sect out of Missouri with help from an Iowa white supremacist militia. Logistical support—assault boats, that sort of thing—came down from British Columbia."

Uriel shook his head in amazement. "What the hell, Azrael? Every religious organization on the planet want my girl dead? How can that be true?"

"Not every one, Uriel. Not the Catholics, of course."

"Of course. They're running the plays for God's excision."

"And not the LDS, not these folk," Azrael said, gesturing expansively at the others in the restaurant. "LDS trying to keep her alive, you know."

"I know. Trying to take her into their protection. Fat chance of that."

Azrael nodded. "Might not have a choice, the way things are going."

"Not going to happen, buddy," Uriel said, shaking his head. "Not her style. But one thing at a time: Why does almost every religious crazy want her dead?"

Azrael stood up and stretched. "Just one, simple reason, my friend: If the girl is dead, she can't be excised. Simple as that. Pay the bill and I'll meet you outside. Gotta go to the bathroom."

Kandahar Province, Afghanistan
"Contact, contact," the comms speaker crackled.

"Oh, fuck," Julius breathed.

"Say location."

"Six hundred yards short of waypoint, just below the ridgeline," Reggie's voice said over the speaker.

"Damn it, I told them," Julius said.

"Single male, leading a donkey."

The driver snorted a laugh. Julius turned crimson and turned to look out the window again.

"Say again, Reg. Is contact armed?"

"Single male, no weapon I can see. Moving to check him out now."

"Negative, Reg. Hold short, we are two minutes from your position. Wait for us. Do not engage."

"Seriously, Cap'n? He's one guy and a fuckin' donkey."

"Hold short, maintain visual. Do not engage."

"Copy that."

The driver chuckled again. "Dude," the driver said, "you got the C.O. good and spooked, sounds like. Bet when he gets a hold of you, gonna tear you a new one, priest or no." He gave Julius a wink.

When Julius and Grace walked to the front of the convoy, they found the SEALs surrounding a young man kneeling in the dirt, hands on the back of his head. His donkey scratched at the dirt nearby.

"Says he's going home," one of the SEALs said, translating. Reggie stood behind him with his weapon at combat ready.

"Where's that?" the C.O. asked.

The translator asked and the kneeling man said in accented English, "Miami Beach."

"Great," the C.O. said. "A real joker. Well, ask him where he's coming from. And I don't want to hear any bullshit." He spat in the dirt.

The translator had a brief exchange with the prisoner. The prisoner spat in the dirt a few inches from the C.O.'s boot, but didn't look up to make eye contact.

"He says he came up from the valley on the other side of this ridge. Says it's the camp for many thousands of *mujahedin*. He says he was just talking with Osama bin Laden. That bin Laden is the leader in the camp and is planning a great war on America."

"Yeah, right. Tell him to keep acting like a smartass and I'll see to it he really can have that conversation. Everybody in this damn country's got an attitude." The C.O. looked up and saw Grace and Julius. He spat again. "Anything?" he asked one of the other SEALs. The sailor finished going through the donkey's saddlebags and shook his head. "Fine. Let the smartass get on his way home. *Assalaam alaikum*, asshole."

As the man moved off down the ridge with his donkey in tow, Julius approached the C.O. with Grace following behind.

The C.O. spat on the ground again and shook his head as Julius stood before him.

"You want to tell me your fuckin' problem, Father Zimmerman?" the CO asked, staring up at Julius.

"No, sir," Julius said.

"Well then, Father, at least tell me what gives you the balls to compromise my mission by fucking with my comms, huh? You want to explain why in fuck you called alert for an ambush on my convoy? Hmm? You want to clarify your reasoning there, Father?"

"I was mistaken, Captain. Sorry."

"Sorry? That's your reason? I want to know why in fuck-all you felt the need to do what you did. Now, Father."

Julius shrugged. "Like I said, Captain, I was mistaken. The situation reminded me of a similar episode and I felt compelled to warn you of what I thought was a possible ambush. I was wrong."

"On what possible fucking basis could you possibly feel that driving along this shitty road in Afghanistan reminded you of singing *a cappella* at your butt fuckin' seminary,

Father? Am I missing something here, Zimmerman?"

Julius sighed.

"Well, Zimmerman?"

Julius reluctantly unbuttoned his right shirt cuff and rolled up his sleeve. He let the CO take a look at the tattoo of a small red seal standing on its hind flippers.

"Ho-ly shit. Well, fuck me," the CO whispered, shaking his head.

Julius rolled down his sleeve and rebuttoned the cuff.

"Won't happen again, sir," Julius said.

"Damn right, Navy," the CO replied, moving off.

Kandahar Province, Afghanistan

The film crew unloaded their equipment from the trucks. The ridge line above them led to a series of sawtoothed mountains, imposing and apparently unscalable. The crew was not excited about the impending climb.

Julius stood a couple of steps away from where the CO stood with his SEAL team, looking up at the ridge.

"No fuckin' way, Cap'n," one of the SEALs said, spitting. "Need technical gear, at least. And some skills. These civvies, with their cameras and shit? Not gonna happen."

Reggie pointed off slightly to the right. "That's where the dude with the donkey was coming down. No way he went over those peaks with that donkey. He didn't have any kind of climbing gear. And I was watching as he came down, while I was waiting for you—he just kinda appeared, right there." He pointed slightly higher.

"Okay," the CO said. "You lead. Backtrack the donkey man's route, let's see where it leads us. Greg, Bill," he said to the other two members of the squad, "you follow five hundred yards behind with the rest, one leading and one rear guard. Stay sharp," he added, nodding to Julius.

The entire group moved slowly up the ridge line, following Reggie's lead.

"Oh, here we go," Reggie said, only two hundred yards up-hill. He stepped to the left and disappeared.

"Where'd you go, Reg?" the CO called on comms from far-ther down the ridge.

"So cool, Cap'n. Slot canyon, hidden behind that big out-cropping. Looks like a dried up river bed, I think."

"What's in front of you?"

"The canyon takes a ninety degree turn twenty yards in-side. Can't see anything past that."

"Hold position. Sounds like a perfect spot for an ambush."

"Sure as hell is, Cap'n," Reggie agreed. "Holding."

Grace trailed Julius as they picked a path upwards along the rocky trail, well behind the SEAL team.

"You okay, Julius?" Grace asked, staring at his sweat-soaked back. Julius gave a tremulous thumbs-up but said nothing. "You remember any of this?" Julius shook his head. She reached forward and slapped him on the backside. "Gonna be okay, Julius," she assured him.

"Yeah, gonna be great," Julius said, stopping to let Grace come up beside him on the narrow trail. "Tell me again why you and I are climbing this fucking ridge instead of flying to Ukraine. The gateway out of this mess is waiting there, right? Not here. So tell me what we're doing in this hell hole. Huh? Tell me that again, Grace."

Grace grabbed onto his belt to help pull herself up over a large rock. "Come on, Julius, you know why."

"No, I don't, Grace."

"I gotta meet this guy, that's why."

"What guy? The guy I killed in a past life?"

"You didn't kill anybody, Julius. Stop it. If saving my butt means setting this poor asshole up for my con, I gotta at least look him in the eye, don't I?"

"I think I killed this guy, Grace. Him and his whole family."

"Shut up, Julius, and just keep moving, okay?"

They came to the entrance of the slot canyon. Julius hesi-tated, shaking his head.

"I'm not going in there," he said. Grace took his hand.

Arthur and Gabriel stepped up, panting. "Are we there yet?" Arthur asked.

"Come on, Julius," Grace said. "It'll be fine. Hold my hand."

"How about you hold my hand?" Gabriel asked. "Looks like a good place to get killed."

Julius nodded and swallowed hard, but let Grace pull him into the narrow defile.

"No problem," Gabriel said. "I'll just hide behind Arthur, then." He pushed Arthur ahead.

When they emerged from the end of the narrow, twisting canyon, they were greeted by the vista of a verdant, broad valley spread below them, stretching along a sparkling blue river. Tall crag-peaked mountains ringed the valley on every side. Grace whistled in amazement, coming to a halt to take in the sight.

"Holy shit, it's Shangri-La," Arthur said, coming up alongside her and scanning the scene below. The CO nodded appreciatively from where he sat on the rocks on the flat escarpment just beyond the slot's exit. He and the other members of his team were surveying the valley with binoculars. Reggie lowered his field glasses.

"Nobody on the ridge lines, nobody above us, Cap'n, as far as I can tell," Reggie said.

"Could be dug in, we'd never see 'em until they opened fire," another member of the team said. The CO nodded again, not taking the binoculars from his face.

"Donkey guy wasn't kiddin'," the CO said. "Several thousand, at least, down there."

"Gotta be more," another SEAL said, drinking from his canteen.

"May I?" Grace asked.

"Greg," the CO said, "give the lady your binocs."

"Be my guest," the big man said, smiling. "Small end go against your eyeballs, ma'am."

"Oh, is that how these things work?" Grace said, taking the

field glasses. She scanned the scene below them. "Lots of women and children. Looks like they're getting ready for a party or something. Do the Taliban have parties?"

"Wedding, I think," the CO said, pointing. "Middle of the village square, there."

Greg suddenly dropped onto one knee and brought up his weapon, pointing past Grace.

"Get outta the way, Ma'am," Greg barked, pushing Grace aside.

The CO dropped his binoculars and looked down the escarpment to the left where Greg was aiming.

"What?" the CO asked as Grace fell onto her face, the binoculars cracking against her forehead.

"Somebody approaching up the trail," Greg said, sighting with his rifle.

"Hey," Grace protested as the CO grabbed her by the back of her shirt and dragged her behind the rock. He stepped over her and knelt, also bringing up his weapon.

"Bill?" the CO asked, keying his neck mic, not taking his eyes off the trail.

"No joy," Bill said over the comm from his position above them on the ridge line. "I'm blocked."

"Shit," the CO said. "Reggie, status?"

"Clear behind," Reggie said over comms.

"Okay," the CO said, "fall back to the canyon, now. Greg, cover, weapons free. Let's go, people," he said, reaching to grab Grace, who had just now sat up and was rubbing blood-stained dirt from her face.

"Oh, hell," Grace said, knocking the CO's arm away. "Quit doing that, asshole." She stood up and shook her head to clear it. She stepped past the CO and headed down the trail. "They're having a wedding down there. You think maybe they're pissed off we didn't RSVP?" She stepped past Greg as well. Greg looked sideways for a moment and tried to knock her back with his elbow without lowering his rifle. Grace knocked his arm up and elbowed him in the ribs, then knocked his weapon aside. "Shit, guys, take it down a notch, will you?" she said, walking down the trail to see who was coming. Julius shook his head as he sat and watched her go.

"Hey, Grace," Gabriel called. "You think that's a good idea?" He looked over at Julius who shrugged. "Don't shoot her," Gabriel said to Greg.

"Gotta admit, it's tempting," Greg said, aiming once again past her as she walked down the narrow trail that snaked beneath the ridge.

Kandahar Province, Afghanistan

Grace stopped when she saw the girl approaching up the trail, head down and laboring up the steep trail.

"Hey!" Grace called, "Are you a good witch or a bad witch?"

The girl stopped and looked up. She shook her head.

"Then you better stop right there and do this," Grace said, raising her hands above her head.

The girl raised her hands and started walking up the trail again.

"Tell her to get on her belly," the CO yelled from behind Grace. The girl stopped at the sound of his voice momentarily, dropping her hands to her sides. She began walking towards them again. "Get back here, ma'am," the CO ordered to Grace. "Get behind me. Greg?"

"*Tawaqquf!*" Greg yelled at the girl, still approaching. "Stop right there!"

The girl shook her head and kept coming closer.

"Cap'n?" Greg asked.

The CO started forward to reach Grace. "If she takes five more steps, take her down."

"Oh, fuck this," Grace said, stepping ahead out of the CO's reach. Grace half slid and half stumbled down the rocky trail towards the approaching girl. "Better do this, sister, or they're gonna shoot your ass." The girl stopped and raised her hands, mimicking Grace. Grace stepped up to her and smiled. The girl, dressed in a bulky dress that reached her ankles, smiled back.

"*Assalaam alaikum,*" the girl said.

"That's what they say just before they detonate," Julius said, coming up from behind. Grace turned and smiled at him.

"She can't be more than fourteen or fifteen," Grace said.

Julius shook his head at that and turned to the girl. "*Assalaam alaikum,*" Julius greeted her. "*Show me your hands,*" he added in Pashto. The girl stretched out her hands to show they were empty. "Pat her down," Julius told Grace.

"I don't think that's—"

"If you don't, then I will, and that won't be considered friendly," Julius said sternly, smiling still but not taking his eyes from the girl's hands.

Grace stepped forward to stand in front of the girl. Grace smiled and shrugged apologetically, then reached out and patted at the girl. The girl felt as thin as a rail under the bulky dress. Grace stopped when she felt the knife in the girl's pocket.

"What's this?" Grace asked, pointing.

The girl withdrew the wicked looking four bladed knife and held it out.

"She's got a knife, Julius," Grace said, stepping back.

"I see that."

"What should I do?" Grace asked, no longer smiling.

"Put it on the ground," Julius said in Pashto, and the girl put the knife carefully on the ground. "Come," he added. He turned and led Grace back up the trail, the girl following.

"Thanks, Julius," Grace said, relieved. "What changed your mind?"

"That idiot was yelling at her in Arabic," Julius said, nodding up the trail to where Greg was still pointing his gun at them. "Just didn't want to see a little girl get nicked because the guy's a moron, that's all."

When they reached the level escarpment, Arthur and Gabriel rejoined them. The CO gestured for the girl to lie on her stomach, which she did. Greg bent to pat her down.

"I already did—" Grace began, then stopped at the glare from the CO. "Thanks for not shooting us," Grace added.

Greg finished patting her down and nodded, and the girl was invited to sit on a convenient rock. The rest stood around as Julius questioned her in Pashto.

"Her name's Hila," Julius said. "She says we are welcome to their valley." Greg snorted, still holding his rifle across his chest at the ready. He spat on the ground.

Julius continued, "She says it was her brother we saw earlier, with the donkey. That there's militia in the area, but none in her valley. No weapons. Only peaceful, god-fearing people who follow the teaching of the Mahdi." The girl sat, smiling demurely.

Grace smiled back at the girl. She's pretty, Grace thought. While she had kind of sad, doe-like eyes, everything else about her seemed tough as wire. "Ask her if she's the one getting married," Grace said.

As Julius finished the question, the girl reddened and giggled briefly, then looked at the ground and shook her head, speaking.

Julius said, "She says she is too young to marry. Two of the villagers are to be married by the Mahdi, and she was sent to invite us."

"What does Mahdi mean?" the CO asked. "Who is this guy?"

Julius asked the girl something and she answered at great length.

"The Mahdi," Julius said, "is the Chosen One. The Messiah, she says."

"Well, fuck me sideways," Grace whispered. "It's started."

"Well, then," the CO said, slinging his weapon on his shoulder. "Tell her to take us to her leader."

Julius translated this to the girl, but she said nothing. Instead, the girl sat, unmoving, seemingly transfixed by something.

"What is it?" Julius asked her. "What's wrong?"

The girl stood up and walked up to Gabriel. Greg started to bring up his rifle as the girl took Gabriel's hand and lifted it, looking at his ring, amazed. She looked up at Gabriel and said something, then dropped to her knees, head bowed.

"O-kay," Gabriel said, taking a step back.

"Don't get any ideas, Gabriel," Grace said, pulling the girl back up standing. "What did she say, Julius?"

"Something about his ring," Julius said.

Gabriel raised his hand with the big Claddagh ring. "This?" Hila nodded, eyes wide.

"She said you are like the Mahdi," Julius said, "that the Mahdi has the very same ring."

"An Afghani with a Claddagh?" Gabriel asked. "I don't think so."

"She insists that it is the same ring, that it is some kind of sign. That she gave the Mahdi this same ring, and now you have it as well."

"Well, where did she get it?" Gabriel asked. Julius asked her in Pashto.

"From the bottom of a well," Julius translated.

"Well that makes no fucking sense at all," Grace said.

Greg looked over at Gabriel's ring. "Hey, Cap'n," Greg said. "He's got the same ring Eli wore."

"No shit?" the Captain said, not looking over. "Let's move, gentlemen."

Kandahar Province, Afghanistan

Grace sat heavily on the rock Hila had been sitting on a few minutes before. She shook her head, thinking.

"Something's not right," Grace said to no one in particular. The others had started to get ready to move off down the path into the valley. Grace looked up at them and shook her head more forcefully. "Hold up. Something's not right." Grace threw a rock that bounced off Greg's helmet. She looked at her husband's ring, then at her husband.

"What is it, hon?" Gabriel asked. "Let's go see this guy. That's what we came here for, right?"

"Yeah, it is," Grace said. "But why does he have your ring?"

"Hell, I don't know, Grace," Gabriel said. "You tell me."

"I don't know, Gabe. I don't know. But it doesn't feel like it's right, that's all. This guy's a shill, a player in this con we're running. He's not supposed to have your ring."

"Well, hon, come on," Gabriel said., "It's just a ring."

"No, Gabe, I told you," Grace said, reddening but keeping her voice soft. "It's not just a ring."

Gabriel sat down near Grace.

"Are we going or not?" the CO asked.

"Hang on," Grace said. "This is important."

"Yeah?" the CO said. "Well, my orders say that escorting this stupid film crew into that valley is pretty important. We need to move out."

"That ring," Grace said, pointing, "is a problem. That ring goes down there," she said, jerking her thumb over her shoulder at the valley below, "and we got a problem. We all have a problem."

"Lady, you are making no fucking sense," the CO said.

"Julius, ask her about finding the ring in a well."

Julius asked and got a long story in return. When Hila stopped talking, Julius raised his eyebrows and said, "Hunh."

"Hunh, what?" Grace asked.

Julius took a deep breath and sighed. "Well, Hila says her home is a few miles east of here. That the Mahdi came to her home—as a pilgrim, I think she said, I'm not sure of the word she used, maybe 'beggar'—and warned her that her house was going to be blown up the next day. That when she drew water from her well to give to the Mahdi, the ring was in the bucket. That night, a truck load of *mujadin* came to their house, so she ran away. The next day, their house was destroyed, just as the Mahdi predicted. It was then that she realized that he wasn't just a pilgrim, that he was Mahdi. So she gave him the ring."

"Hold it," the CO said, interested in spite of himself. "What does she mean, her house was destroyed?"

Julius asked Hila the question and listened as she spoke, watching her trace two fingers in an arc from above her head down to her other hand, and then saying, "Boom."

"Predator strike," Glen said. The CO nodded.

"How'd this Mahdi dude know in advance about a drone kill?" Glen asked.

"Good question," the CO said. "And who was the HVT? They don't pull the trigger on those things for *mujahedin* regulars."

"She says her family were all killed," Julius said. "Just her and her brother got away."

"Because this Mahdi guy warned them," the CO said. "Something's not right."

"That's what she said," Glenn said, nodding at Grace.

"Shut up, Glen," the CO said, scratching his chin. "I don't care about that shit. That Predator is tasked from Nevada, stateside. No way some dumbshit pilgrim knows where a strike is targeted. Hell, those pilots in Vegas don't even know until the fucking President tells them to pull the trigger on some target they've had under surveillance for days, sometimes weeks. And we should've heard about it right after. We should've gotten orders to check the kill zone immediately, to do BDA and collect specimens. We're the only SpecOps in this whole sector."

"What's BDA?" Arthur asked. "What specimens?"

"Bomb damage assessment," Julius answered. "Take pictures, collect DNA, to see if they got the target they were after."

They were all silent for a bit, considering this. Julius asked Hila more questions. Hila put her fingers to her lips, shaking her head.

"What's she saying?" Grace asked.

Julius turned to Grace, puzzled. "I didn't get it the first

time around, but now I'm sure of it. She says that this guy—the pilgrim, the Mahdi, whatever—doesn't speak." He shrugged.

"What do you mean?" Grace asked.

"He's a mute," Julius said.

"You have got to be shittin' me," Grace said, wide-eyed. "The dude we're setting up to be our shill, the key player in this whole damn con—can't talk?" Julius nodded. Grace slapped her forehead. "Oh, fuck me sideways," she added. Glenn laughed, then stopped at the look he got from Grace.

There was silence again. Grace stood up and looked out over the valley. She picked up a rock and threw it over the cliff at the village far below.

"Did you know?" Grace asked Arthur.

"Know what?"

"That our guy can't talk," Grace said, reddening. "Don't play stupid with me, Arthur."

"Don't yell at me, Grace," Arthur said. "Yeah, I knew. Gabriel knows, too. I told him."

Grace wheeled on her husband, who took a step back, arms raised.

"It's okay," Gabriel said. "We got it covered. Don't worry, hon."

"Don't worry? Are you serious?"

Grace turned back to face the group. She pointed at Gabriel. "You can't go down there, Gabe. This is fucked up."

"You say that because he's got a stupid Claddagh ring?" Gabriel asked. "Come on, hon. Mine isn't the only one. We talked about this."

"No—this is a problem. It'll be bad," Grace said.

"Is it like crossing the streams, Professor Venkman? That kind of bad?" Arthur asked, smiling. "All life as we know it will stop instantaneously and every molecule in our bodies will explode at the speed of light."

"Total protonic reversal!" Glen added, smiling.

"Shut up, Glen," the CO commanded.

"Shut up, Glen," Grace echoed. "I'm serious. The two rings, in the same place--not good. Not good," she repeated, shaking her head as she paced.

"Why, Grace?" Gabriel asked.

"I don't know. And now you tell me this guy is deaf and dumb? How can that be right? How are we going to pull off a con like this when my shill can't talk? Huh? How do we pull that off?"

"I don't know, hon," Gabriel said. "He's not deaf, though. Just dumb." He smiled at her.

"Fuck me," Grace said. She sat down again. She sat, thinking. "You've gotta fix this, Gabe,"

"What do you mean?" Gabe asked.

"I mean I need you to make this work, that's what I mean," Grace said, standing up again in front of her husband, hands on hips. She pointed back up the trail the way they had come. "You and F-troop here," she said, nodding at Glen and the CO, "need to find out why your ring got into this girl's well."

"What?" Gabriel said. "Who cares? He's got it."

"Pretty sure I know," Glen said. "Eli brought it in-country, but it wasn't with his things after he was KIA. Must've tossed it into the well at some point, maybe while on patrol."

"Why would he do that?" Gabriel asked.

"I don't know," Grace said. "And I don't like it. Gabriel, you need to fix this. Take Artie with you."

"What?" Gabriel and Arthur both asked.

"I'm not leaving you here," Gabriel said. "That's nuts."

"Don't give me attitude, Gabe. I've got enough *tsuris*," Grace said. "These guys will give you two a lift back."

"Listen, lady, you're not the one giving—" the CO started.

"No, you listen," Grace said, rounding on the captain. "You said yourself you need to go check it out. So go check it out, and take these two back with you."

"My orders are—"

"Yeah, I know. To get the crew to the valley. Well, there it is. I think we can find our way from here, Captain. Mission accomplished."

"You don't think I should go with you, hon?" Gabriel asked. "You don't know what you're walking into down there."

"Julius will have my back, Gabe," Grace said, nodding at Zimmerman. "Don't worry about me. I need you and Arthur to fix this. The whole thing is fucked. Which means I'm fucked. You need to make this work. The ring, the con—the whole game depends on it. Fix it."

"Fix it how?" Gabriel asked.

"I don't know, hon," Grace said, standing on tiptoe and kissing her husband one last time. "But I know you will. You always do." She turned to Arthur. "You, too, Artie. Don't screw this up."

"What, no kiss?" Arthur asked.

CHAPTER 11

Kandahar Province, Afghanistan

Arthur, Gabriel, and the SEAL team passed the rest of the film crew heading up the mountain trail as they headed back down to the road. Then they loaded into the trucks and headed off to find the girl's home—or what was left of it.

Hila and Grace led the rest of the crew down the steep trail to the valley. As they walked, Julius translated as the two women questioned one another. Hila wanted to know why Grace had come, how she had heard of the Mahdi, why a film crew was shooting a documentary about the man. She seemed unsurprised, despite Grace's vague responses, assuming that the world would want to know about the arrival of the new Savior. Grace, however, pressed the girl for details about the Mahdi, and about life in the valley. Despite half an hour of questioning as they descended the trail, Grace was still unsatisfied.

"I don't get it, Julius," Grace said. "Ask her again."

"Sorry, Grace," Julius said. "She keeps saying the same thing, but I'm not really getting it. He can't speak, I'm sure of that much. Not that he doesn't speak—he can't. He's a mute."

"But she says she understands him when he talks."

"She's not saying he talks. It's a different word—that's the part I'm not getting. She says he—I don't know, it's the same word as 'think' or 'understands.'" Julius shook his head. "I'm not getting it. Sorry. My Pashto is more than a little rusty."

Grace snorted. They rounded yet another switchback on the trail and were greeted by a vista of the village spread out over the valley floor, now only a few hundred feet beneath them. Grace swept an arm across the scene below. "And how do these people eat? There's hardly more than patchwork gardens down there. And no poppies. How do all these thousands of people survive?"

Julius asked the question to Hila again, and again the girl replied with a satisfied smile, nodding to the bustling village below.

Julius said, "Same thing, Grace. She says the Mahdi provides for all. That no one is hungry."

"Sounds like a damn cult."

"Even cults need food, though. All those people gotta eat."

"Ask her where the food comes from," Grace said.

Hila gestured with raised palms to the sky, then smiled as she pointed at the valley floor, speaking to Julius. After the exchange, Julius shrugged and said, "From—"

"The Mahdi," Grace said, kicking at the rocky trail. "Yeah, I got it." They reached the point where the trail landed on the floor of the valley. "Let's go meet this guy."

Kandahar Province, Afghanistan

Grace, Hila, and Julius led the dozen members of the film crew down off the trail and onto the path that became the main dirt road of the village. Bogart hung back, discussing camera angles with his cinematographer . One of the cameramen moved back up the trail to film their arrival. They paused as Bacall positioned Hila for an interview, framed by the village stretching before them. Neither one understood a word the other was saying as they pretended to converse for the camera. Then they continued on into the village.

Julius would've been more anxious about their arrival had Hila not been so obviously happy to lead them onward. The young girl certainly appeared without guile as she pointed out the sights around them. The street was lined with tiny neat huts on either side, each with a well tended garden in front.

"Where is everybody?" Bacall asked. "We need some locals waving colorful scarves, people."

Julius conferred with Hila, who encouraged them onward. "At the wedding, she says," Julius explained. "She says we should hurry, we don't want to miss it."

Bogart agreed and sent a cameraman running ahead.

They arrived to find the entire population of the village, thousands and thousands of people of all ages, children running about, thronging the central square. Everyone smiled and urged them on, the dirt road becoming a well-manicured path leading through a wide gap in the crowd to a raised central stage. As they approached, they could see the young wedding couple on stage, dressed in ornate clothing beneath an arbor, waving to them. Grace and Hila waved back as they approached.

A tall, shaven-headed man appeared from behind the couple and beamed down at them. He was dressed in a long white robe; a traditional enough outfit, but striking nonetheless.

"He's a white guy," Bacall said. "Hell, he looks like a Brit."

"No shit," Grace said, staring up at the man.

"Lawrence of Arabia," Bogart said from just behind them.

"Peter O'Toole had hair," Julius said.

They stopped as Hila abruptly dropped to her knees and pressed her forehead to the ground. The Mahdi gestured for her to rise and she did so, leading the new arrivals to an open area reserved for them before the stage.

Grace looked around at the crowd, now quieting as all stared at the stage. Grace watched as the Mahdi smiled in welcome to them, then took up a position to officiate the wedding. It was silent, though as she watched those around her, it was obvious that the ceremony had begun.

"What the hell?" Grace asked Julius next to her. "Is he saying anything? Do you hear anything?" Julius shook his head, watching the ceremony. "Is it like a pantomime or something? Are Moslem weddings just done with gestures?"

"Uh, I don't think so," Julius said, looking around.

"Well, this sucks," Bacall said. "What the hell kind of ceremony are they doing? If they're not going to say anything, can't they have some music or something? This is the most depressing wedding I've ever seen."

The bride and groom began speaking in turn, each looking between their betrothed and the Mahdi as they completed their lines.

"Well, at least they talk," Bacall said. "Cute couple. We'll need to interview them, after," she said to her husband. Bogart nodded.

The Mahdi raised his hands over the heads of the bride and groom.

"Holy shit!" Bogart said, clapping his hands to the sides of his head.

The crowd broke into loud cheering, applauding enthusiastically as the now husband and wife took each other's hand and turned to face the crowd, smiling.

"Did you just hear that, too?" Julius asked of Bogart, confused.

All at once, the crowd threw vollies of white flowers at the stage, clouds of white petals arcing over their heads as Julius turned to Grace, asking, "Did you hear him? I thought I could hear him, in my head. Did you hear that, Grace?" He stared at her as hundreds of tiny white petals rained down all about them. "Grace?"

Grace's eyes rolled into the back of her head and she collapsed on the ground at Julius's feet.

Grace was awake, but she couldn't move. She didn't know why, or where she was lying.

She tried to speak, but something was in her mouth, between her teeth. Grace fought to sit up, but a hand pushed her head back gently.

"A bheith go fóill, beag amháin,"
a woman's voice said.

Grace tried to shake her head as it was being restrained, a leather strap across her forehead. She couldn't see the people doing this to her, didn't know what they were doing, all she could see was the stained ceiling tiles and then —

White.

Grace tried to open her eyes, didn't know if they were open or closed. She saw snowflakes, thousands of snowflakes, little points of white, shining white and leaving pearly streaks behind as they fell from above, white points of light drifting down onto her face.

Grace had never seen snow before. She tried to stick out her tongue, to feel the snow fall on her tongue, cold and wet, but all she could taste was blood.

Salt Lake City, Utah

When Uriel came out of the restaurant, he found Azrael holding the door of a taxi open for him. Uriel got in.

"Where to, gentlemen?" the taxi driver asked after Uriel closed the door.

"Depends," Azrael said. "What is the fare to Granite Mountain, young man?"

"Granite Mountain? Almost an hour, give or take. I can get you there for fifty bucks. Why? Nothing to see out there."

Azrael turned to his friend next to him in the back seat. "You have fifty dollars?"

"Even enough for a tip if we get there alive," Uriel assured him.

"There you go, driver," Azrael said. "Even a tip if you get us there in one piece."

The driver put the car in gear, shaking his head at them in the mirror. "I'll get you there, gentlemen. Not sure what you'll be doing once you get there."

After a pleasant half hour drive out of the city, during which Azrael and Uriel caught up on a century's activities since they had last crossed paths, the taxi deposited the two in a nondescript parking lot on the side of the mountain. The taxi driver, like any good Mormon, felt guilty about taking Uriel's money to leave them in the middle of nowhere with no prospect of getting back to town. Uriel shared the man's concern as, at Azrael's cheery urging, he handed over the fare with the promised tip. The taxi made off with the driver shaking his head as he watched the two recede in his mirror.

"We're on the side of a mountain, Azrael," Uriel noted, looking about at the wilderness.

"Indeed," Azrael said, striking the rough terrain with his cane as he led off along an unmarked trail. "This way, my friend."

"We're way too old to go hiking up a mountain," Uriel protested as he followed. "You should know that, old man."

"It's not far, don't worry," Azrael reassured him.

Not more than five minutes later, the trail rounded a rocky outcropping to reveal the hewn face of the mountain, inset with three giant cement arches framing large, blast-proof steel doors. Azrael stopped, breathing heavily as he leaned on his cane with both hands. He nodded to the scene in front of them, too winded to speak.

"Holy shit," Uriel said, coming up behind and seeing the huge edifice cut into the side of the mountain. "What is this, a missile silo?"

"No, not government," Azrael huffed, finally regaining his wind. "Mormons, brother. You're looking at the Granite Mountain Records Vault of the LDS Church."

"Records Vault? Looks like something designed to survive a nuclear apocalypse," Uriel said, shaking his head in amazement.

"Exactly," Azrael said. "Come on."

"We going to take the tour?"

"The Jewish version, yes."

Uriel followed the little old man along a side trail, mostly downhill, Uriel was relieved to find. They came to a small, nondescript door set into the stone, well away from the larger entrance. Uriel watched as Azrael fished inside his shirt and came out with an identity card on a lanyard. He held the card against a plate set in the rock. The door opened with a click. Uriel followed his friend inside.

"Been here before, I guess," Uriel said.

"Dozens of times. Took the tour so many times I could give it myself."

"Not meaning 'the Jewish version.' "

"No. This is my own special tour, just for you." He led Uriel along a long tunnel, smoothly cut into the mountain, lit by reflected light from the ceiling. It was pleasantly cool compared to the outside.

"You want to tell me what this place really is?" Uriel asked, his voice rumbling with a gentle echo from the passageway.

"That part, up front," Azrael said, gesturing toward the main entrance to their right, "houses a massive data storage facility, just as advertised. The Mormons have amassed genealogical records going back more than a century, the most complete and accurate database of the earth's souls ever achieved."

"Well, that's a damn scary concept," Uriel said, looking about. The passageway had opened onto a large concourse with other tunnels going off in every direction. Dozens of people, dressed in black slacks and white shirts, were walking purposefully, some in pairs conversing, most singly. As they watched, the occasional electric cart or truck hummed past along the wider corridors. "Nobody gonna give us a hard time about wandering about?"

"I got my pass," Azrael said, smiling as he showed off his lanyard, imprinted with 'Church of the Latter-Day Saints.' "You should probably employ your trick of not being noticed, Uriel. They don't see many 'people of color' in this facility."

"Not surprised. What's the next stop on this Jew tour?" Uriel asked.

"This way," Azrael said, pulling his friend by the elbow as they crossed the busy concourse. He smiled at the occasional passer-by that made eye contact. "Behind us, like I was saying, are the facilities to accumulate and catalogue the genealogical data. Amazing facility, makes the server farms at Google look modest in comparison. And always expanding, faster than an Arizona suburb. They're like ants in this mountain.

"You're damn right about how scary the concept is, Uriel," Azrael continued, leading down various passageways as he spoke, the number of people around them dwindling noticeably as they walked. "Ostensibly, the idea is to track good Mormons into the afterlife, or some such. Except the truth is that they're amassing data on everyone, not just Mormons."

"I remember hearing about that," Uriel said, following the other man around a corner into yet another passageway, this one sloping gently downward. "A Jewish organization found out that the Mormons were doing something with the records of Holocaust victims or some such."

"Yes, yes, exactly. That was a significant security breach, that. The Church was extremely upset and embarrassed by the leak, had to come up with a song and dance about post-mortem baptisms—complete crock of shit, of course, but with just enough truth to conceal what they're really up to."

"Which is what, exactly?"

"Which is this," Azrael announced, using his card to unlock a metal door which slid upwards silently into a slot in the rocky ceiling.

Salt Lake City, Utah

For a moment, Uriel couldn't see anything. The light was dazzling after the relative gloom of the underground passages. He blinked in the bright sunshine, realizing that he was looking at the sky outside. Below them stretched a bowl-shaped valley, verdant and idyllic, a small river running through the middle before disappearing through a defile in the mountains some miles away.

Azrael took Uriel by the arm and walked him out onto the broad stone balcony that overlooked the valley. Uriel looked about, taking in the scene. He walked along the railing as the balcony followed the face of the mountain from which they had emerged. Azrael followed.

"It's a town," Uriel said, nodding at the scene below. "No industry, but lots of housing from the looks of it. School?" he asked, pointing to a large building in the valley below them with a track adjacent. Azrael nodded. Uriel scanned the scene below him. There were hundreds of people moving about, small as ants far below. The roads were narrow and winding, Uriel noticed, with people walking or riding bicycles. No cars or trucks, though. "Strange," Uriel commented. "No roads in or out. Just the river."

"You are a perceptive man, my friend." Azrael nodded, pointing at the high mountains ranging in a circle around the valley.

"Huh," Uriel said, noticing. He scanned the small town below again. "Where's the church? Don't see a steeple."

"Synagogues don't have steeples, Uriel," Azrael said.

Uriel turned from the railing to face his friend. He was speechless for a brief moment, taking in this last statement.

"You are fucking kidding me. They weren't just baptizing six million dead Jews, is that what you're saying? They're..." Uriel let the last part hang in the air, unsaid.

Azrael nodded, his expansive gesture taking in the people in the valley below.

Uriel looked at the town again, shaking his head. "Holy shit."

"We should go," Azrael said, heading back through the door to the underground passage into the mountain.

Back inside, Azrael moved along the passage at a more rapid pace than Uriel would've thought possible for such an elderly man.

"Why?" Uriel asked, Azrael's cane clicking on the smooth floor as they walked back up the passageway.

"This isn't a good place to discuss that," Azrael said. "This way." He turned them down a different passage from whence they had come. "I'm hoping this works."

"Hoping what works?" Uriel asked, keeping up with the little man's quick strides.

"I've got an idea for a shortcut back," Azrael explained. "Maybe."

"Okay. But listen, that wasn't no six million back there in that little town," Uriel said.

"No, there's about three thousand currently, I believe. It varies."

"Why does it vary?"

"Because they don't stay here. It's just temporary, to acclimate them following their return. One assumes the whole process to be a bit of a shock, psychologically at least."

"Yeah, I'd guess that's true. Out of the oven, into the—"

"You are shameless, Uriel," Azrael admonished.

"Yeah, whatever. So where do they go after they get used to the idea that Hitler's dead and all's right in the world?"

"Everywhere. The Church relocates them, families reunited whenever they can, all over the world. Some back to Europe, to their ancestral homes, if the returnees really want it. Most don't, of course. You understand."

"Sure as hell do," Uriel agreed. "Not like they can just move back into their old place. No sense going back there. Poland? I think not. Not like that worked out for them after the war. Or like they could exact revenge on the vermin that helped get them shipped off to the camps in the first place. A couple generations too late."

"Yeah, I'm pretty sure that sort of thing is discouraged by the Church authorities," Azrael said. "Here we are, I think. Hope this card works on this one." Azrael opened the door with his pass, smiling with his success. They entered a large room, identical to the baptismal fount room in the Temple.

"All right, Uriel," Azrael said, taking his hand. "Let's see if I understand how this thing works."

Azrael led Uriel around the large, circular fount twice clockwise, then back a half-circuit before stepping out through the door. When they exited, they were back in the sunshine of Temple Square in downtown Salt Lake City.

"Wow, I'm impressed," Uriel said. "Damn witchcraft saved us taxi fare."

Kandahar Province, Afghanistan

Grace held her eyes tight shut, listening. Not just listening —something else, as well. She could hear Julius's voice, his soft timbre, inflected in question. But the answer came not to her ears, but in her head. The sensation of a man's voice, the faintest tang of a brogue nearly lost in decades spent traveling the Middle East, the sound of an easy, open laugh— but not sound. Something else, more immediate, more intimate, coming not from without, but arriving directly in her mind. She knew this feeling very well.

Grace sat up, too fast, and nearly swooned. Julius caught her by the shoulders before she fell off the small cot upon which she lay.

"Hey, Grace," Julius said. "Slow down there. You okay now?"

Grace said nothing but stared at the man sitting on a low stool across from her. The Mahdi was dressed in a more casual caftan now, undyed and open at the throat showing a tan chest. He smiled at her.

"*Hello.*"

Grace shook her head. She turned to Julius who was seated at the foot of the cot. "You can hear him, right?" Grace asked Julius.

Julius nodded.

Grace looked at the other man. "I know what you're doing," Grace said to him. The other man inclined his head slightly, questioning. He appeared to be in his late thirties, maybe early forties. It was hard to tell, since his head was shaved, his only facial hair reddish blonde eyebrows above a tanned, lined face. "Can you talk?" Grace asked him.

The Mahdi shook his head.

"Great." Grace stood unsteadily, refusing Julius's steadying hand. She paced about the small hut, examining several small trinkets lying about. "Can you read my thoughts?" Grace thought inwardly, but there was no reply. "Huh," she said aloud. She stood before the Mahdi again. "You can't read thoughts, then? Just project?"

"*So it seems.*" The man smiled at her.

"Everywhere? Do you ever leave this valley?" Grace asked.

"*Just here.*"

Grace nodded.

"What, Grace?" Julius asked. "What's going on?"

Grace sat back down on the cot and smiled. "Impressive," she said.

"What's impressive?" Julius asked.

"I know how he does it," Grace explained. "It's a neat little trick. But I'm the one who invented it, Gabriel and I."

"What did you invent?" Julius asked.

"The technology he's using to project his thoughts. Only we just had the sensing side of things back then, not the projecting. Makes sense though, it's not that much of a jump. I'm sure Parnell's government project had something to do with it, too."

"You lost me, Grace."

Grace ignored him. "Do you know Parnell?" Grace asked the Mahdi. The Mahdi shook his head. "Are you Mormon?" Again, he shook his head.

"Seriously, Grace?" Julius said. "Does he look Mormon?"

"Shut up, Julius," Grace said, tempering her words with a pat on his knee. "How then?" she asked the Mahdi.

The man shrugged. *"It just is."*

"No, it isn't 'just is.' It's a machine, a technology. You didn't set it up?" The man shook his head. Grace sat quietly, thinking, elbows on knees and finger tapping her lips. Sounds of music and laughter came from outside.

"We're missing the party," Julius said.

The Mahdi smiled and nodded.

"This can work," Grace announced, standing. She smiled at Julius and the Mahdi. "We should celebrate."

Purgatory

Elliot sat in the control room, staring at the monitors. He was fascinated with this new surveillance, now provided by the quantum entanglement phenomenon. Despite a professional lifetime in the field of satellite imaging and surveillance, he had never seen anything like this. At will, he was able to swoop his point of view from miles above the valley to shoe-top level, swing his vantage point in every conceivable direction, peek into windows or stare down alleyways. Even more remarkably, he had selective audio as well, seemingly tied to his visual point of view. He gawked at the images, hypnotized, listened to conversations in the village square, mingled invisibly with the villagers moving about the fields.

"This is fucking unbelievable," Elliot said aloud.

Behind him, Gödel chewed a hangnail while he sat in the semidarkness. "*Das Auge des Gottes, wirklich*," Godel muttered.

"What's that, Kurt?" Elliot asked, not taking his eyes off the screens.

"*Ja*, fuckin' unbelievable," Gödel said.

"Looks like they're having a wedding," Elliot said, pointing at the screen.

Gödel spat a piece of fingernail onto the floor.

"Hey, you know what we should do?" Elliot asked, spinning his chair to look back at Gödel for a moment. "Arthur says we're supposed to be making this guy into the Second Coming, right? The Messiah? That's what this is all about, right?"

Gödel studied his fingernails, wondering how this idiot was supposed to help him work out his problem with quantum entanglement theory.

"Well, if that's the idea, we should go all 'Cana' on this, you get me? Have the dude wave his hands over some barrels of water, and that materials guy—what's his name?—whatever, we have him do some kind of bioenzymatic miracle and replace the water with a great Chardonnay. How cool would that be, right? Am I right?" He spun his chair again to see if Gödel was appreciating his idea. The mathematician was now gnawing on his thumbnail. "You don't think that's a great idea?"

Gödel looked up at the other man and shook his head. "*Nein*, I do not. I think they are Moslems, *ja*? They don't drink the spirits." Idiot, Gödel didn't say aloud.

"You're kidding? Really, no alcohol of any kind at a wedding? How do they dispel the feeling of looming disappointment? Not enough water in that whole valley to drown that out, am I right? Am I right?" He winked at Gödel, who was not making eye contact.

The mathematician looked up, staring. "What did you say?" Gödel asked.

"Not enough water in—"

"*Ja, ja, ja!*" Gödel said, pounding his hands on the table. "*Das ist est! Du bist win genie!*"

"What? I'm a genie? What are you talking about there, Kurt?"

"Not genie, you idiot, '*genie.*' German. You are genius!"

"I am?" Gödel nodded madly. "How so?"

"I need paper and pencil. Right now, I need to write." Elliot didn't move. "Now! I need to write this!"

"There's no paper and pencil, *herr Doktor*. Here, use my laptop," Elliot recommended.

"No, no , no," Gödel protested, shaking his head as he paced in circles around the table. "Blackboard, then."

"There's a whiteboard back in the conference room," Elliot said.

"Take me!"

"We just came from there, it's just down the hall."

Gödel grabbed the other man's arm and dragged him out of his chair. "We go."

Elliot sat at the conference table and watched the mathematician's back as the other man rapidly scrawled unintelligibly on the whiteboard. Occasionally, Gödel would curse and wipe away whole sections with his shirtsleeve.

"Nobody can read that, you know," Elliot offered. Gödel ignored him. "At least tell me why I'm a genius, Kurt. I mean, it was my idea, right?"

Gödel wrote, erased, wrote more, circled one part and put a huge question mark next to it, then shook his head and dropped into the chair next to Elliot. He reached over and grabbed Elliot's hand, shaking it vigorously.

"Genius," Gödel assured him.

"Yeah, I know. Tell me again, exactly, why I'm a genius?"

"The water, you said. 'Not enough water.' Brilliant. The ring, it was in the water..."

"It was thrown in the Potomac River, they said," Elliot said.

"*Ja*, thrown in river—but never landed in river. In a different time, different ring. Somebody else took the ring. Somebody throws it into the well in Afghanistan. Water, time; time, water. It is the same, yes?"

"I'm sorry?"

"Of course it is. Just the same. But a different time."

"Hold it, Kurt, buddy, you're kinda losing me there," Elliot said, but Gödel rambled emphatically on, ignoring him.

"It is just topology—a Noether ring. The water is in the well, not enough in the valley; no, there couldn't ever be enough water to bring the ring to our valley, but there is enough time, you see? We have the discontinuity in time, all the time we need, so there is enough water, you see? With enough time, the water is enough. A mechanism must be found. It is all one. A Noether ring. You are truly genius, my friend, Elliot." He grabbed Elliot by the shoulders and shook him, smiling like an idiot.

"Right. Of course I am. But what do you think about the wine idea?"

"*Ja, ja*, they must have wine. We must!" They left to find Arthur.

Purgatory

Gödel sat smiling and scribbling on a pad of paper he had finally found. He ignored the discussion going on between Elliot and the woman in charge of materials management.

"I don't care, Libby," Elliot was saying. "Just get a couple of barrels of Chardonnay to appear right there, in the middle of the village square."

"I can't materialize shit from thin air, Elliot," Libby said.

"I'm not Scotty and this tech isn't a fucking Star Trek transporter, asshole. It's impossible."

"Quit whining, Scotty" Elliot continued. "Then change something that's already down there into Chardonnay, I don't care. This is important."

"Is it? Is it really?"

"Yes, it is. So fire up your little autonomous chembots and do a little 'water into wine' action, *capisce?*"

"It's not enough that I gotta feed a few thousand mouths down there every day? That's not good enough for you?"

"Come on," Elliot cajoled. "It's a wedding. Be a sport."

The woman rolled her eyes. "I'll see what I can do." She left and Elliot plopped down in the chair next to Gödel.

"You found some paper, huh?" Elliot asked the mathematician.

"*Ja*, and pencils. Now I can really work."

"So, did you figure it out? Or are we all totally screwed?"

"No, not screwed. It's good. All good."

"Glad to hear it," Elliot said, starting to get up.

"You see, it is like you said, like I was telling you. The ring was in the well. In the fullness of time, someone, at some point has put the ring in the well. It must happen."

"It must? Why?"

"I told you, it is in the mathematics. It is topology, Elliot. Time is like water, they describe a Noetherian ring. The Krull dimension need not be finite, not for a Noetherian ring. So it is that the ring must be in the well."

Elliot stared at the other man, dumbfounded. "Why did the ring get into the well?"

Gödel rolled his eyes. He said, "Because it has, that is why."

"Oh. Like that makes any fucking sense."

"It does make any fucking sense. You can see yourself," he said, gesturing to the screens above them.

"Math, *herr* Gödel," Elliott said, rising from his chair, "can be pretty crazy."

"*Ja*," Gödel agreed, "but always beautiful, Elliot."

Kandahar Province, Afghanistan

The Mahdi, it turned out, was a helluva dancer. The music was provided by a band of villagers that shifted seismically between traditional Arabic wedding tunes and Irish folk music. The Mahdi was thrilled to have a partner in Grace that knew all the old Irish folk dances and was willing to learn the Arabic ones. Breathless, they joined Julius at the head table. He clapped as they approached.

"Nice," Julius said, smiling. "I thought you two were going to dance yourselves to exhaustion."

"Your friend is quite a dancer," the Mahdi intoned, collapsing into a chair next to Julius.

Grace dropped into the chair on the other side of Julius, only mildly out of breath and smiling.

Julius beamed at her, realizing that this was the first genuine smile he had seen from her since New York. He raised his glass in toast.

"What are you drinking?" Grace asked. "I need some."

"The same thing everyone is drinking, Grace," Julius said. "Water."

"Water? At a wedding?"

"A Moslem wedding."

Grace took the glass from Julius and drank down half, making a face. "Warm water! You can't call this refreshment, Moslem or whatever." She gestured to the wedding couple who were smiling at them from the other side of the table. "Come on, Mahdi! It's the happiest day in their lives. You can't expect them to get through this on water, can you?" Mahdi looked at her, not understanding.

"Perhaps you brought something stronger with your film crew?"

"I'm sure they did," Julius said, "but good luck getting them to share any."

Grace leaned across Julius to confront the Mahdi. "You're their leader, Mahdi-san. And our host." She banged her fist on the table in front of him. "Drinks!" She gestured around the table at the other guests, all nodding and smiling back at her. "Your guests—your flock—need drinks!"

The Mahdi looked sheepish and made a half shrug.

Grace wouldn't back down. "We've got all this food," she said, gesturing at the table, "we've got music. No drinks!"

"I'm not sure how it is done."

"You're not sure?" Grace was incredulous. She wheeled around and confronted a young man in a caftan carrying a large tray of sweets. "Hey, buddy," she said to the man, standing and taking his tray. She put it on the table. "Eat this," she said to the wedding couple. She turned back to the waiter, if that was what he was, and put her arm around his shoulder. "Julius," she said, "tell this young man that the Mahdi commands the he bring wine for the table. No, no—the Mahdi commands that wine be served to all the guests."

"The Mahdi does not command."

"Tell him," Grace said, making a face at the Mahdi. "Tell him the Mahdi desires he bring wine for our guests." Julius translated. The young man looked between the three of them, confused. "Go!" Grace commanded and smacked the young man on the buttocks. The youth blanched and looked like he would faint for a moment, before nodding once and running off in the direction from where the food had been appearing.

Julius had his head in his hands. The Mahdi shook his head, bemused.

"Grace," Julius said, "you can't do that here."

"I think I did."

Ten minutes later, the guests were served a refreshingly chilled Zinfandel.

"Now that's more like it," Grace said, toasting the couple.

Kandahar Province, Afghanistan

That night, Grace sat on a pallet across from the Mahdi, sipping at a steaming cup of tea, the darkness inside the hut held back by several candles sitting on the low table be-tween them.

"You dance a fair jig for a Messiah," Grace said, smiling.

The man shook his head as he cupped his hands around the hot tea, savoring its warmth. It had turned chilly with nightfall.

"I am no messiah, Grace."

"It's what your people call you. It's what Hila calls you."

"People call me many names."

"Well," Grace said, laughing, "that's something else we have in common, then."

The Mahdi laughed with her.

"You mean, in addition to our shared love of Irish folk music?"

"No, I mean in addition to being marked for death."

The man's smile vanished.

"Someone wants me dead?"

Grace took a sip of her tea and nodded.

"Who? For what reason?"

"The same one who wants me dead."

The Mahdi leaned forward, concerned. *"And who would that be, Grace?"*

"God."

The Mahdi gave a short, guttural laugh, almost spilling his tea.

"It is no great revelation that God wants us all to die at some point, is it, Grace?"

Grace set down her cup. She looked the other man in the eyes, studying him. He held her gaze, unblinking, his smile deeply creasing his face with open amusement.

"What is your real name, then?"

The Mahdi shrugged. *"I have used many names, Grace. Which is real, I cannot say."*

"How about the one you were born with, then?"

The Mahdi shook his head. *"That one I do not know."*

Kandahar Province, Afghanistan

There was a gentle knock on the door of the Mahdi's hut.
"*Come.*"

Hila entered, carrying a tray with wine and cheese left over from the wedding celebration earlier. She set the tray down on the table between the Mahdi and Grace.

"How may I be of service?" the young girl asked in Pashtun. She stole a glance at Grace, then looked downward.

"*I want for nothing, child. Thank you for this kindness,*" he said, gesturing to the tray. Hila bowed and turned to leave, making eye contact again with Grace before wishing them both a good night and exiting the hut.

"The girl cares for you, I think," Grace said, breaking the cheese in pieces and handing a portion to the Mahdi, taking one for herself.

"*Hila thinks that she is my mother, I believe.*"

"Maybe."

"*You believe she wishes something else?*" He smiled at her slyly. "*I am at least twice her age.*"

"Let's just say that I've seen that look before. She'll be watching to see when I leave your hut."

"*No doubt you are right in that regard.*" He ate his cheese and took a sip of the wine, letting the silence extend. "*She is tough, that one. An orphan. Her family was killed in a drone strike.*"

"How did she escape?"

The Mahdi looked at her. "*I warned her.*"

"Did you? Just her? Not the entire family?" The Mahdi took another sip of wine and said nothing. "How did you know? About the strike?"

"*It is one of the things I am allowed to know. Sometimes.*" He set down his empty wine glass. "*Her brother also survived. You met him, I believe. He was leading a donkey.*"

"Yeah, I guess I did. Not as nice as his sister, my impression."

"*Not as nice.*" He waited for Grace to finish her wine and set down her cup. "*Perhaps we shouldn't keep Hila waiting to see you leave."*

Grace nodded. They both stood. *"Good night, Grace. Welcome to our home, once again."* Grace left the hut. She smiled at the girl sitting cross-legged near the path, whittling at a long piece of wood with her wicked looking knife.

"Salaam alaikum, Hila," she said.

The girl looked up from her work and nodded in reply.

Grace found Julius sitting outside their hut.

"What are you drinking?" she asked, sitting down next to him. The night was cold and the sky clear black save the light from the single bright star overhead.

"Wine. From the wedding."

Grace took the cup from him and finished what remained.

"That was actually pretty good," she said. "Amazing."

"Amazing that I just let you drink the rest of my wine?"

"No, that they can come up with wine that good on a moment's notice."

Julius shrugged. "Whoever *they* are. You know what's not so amazing?"

"What?"

"That was the last of it."

"Oh."

"How'd it go?" Julius asked.

"What?"

"Your talk with Mr. Mahdi."

"Not sure." Grace thought for a bit. "I almost told him."

"Told him what?"

"What's going on."

"Really? Could you tell me, then?"

Grace gave him a kick in his shin.

"Yeah," Julius said. "That's what I thought. But you didn't tell him, did you?"

"No, I didn't. Or I started to, but he didn't believe me."

"Not surprised. You think it's a good idea—to tell him that he's the fall guy in your little con game?"

"Probably not. Definitely not."

"So why, then?"

Grace shrugged in the gathering dusk. "He seems so nice."

"Yeah, he does. Too nice, you think?"

"Too nice to fuck over, you mean?"

"Yeah," Julius said.

"Doesn't matter any more. Look at that," she said, gesturing to the star above them. "It's already happening. And he believes it."

"You think he believes he's the Savior Returned, huh? I didn't really get that impression."

"Oh, not yet. I get the feeling that he doesn't know what he is. But he's not fighting it very hard, either. He's not asking many questions. Like the wine—he just smiles and drinks and chooses not to look behind the curtain, you know?"

Julius nodded. "But it's not too late for him, Grace. The setup is here. I don't understand how Arthur and Gabriel arranged it, but obviously all the dominos are lined up nicely. The question is, are you going to give him that little push."

Grace didn't answer. Instead, she stood up. "Let's get some sleep, Padre."

IS NOT MY WORD LIKE FIRE, SAYS THE LORD.

Kandahar Province, Afghanistan

Grace awoke with a start, her heart racing. For several moments, she didn't know where she was.

"Grace."

Grace turned to see Julius's face close to hers in the thin starlight.

"Are you awake?" Grace nodded. "Are you okay?" Julius asked. She felt him take her hand in his.

Grace shook her head.

"Bad dream," she said, sitting up.

"Me, too," he said. Julius sat up next to her and together they listened in the darkness. He turned to her. "Do you hear that?"

Grace nodded. The village was awake. Not the sounds of daytime awake, but a soft susurration permeated the night air. The sound of a thousand couples consoling one another was on the night wind. Somewhere close, a baby cried softly.

"The sky was on fire," Julius said softly.

Grace nodded next to him in the darkness. "And then everything was on fire," she said.

They stared at one another.

"And then I was on fire," Julius said.

Grace nodded.

"Everyone was."

Julius looked at her in the darkness. "Did you do this?" he asked softly.

"What do you mean?"

"The dream. Was it like the wine? Like all of this?"

"I don't know, Julius."

"Please, Grace," Julius said, squeezing her hand. "Don't hurt these people. It's not worth it."

"I'm not going to hurt anyone," Grace said, pulling her hand away. "It was just a fucking dream, Julius."

The next morning, they quickly realized that it wasn't an ordinary dream. Just as Julius and Grace had realized that they both had shared the same dream, neighbors and friends discussed how they had the same dream as their partners, then were shocked to learn that their neighbors and friends had had the very same dream. Was it a dream, then? It had been short, intense, disturbing—waking the sleeper in a panic, turning to their lover for consolation and finding him or her in equal need. The village gathered in the square as midday approached. At the edge of the crowd, the film crew was setting up under Bogart's direction. Bacall held a small microphone as she interviewed a bearded man holding the hand of his young son, a member of the documentary team translating from behind her shoulder.

The Mahdi walked among the restless crowd, nodding, consoling, placing a hand on a shoulder or kneeling to hug a small child. Eventually, he mounted the steps to the dais in the middle of the square and looked out at the people gathered below him.

"*I, too, had the dream,*" he began, hands clasped before him, head slightly tilted. He gestured to the sky. "*I don't know what it means. I don't know if it means anything. I only know that it is a beautiful day. Let us spend it dreaming of more pleasant things. Peace to us all.*" He descended the stage.

"Well," Zimmerman said, turning to Grace next to him in the crowd, "I feel much better now. How about you?"

Grace opened her mouth in rejoinder but closed it, seeing the Mahdi approaching through the dispersing throng.

"*I am glad to see you, Grace.*" He smiled at them both. "*And you as well, Father Zimmerman.*"

They smiled back.

"*I'm hoping that you'll join me for tea later.*"

"Of course," Grace said. The Mahdi nodded and left.

Julius waited for him to get out of earshot. "He's scared."

"Or pissed," Grace added.

"Maybe both," Julius said.

As Grace entered the little hut, the Mahdi stood from where he was tending to the pot of water boiling on the small grate. He smiled at her and gestured for her to sit. She did so and the Mahdi busied himself with the preparation of the tea.

"*Will Father Zimmerman be joining us?*" the Mahdi asked without turning around.

"I'm not sure," Grace said, trying to get comfortable on the low cushions. "I haven't seen him for a while."

"*More tea for us, then,*" the Mahdi said, smiling as he carried over the pot and two small handleless cups which he set on the low table between them. He poured and proffered one of the cups to Grace. "*Sláinte.*"

"Salaam alaikum," Grace said, taking a sip.

The Mahdi set his cup down and eyed his guest with interest. *"I do not wish to be rude, Grace,"* the Mahdi began, *"but I wonder why you are here."*

"You asked me to come by for tea, remember?"

"Of course. But I mean to ask, why did you come to this place? This valley?"

"Your valley, you mean?"

The Mahdi inclined his head. *"This is not my valley."*

"Isn't it? Aren't these your people? Your disciples?"

"Disciples? Not at all. These are not 'my people,' as you call them. They are not anyone's people."

"You were telling me last night how you brought them here. Like Hila."

"Hila, I brought here. And her brother. A few others. But these people live here, many lived here before I found the place."

"So when did you become their leader?"

"I am not their leader."

Grace shook her head slightly and sipped her tea. "You may say so. Mahdi."

"I cannot help what people call me."

"I don't see anyone forcing you up onto that stage in the square, Mr. Mahdi."

The Mahdi took a sip of tea. *"You haven't answered my question, Grace."*

"I'm sorry. What was the question again?"

"Why did you come here?"

Grace shrugged. "I was in the neighborhood."

The Mahdi poured more tea. He waited for Grace to elaborate, which she did not.

"And your film team? What is it you wish to make a movie about?"

"No clue. They're not my crew. Zimmerman and I just hitched a ride on their plane, on our way to the Ukraine. We're just sightseeing, you could say. Just passing through."

"You are not their boss, then?"

"Nope. That would be the short, ugly guy. Actually, I think

the lady is really the brains of the outfit. That's just my opinion, though."

The Mahdi considered this. *"What is in Ukraine?"*

"Pechersk Lavra. In Kiev."

"What is that?"

"A church," Grace said.

"A very long way to go to visit a church."

"I hear it's nice."

The Mahdi set down his cup and leaned over the table, staring fixedly at Grace. *"Are you an angel, Grace?"*

Grace spat tea onto the other man's face.

"Oh, shit. Sorry, Mahdi. Sorry." She attempted to wipe the Mahdi's face but he leaned away, wiping himself with the back of his hand. "Sorry. Now that was not very angelic, was it?"

"You don't deny it."

"That's funny. The really funny thing is, you're the second person to ask that."

"Am I? And who was the first?"

The door of the hut swung open with a thud. Zimmerman stood in the doorway, ashen and wild-eyed. He held a baby in his arms.

"Him," Grace said.

Kandahar Province, Afghanistan

"Grace!" Zimmerman exclaimed breathlessly, "we have to leave. We have to!"

"Good afternoon, Father," the Mahdi said. *"Please come in and join us for tea."*

Julius shook his head. He stared at Grace. Behind him, a man and a woman crowded the doorway to the small hut.

"Hi, Julius," Grace said. "Who you got there?"

"This is the baby," Julius explained, coming into the hut to show Grace the baby in his arms. "We have to go, Grace. This is him. He's alive."

"Yeah, he looks alive. He's cute, Julius. Who is he?"

"That is Faakhir," the Mahdi answered. *"Those are his parents,"* he added, nodding to the couple standing in the door of the hut.

"This is the baby I killed, Grace," Julius said, kneeling so that Grace could look at the baby. "He's alive."

"Yeah, that't great, Julius. Like I said, I never thought you killed anyone."

"But I did, Grace. Before. I know, from the pictures. This baby, those people standing there—they are the ones I killed, before. We have to go, before something bad happens. Right away."

"I don't understand," the Mahdi said. *"This is a good family. I know them well. They and their relatives travelled with me to this valley, almost a year ago. It was very perilous."*

"We have to go," Julius insisted, still kneeling with the baby in his arms. The baby began to fuss. Julius looked down at him with wide, moist eyes.

"Yeah, Julius, you said that. Listen, I think you should give the cute little baby back to his nice parents now, okay, hon? They might be getting a little concerned, what with all the talk of you killing their baby and all." Grace nodded to the mother and she came forward and silently took the baby from Julius. Julius watched them leave and sat heavily on the floor at Grace's feet, his face ashen.

The Mahdi looked down at him.

"I don't understand, but you are obviously very disturbed, Julius. Why do you think that you could have killed Faakhir?" He turned to Grace. *"Why would he think he would do such a thing?"*

"He wouldn't," Grace said, rubbing the back of Julius's neck as he leaned against her legs. "He was here, before. With the military. Things happened."

The Mahdi nodded knowingly. *"I see. Father Zimmerman, please, be at ease. Sit up, here in this chair. I will get you a cup for tea."*

Julius was seated at the low table, more composed, when the Mahdi returned with a fresh pot and an additional cup. He poured tea for all of them. *"We were hostages together,"* the Mahdi explained. *"Held by the Taliban for almost two months. It was only grace that allowed us to escape."*

"All of you?" Grace asked.

"Yes," the Mahdi said. *"There were ten of us."*

"Five adults. Two men. Three women. Four children. Three little girls, and this baby. A baby boy," Julius said softly. He cradled his cup of tea with both hands, which were shaking.

"Yes, that is exactly true," the Mahdi said. *"How did you know, Julius? Did Faisal's parents tell you the story?"*

Julius shook his head and said nothing. He tried to drink but his hands were shaking so hard the tea spilled.

"How did you escape?" Grace asked, more to change the direction of the conversation away from Julius than out of any real interest.

"As I said, grace. Or luck, if you prefer. One night, almost the entire group of our captors was away. We were left with only two guards. I was able to overcome one of them."

"Really?" Grace asked. "And the other one?"

"He died, I'm afraid."

"You killed him, you mean," Grace said, looking at the man with a fresh appraisal. The Mahdi sipped his tea. "Well, Mahdi, you are quite the badass it seems."

The Mahdi shrugged and set down his cup. *"Luck."*

Julius set down his cup and turned to Grace. "We have to leave this place, Grace. I can't stay here." He stood. "You're going fuck all this up." Julius left the hut without a word or gesture to their host.

The Mahdi watched Zimmerman leave his hut. He turned back to Grace.

"Not the way one should talk to an angel," he said.

"I think Father Zimmerman has moved on from his first impression," Grace said, sipping tea. "How 'bout you?"

The Mahdi shook his head and poured more tea.

"Your arrival has occasioned many small miracles, it seems. What else am I to think?"

Grace shook her head. "Call them miracles if you wish. We both know better."

"Do we?"

"You see what you wish to see. You've pretended not to see a helluva lot, I'm sure, for some time before I came to your little valley of miracles."

"It is not my valley," the Mahdi protested.

"Yeah, right."

"I told you. I came to this valley as a refugee, a pilgrim. Most of these people lived here long before I arrived."

"Some were here, I'm sure. I doubt 'most.' I see them arriving every day. They come because of you."

"Why would they come because of me?"

"Because you are the Mahdi."

The man made a sour face and shook his head. *"I don't think you know what the word means."*

"It is not me who pretends not to know what it means. You refuse to listen to what your people name you, because—"

"Because they are not 'my people!' "

"Because your fear is stronger than your faith."

The Mahdi looked levelly at his guest and said nothing.

"And since you lack faith, you look for a sign, for proof that you are worthy. You fear I'm some kind of angel, a messenger, and that I'll tell you that you are chosen, that you are special, that you really are the Mahdi. That it is god's will that you lead these people."

"I want no such thing," the Mahdi protested, pushing away from the low table and sloshing tea from the cups.

"Of course you don't," Grace said to his back as he stood and paced about the small hut. "Only a fool would want such a thing. But you're not a fool. Not nearly fool enough to be blind to what is happening here."

The Mahdi stopped pacing and turned to face his guest.

"Father Zimmerman is right. You are no angel."
"Bingo."
"And you should go."

Kandahar Province, Afghanistan

That night, the fire dream returned to the people of the valley. And again the next night.

The film crew shot scenes around the valley as the populace became increasingly agitated. Everyone, children and adults, glanced up at the sky with trepidation as they went about their lives. A camera was set up in the main square, fixed upon the small raised platform, waiting.

The Mahdi walked about the village, comforting those who approached, but he was met with increasing concern. Everywhere, faces turned to him with anxious expectation. He retreated to his hut.

Julius sat on the end of the small bed, his kit packed, begging Grace to let them leave. Grace waited. She avoided the hut where Julius sat and worried, she avoided the hut where the Mahdi sat and brooded. She waited for the fire to come down from the sky. The entire village waited.

On the seventh night, the plutonium reactor powering the satellite that orbited over their small valley went supercritical. Without a sound, the night was turned to day with an incandescence more bright than the desert sky at noon, a brightness that burned cold and pure white for several minutes while everyone in the village cowered beneath a sky that glowed hot-white from horizon to horizon. When the whiteness faded into a shower of a million falling points of light and the black of night returned, the stars were gone and Grace was catatonic.

Grace heard the voices but couldn't see. Her eyes were open she was sure, but she only could see shades of white everywhere. She was in a room, but it was snowing.

White sparks drifted down from above. Grace tried to move her arms, to sit up, to speak. Nothing worked.

"The child of a priest, doctor! A priest!"

"Shuss, nurse. You know no such thing."

"I do, too. Everyone speaks of it. It's why the girl is cursed. It's why she's the way she is."

"You speak like an old washer woman. Be silent."

"The child of a priest, doctor. The child of a priest is an abomination to God."

"Shuss up and hold her arm there. I need to get this done, there are others waiting."

"What setting, doctor?"

"The same, of course. Now hold her, dammit."

Suddenly, the white sparks hummed and danced, stuttered and flew up, up and away, as she tasted blood, biting on the leather block, the rhythmic thudding of her legs beating against the metal frame of the bed as she convulsed, then only white, the smell of slightly burnt flesh as tendrils of white smoke rose from her temples and chased the white sparks across her vision towards the white ceiling, everything white...

Purgatory

"Well, I hope you're happy now," Elliot said in disgust. "It's toast. Just like I told you. No more recon satellite. My work is done here."

"Not quite," Arthur said from across the conference room table.

"What do you mean, 'not quite?' " Elliot asked. "Didn't you hear what I just said? It's gone. Vaporized. Poof!"

"We need you to task us another satellite," Arthur said. He smiled.

"You are not serious."

Arthur nodded.

Elliot opened his mouth to speak, shut it again, opened it, then said, "Why? You have your magic quantum surveillance decoder ring, anyway. You don't need my satellite. It was just a stupid 'Star of Bethlehem' lightbulb. A bulb that just went *p'ffft.*"

"Yeah, that's why, Elliot. We still need a star. Something that can be seen from farther away, though. And during the daytime. All the time, actually. And it needs to move."

"You're nuts, you know that? It would take a miracle to snag another bird."

"Miracles are what we do, Elliot."

Another satellite would've required an act of god. So Elliot got them a drone. It was a new, top secret model that flew silently and was so stealthy as to be nearly invisible. Except for the incandescence that Arthur insisted upon, of course. That was provided by Elliot's sabotaging of the drone's laser designator device so that it painted a defocused beam across a swath on the ground. At night, it could be seen for a thousand miles in every direction. At least this time he didn't need to make a plutonium reactor go critical, Elliot reflected.

Kandahar Province, Afghanistan

Grace awoke in the hut she shared with Julius. Julius stood over the small stove, heating a pot of tea.

"Still haven't left, Julius?" Grace asked. Julius turned and smiled weakly at her. He shook his head and poured them each a cup.

He sat on the foot of the bed as Grace propped herself up against the wall behind. She took the cup he offered and blew the steam away.

"Found you out there, lying on the green," Julius said.

"Well, thanks for not leaving me there, Julius."

"You're welcome, Grace."

"How many times have you saved my sorry ass?" she asked, smiling at her friend.

"I haven't been counting."

"Lucky for me, then. I must've saved your'n once or twice, though, since we started down this road," Grace said, slipping into the slightest brogue.

"Just the once, Grace."

"Ah, but it was a good one, that. Wasn't it, Julius?"

"It was, Grace."

Grace drained her tea and set down the cup. "You're right, Julius. We should leave this place."

Julius shook his head heavily. "Doesn't matter now."

"Doesn't it? Not afraid of strangling that nice family any more, of smothering that pretty baby in your sleep?"

Julius shook his head. "Everybody's gone, Grace. While you were out."

"What do you mean?"

"Just that. The Mahdi led them away, and everybody followed. Every last soul, with the film crew in tow to document the whole thing, I guess. I think we're the only ones left in this little valley."

"Where is he taking them?"

"To Jerusalem, he said."

"That's a pretty long walk, Julius."

"Yeah," he agreed, stretching out on the bed next to her. "A pretty long walk."

"Too long for us, you think?"

He turned to face her. "Far too long for us."

CHAPTER 12

Salt Lake City, Utah

"Are you crazy?" Parnell asked Uriel, pulling him to the side of the hallway in the Joseph Smith Building. His eyes were wide with fear. "You can't say shit like that here!"

"Take your hand off me, Charles, or you'll have to find somebody to sew it back on."

Parnell let go. "Just shut up, then, Earl," Parnell said in a harsh whisper. He looked over the man's shoulder to where the other two stood. "Tell him to shut up." *Julius* shrugged, hands in pockets. Azrael looked bored.

"Where then?" Uriel asked.

"Not here, that's for sure. Not in Salt Lake, period."

"We could go back to Granite Mountain," Uriel said.

"Granite Mountain?" Parnell asked, eyes widening even further. "You guys didn't go to—" Uriel nodded. "Aw, hell's bells," Parnell said. "I gotta get you jokers out of here."

"I know a nice little deli," Azrael offered.

They ended up huddled in a back booth at a dive bar in downtown Salt Lake City, ignoring Parnell's paranoid rantings about there being ears behind every wall. The beer was warm and the popcorn was stale. Parnell scowled as his elbow stuck to something on the table. He looked around nervously.

"There's nobody here, Parnell," *Julius* assured him from across the table. "Not even a bar maid. At least, not for the last twenty minutes."

"She just had to notify the Prophet that we're here drinking. She'll be back," Azrael teased. "And she's waiting until the food turns cold and congealed before she serves it."

"Go ahead and joke," Parnell said, his voice low and conspiratorial. "You guys have no idea what's going on here."

"Oh, yeah? Well, why don't you explain it to us, Charles?" Azrael encouraged.

Parnell hunched over his glass of warm beer and glanced about, but said nothing.

"We know about the Jews being brought back, up on the mountain," Uriel provided.

Parnell grabbed his wrist. "Shut up about that, Earl. I told you. Not here."

"You said that back in the Temple Square, Chuck."

"About ten times, actually."

"Yeah, well, I'm telling you again. You jokers don't know what we're up against here. We're in the belly of the beast. I mean, literally."

"So, tell us."

Parnell took a deep breath and sighed expansively. He whispered into his beer mug. "That's just the tip of the iceberg, the Granite Mountain project. You've got to know what these crazy bastards are up to. They're—"

"—Trying to light the fuse on the Apocalypse," *Julius* interjected. Parnell looked up at him sharply. "Well, come on, Charles. I mean, it's not terribly obscure, is it?"

"So that's why the Mormons are bringing back Holocaust victims? How so?"

"Returnees are all over the world now," Parnell explained. "Waiting."

"Waiting for what?"

"I don't know, Earl. For the Apocalypse, I guess. Only it's not natural, or fate, or biblical; whatever you want to call it. The Church has systematically brought them back, set them up around the world, and now they wait."

"Like an army. A secret army."

"Or sleeper cells. Dead Jew Army of the Apocalypse."

"Whatever."

"How many, Charles?"

"Hard to know exactly."

"Make a guess."

"From what I've seen, just in the years since I've been here —at least ten thousand."

"Are you kidding?"

Parnell shook his head. "Could be a lot more. A whole lot more. Not less, believe me."

"So what are they waiting for?"

"Gabriel's trumpet," Parnell said, trying to take a gulp of his beer but thinking better of it before the glass got to his mouth. He set the mug back on the table. "Like I said, that's only a small part of what's going on."

"So what else?"

"Political maneuvering. Subterfuge. Incitements. The Returnees aren't the only army the Mormons have abroad, you know. They have a worldwide force of missionaries, just to name another one. And money. Hundreds of billions set aside, funding god-only-knows-what."

"Wow, Parnell. You are quite the conspiracy theorist, aren't you?"

"This isn't theory, Julius," Parnell hissed. "I've seen it. You saw it, Earl. How quickly they were able to react to the situation in New York. Twice. That's not theory, gentlemen. That's a sophisticated operation."

Uriel was forced to nod in agreement.

Azrael agreed. "But to what end, gentlemen? I mean, I see that the Apocalypse is a type of end in itself, of course. Pardon the pun. But why are they doing this?"

"You're a Jew," Parnell said. "You don't understand how Mormons think."

"Well, that's true," Azrael said.

"Jews are just waiting, aren't they? You were told you were chosen thousands of years ago, so all you do is wait. The Messiah will come, and then you'll get what was promised you."

"And the Mormons?"

Parnell shook his head. "Different attitude altogether. They're not waiting for God to appear—or reappear. The Prophet—the President, if you want the politically subtle approbation—is taking the initiative. It's his calling—his mission. And since all this shit has happened with Helena, and you, whatever you are," Parnell nodded at *Julius*, "and this asshole," here he jerked a thumb at Uriel next to him in the booth. "Well, now I think I understand a helluva lot more of what's up."

"Which is?"

"The Prophet isn't like what we think of as the prophets in the bible. The Prophet—the President—is a Returnee. I'm sure of it. But not like the others, if you know what I mean."

"Which I don't."

"Not like the others, how?"

"Not like Helena, or the others who have died in the past and somehow come back."

"Then what is he? I don't understand."

Uriel whistled softly under his breath. "You think he's from the future? That he not only came back from the dead, but back from having died in the future?" Parnell nodded. He managed a gulp of his beer this time. He gagged and fought the temptation to spit it back in the mug.

"I think every one of 'em has come back here to lead the Church. Every President, every Prophet, maybe going all the way back to Smith. Some of 'em even said as much, you know."

"Who? Said what?"

"Snow. Lorenzo Snow, for one. Back in 1898. He must've been a crazy bastard, a real loose cannon. Said all kinds of shit that the Church had to paper over later on. But he made it pretty clear what was up: 'What man now is, God once was. What God now is, man will be.'"

"And you think he meant that what we call God is really

just a dead guy from the future..."

"...who comes back to Earth to play god?"

"Yeah. Pretty much."

"Do you believe that?" *Julius* asked.

"Doesn't matter what I believe, or what you believe. They believe it. Not just believe it—they're acting on it."

"That's why the Church is working to bring on the Apocalypse, you mean?"

"Exactly."

"Can they do it?"

"They think so. And they've been working on it for almost a hundred years."

Azrael looked about at his companions. "These *goyim* are more *mushugannah* than most, that much is clear."

Uriel looked at his friend. "There may be more to it than that, old man," he said. "They may be right."

Salt Lake City, Utah

"It doesn't matter if it's true or not, if these people are crazy or not," Uriel said to his companions. "What matters is what's happening now, what will happen if we don't do something."

"Which is what, exactly?" *Julius* asked.

"The Apocalypse," Parnell intoned.

"Don't even know what that means," Uriel said, shaking his head. "Don't give a shit about any Apocalypse. But I do care about whoever is this God that's setting to take out Grace."

Parnell stared at him. "Why? Who gives a shit? I sure as hell don't."

"Parnell, for a fairly smart guy who's been around for a really long time, you can be pretty fuckin' stupid," Uriel said. "You just don't like her, that's your problem. Won't let you see what's happening here."

"Which is what, then?" *Julius* asked again.

"We're standing on a knife edge here," Uriel answered. "An

inflection point in time that is so critical, God His'self feels He must intervene. Something about Grace, that's the key to this thing. It all turns on her."

"I say let Him take her out, then," Parnell said.

"Then we're screwed," Azrael said. They all looked at him. "It's pretty clear that Grace's part in this is our part: our free will, our ability to affect our fate. That's why she's the target."

"And if she is killed?" *Julius* asked.

"Killed? I don't know," Azrael said. "But if God succeeds in having her excised, then a door closes on all of us. Free will —Man's ability to stand up to God, whoever that really is— ends with Grace."

"Bullshit," Parnell said. "Why is she so special?"

"I don't know," Azrael admitted. "I just see the machinations surrounding her, see the lengths that the Lord is going to, and I can see only one explanation."

Uriel nodded his head. "Agreed," he said.

They sat in silence for a bit.

"Let's say what you say is true," *Julius* began slowly. "That for whatever reason it's in our interest to save Grace, or whatever. How do we do that? What power do we have against God?"

"Her plan, her 'big con,' " Uriel explained, "was to set up someone more important than her to take the fall. Make it in God's interest to change His focus from excising her little ass to saving the world from this other guy."

"Some plan," Parnell snorted.

"I think it's a good plan," Azrael said.

"So do I," Uriel said.

"Is that because it's the only plan?" *Julius* asked.

"Only partly," Uriel said. "Mostly."

"Well," Parnell said, "I, for one, don't give a shit about Grace or her con. I do feel pretty strongly about preventing a bunch of self-important crazy people from bringing about the end of the world."

"Sounds pretty righteous when you put it that way," Azrael said. "Exactly how do you plan to do that?"

"I'm working on it," Parnell said. He slouched back in the booth.

"Work all you want, Parnell," Uriel said. "I don't see you stopping these Mormons, not after what I've seen in that facility under the mountain, especially now that you're telling me that they've been working on this for a hundred years or so. Too far along, way too much momentum."

Julius and Azrael nodded.

"So what are you saying, Earl?" Parnell asked. "Just sit back and watch the fire rain down? Pray for the Rapture? Fuck that, Earl."

Uriel shook his head. "No, that's not what I'm saying, Charles. Listen: it can't be stopped. But it can be turned."

"What do you mean?"

"Use all their hard work and preparations against them, that's what I mean. The machinery is in place and ready to be sprung, you say. So use that momentum, the force of their zealotry, to our advantage. Hit the 'go' button before they're ready. Use their enthusiasm against them. Instead of trying to stand in front of the train, release the brakes now, buddy. Push the pedal down and get this sucker rolling so fast it goes right off the rails."

Parnell considered. "That might work," Parnell said, nodding.

"It's a good plan," *Julius* added, "It might just help Grace as well."

Uriel winked at the priest.

"Only one little worry," Azrael said.

"Yeah? What's that?" Uriel asked.

"What if the Mormons aren't completely crazy? What if what they've been doing really is the Almighty's plan? Then what?"

"Then," Parnell said, "we've triggered Armageddon."

"And in that case, gentlemen, we won't have to worry

about what comes next," *Julius* said.

Salt Lake City, Utah

"So, Earle," Parnell said, leaning back into the conversation. "How do we do this?"

"No clue, Chuck," Uriel said. "That's not my problem. My friend Azrael and I need to move on. You and the preacher here will have to light the fuse on this end."

"What? Why? You're leaving it to us to save the world?" Parnell asked.

"Yeah, Chuck. Save the world or get fucked trying. The two of you. I'm sure you'll figure something out."

"Where are you guys going?" *Julius* asked, not entirely pleased with the team he had just been drafted onto.

"We," Uriel announced, clapping Azrael on the shoulder, "are going to save our girl from God Almighty." More softly he said, "Let's see if your magic bathtub can get us to Afghanistan, buddy."

"I'm not sure there are Mormons in Afghanistan."

Kandahar Province, Afghanistan

Hila walked alongside the Mahdi. She stole the occasional sidelong glance at him, noticing with satisfaction his new bearing; that of a leader. He wore the ring she had given him on his left hand, and with his right toggled the road with the long staff she had fashioned for him from a gnarled branch of ironwood she found in the valley. Behind them walked the thousands who had lived with them in the valley.

"Where do we go?" Hila asked as they walked.

"We follow the light that goes before us," the Mahdi said in her mind.

"And to where is it taking us?"

"Jerusalem," he replied.

"Is that far?"

The Mahdi nodded at this.

"More than a day's walk?"

The Mahdi nodded.

"Where will the people sleep?"

"The people will sleep where we lie at the end of the day, little one."

Hila didn't like it when the Mahdi called her that, but she said nothing of this, so great was her respect for the Mahdi.

"What will the people use for shelter?"

"If shelter is needed, it will be provided."

"By whom will the shelter be provided, Mahdi?"

The Mahdi turned and smiled down at her as they walked.

"You ask a lot of questions, Hila," the Mahdi said, eyes twinkling.

Hila smiled back. She liked how it felt when he made her name ring in her mind like that.

"Not nearly so many as the old men will ask when their feet get sore and their bellies complain of not eating," she said.

At this he nodded again.

"We shall see."

Kandahar Province, Afghanistan

"There you are," Uriel said, " 'Bout time, girl. Getting sunstroke, sitting out here all morning waiting for you two."

Grace looked up to see Uriel sitting on the edge of the low stage. She let go of Julius's hand and stopped in her tracks, shading her eyes in the sun.

"Earl?" Grace asked. "How in hell?"

Uriel waved them over as he swung his legs, dangling over the edge of the stage.

"This here is my particular friend and traveling companion, Azrael," Uriel said, introducing the old man sitting on the pallet by his side. "Azrael, I told you they were still here somewhere."

Julius walked up and shook the hands of the two men.

"And this is the good Father Zimmerman," Uriel said. "The

other one."

"Julius," Julius corrected.

"He doesn't like to be called 'the good Father' right after he's slept with me," Grace said, smiling. "Cognitive dissonance, I think it's called. I'm Grace," she said, shaking Azrael's hand. "Thanks for saving my life in Chicago."

Grace and Julius sat down in chairs in front of the stage.

"You two just missed the party," Grace said, smiling. "And the fireworks."

"We passed the parade on our way in," Uriel said. "Very impressive. Never seen an entire village up and walk away like that."

"Last time I saw something like that was in Sodom," Azrael said. The others looked at him. "What? It was a different kind of thing, I admit. Just saying it looked similar."

"So what brings you to our little valley, gentlemen?" Grace asked.

"You gotta ask, girl? This is your game, after all. Knew you'd need some help now that the gun's sounded," Uriel said.

"Why, Earl? What happens now?" Julius asked.

"The End, that's what. The End happens now," Earl said, standing. Azrael nodded his assent.

"And all I was thinking was that we should find some breakfast," Grace said, standing.

"Every End has to have a beginning," Uriel said. "Let's begin with breakfast, then."

"Breakfast would be a good start," Azrael agreed.

Purgatory

"Okay, people, settle down," Arthur intoned from the head of the conference table. Gabriel rapped on the table top next to him. The dozen attendees stopped talking and looked at him.

"Our group is on the move. This is it, folks. Getting close to the end game here."

"Which is what, exactly?" somebody asked from the other end of the table.

Gabriel shook his head. "We don't know that yet."

"Great. So we're all just wingin' it, is that what you're saying?"

"No, I'm saying that we're not at that point yet. Right now, we have a little over three thousand men, women, and children who have started walking across some of the most inhospitable and dangerous territory on the planet, and it's our responsibility to take care of them."

"Yeah, exactly why is that?" the guy at the end of the table asked.

"Because we put them there," Arthur explained with exasperation. "Look, you all volunteered for this. Whether you thought it was a good cause or a fun project or you were just bored, you're here now, so let's move on, okay? We've got work to do."

Arthur was pleased that this was met with a general yawn.

"Great, thank you. Day one, the party has left the valley. I believe the destination has been set as Jerusalem. Is that correct, Elliot?"

Elliot nodded. "Yeah, boss. Just confirmed by the Mahdi himself. Conversation with the girl."

"We can just call him by his name. It's Tiernan, I think," Arthur corrected. "No need to get crazy on this end, Elliot. The girl's name is Hila."

Elliot shrugged.

"Well," a middle-aged woman with thick rimless glasses began, "it's a challenge, of course. With a caravan of motor coaches, it's about a 45 hour drive, more or less."

Arthur shook his head. "No coaches."

The woman looked up. "What do you mean?"

Arthur smiled and said, "They need to walk the whole way."

The guy at the end of the table slapped his forehead. "You're shittin' me, Arthur. For real?"

"'Fraid so," Arthur said.

"That's," the woman vigorously worked at a slide rule she had produced from her lab coat, "that's over 730 hours of walking, Arthur. Maybe they can walk ten hours a day, tops."

"There's children and old folks in that group," somebody interrupted.

"Whatever, say eight hours walking a day, with breaks for lunch and all. You're talking about supporting a group of thousands of people for over two months on the open road."

"You think that's a problem?" Elliot chimed in. He tapped on his keyboard and a map appeared on the conference room wall with a dotted line indicating the route from Kandahar to Jerusalem. He stabbed a finger at the bright red dotted track. "How about the fact that these poor buggers will be walking across Iran, Iraq, and Syria? Assuming they even survive the walk out of Afghanistan. Could you pick a more dangerous trek? I don't think so. You'd be better off sending these guys across the Sahara. Hell, I'd give them a better chance of surviving a walk across the moon."

"If it were easy," Arthur soothed, "it wouldn't be nearly so dramatic, would it? Not nearly so—biblical."

"So that's what we're going for here? Old Testament dramatics? Hell, Arthur, the Exodus was only from Egypt to Canaan. A walk across Central Park by comparison."

"Why Jerusalem?" the guy in the back asked. "Let's give them a more workable destination. Problem solved."

Arthur shook his head. "Jerusalem. Let's concentrate on the problem at hand. We have first-person intel on the ground, no problem there. We have surveillance from the drone, so we have good situational awareness. We have guidance, what with Elliot's drone painting the way. That was good work, by the way, Elliot. I like the laser thing."

"Thank you. I try."

"So these are our current challenges: Food. Shelter. Security."

"For three thousand men, women, and children?"

"That's for a start. We expect that the number of pilgrims will grow exponentially as the trek progresses."

"Exponentially? Figuratively speaking? Or literally?"

"I'm not sure what is which," Arthur said, "but I mean 'really a lot more people.' As in, a whole lot. How's that?"

"Well, for a start," the woman in the glasses said, putting away her slide rule in her breast pocket, "you might want to turn off that stupid beacon. Security will be tough enough without signaling every Taliban cell in the area that we're walking through their back yard."

"Actually, Sally," Gabriel said, "we can't do that. The whole idea is that everyone knows they're coming. It's part of the whole 'pilgrims to Palestine,' 'join-our-movement' thing."

Sally leaned back in her chair and tossed her pencil up where it stuck in the ceiling. "I give up. This is ridiculous."

"It's not that big a deal, Sally," Elliot said. "We've got over-watch of the entire region. We'll know if any bad guys are showing interest. And we got firepower."

"Um, actually, Elliot," Arthur corrected, "that's another thing. No explosions."

"What do you mean, no explosions? I got Hellfire missiles on this bird. What's more Old Testament than that?"

"Yeah, I know. Just keep them in reserve. You know, for emergencies."

Sally said, "You'll have you're first 'emergency' about six hours after this flock of lambs leave the protection of that valley. That whole area is filled with bad actors."

Arthur turned to one of the other engineers. "Pam?"

A young woman halfway down the table leaned onto her elbows. "I think we should have effective passive deterrence along the majority of the route corridor, Arthur."

"What does that mean?" Sally asked.

"Mobile microwave emitters flanking the pilgrims," Pam explained. "The lambs won't even know they're there. If any wolves try to get close, though, they'll get a pretty nasty welcome."

"Even if they're in a vehicle?"

Pam nodded.

"And Elliot," Arthur added, "if you see a more determined threat, you stay in contact with Pam. She's got some other resources as well, right?" Pam nodded again.

"Who is this gal?" Elliot asked the guy sitting next to her. The guy shrugged.

"Pam, could you meet with Elliot for a few minutes after this?" Arthur asked.

"Sure," Pam said, smiling at Elliot.

"Great, thanks," Arthur said, checking off items on his yellow legal pad in front of him. "Security is done, then. Shelter. Aaron?"

Aaron touched a button on the console on the table and a picture of pop-up tents appeared on the screen next to the map. "We prepositioned a few thousand of these at a point we expect the group to stop on the first day. We'll have to see how they work, whether they decide to pack 'em up and carry them or if we need to just keep providing them along the way. It's not luxurious, but they're Mylar, nice and warm at night, reflect the sun in the daytime. Keeps the rain off, too, if it ever rains. Which it doesn't. Sleeping rolls, washing supplies, clothing, water. We can stay ahead of the group and be sure there's plenty. With those microwave doohickies, doesn't sound like we have to worry much about looting. It's just scheduling and supply chain management. We got this."

"Excellent, Aaron. You let me know if you need more people on this," Arthur said. "Let's move on to food, then."

"We could've just added caches of MRE's, wouldn't be a problem," Aaron added.

Gabriel shook his head.

"Scotty?" Gabriel asked.

Libby looked up from doodling on the agenda in front of her. "You do realize that my name isn't Scotty, right?"

Elliot smiled at her.

Libby rolled her eyes. "Middle school humor," she muttered. Then, "It's all set. Manna from heaven. Twice a day and once at bedtime."

"Seriously?" the guy in the back snickered. "MRE's not biblical enough?"

"Don't think so," Gabriel said. "Do I want to know how it tastes?"

Libby looked hurt. "It tastes great, of course. Like manna from heaven, it's got to taste great."

"And you can deliver on the move?"

"That's what you asked for, isn't it? Just give me time and place, it'll rain food. Focused APM, pinpoint geosynchronicity. Enough to keep 'em happy and then some. On-time delivery guaranteed."

"Swell. The great pilgrimage will be trailed by a horde of rats and mountain lions," the guy in the back commented.

"Anything that doesn't get eaten or wrapped up airtight disintegrates in a couple of hours. Nothing left but dust." She turned to Arthur. "But I can do water, too, if you want. I mean, rain is easy, comparatively."

"I'll let you know," Arthur said. "For right now, we'll go with bottled water, thanks." Arthur and Gabriel scanned around the table. "Okay, then. Nice work, group. Back to work."

> *SUBMIT TO THE LORD WITH FEAR,*
> *AND WITH TREMBLING*
> *BOW BEFORE HIM;*
> *LEST HE BE ANGRY AND YOU PERISH;*
> *FOR HIS WRATH IS QUICKLY KINDLED.*

Purgatory

The work group was back around the conference table.

"Look," Arthur explained with exasperation, "they've

been in a complete vacuum ever since this thing started. The Senator has worked hard to scrub every scrap of intel or reporting about our guy. The world knows something is going on, something big—but they have no clue what it is."

"Some references have gotten out," Libby argued.

Arthur nodded. "Of course, of course, Scotty. Spec Ops reported back up the chain, of course, got everybody in the military asking a thousand questions. That guy with the donkey been screaming bloody murder all over Taliban country. That got back to the Pakistanis, which got the Indians wondering what the hell was up. Russia, France, Great Britain, China—we've seen 'em all move their birds to get a better look at our little Shangri-La. And the Senator has squashed every inquiry with a stone cold 'no comment,' 'never happened,' and 'no idea to what you're referring.' You know the kind of pressure been building around this as a result? Intense. Now is the time to blow the lid off."

"You mean the documentary thing?"

"No, not yet. That's for later. But now, we want the dam to break."

"Yeah?" Elliot asked. "Just how do we do that, Arthur?"

Arthur smiled at him. "I'm glad you asked, Elliot. I want you to blow something up."

Elliot smiled broadly. "Really, boss?"

Arthur nodded. "Just don't hurt anybody," he said, wagging a finger at Elliot.

"Course not."

As the meeting broke up, Libby stopped Elliot as he started to leave.

"Hey, good looking," Libby said. "Got a second?"

"For you? Sure, Lib."

"I've got a little problem I could use your help with," she said. "Have a seat."

"I'm here for you, baby." He sat down.

Libby sat down next to him and tapped on a keyboard. She pointed to the wall screen.

"There's my problem," she said.

"Oh," Elliot said. "That might be a problem, for sure. Where is it?"

"Two days out from their current position."

"How close to their line?"

"Dead smack on."

"Go around?"

"Not a chance. The terrain is a nightmare in that area. That's why it's there."

The two sat and stared at the recon photo of a large Taliban stronghold. After a bit, Elliot pointed to the side of the image.

"What's that?" he asked.

"Ammo dump, I think. We see a lot of truck traffic in and out of that area."

Elliot smiled. "Must be a really, really big one," he said.

"Makes sense," Libby agreed. "No place else to store shit around there. Too mountainous." She looked at Elliot, who was still grinning like an idiot. "Hold it. You're not thinking of..."

Elliot nodded.

"But the boss said for you not to kill anyone."

"Do you think he meant bad guys, too?"

"Yeah, Elliot. I think he meant those guys, too," Libby said, pointing at the screen.

"But they're going to jump all over our parade, Libby," Elliot protested. "We gotta take them out. Two days, you said."

She nodded. "I guess we should talk to Arthur about it," she said with a sigh. She started to get up from the chair.

"Not so fast," Elliot said, putting a hand on her arm. "Just give me a little while to think about it, okay?"

She patted his hand, then gently removed it from her arm. "Sure, Elliot. But be quick. Get back to me tomorrow, then."

"How about tonight?" Elliot said, as Libby got up to leave.

"Tomorrow will be fine," she said, leaving.

Kandahar Province, Afghanistan

The small group breakfasted under the shade of the only tree that stood, gnarled and sparse, in the middle of the village green.

The four had spent some time rummaging through the now desolate village for left-behinds, of which there were many. Azrael had found dishes and cups, as well as a teapot. Uriel had discovered the storehouse, still miraculously refrigerated, and presented Grace and Julius with rashers of bacon (in the middle of a Moslem country, he marveled), a dozen fresh eggs and rounds of fresh-baked flatbread. Grace and Julius had prepared the meal, and now the four sat, eating, beneath the shade of the tree.

Uriel asked, "So what, exactly, did you say to this man, Grace, to get him to play this fiddle game of yours?"

Grace shrugged in response.

"It's not so much what she said, Earl," Julius supplied. "It's more about what she didn't quite say. Isn't that right, Grace?"

But Grace said nothing.

"What didn't you say?" Azrael asked.

"She didn't say that this whole setup was carefully staged. A setup to get the poor sod thinking he's something he's not."

"He was here when we got here," Grace explained. "It wasn't me doing the setting up. He had already bought in, as well he might. A man unable to speak, suddenly able to communicate to a whole crowd of admirers just by projecting his thoughts. Pretty heady stuff, that."

"And that wasn't you, Grace?" Uriel asked.

Grace shook her head without conviction. "I never even met the guy before."

"Oh, that's malarkey and you know it, Grace," Julius said. "You said yourself, not two minutes after hearing the guy in our heads, that it was based off your work. The stuff you and Gabriel invented, you said."

Grace flushed angrily. "That was decades ago. I didn't set this up. Maybe I made it possible in some way…"

"Yeah, that's bullshit, Grace," Uriel interjected. "Where's Gabriel now?"

"I don't know. He left before we entered the valley."

"Exactly," Julius said. "He left because you told him to make this thing work. 'Make the mute guy into the Messiah,' you told him. Which, obviously, he somehow was able to do."

"You may be right. I don't know," Grace said sheepishly.

"Well," Azrael soothed, "your late husband does seem to have accomplished quite a bit. But what pushed them out of the valley? Got them to move?"

"More of the same mind-fuck technology," Julius said. "Communal dreams of fiery death from the sky. Which, of course, Grace also had nothing to do with."

"You got a problem this morning, Padre? You want to talk about it with our friends here?"

"Yeah, I got a problem. I mean, I know I signed up for this little mission to save your ass and all—"

"Exactly, Julius. You signed up, and I thanked you for it. About a dozen times. So quit whinging."

"But this has gone a long way beyond just saving your ass, that's my problem. There are some serious machinations going on in this little valley."

"Oh, hell, Julius," Grace said. "You're just scared. You found that little baby alive, and all those nice people you thought you killed, and now you're scared shitless all over again."

"You're damn right, Grace," Julius said, reddening. "Damn right. I did something terrible a long time ago, and now it seems like it never happened. I've been given another chance. So I don't want to fuck it up, okay? I don't want to keep pushing this until maybe it all happens again."

"That won't happen," Grace said.

"You don't know that, Grace," Julius. "You can't know that, because you don't know why it happened before. You weren't there. I was."

"The good Father does have a point," Azrael said.

"No, he doesn't," Grace insisted. "Nobody's going to kill that family."

"You mean, that family that's now walking across Afghanistan, because of you?" Julius asked.

"That's enough, Zimmerman," Uriel interjected. "I understand what you're saying, and you're right that people may get hurt. But you're wrong if you thought that this was just about saving your girlfriend here. It never was just that."

"She's not my girlfriend."

"So what is it, then, Earl? If it's not just me, what is it?" Grace asked.

"I'm not sure anymore, Grace. I thought I knew. It was about your invention, about the mind-reading—"

"That wasn't me, that was Gabe," Grace said.

"No, it was you, too. And it was particularly something that you did, something that was so fundamental, you were a threat."

"A threat to who?"

"Not just who--what. Not just to Him, to everything. The whole system, the universe as it exists. You fucked with something fundamental, and it required a reaction."

"You pissed off God, I'm afraid," Azrael nodded.

"Bullshit," Grace proclaimed. "What I did wasn't that big a deal."

"Maybe it didn't seem like that big a deal," Uriel said. "It was important enough, though, to get His attention. To put in motion the plan to get you erased, permanently. When you came back to us, it gave them the opportunity to erase whatever you had done."

"Ideas don't just die, Earl," Grace said.

"You're right, Grace. But it can be buried, buried so deep only God would know. That's the way it's supposed to be. You're playing Prometheus here, that's what upset things."

"Well, I came back and fixed it. I put that genie back in the bottle. God should thank me, not be fucking with me still."

"You might have a point, Grace," Azrael said, "if your friend here hadn't gone back to get you."

"I didn't ask him to do that," Grace protested.

"That doesn't matter, Grace," Uriel said. "What matters is that it happened."

"What happened, exactly?"

"I don't know what happened, exactly," Uriel said, shaking his head. "Maybe it hasn't even happened yet. But it's important enough to get the attention of God Himself. To get Him to intervene in our little tragedy."

"Which is why, Julius," Grace said, "we have to play this out."

"And let this Mahdi guy take the fall for you," Julius said.

"To take the fall for all of us," Uriel said.

Purgatory

"Holy shit, Elliot," Arthur exclaimed. "What the hell was that?"

The rest of the occupants applauded in the darkness of the conference room. They had just watched a very large explosion on the wall monitor.

"Show it again, Elliot," someone said from the back.

Elliot, smiling, dutifully replayed the recording. On screen, a missile-viewpoint camera swept down from great altitude and soared into the midst of a large military compound. Then the view changed to an overhead view of the entire compound exploding, followed by a series of secondary explosions building to a crescendo worthy of a Macy's July 4th celebration. A couple people clapped again.

Libby leaned over to Elliot and whispered, "He said not to kill anybody, asshole."

"I told you not to kill anybody, asshole!" Arthur yelled at him, bringing up the lights as the recording started another loop. "And stop showing that, dammit."

"You wanted a big boom, boss. That was a very, very big

boom. I'm pretty sure they got that on all the recon sats, that's how big it was."

"Shit, Elliot, the damn BBC got it. It's all over the World News."

"You're welcome," Elliot said, leaning back in his chair with his fingers knitted behind his head, smiling.

"That's not the PR we're looking for, Elliot. Not killing hundreds of people, just before the Movement arrives. Not good."

"I didn't kill anybody, boss," Elliot said.

"Libby said it was a Taliban redoubt. Obviously, that was a pretty damn huge ammo dump, Elliot. There must've been at least a hundred Taliban there. And now there's a smoking hole in the ground."

Elliot leaned forward and tapped the keys to bring up a new video. "This," Elliot said, "is four hours before I blew up that dump." The lights went back down and the group watched as the screen showed dozens of trucks and scores of men on foot rapidly leaving the compound in all directions.

"Oh," Libby said. "Why are they all running away?"

"I fired an unfused Hellfire missile into the middle of the base four hours before sending in the real thing. Kind of a warning shot, you could call it." He showed a close-up of a white missile half buried in the ground of the compound. On it's side was clearly written, "RUN AWAY!" in large crude letters.

"A dud?" Elliot nodded. "A warning shot?" Elliot nodded. "You think they all got out?"

Elliot shrugged. "Looked like it to me, boss. Anybody stupid enough to be hiding under a desk got vaporized, that's for certain."

"Oh," Arthur said, bringing up the lights, "Okay, then. Hopefully, nobody that stupid. Nice work, Elliot. Nice, big boom, that."

"And those guys had to be moved, boss," Libby said. "Our party is one day out from that location."

"Yeah, Libby. Had to be done. No doubt." Arthur killed the view screen. "Okay, people. The lid is off. Let's talk publicity, then."

Kandahar Province, Afghanistan

"So what do we do now?" Julius asked. They had finished their breakfast.

Uriel stood and stretched. "Time to go, I think," he said.

"Go where?" Julius asked.

"Out of dodge, Julius," Grace said. "That's how the fiddle game works. You gotta be outta town before the curtain falls."

"Indeed," Uriel said. "Get Grace to a gateway, while our con works the mark."

"Which is where?" Julius said.

The four moved off across the village green.

"Only natural gates now," Uriel said. "And the only one of those I know of for certain is still the one in Ukraine. Parnell gave me the low-down, before we left him in Salt Lake City."

"How the hell would Chuck know about a gate in Ukraine?" Grace asked.

"And how are we supposed to get there?" Julius asked.

At that moment, a single bolt of white lightning silently gathered above them from a perfectly blue, cloudless sky. The sound of an unearthly sizzle drew their eyes up, and with a brilliant flash the bolt stabbed down and struck at the tree under which they had been seated moments before. The four were knocked to the ground as the rumbling explosion of the tree bursting into flames rolled over them.

Grace looked up as she fell, a purple sky streaked with the first rays of sunrise above her. She felt the place where the man had struck her in the chest, his face in shadow, his voice soft and apologetic. "Someone who loved you," he said, and then she was falling, the white curtain flapping about her like broken angel's wings, just before she hit the water and every-thing disappeared, again, everything except sunshine refracted like bright diamonds though the water's surface above.

Kandahar Province, Afghanistan

Azrael levered himself upright with his cane and stag-gered back to the smoldering remains of the gnarled old oak. The others followed and stood behind him, staring. In the re-mains of the blasted tree trunk, smoke curled from a series of strange letters glowing like orange embers.

"What is it?" Julius asked, the first to find his voice.

Uriel shook his head.

Azrael traced the curves of the letters with the tip of his cane.

"Is it Arabic?" Grace asked, her voice shaking.

Julius shook his head.

"Aramaic," Azrael said.

Grace looked at him, then at Uriel.

"He's really old," Uriel explained.

"So what's it say, old man?" Julius asked.

"It says, 'I come,'" Azrael said, dropping the tip of his cane to the ground and leaning on it heavily. "Maybe, 'I am com-ing.' It's been quite a while since I've read Aramaic. The con-jugations are tricky."

"I think we get the general idea," Grace said.

"Who's coming, do you think?"

"I don't think we should wait around to find out," Julius said.

"Where are we going?" Grace asked.

"We're going that way," Uriel answered, pointing up the path that led from the valley.

"Yeah? And then where?" Julius asked.

"No need to worry about that," Uriel said.

"No? Why not?"

"Doubt we make it that far," Uriel said, staggering for a moment. He began to walk, and the others followed.

Purgatory

"What the hell was that?" Arthur demanded.

The workgroup sat around the conference table, watching the scene replay over and over again on the big viewing screen on the wall.

Arthur pointed at the screen. "Anybody?"

They all watched the surveillance video of the lightning strike to the tree, repeating over and over.

"Elliot?"

Elliot shook his head. "This is all I got, boss. Just the overhead from the drone. The real surveillance is with the guy wearing the ring, remember? And he's not in the valley anymore."

Arthur scowled at the man across the table. "Don't get sarcastic with me, Elliot. Look at that. Out of a clear, blue sky, no less. We're the only ones supposed to be playing this kind of shit. You know that, right?"

"Well," Libby said, spinning her pencil on her finger thoughtlessly, "looks like somebody else decided to join the party."

"Yeah, Libby," Arthur said, "that's the point I'm getting at here. Who?" Libby shrugged. "That bolt could've just as easily hit Grace, or any of those people sitting there in the valley. Hell, people, it could fire off again, but this time take out our whole parade. I need some answers."

"It came outta nowhere, Arthur," Elliot explained. "There's no trace of the energy source. It's like a window just opened up and 'Zap!' Then it was gone."

"That's not possible," someone else protested. "That must be like a kajillion joules. It had to come from somewhere."

"Well, it didn't. I said, 'Zap.' Term of art. Means it came from nowhere. And I don't think kajillion is even close," Elliot repeated. "More like a million kajillion."

Arguing around the table ensued. Gabriel raised his hand but nobody took notice. He banged on the table and the arguing raggedly ceased.

"It did come from somewhere," Gabriel explained. "Somewhere else. Somewhere we can't see."

"Like where?" Elliot asked.

"Like us," Gabriel said.

"From here?"

Gabriel shook his head. "Not here. Like here. Another plane of existence or whatever." He sighed. "It was going to happen, we knew that. It's the whole point."

"What's the whole point?" Arthur asked.

"The con. To get Him in the game," Gabriel answered.

"Who?" Arthur asked.

"God."

Helmand Province, Afghanistan

The Mahdi and his followers, now numbering over six thousand, swept like a flood into the ancient city of Shindand. Two days later, the Mahdi led his legions through the city gates once again, but now he was at the head of ten thousand souls, and the city he left behind was nearly deserted.

Hila walked beside the Mahdi, squinting ahead into the distance.

"*You are troubled, my child,*" the Mahdi said. He smiled at her, as she had ceased being a child many miles back along their journey together.

"It is my fate, Father," she answered, no longer resentful of the endearment. "Nothing troubles you, so I must be troubled for both of us."

The Messiah brushed his hand against hers. Hila stumbled, but the Mahdi caught her, smiling. She blushed slightly, and said, "The border to Iran is ahead, Father. They are preparing for our approach."

"It is good that they should be prepared, is it not?"

"Good for them, perhaps. I'm not so sure it is good for us."

"Then we will wait until we get there, little one, and then we will see."

Kandahar Province, Afghanistan

The four sojourners did make it up the path out of the valley. The four stood on the rocky plateau, old Azrael leaning on his cane and wheezing heavily. Julius looked back down at the valley below, now deserted. Uriel frowned at the narrow cleft in the rock before them.

"You guys coming?" he asked, then stepped inside. Grace followed.

She immediately knew that something was wrong. Uriel had disappeared around the bend in the rocky passage, only a few steps ahead. As Grace quickened her pace to catch up, the passage continued to curve impossibly ahead of her. And instead of deepening shadow, the narrow passage seemed to be getting brighter.

Grace opened her mouth and shouted for Uriel to wait up, but she couldn't hear her own words. Instead the walls around her were growing softer, more indistinct, and the entire passage brightened to a brilliant white that suffused her vision. She stopped and turned about, but everywhere was the soft, bright whiteness, without interruption, even beneath her feet. She reached out her hands to steady herself against the rocky walls which she knew to be only a foot away on either side, but her hands found only emptiness. Words came into her mind, like a breeze across her face...

AM I A GOD NEAR BY, SAYS THE LORD, AND

NOT A GOD FAR OFF? WHO CAN HIDE IN SECRET PLACES SO THAT I CANNOT SEE THEM? DO I NOT FILL HEAVEN AND EARTH? SAYS THE LORD.

I HAVE HEARD WHAT THE PROPHETS HAVE SAID WHO PROPHESY LIES IN MY NAME, SAYING, "I HAVE DREAMED, I HAVE DREAMED!" HOW LONG? IS NOT MY WORD LIKE FIRE, SAYS THE LORD, AND LIKE A HAMMER THAT BREAKS A ROCK IN PIECES?

Kandahar Province, Afghanistan

The words faded but the bright soft whiteness did not. Grace turned slowly about, looking for a way ahead, but there was no detail, no form, nothing upon which to focus. She started to feel dizzy, thought she might be toppling, when someone grabbed her hand and pulled, hard. She came stumbling out of the whiteness and blinked as Uriel caught her up roughly.

"What?" Grace asked, dazed.

"Steady on, girl," Uriel said, holding her until she felt her legs solidify beneath her. "You're just fine."

Julius and Azrael emerged from the rocky cleft behind them.

"What's wrong?" Julius asked. "What happened?"

Grace pushed away from Uriel and swayed momentarily.

"Nothing. I'm just fine," she said, and then collapsed face down onto the dirt.

A thousand little holes in a yellow stained tile ceiling. Thousands of little holes. Women's voices, at a distance. No more pain. Thick warmth oozing down her thighs.   Please, no more pain.

"It won't cry, Mother."

"What is it you say?"

"It doesn't cry. See."

"Give it a lick, then. Give it something to cry about."

"You think I should?"

"Yes, yes. Don't be a simpleton, child. You must, to get the baby to breathe. Quickly."

"It is breathing, Mother. And he's as red as a strawberry. Look. He looks like he's crying, but he's not making any sound."

"You're making no sense at all, girl. Let me see the baby. Tend to the strumpet, she's bleeding and making a mess."

CHAPTER 13

Kandahar Province, Afghanistan

"Shit, shit, shit," Julius muttered, cradling Grace's head in his lap.

"Stop worrying there, Father," Uriel admonished. "Girl'l be fine. Give her a moment."

Azrael looked about nervously. "Not entirely sure we have a moment, Uriel."

"Don't start, Old Man," Uriel said. "We knew it was coming. Just the overture playing."

Azrael nodded. He carefully settled his *yarmulke* on his head.

Grace opened her eyes and struggled to sit up. She got halfway, then started to fall back. Julius caught her and held her up.

"Just rest for a second, hon," Julius said. He looked over at Uriel anxiously.

"What did you see, girl?" Uriel asked her.

Grace shook her head woozily. "Didn't see anything. Just all white, like. But the voice, in my head."

"Like the Mahdi?" Julius asked.

Grace shook her head again. "I guess, but nothing like that. So much—I don't know—bigger. Like it would burst my head, it was so strong."

"What did He say?" Azrael asked.

Grace took a deep breath and sighed. "That He is a God nearby. There's no place to hide. Something about false prophets."

"Jeremiah 23," Azrael said.

"What?" Grace asked.

"It's scripture," Julius offered.

"Guy loves to quote Himself," Uriel offered.

Grace looked confused. She turned to Julius, who was still supporting her. "It said 'is not My word like fire?' I think—I think it was talking about the dream."

"That was no dream, Grace," Uriel said, offering her a hand. "You know that. That was your con working."

Julius stood up as well. "You think that whatever just happened to Grace was some kind of warning, then?"

"Warning? Nah," Uriel said, shaking his head. "God doesn't need to make threats, bubba."

"That really was…?" Grace began, swaying a little again before Julius steadied her.

"Sure as shit, girl," Uriel assured her.

"What was it then, if not a threat?" Julius asked.

"Just saying He knows what's up, is all," Uriel explained. "That He's taken notice." Uriel looked sharply at the shaken Grace. "Better suck it up and get a move on, Grace. Show's started. This is what you been playing for, right? Game on, girl."

Grace swallowed hard. She dropped Julius's arm and started to move off down the trail.

"Atta girl," Uriel said, moving off behind her. "Gettin' exciting now, Azrael." He smiled and clapped his friend on the shoulder, staggering the old man.

Kandahar Province, Afghanistan

The children laughed as they ran about, catching pieces of manna as it floated like petals from the sky. The adults were more circumspect as they gathered the food into baskets they held under one arm, but even they couldn't help smiling as they did so. Others distributed bottles of water and packages of linen clothing that they had come upon as the twilight gathered. The group gathered in small communities and ate, and bathed, and massaged their feet, surprisingly good-spirited after a week's walking on the road past Kandahar.

Hila watched as the men set up the large tent for the Mahdi.

"*What troubles you, child?*" the Mahdi asked her as they ate their evening meal together.

You calling me 'child,' she wanted to answer. Then she wondered if he could read her thoughts as she heard his.

"*No, I can't,*" came the reply. He smiled at her kindly.

Hila laughed in response. "Everything troubles me, Mahdi," she answered. "We are not safe here, on the road. It is far to Jerusalem. So much trouble lies between here and there."

"*You are too young to be so old, Hila,*" the Mahdi replied. "*You try to see too far. Look at what is in front of you. Look at me. No one will harm us.*"

Hila shook her head. Perhaps the Mahdi was right, but she felt that somebody should worry. She turned to the sound of a commotion from farther up the road, peering into the gathering twilight.

She stood up. "You see?" she asked of the Mahdi, who was still sitting. "Something is happening. We should go see."

He waved her back to sitting. "*Eat, rest. We've walked far today.*"

"It might be trouble."

"*It might be. In which case, I'm sure it will find us in due time.*"

She scowled at him and ate her manna.

After a few minutes, a large group of men arrived. They were bearded and several carried guns of various types. Hila jumped to her feet. She cursed.

"In due time, my ass," she hissed to the Mahdi behind her. "They are Taliban, Mahdi."

"*That may be, child, but they have as much right to be here as we do.*"

Hila stood protectively, hands on hips. "What do you want?" she demanded of the newcomers.

The leader stepped forward, smiling. "So fierce!" he said. His smile disappeared. "I am told that there is one who leads you, one that calls himself Mahdi. Is this so?"

"What business is it of yours?" Hila said.

He smiled again and his companions laughed. Hila turned crimson with anger.

"I speak of faith, little one, not business," the leader said. His gaze went beyond the girl to the man seated behind her. "The valley is full of rumor, of a great man who has come to lead us. A man of God. I wish to meet this man."

"I don't give a fuck about your rumors," Hila said. "Why do you stop here? Why don't you take your guns and thugs and keep going?"

The leader turned back to Hila. "Because of the light, little one." He pointed up at the sky. Hila followed his finger but saw nothing.

"You're crazy," Hila said. "There's nothing here for you. Go on, then."

The leader shook his head. He slung his gun onto his shoulder and took out a night vision scope from his satchel. He handed the scope to Hila, but kept shifting his gaze to the Mahdi behind her.

"Look for yourself, child," the Taliban leader said.

Hila took the scope from the man and put it to her eye. She gasped in amazement. As she looked up, she traced a beam of bright green light emanating from the sky. As she followed it with the scope, turning, she saw it land squarely on the chest of the Mahdi behind her, bathing him in a bright splash of phosphorescent green. She took the device from her face and handed it back to the man.

"You see?" the leader asked. "You see now why we are here? So tell me, are you he? Are you Mahdi?" the man asked.

"Do you wish me to be?"

The leader, and each of his men, clapped their hands to

their ears. The leader fell to his knees, his gun clattering to the dirt beside him.

"With all my heart," he said, head bowed.

Herat Province, Afghanistan

As the Mahdi led his pilgrimage up the highway to the city of Herat in northern Afghanistan, their numbers swelled to over twenty thousand. Hundreds joined their ranks every day as they walked, the procession stretching for miles along the road. Helicopters buzzed overhead, some from the military investigating what was afoot in the rough countryside, others from news organizations trying to make sense of the mass of humanity below. Where before there had been only rumor and silence, now there existed a palpable movement, a swelling presence; but still, no one quite knew what was happening.

The story of the pilgrimage was lit anew with the large explosion of the Taliban stronghold in Lashkar Gah. No one knew how to connect the event to the pilgrimage, but the proximity seemed more than a coincidence. The stories of a great man, a man of God, a man who did not speak but whose mind reached out to touch those who wished to follow him —stories of a divine grace that protected the pilgrims from harm, fed them, sheltered them, spread like a wave before the pilgrims. Along their path, people left their homes to line the sides of the road in anticipation. As the pilgrimage passed, many felt compelled to join their ranks, walking away from their lives with just the clothes on their backs. Whole families joined the movement, bands of Taliban fighters, beggars and chieftains—all joined, stepping into the mass of humanity and welcomed by their fellow pilgrims, old and young.

The human river rolled north along the road to Herat. Whenever they passed a city or town, almost no one remained behind, such was the force of their movement now. Civic and religious leaders either joined the throng or were left behind, shaking their heads, ministering to no one.

Kandahar Province, Afghanistan

Grace and her three companions descended the rough track back down the mountain to the road to Kandahar. Grace kept looking about, fearful.

She looked up at the cloudless blue sky. "He could just strike us down with a bolt of lightning right now, out of a clear sky. Like back at the tree."

"True," Uriel said. "Wouldn't worry 'bout that, child."

"You wouldn't? Why not?" Grace demanded.

"He would've done it already, Grace," Azrael said consolingly. "He won't be striking you down."

"Why not?" Julius asked, still walking beside Grace.

"Don't know that," Uriel admitted. "Don't know why, but for some strange reason just killing you doesn't seem to be what He has in mind. Something else, though."

"Excision," Azrael supplied.

"Yeah," Uriel agreed.

"But why isn't killing me good enough?" Grace asked, stumbling forward down the rocky path. "Why does it have to be excision?"

"Don't know that either," Uriel said. "You should be glad of it, whatever the reason. Elsewise, you'd be long dead, girl."

"Wouldn't mind being dead," Grace muttered.

"I think you would," Azrael said.

Julius grabbed Grace's shoulder, stopping her.

"What?" Grace asked.

Julius pointed to a bend farther down the track. At the side of the path, a low scrub tree burned brightly.

"Seriously?" Uriel asked. He brushed past Grace and Julius and headed down the path.

Azrael nodded at the other two to follow Uriel. Grace shook her head.

"It does no good to stand here, child," Azrael said softly.

Julius took Grace's arm and led her ahead, Azrael following.

As they approached the burning tree, the flame grew intensely bright, the heat assaulting the four of them as they stood before it, waiting.

When nothing more happened, Uriel said, "Okay, then. Nice touch. Moving on—" He started to move past. He froze as the flames jumped across the path, then rose in a towering wall of flame that circled about them, the heat intensifying, now from all around, climbing above them, causing the four to cower together. Azrael raised his cane defiantly and began to speak in Aramaic, raising his voice over the crackling of the flames. In seconds, his cane burst into flames and he threw it aside. He stopped talking.

THE BEGINNING OF HUMAN PRIDE IS TO FORSAKE THE LORD; THE HEART HAS WITHDRAWN FROM ITS MAKER.

HE REMOVES SOME OF THEM AND DESTROYS THEM, AND ERASES THE MEMORY OF THEM FROM THE EARTH. PRIDE WAS NOT CREATED FOR MEN, OR VIOLENT ANGER FOR THOSE BORN OF WOMEN.

Kandahar Province, Afghanistan

The flames retreated, guttered, then flickered out. The furnace-like heat was replaced by the usual oppressive dry wind of Afghanistan.

Uriel spat on the charred ground before them. "I swear the Guy's got one good trick and that's about all," he said.

Grace clung to Julius, shaking uncontrollably.

Azrael kicked at the burnt pieces remaining of his cane. "Had that one for two hundred years, at least," he sighed. "Gift from the last wife."

Grace gradually found her voice, her shaking coming under control slowly. "It said…" she quavered, trailing off.

"He said," Uriel said, rounding on her, "'He erases the memory of people like you from the earth.'"

"Sirach, chapter ten, verse twelve," Azrael said.

"Not helpful, Azrael," Uriel said.

"Excision," Julius whispered.

"Yeah, excision," Uriel agreed. "Brilliant, Father. Subtle, He ain't. And we're not getting any younger, standing here in this sun. Damn, I feel like a piece of burnt toast. Move!"

Purgatory

"Guys!"

The members of the work group continued to argue around the big conference table.

"Guys!"

Libby appeared in the doorway, white and trembling.

"Guys!" she screamed into the room. Everyone stopped talking and looked over to her.

"What, Libby?" Arthur asked.

She pointed a shaking finger at the large monitor screen on the side wall of the conference room. On it, a red-orange flare was blossoming across the screen, obliterating the image of the ground below.

"Holy shit," Elliot whispered. "What the fuck is that?"

Libby dropped her arm. "I was sitting in the control room when it started," she explained. "It started just outside the valley."

"Is it the Mahdi's group?" Arthur asked.

"No, way behind. Just the other side of the ridge from the valley," Libby explained. "But," she said, voice cracking, "it's really big. Off the charts, big."

They all watched as the flare obliterated the entire scene on the monitor.

"God damn," Elliot whispered.

"Yeah, probably," Gabriel agreed.

Libby sat and took a deep breath. "What does it mean?" she asked.

"It means," Gabriel explained, "that we've got His attention, that's what it means. This shit just got real."

"So now what?" Arthur asked.

"Now we play Messiah," Gabe said. "And see if He wants to play along."

"No fucking way we can play in that league," Elliot said. "I don't have much of a feed, that whatever-it-is knocked the drone offline, but—" he tapped furiously on his keyboard, staring at the screen in front of him, "that's like thermonuclear output. We can't do that shit."

"We find a way to do that shit, Elliot. We have to find a way."

Elliot threw his hands up and leaned back in his chair. "I'm not God, Jim, I'm just an engineer."

There was silence in the room.

"Then we're fucked," Gabriel said. "And so is Grace."

Gödel raised his hand from the other side of the table. No one noticed, so he waved it about a little bit until he got Gabriel's attention.

"Yes, *herr Doktor*?" Gabriel asked, sighing.

Gödel cleared his throat nervously. "We do not have such abilities as we see there," he said in his thick accent, pointing toward the completely blank screen. "We need help, I think."

"Yeah, Doc, I'm with you," Elliot said. "We need help. You got anybody in mind? Because I don't see anyone at this table that's gonna be much help. No offense, Nick."

Tesla looked up from his spot at the table. He looked about to try to discern who had mentioned his name but was met with blank faces. He went back to sketching on his notepad.

"My point, exactly," Elliot added.

Gödel nodded. "More dead mathematicians, Gabriel. We

need to get with us *Doktor* Noether."

"Noether? Never heard of Noether. Who is he?" Arthur asked.

"Noether? As in the Noether theorem—that Noether?" Elliot asked. "Why don't you just get Einstein here while you're at it, doc?"

Gödel nodded more vigorously at that. "Exactly, Elliot. She is a she, not a he. Emmy Noether. I believe you are correct, Elliot. They are very close friends, you know. We get Emmy, I do not doubt that Albert also joins us. Then we are good to go with this God game, no? Then we are serious shit. Emmy is who we need."

"Sure, Kurt. No problem. I'll get right on it," Gabriel said.

"If you want, I will talk to them," Gödel offered. "If you can get me back to Princeton, I will talk to him."

"Who?"

"Albert," Gödel explained. "We have access to closed time-like curve, I go back to Princeton and walk with Albert, telling him that we need him and Emmy. They will help, I think."

"Princeton when?" Gabriel asked.

"1955, please."

"But it says here Noether died in '35, Kurt," Elliot said, tapping his screen.

"*Ja*," Gödel said, smiling. "That is why Albert will help us. He missed her terribly, you know."

Kandahar Province, Afghanistan

"What?" Uriel asked, giving Grace a shove in the back as they walked down the mountainside. "You rattled, girl?"

Grace only managed to nod as they trudged along the rocky track.

"What did you think was gonna happen?" Uriel continued. "You thought you'd have a friendly little chat with Him over tea and crumpets? Put your hand on Our Lord's knee, maybe show a little cleavage as you sweet talk Him into buying your little game, girl? That what you thought?" Uriel pushed her again and Grace stumbled. Julius wheeled on the other man.

"Leave it, Earl," Julius snarled. "We're all a bit rattled."

"We are? I'm not," Uriel said. "You rattled, Azrael?" The old man shook his head slightly as they walked along. "Naw, Azrael not rattled. And he's just an old geezer with a burned-up cane. You know why we're not rattled, son? Because old Azrael and me, we ain't stupid, that's why. We know what we're playing at. You and your girlfriend, though, that's another story, isn't it? Sounded pretty smart when you started this *schtick*, setting up God real good. Helluva grifter, eh girl? The big con. You ever stop to think you might be the one being played here? Huh? Ever think you might not be the smartest player in this game, after all?"

Grace pulled up short and spun on her heel, shoving Uriel in the chest. He stumbled back but managed not to fall over.

"What do you want from me, Earl? You want me to say I fucked up? Want to hear me say I'm scared? Well, yeah, Earl —I'm scared. Maybe I fucked this up for good. Maybe I'm in way over my head. Maybe I got all the people I care about completely fucked with me. What the fuck do you want me to do about it, anyway?"

Uriel smiled at her, then at his friend. "You see, Azrael? I told you she was tough. And not as stupid as most." He turned back to Grace. "I want you to tell me that we're gonna finish this. That you're not going to quit on me, girl. Because that little scene back there ain't dink compared to what's waiting for us."

Grace smiled weakly and started walking again.

"Shit, Earl," she said as she walked, "now you're just trying to scare me."

"Scared or not," Julius said, walking beside his friend, "not like we can turn things back at this point."

They walked on in silence for a while.

"It's not gonna work, is it?" Grace asked finally.

"No, it ain't," Uriel said. "Not the way you figured, anyway."

"No fiddle game?" Julius asked.

Azrael shook his head. "He doesn't play the fiddle. That's the other guy."

"Lord above must've seen that coming from a mile away, anyhow," Uriel added. "He can play both sides of that game and leave you breathless."

"Then I'm fucked," Grace said.

"We're all fucked," Julius added.

"Well, Grace probably is, anyway," Uriel said. "Azrael and I gonna be okay, regardless. You, Julius, are already, irrevocably, fucked."

"Well, that's a relief," Julius said.

"Just givin' up then, huh, Gracie?" Uriel asked.

"You just said it wasn't going to work, Earl," Grace said.

"You're little fiddle game won't, that's a fact. What else you got, girl? Gotta move on to Plan B. Always have to have a Plan B. That's the nature of the grift."

Grace shuffled to halt. They had reached the bottom of the mountain, where the path dropped onto the road. She sat down on a large rock, shaking her head. "Doesn't matter what I think. He's going to know, like you said."

Uriel sat down on another rock, wagging his finger at her. "Didn't say that. He knows what you're doing, that's true. But He doesn't know what's in here," he said, tapping his chest. "He doesn't know why you're doing it. That's your edge, Grace."

"He knows why, Earl. Because I'm trying not to get excised."

"Can't be just surviving," Azrael said. "Has to be something worth surviving for. That's something He can't know."

"Maybe," Julius said, sitting down next to Grace, "we just need to run like hell."

Uriel nodded. "Best idea you've had so far, Padre."

EVAN GELLER

Kandahar Province, Afghanistan

"I thought He knew everything," Julius said, still sitting next to Grace.

"Why? Because He wrote that in His book?" Uriel asked. "Just propaganda, that's all that is. He knows a lot, don't let me kid you. Pretty much everything that happened, if He has a care to. Almost what's happening, too, as it happens."

"But not the future?" Grace asked.

"Yeah, He knows that, too," Uriel admitted.

"Oh. Great." Grace said, her head hanging.

"But only His future," Azrael added.

"What does that mean?" Julius asked.

"Look, God—the current God, that is—comes from the future, you know," Azrael said.

"What do you mean, 'the current God?'" Julius asked.

"Just what I said. The guy being God at this particular time," Azrael said.

Julius opened his mouth to say something and just shook his head instead.

"This one's been at it a long time, of course," Azrael continued. "Over two thousand years. But He's not the first. Don't think he's even the second."

"He's not the Creator, then?" Julius asked.

"Course not," Uriel said. He spat. "That's ridiculous."

"He only knows His future," Azrael continued. "The future He came from. But time is fluid, and the future He came from —the one that leads from where we are now—well, that's not set in stone. No one really knows how this all plays out. Not even Him."

Grace kicked at the dirt under her boot. "I never really believed it was Him."

"What didn't you believe, child?" Azrael asked.

"Never really believed He even...I just—I didn't really think it was really God that wanted me excised, you know?" Grace replied, looking up at the old Jew.

"Who'd you think was playin' for you, girl?" Uriel asked.

"I don't know. I guess I was hoping it was just Donovan or the Church or somebody. Somebody—normal."

"Somebody we actually had a chance of getting past," Julius added.

"Donovan's just a pawn," Uriel said, squatting. He picked up a rock and examined it closely. "No, girl. It's God after your immortal soul. That's just a fact. Told you that a bunch of times. Lots of people told you that."

"But why, Earl? What have I done to piss Him off?"

Uriel carefully held the small rock between his thumb and forefinger in front of his face. He squinted at it. He didn't say anything for a moment.

"It's a rock, Earl," Julius said, interrupting his reverie. Azrael settled onto a boulder with a grunt.

Uriel looked up from his study of the rock. "Hmm? Yeah, that's the million dollar question, Gracie. That is the question." They watched as Uriel held the small rock steady in front of him, then carefully released it from his pinch. The rock stayed in place, turning slowly in midair. Uriel smiled at it.

Azrael shook his head. "It is indeed the fundamental question in our situation," Azrael said. "Unfortunately, we don't have the answer."

"But we have to know," Grace said, trying not to stare at the floating rock. "If we don't know why He wants me excised, how are we going to stop Him?"

"Yeah," Uriel agreed. "That's a bit of a problem."

Grace and Julius watched the rock slowly rotate in midair.

"I haven't done anything," Grace murmured. "I mean, I did kill a priest, but that doesn't get a person excised, does it?"

"Not in the least," Azrael said. "No offense, Father Zimmerman."

"None taken."

"Doesn't even have to be something you did," Uriel explained. "Might be something you didn't do."

"Like sin," Julius said. "For what we have done, or left un-done."

"Might well be something you're going to do, but haven't done yet."

"Well, I won't do it, then," Grace said, exasperated. "Shit, Earl, I've been dead already. I'll just go back to being dead. I won't bother anybody."

"But that's the point, isn't it, girl?" Uriel said. He held his hand under the rock and it dropped into his palm like a string had been cut. "You've done a lot, 'specially after you were dead. Pushed shit back into the past. Hell, Grace, you're the first person I ever seen work both sides like that, before and after."

"My sister..." Grace said, then trailed off.

"Twins," Azrael explained to Julius's questioning expression.

"So, I'm screwed," Grace said. "I've either already done the thing He doesn't want me to do, or I'm going to do it even if I don't want to because I don't know what it is I'm not sup-posed to do. And when I do it—"

"Or if you've done it already," Julius added helpfully.

"I get excised."

"Yeah, pretty much," Uriel agreed. He tossed the small stone to Grace, who caught it.

"What is it?" Grace asked, looking at the brown, feature-less stone in her hand.

"It's a rock," Uriel said.

"I see that. Is it some kind of special rock?"

"Looked pretty special when it was floating there, didn't it?" Uriel said, winking at her. Grace nodded.

"God, I hate when he starts with the parables," Azrael said. He stood and dusted off his pants. "Our ride is coming," he announced.

Kandahar Province, Afghanistan

They looked down the road to where a cloud of dust approached.

"Our ride?" Julius asked.

Azrael nodded. "I'm too old to walk back to Kandahar," he explained.

"You're planning on getting a ride with the Taliban?" Julius asked, staring at the approaching vehicles.

"Course not," Azrael said. "I paid one of the locals, before we left."

"Well," Julius said, standing and squinting into the distance, "your local yokel decided to discuss your travel arrangement with the militia. Of which about a dozen are coming this way."

Azrael shook his head in disgust. "I dislike this country more and more, I must say. I paid that man a significant sum of money—in advance."

"Shocking," Uriel said.

Julius stood and looked at the approaching vehicles, now clearly a pair of white pickup trucks, each carrying armed men.

"Do we have weapons?" Julius asked.

"I have a few knives," Uriel said. He spat.

"I'm afraid my cane is ashes," Azrael apologized.

"What are we going to do?" Julius asked. He looked down on Grace who remained sitting, rubbing the stone in her hand.

"Get shot, looks like," Uriel explained.

"Probably quite a few times," Azrael agreed.

"What? We have to do something. Hide or something."

Uriel gestured at the landscape around them. "Don't think that's a very practical idea, Father. Besides, I think they know we're here. Seeing as they drove all the way out here just to meet us."

"Well, we can't just stand here and let ourselves be killed," Julius stammered.

"Killed? Nobody said anything about getting killed," Uriel said.

EVAN GELLER

"But you just said—" Julius said.

Azrael put a hand on the priest's shoulder. "We don't die, Father."

"Neither do you," Uriel said.

"What? What are you two talking about?"

Uriel shook his head. "Told you, back when we met your alter ego, back there in New York City. The other Zimmerman gets to die. Not you."

Julius looked back and forth between the two old men.

Azrael squeezed his shoulder. "Sorry, Father."

Julius dropped back down on the rock next to Grace. "I don't understand," he said.

"Told you, son. You got snookered, while you were back saving Gracie. Never would've sent you back like I did if I thought such a thing could happen. I am sorry, Julius." The old black man looked down at him for a moment, then turned back to the approaching trucks. "You must've noticed, Julius," he continued. "You're not the same. Only partly here. Sometimes, people see right past you."

"Just like him," Azrael added, nodding at Uriel.

"Yeah," Uriel said. "Just like me."

"Not exactly, though," Azrael added. "Uriel here was special. Before the Fall," Azrael said, nodding respectfully.

"None of that matters now," Uriel said bitterly. "Only thing matters now is that those clowns coming down the road only a threat to Gracie, here. Not us."

Grace looked up at that. "Why are they a threat to me, then?"

"Because, you girl, can die. You know that. And if you do, you will be well and truly fucked. Which may well and truly fuck everyone else."

Grace nodded.

"And these guys," Uriel continued, "most likely want you dead. Can't think of a lot of other reasons they came all the way out here."

Julius said, "So what are we going to do?"

Uriel spat. Azrael shrugged.

"That's all you got?" Grace asked. She watched as the trucks bounced over the rutted road, now close enough to see almost a dozen Taliban aboard, many with guns slung over their shoulders.

"Let's just see how this plays out," Uriel said.

"Really?" Julius asked. "That's the plan?"

The trucks gouged to a halt in a cloud of dust just short of where they stood. A gaunt man in a black and white keffiyeh stepped down from the lead truck and walked up to Grace, ignoring the others. He stared at her, then gestured for her to get in the truck. She looked at Uriel, who shrugged. Grace walked to the truck and got in, the man climbing in beside her. Uriel, Azrael, and Julius climbed into the back of the pickup. The trucks moved off, making a broad turn before heading back through the cloud of dust and up the road from which they had come. Julius sat next to Uriel on a pile of frayed carpets. Azrael sat across from them next to a young bearded man with an AK-47 across his lap.

Julius turned to Uriel beside him. "I thought you said these guys were going to kill her," he said.

"What makes you think they're not?" Uriel asked him.

"They could've just gunned us down back there."

Uriel shook his head. "Far as they're concerned, we don't count."

"So you keep saying. But they could've just killed Grace as easily as putting her in the truck."

"Can't lie to you, Zimmerman," Uriel said. "I don't have a great deal of insight into the current situation."

"But you think you know why so many people want to kill Grace."

"I think I know a lot of things. Doesn't mean I know anything."

"Why do they want to kill her? Same reason as God?"

"No. If God wanted Grace dead, she'd be dead. God kills people every day, obviously. God wants her excised, not dead."

"So why would others want her dead?"

"Because if Grace is dead, she can't be excised, can she?"

Julius had to think about this for a minute.

"You're saying that something or someone is working against God, against his plan to have her excised?"

Uriel nodded.

"Who?"

"Devil if I know," Uriel said.

Julius hung his head at that.

"Maybe," Azrael said from across the truck bed.

April 15, 1955 Princeton, New Jersey

Gödel strolled beside his friend, admiring the young students who walked briskly past.

"Of course I miss her," Einstein said. "She was truly brilliant. And funny, as well. Those two traits rarely exist side by side, you know, Kurt."

"If you say so, Albert."

"I have known many women, Kurt. Always either brilliant or pleasant. Never both. Did you ever meet my first wife?"

"I don't believe I ever had the pleasure, Albert."

"It wasn't. Brilliant, but not pleasant. Emmy was the exception, bless her."

Kurt sighed under his breath. "And you, Albert? Also an exception?"

"I dare say, wouldn't you, Kurt?"

"I reserve judgement," Gödel answered with a smile. "Listen, my friend," Gödel continued before Einstein could protest. "I have a little proposition for you. Are you interested?"

"A proposition? That relates to Emmy? What type of proposition?"

DO NOT FOR A MOMENT BELIEVE THAT I AM NOT AWARE OF YOUR TERRIBLE PAIN. I KNOW THE PAIN

THE WISE SILENCE OF GOD

OF YOUR LOSS, OF YOUR HOPELESSNESS, THAT YOUR DEEPEST FEAR IS THAT YOU ARE FORSAKEN. YOU LOOK UP FROM THE DIRT AND SEE ONLY DARKNESS. YOU CALL OUT AS THE ONES YOU HOLD DEAREST LEAVE YOUR WORLD AND LEAVE YOU BEHIND, WITH NOTHING BUT YOUR UNSTEADY FAITH TO SALVE THE WOUND.

WHY DO I MAKE YOU SUFFER SO?

YOUR GOD COULD LET YOU SEE THE REALITY THAT LIES BEYOND. I COULD SHOW YOU THAT THE GREAT MASSES OF DARK MATTER WHICH SURROUND AND ENGULF YOUR LITTLE STAGE ARE NOTHING LESS THAN THE SOULS OF ALL; THOSE THAT WERE, THOSE THAT WILL BE. THAT THE PROPERTY OF DARKNESS IS BUT A VEIL THAT I HAVE DRAWN BETWEEN YOU AND THOSE THAT ARE LOST TO YOU. THAT THESE ELEGIAC ELEMENTS ARE THE VERY SEA THROUGH WHICH YOUR LITTLE ISLAND SAILS, SO TURBULENT AND STORM-TOSSED. YOUR GOD COULD ENLIGHTEN YOU TO THIS SIMPLE TRUTH, AND IN SO DOING, TURN THE WEAK GLOW OF FAITH'S FAINT CANDLE FLAME TO THE BURNING BRIGHT KNOWLEDGE OF YOUR FUTURE FOREVER; FAMILIES REJOINED, LOST CHILDREN RETURNED, ALL SUFFERING ENDED AND FORGOTTEN.

YOUR GOD COULD DO THAT.

ALAS, NO. YOUR GOD, MY CHILD, IS GOING WITH A DIFFERENT APPROACH.

Kandahar Province, Afghanistan

"Maybe we should try to do something," Julius said. "You know, before they try to kill Grace."

"You're probably right," Azrael agreed.

Uriel nodded.

"Shouldn't be too hard," Julius continued, "since we can't be killed or anything."

"Not very hard at all," Azrael said. "I'd be happy to distract this young man while you take his weapon and shoot him."

Julius looked back and forth between his two companions.

"Or maybe not," Julius said after a bit. Uriel stared at him, eyes narrowed. "I'm just saying, there must be another side to all this. Isn't there?"

"Another side to what?" Azrael asked.

Julius paused, staring back at Uriel.

"Like you said, there are other forces involved here. I mean, we're in the middle of something. I saw it back in the valley, with the Mahdi. This isn't just about us."

"Isn't just about Grace, you mean," Azrael said.

"Yeah. I've been on her side, you know, the whole time since I met here, don't get me wrong. I've saved her ass a bunch of times, you know that. Shit, I died for her." He stared at Uriel and waited, but the old black man only stared back. "But we've officially taken this too far. The situation is changed."

"Changed how, Father?" Azrael asked.

"The whole situation is changed. Reality is changed. I mean, those people I had killed—they're alive now. That little baby is alive now, somehow. The Mahdi was able to save those people. I'm thinking we shouldn't—I shouldn't—screw that up again."

"You think helping Grace might bring back some past

transgression?" Azrael asked.

"Well, isn't that how this works?" Julius asked, looking at Uriel but getting no response. "We're talking about setting up this Mahdi guy to take the fall for Grace, right? That's the whole plan, right? That's the con she's running. But maybe that's not right. We set up the Mahdi, we save Grace--maybe. But at what price? Who suffers for her gain? If the Mahdi isn't around to save those people, what then? Who are we to say that Grace's life is more important than the lives of that family, of that little boy? Especially if it really is God's will that we're trying to go against here? What gives us the right?"

He looked between Azrael and Uriel, waiting.

The truck bounced over the rutted dirt track, then climbed a short embankment and turned onto a paved road.

"You done?" Uriel asked. "Or maybe we should get Grace back here, let her weigh in on your proposal?"

Julius flushed and looked down. "I care about her, you know that. I wouldn't have done what I've done if I didn't. It's just—"

"You care about yourself just a little bit more, Father," Azrael said.

"No," Julius said, turning on the old man. "That's not it. You said God wants her excised. There's got to be some reason, some higher plan."

"Does there?" Uriel asked. Julius looked back at him and nodded. "Maybe there does," Uriel agreed. He spat onto the bed of the truck between his feet. "Which is why is doesn't matter that you want to throw your friend under this bus."

"I don't—"

"Shut up, Zimmerman," Uriel said. "Don't matter, one way or the other what you want or what you're willing to do. Because there is a higher plan, something more important than a few more dead babies in the world, or Grace being excised from this existence forever, or whether you have an easier time sleeping at night. You think I'm spending my time in the back of this fuckin' truck because I give a rat's ass about your conscience, or if that girl ever existed? You think any one of your immortal souls counts for anything to me? Hell no, Padre. Hell no. A higher plan, is right. That's why He's playing this game, that's why we're in this shit. You want out? Good luck with that, Julius. Stakes are a damn lot higher than your guilt over getting some family killed. Damn lot higher."

Uriel stared at him, judging. Julius dropped his head and sighed deeply.

"I don't know what to believe," Julius said.

"Why should you?" Uriel said. "Nobody else does, either."

Azrael clapped Zimmerman on the back. "Have faith, Father. Have faith."

Purgatory

"On a more practical matter," Arthur interrupted. He pointed to the map projected on the monitor on the wall. "Our parade is approaching the border with Iran."

"Yeah," Libby said. "Making pretty good time, considering."

"Yeah, amazing," Arthur agreed. "Only I don't think the Iranians are keen to see them cross their border. Elliot?"

Elliot nodded from the other side of the table. " 'Fraid not, boss. The Iranians have moved a brigade of Revolutionary Guards to the border crossing with Afghanistan. Doesn't look like a very friendly reception."

CHAPTER 14

Kandahar Province, Afghanistan

The truck crunched to a halt just short of where the dirt road climbed an embankment to the paved highway. They heard a commotion from within the cab of the truck, followed by the driver getting out and getting back in on the passenger side. The truck started again with a jerk, then moved along faster once it swerved onto the paved highway.

"Where are they taking us?" Julius asked. Uriel shrugged. "Ask this guy," Julius said to Azrael, gesturing.

Azrael had a brief exchange with the young man with the automatic rifle. At its conclusion, the man drew his finger across his neck, smiling at all three of them.

"He said—" Azrael began.

"Yeah, we got the gist," Julius said. "I'm thinking maybe we should do something. You know, before we get to wherever these guys want to take care of business."

"Don't think we have to worry 'bout it," Uriel said, looking over the cab of the truck and shielding his eyes.

"Did you miss this dude's subtle little gesture, there at the end?" Julius asked.

"No, I saw it. Just seems the plan's changed, is all." He pointed ahead.

The other two looked down the road they were traveling. In the haze ahead, an airport loomed up from the twisting landscape.

"Huh," Julius said, looking. "That's a funny place to kill a person."

"Yeah, looks like someone changed the plan without telling this guy," Azrael said.

"Think he'll be upset?" Julius asked.

"Maybe," Uriel said. "He seems to like that gun."

"Probably best to relieve him of the weapon, Julius," Azrael advised.

At this point, the young man noticed the airport, too. He was, indeed, upset. He pounded on the roof of the truck cab until he felt Uriel's knife at his throat. Julius took the rifle. He turned and fired on the following the truck's tires, disabling the vehicle as their own truck continued on the highway to the airport. Julius threw the weapon away as they sped off. The young man resumed banging on the roof of the cab.

The truck slowed and pulled off to the side of the road, rolling to a stop. The driver's side door opened and Grace got out, swearing.

"Who the hell is pounding on the roof?" she demanded, glaring at the man standing up in the bed of the truck. Azrael nodded at him. "Well, what the fuck do you want?"

The man began yelling at Grace in Arabic.

Grace shook her head. "I got no time for this," she said.

"He's asking where his friends are," Azrael translated.

"Oh," Grace said. "Tell him to hold on a second." She walked around the front of the truck and pulled open the passenger door. One of the men climbed out, pale and shaking. He stood next to the truck, arms raised. Grace reached back into the truck and pulled out a second man—the one wearing the kaffiyeh—who fell out of the truck and onto the dirt, unconscious.

"Azrael, tell the young man to come down here so we can be on our way, please," Grace said. Azrael translated. The young man looked confused. Grace stepped over to the man standing next to her and spoke something in his ear. The man nodded, then gestured for the young man to come down. He yelled to him in Arabic as well. The young man clumsily jumped down.

"Thank you," Grace said. "You guys want to ride in here?"

"Julius will join you," Azrael said. "Uriel and I will continue to enjoy the fresh breeze, I believe."

"Whatever," Grace said, walking over to climb back in the driver's seat. Julius jumped down and, smiling apologetically to the two men standing next to the truck, climbed into the passenger side. Grace pulled the truck back onto the highway and accelerated towards the airport.

"Hi," Julius said.

"Hi."

"I was pretty sure those guys wanted to kill us," Julius said.

"Yeah, probably."

"Talked them out of it, huh?"

"Not really. But once the big honcho guy cracked his head on the windshield back there, and I waved his pistol at the other guy's head, they decided to let me drive."

"Oh."

"Throw that thing out the window, will you?" she added, nodding at the gun on the dashboard.

"You sure? Might come in handy, never know," Julius said.

"Pretty sure it's loaded," Grace said. "Makes me nervous."

Julius shrugged and tossed the pistol out the window.

"So, where're we going?"

"Airport, Julius. Fly away home."

"Can we do that?"

"Baby steps, Julius. Baby steps."

"Yeah? So what's baby step number one?"

She turned to look at him, then stole a glance out the back window.

"Step one: run away as fast as we can."

"Pretty sure that's not gonna be fast enough, Grace."

"Yeah, but we're running *away*," she explained, turning front again. "So we're going to make God choose—does He want me, or does He want to go after the other guy."

"Why can't He do both? He's God."

"Because, Julius," she explained, blowing a lock of her hair up off her forehead as she drove, "that wouldn't be fair. Even God has to make choices, right?"

"Not sure I heard anyone say this was supposed to be fair," Julius said.

"We just have to trust that Gabe and Arthur are making the other guy a bigger pain in the arse than I am."

"Yeah? How are they going to do that?" Julius asked.

Grace shook her head, driving faster now. "That's not our problem."

Bagram Airport, Afghanistan

They saw the plane as soon as they passed the gate to the airport, the big black 747 that had carried them here.

Grace smiled at the sight as she drove the truck towards the ramp.

"Looks like Arthur's looking out for us," Julius said.

Grace nodded. "Hope so, Julius. That is, after all, his job."

"What's that?" Julius asked, squinting through the dirt-smeared windshield.

"It's an airplane," Grace answered.

"No, that," Julius said, pointing ahead.

Grace saw it then. A shimmering curtain vaguely stood between them and the plane, like air rising from hot pavement on a summer's day.

"Maybe we should stop. Or at least slow down, huh?" Julius suggested.

Grace pushed the accelerator to the floor. The truck leapt forward, nearly sending the two old men behind her tumbling.

"Yeah, maybe," Grace said.

"Should we jump?" Azrael asked, holding on tightly to the side of the truck, staring at the strange curtain quickly approaching.

"We're too old to jump," Uriel said.

"Pray, then?"

"Too smart for that," Uriel said, smiling.

"Probably wouldn't help anyway," Azrael said.

"Never has before," Uriel agreed.

The truck was still accelerating when it passed through the curtain of air, but without the slightest sensation of slowing, it came out the other side, stopped dead. Grace and Julius looked at each other, puzzled. The plane was gone. The airport was gone. Everything, it seemed, was gone. A featureless grayness rapidly spread before them in every direction. As they watched, the truck disappeared from beneath them.

"This can't be good," Julius said, but Grace heard him as if he were already a great distance away. She saw him reach his hand across the seat towards her, but as she reached her hand towards his, Julius too faded into the grayness and was gone. She twisted to look behind her.

She was alone. Alone in a gray fog.

The Director of the St. Brigid's Mental Health Hospital stood appalled, listening to the animal screams emanating from the room at the end of the hallway.

"Jesus, Mary, and Joseph," the doctor cursed at the coterie of physicians and nurses attending his morning rounds. "What in God's name is going on down there?" The screaming modulated into a desperate wailing, then the sickening smack of a body being thrown against a wall, which started the screaming anew.

"It's the girl, sir, the one we were

discussing yesterday," the nursing director answered, trying not to look in the direction of the awful sound.

The Director strode purposefully down the hall, followed by his entourage, their heads down and jaws clenched at what they already knew they would encounter. The Director came to the door of the room from which the pitiful sound continued to emanate, his face reddening as he watched the source of the inhuman screaming through the small window set in the door, watched as the girl, naked and bloody, threw herself about the room, first at the walls, then onto the floor, finally causing the Director to flinch back as she crashed into the heavy metal door inches in front of his face.

"MY BABY, MY BABY, MY BABY, GIVE ME BACK MY BABY, MY BABY, MY BABY, GIVE ME MY BABY…"

The Director turned to face the others. He stared at them, fists balled at his sides, all flinching at the sound of their patient crashing against the door yet again, the wailing even more piercing than before. "You tell Dr. McIntosh," the Director said evenly, barely raising his voice to be heard over the awful din, "that I wish this patient to be sedated and restrained at once. And that once he has seen to the safety of his patient, that he report immediately to my office. Is that clear?" They all nodded. The Director stared again through the window and shook his head. "And bring her as well." He strode purposefully away as the girl's face appeared, tear-stained and encrusted with blood, pressed against the window, her mouth twisted in a scream which chased the Director back up the hall to his office.

Thirty minutes later, Dr. McIntosh and the nursing supervisor sat across the desk from the the Director. The patient, restrained in a canvas straight-jacket and leather straps, slumped unresponsive in a wheelchair just inside the door. An attendant periodically dabbed at the spittle from the young girl's mouth so as to prevent it from soiling the carpet.

"Dr. McIntosh," the Director began, "how long have you been employed in my hospital?"

"Almost two years, Dr. Murphy,"
the young man stammered.

"And in the almost two years spent working in my hospital, have you ever—even once—witnessed a patient so completely uncontrolled, so painfully and obviously under-medicated, as the spectacle which I was forced to witness on your ward this morning?"

"No, sir, but you must understand—" the young psychiatrist started, but then halted under the older doctor's withering gaze.

"What must I understand?" the Director asked.

The younger man sat speechless and could only shake his head.

"The girl is medicated on a regular basis," the nursing supervisor volunteered. "She is receiving dosages greatly in excess of the therapeutic limit, without interruption, I assure you, Dr. Murphy. I am sorry that you had to see such behavior on my unit, but I must—"

"You must what, Miss Withers? You are sorry I witnessed the gross mistreatment of your patient or that the mistreatment is due to such professional incompetence? I will not tolerate a patient in my hospital to suffer in an animalistic state such as the one which I just witnessed. There can be no excuse." He turned back to the staff doctor. "Present the case, Dr. McIntosh."

"It's the same patient I presented on treatment rounds last week, Dr. Murphy," the young man said, puzzled. The Director continued to stare at him. "Very well. The patient,"

he began, coughed, swallowed hard, and re-
started, "The patient is a thirteen year old
Caucasian female, involuntarily confined to
treatment at the behest of the Mother Superior,
Sisters of Mercy orphanage. Shortly after her
arrival, she was determined to be pregnant and
began—"

"You are mistaken, Dr. McIntosh," the
Director interrupted. The other doctor
looked at him, confused, but the Director
only waited for him to continue.

Dr. McIntosh continued, "She began a
regular series of therapeutic electroshock
interventions, combined with Thorazine
injections around the clock until such
time as her gravid state—"

"You are mistaken, Dr. McIntosh," the Dir-
ector repeated, again interrupting the presen-
tation. The other man gaped at him, again
silenced by his confusion. "Your treatment regi-
men has failed, Dr. McIntosh, because you have
made an error in diagnosis."

The other man was flabbergasted.
"Of course, the girl is schizophrenic,
I was getting to that, but—"

The older man shook his head. "Your diag-
nosis of pregnancy is in error. Your patient

423

is intractable to your therapeutic medications and electroconvulsive therapy because you are not treating her underlying psychotic delusion."

McIntosh stared, puzzled.
"What delusion?"

"That the patient was ever pregnant."

The other man opened his mouth to speak but no sound came out. Again, it was the nurse who managed to respond.

"But Dr. Murphy," the nurse said, "when the girl came to us, she was pregnant. She delivered a baby boy, two months ago, as you well know. Her pregnancy is not a delusion."

"Where is the child?" the Director demanded.

"Why, it has been transferred, of course. To the Sisters, to the Home for Wayward Girls in Galway. We have no facilities to care for—"

"There is no child," the Director said.

"I don't understand," the nurse said.

"There is no child, no actual baby, here in this hospital?"

"No, of course not, Doctor."

"There is no baby. And the girl, your patient, was never pregnant," the Director explained.

"But of course she was," the

nurse protested. She lifted the patient's chart from her lap. "It's all documented. Of course she was."

"Show me," the Director said, leaning forward on his desk.

The nurse stood and opened the thick chart on the desk before him, bending over to indicate the pages documenting the girl's labor and delivery. She straightened as the Director appeared to be reading the indicated section. The nurse gasped as the Director carefully and deliberately tore the pages from the chart and deposited them in his waste bin. He closed the chart and held it up to the nurse.

"There is no baby. The girl was never pregnant," he said sternly. The nurse stared at him, then took the chart back and held it against her chest, arms crossed. "You may go now, Miss Withers." The Director waited until the door had closed behind the nursing supervisor. He addressed the young psychiatrist. "Your treatment is failing, Dr. McIntosh, because you have not addressed the underlying cause of your patient's psychosis. For this reason, you are allowing your patient to suffer in a most inhumane manner. Look at her, look at what you've done!" the Director said, pointing to the patient slumped awkwardly in her chair. "It is your professional duty, doctor, to direct your therapy to the complete elimination of the girl's belief in the existence of a baby, or even of having ever been pregnant. Do you understand? Electroshock, certainly. Thorazine, certainly. But these treatments, and any other you deem appropriate, must be directed to utterly burning out that part of her memory which is the source of her suffering. What I just did to that chart, you must do to her mind." He stared at the other doctor.

"I'm not sure I agree..."

"I care not in the least what you're sure of, or to what you agree, Dr. McIntosh."

"But it seems inhumane to deprive a mother in such a way. To do such a thing will leave her damaged, no doubt."

"Inhumane? You have been treating this girl for over eleven months and her suffering is beyond anything which I have ever encountered in practice. It is you who are being inhumane, Dr. McIntosh, and I cannot abide any inadequacy of therapy which allows a young girl to suffer so. I believe that her only chance at recovery, any prospect for mental hygiene at all, lies in the treatment plan which I have out-

lined. The girl is thirteen, which means that we have three years of compulsory therapeutic intervention in which to try to restore her to some semblance of health. I'm not making a recommendation, Doctor. Treat your patient as I have prescribed or resign your post, but I will not allow a patient in my institute to suffer in this manner. Not for another moment. Do you understand me?"

The young psychiatrist nodded.

"Very well then, Doctor McIntosh," the Director said. "Please keep me informed of your patient's progress."

The younger doctor stood to leave.

"Oh, and Dr. McIntosh," the Director began. McIntosh turned back from the door. "See that she is sterilized as well. As soon as possible. It won't do to have her psychosis set off anew, if by some miracle you are successful in your treatment."

Kandahar Province, Afghanistan

Grace saw a light, small and feeble, seeming at a great distance in the gray fog before her. She wrapped her arms about herself and shivered.

The light grew brighter, yellow. It danced slightly, like a candle. She couldn't tell how far away it was, all grayness above and below.

"*Kneel before the Lord,*" came the command, pure and strong, from all about her. The light danced.

Grace knelt.

"*Dear child,*" the voice sighed, a long pure chord as if bowed of a cello, its resonance tumbling softly from the fog. Grace looked up to see the light was nearer, flickering above her, floating. "*Dear child,*" it came again, "*how do you come before the Lord?*"

Grace didn't understand the question. The light flickered. Finally, she said, "Here I am."

"*The Lord sees His lost child,*" the light flickered in cadence to the words, growing warmer, closer. "*The Lord hears your lament. The Lord comes to you in your time of need.*"

Grace didn't remember lamenting, but she chose not to point this out. Instead, she remained kneeling, head bowed.

"*The Lord knows of your suffering and brings you peace, child.*"

Well, amen to that, Grace thought, but said nothing.

"*The Lord is kind beyond measure.*"

That, Grace thought, sounds ominous. At this, Grace looked up. Still, only the flame was to be seen, so she addressed the flame.

"Your child is grateful for your kindness, Lord. If I may, does the Lord mean to grant me the peace of my death once again? To again be with those I love in the place beyond death?"

"*The Lord is kind beyond measure, and will grant you peace, child.*"

Grace stood and looked levelly into the flame, which seemed much closer now.

"Yeah, I get that. Your child wishes to know what the Lord means by peace, exactly."

"*The Lord is kind, He will cease your suffering, child. Be assured.*"

"Oh, the child is assured," Grace said. "Looking forward to an end of the suffering and all, as the Lord so kindly offers.

It's just that, it's not exactly clear what the Lord means by an end to my suffering."

"An end. To all of your pain and suffering."

"Yeah. Grace gets that part, Lord."

"The Lord's kindness is upon you."

The flame flickered more brightly and seemed to enlarge, or grow closer—maybe both, Grace couldn't tell. She took a step back but nothing changed.

"Just a moment before the Lord's kindness is upon me, if You don't mind. His child does not wish to end this suffering if it means the child no longer exists. Does the Lord mean to excise His child, that His child should not ever exist?"

"The Lord is kind beyond measure, and will ease your suffering."

"Ease or cease, dammit?"

The flame flickered at this, considering.

"Will the child, Grace, cease, then, Lord?"

The flame flickered yellow, then pale green.

"Because," Grace continued, stepping up to the flame, "your child wishes to know what her Lord is offering as kindness. An ease to her suffering, a return to the world beyond this one, your Grace welcomes. But the child will not cease to be, Lord. I will keep on, I will choose to suffer, rather than have the Lord cause me to cease to be His child."

With the softest sigh, the flame guttered, then died. The grayness around Grace faded, and the air became more and more transparent, until she found herself standing on the airport tarmac, Julius beside her. She swayed and nearly collapsed, but Julius caught her and steadied her.

"Donovan was right," Grace said, holding onto Julius to keep from slumping to the ground.

"What was right? Right about what?"

"Others might want me dead," Grace said. "But God wants me gone."

"WHAT IS MAN, THAT THOU
DOST MAKE SO MUCH OF HIM,
AND THAT THOU DOST SET
THY MIND UPON HIM,
DOST VISIT HIM EVERY MORNING,
AND TEST HIM EVERY MOMENT?
HOW LONG WILT THOU NOT
LOOK AWAY FROM ME,
NOR LET ME ALONE TILL I SWALLOW MY SPITTLE?
IF I SIN, WHAT DO I DO TO THEE,
THOU WATCHER OF MEN?
WHY HAST THOU MADE ME THY MARK?
WHY HAVE I BECOME A BURDEN TO THEE?
WHY DOST THOU NOT PARDON MY
TRANSGRESSION AND TAKE AWAY MY INIQUITY?
FOR NOW I SHALL LIE IN THE EARTH;
THOU WILT SEEK ME, BUT I SHALL NOT BE."

Bagram Airport, Afghanistan

Julius helped Grace up the stairs of the black 747, Uriel and Azrael following them aboard. Lauren Bacall met them just inside the door and helped Julius half-carry her to a seat. Grace looked quickly about before collapsing into the chair.

"Where's Gabe? Where's my husband?" she asked.

Bacall came back with a glass of ice water which she handed to Grace.

Bacall shook her head. "We haven't seen him, dear. Just Humphrey and me, and a few members of the film crew."

"Arthur?" Julius asked.

Bacall shook her head. "Not since the valley."

"I don't understand," Grace said. "Why aren't they here? Where else would they go?"

Uriel sat down across from her. He shook his head solemnly. "We won't see them again on this side," Uriel said. "That is, not if we're to succeed."

Grace slumped in the chair. "Why do you say that?"

"Because this is the play," Uriel explained. "You got what you wanted, Grace. You have Him playing your con. But the only chance we have is if your husband has found another angle. Somewhere we're not."

Grace closed her eyes and sighed. "He'll never find another angel like me," she said, and slipped into unconsciousness. The glass of water slipped from her grasp. Uriel caught it before it hit the floor.

Uriel shook his head. "No," Uriel said, "I don't suppose he will."

Bacall walked back to find her husband. Bogart was watching the last rushes from the film they had shot of the Mahdi.

"She's on board," Bacall said. "We're leaving."

"I'm almost done," he replied. "Have a courier ready."

"Is it good?"

He nodded. "Yeah," Bogart said. "It is. Very good."

Bacall leaned over and kissed her husband on the cheek. "Then it was worth coming back?"

"Yeah, I think so."

"I'll get the courier. The captain is going to want to go soon, dear."

Bogart nodded, back at his monitor.

Bacall touched her husband's shoulder. He looked up at her again, impatient. "What? I thought you wanted me to hurry up."

She looked at the screen. On it, an image of the Mahdi was frozen, facing his followers, in mid-exhortation. She looked at her husband again and asked, "Do you think he's for real?"

Bogart laughed and turned back to his screen. "Baby, when I'm done, it won't matter."

Something was missing, Grace knew. Something important had been taken from her. Grace huddled against the wall of the tiny, bare room. She hugged her knees to her chest, feeling the cold of the cement floor against her buttocks. Grace stared about, seeing only the gloom clinging to the green walls, sickly green shadows slow-dancing in time with the pendulum swing of the bulb hanging from the ceiling high above.

Something was missing. Something important. Grace was overwhelmed by how important the thing was, how it was the most important thing in the whole world. What was it? She rocked on the cold, hard floor, trying hard to recall what had been taken. She couldn't remember.

"No, no, no," Grace muttered, shaking her head violently, her grizzled scalp scraping a bloody smear against the wall. "Please, no, please, please, give it back, please," she begged, rocking and shaking her head in rhythm to her pleas. But she didn't know what it was she wanted back.

She only knew it was hers. And it was

important. And they had taken it away.

PART THREE

CHAPTER 15

Purgatory

"Look," Einstein said, "it is just as I predicted. You see how she is?"

"I see she passed out again," Arthur said, staring at the monitor. "She does that sometimes. Does it a lot, lately."

"It's one of her spells, Albert," Gabriel said. "I can call you Albert, right?"

"Of course you can," Noether said. "And please call me Emmy. What do you mean by 'spells?'"

"She's had catatonic episodes like that all her life. At least, as long as I've known her."

"You mean, like fainting?" Noether asked, concerned.

"No, not fainting, exactly," Gabriel explained. "She talks sometimes, while she's having the spell. Sometimes in Irish."

"Well, Gabriel," Einstein said, "she is not 'passed out,' as Arthur put it. She is in a state of critical opalescence."

"Oh, Albert," Noether said, "you give yourself too much credit, dear."

"It is just as I predicted, in my paper," Einstein insisted.

"Albert, not everything in the universe happens because you wrote it in a paper," Noether admonished.

"What is critical opalescence?" Gabriel asked.

"It's a physics thing," Noether explained. "It is of little consequence."

"Little consequence?" Einstein said. He gestured to the screen. "You see that? To that young lady, it is of little consequence? I think not, Emmy."

Noether rolled her eyes.

"I don't understand, Albert," Gabriel said. "If Grace isn't unconscious, then what is going on? Why is she in critical opal-whatever?"

"Critical opalescence," Noether corrected. "She isn't. It doesn't apply, Albert. Let it go."

"But it does, Emmy," Einstein insisted. He turned to Gabriel. "Usually, you see, state fluctuations are controlled by the second derivative of the free energy with respect to density. But when the state is at critical point, the derivative is zero, leading to very large state fluctuations."

"Uh, you lost me there, Albert," Gabriel said.

"So what, Albert?" Noether added. "The sky is still just a pretty shade of blue, Albert."

Einstein threw up his hands. "I cannot believe you just said that, Emmy! The young lady is obviously at some type of critical point state. She is—she is...why, I don't know what she is, but she is, she is—"

"She is what, Albert? Finish your damn sentence so we can go get lunch or something," Noether said.

Einstein smacked his palm on the desk. "She is a thermonuclear bomb about to explode," he declared.

"Really?" Arthur asked.

"No," Einstein, answered, "not really. I'm just trying to make an example."

"Oh."

Noether shook her head. "I'm going to lunch."

Salt Lake City, Utah

Julius and Parnell sat across their third pitcher of beer. Uriel and Azrael had left hours ago.

"Any idea how we're going to do this?" *Julius* asked.

"I'll tell you how we can't do it," Parnell said. "We can't go into the Prophet's office and try to steal the secret code or whatever. I can't even get close to that place."

"No, that's stupid, anyway," *Julius* said. He flagged down a

436

waiter.

"What are you doing?" Parnell asked. "There's half a pitcher there."

"We need food," *Julius* said.

"I like your thinking," Parnell agreed.

They ordered dinner.

"Tell me why it's stupid," Parnell continued, once the food had arrived.

"Because security is tightest at the top," *Zimmerman* explained. "Always is."

"So what are you suggesting?"

"Attack the bottom of the pyramid."

Parnell nodded thoughtfully. "Makes sense. We can get in with the new Arrivals, I think."

"Sure you can."

"And we just stick around long enough to learn what the trigger is."

"Right. Except that's not quite good enough."

"But you just said." Chuck stole half a dozen fries from the other man's plate.

"You could've ordered fries yourself, you know."

"No, I couldn't. I'm on a diet."

"Hate to tell you, but that's not how dieting works." *Julius* pushed the plate away. "Finding out the signal for a group of new Arrivals is where we start. But groups may get different signals, different instructions."

Parnell took the rest of the fries from *Julius's* plate. "Good point."

"So we get the signal from the guy who gives out the signals. Then we have to find out what signal he's looking for that tells him to give the signal. And so on up the line."

"Hmmph. Sounds hard."

Zimmerman shrugged. "You got a better idea?"

"Yeah," Parnell said, "Dessert."

"I thought you were on a diet."

"Yeah, was. And we don't have the time to do it like you're

saying."

"So what's your plan?"

"Steal it from the Prophet."

"You just said you can't get close to him."

"I can't. But you can."

"True. But it's still not going to work," *Julius* said. "Like I was saying, security at the top is tough. No way I'll crack it."

"I think you can."

"How?"

"I'll work the bottom of the pyramid up as far as I can."

"Yeah? And then?"

"And then I'll get caught."

Julius considered this. "And that'll force the Prophet to change the signal." Parnell nodded. Julius considered. "That might work."

Salt Lake City, Utah

It took two weeks for Parnell to infiltrate the newest class of Arrivals in Granite Mountain. It should've been quicker, as Parnell had extensive previous knowledge of the workings of the organization. But much of Parnell's knowledge was dated at this point, not to mention his access codes and ID badge. Thankfully, the low-level administrators were helpful in bringing him up to date. By the end of the second week, Parnell had attended enough briefings to understand the protocols. By two days later, he had a half dozen activation codes, several at fairly high levels within the organization. As this most recent class of Arrivals was dispatched, Parnell graduated with them. He met *Julius* at Feldman's Deli.

"It's scripture, of course," Parnell explained over scrambled eggs and lox.

"Makes sense," *Julius* said. "A reading? Or a sermon?"

"A reading. Not in the usual rotation, of course. A special reading."

"Please tell me it's not from the Book of Mormon. That it's from the Bible."

"Of course it's from the Bible. When these people are sent out, do you think they're sent abroad as Mormons? They're born-again Jews. Literally, I mean. It's an Old Testament verse."

"Then we have them."

YOUR OWN BIOLOGIST, JEAN ROSTAND—HE KNEW:

"SCIENCE HAS MADE US GODS, EVEN BEFORE WE ARE WORTHY OF BEING MEN."

SO DON'T BLAME ME.

Salt Lake City, Utah

"Mr. President," *Julius* began, taking the seat offered. "It is very kind of you to agree to meet with me."

"Not at all, Father Zimmerman," the President said, smiling. "Just give me a minute. I'm just finishing up." *Julius* watched, amazed, as the other man typed on his computer keyboard. As he did so, *Zimmerman* pulled out his cellphone and tapped up a program. Finally, the President looked up from his computer and smiled apologetically. He came around his desk and sat across the low table from his guest. "It's my pleasure. It is good to see you again. Can I get you anything to drink? Water? Tea?"

"Tea would be great, thank you, Mr. President."

The President nodded and crossed to the sideboard. He returned with two cups of tea.

The President said, "I'm sorry our time with Dr. Parnell was so brief the last time. I'm anxious to know what brings you all the way back from Georgetown to see me, Father. Is this a mission of scholarship? A research project? Are the Jesuits suddenly interested in the teachings of the Church of Latter-Day Saints?"

"I assure you, Mr. President, that my fellow Jesuits and I have had a very long and respectful interest in your faith."

"Long, perhaps. Hardly respectful, Father Zimmerman. I'm curious, Father," the President smiled broadly at *Julius*.

"Tell me, Father Zimmerman, how does a true man of faith go from Jew to Jesuit? It seems so—contradictory. It must be a fascinating story."

"Only to the one who has lived it, I assure you, Mr. President. I won't try your patience with my journey. You're a busy man, I'm sure."

The President leaned forward to his guest. "You weren't raised in a devout family. Yours were the kind of Jews that found their way to synagogue during the High Holy Days, am I right? Never really talked about God around the dinner table, talked more about the cost of tickets to get a seat for Yom Kippur." *Zimmerman* said nothing, only stared levelly at his host. "Were you even Bar mitzvah'd, Julius?"

Zimmerman shook his head slightly. "It was a difficult time for my family."

"Difficult? Too difficult to follow the teachings of your faith? Or too expensive, living in Chicago, and all? Those upscale Bar mitzvah's can be pricey. Your Dad decide to buy a boat when you turned thirteen, instead? Promised to teach you to waterski on Lake Michigan?"

It was *Zimmerman*'s turn to lean into the conversation. "The year I turned thirteen, Mr. President, my brother nearly died of leukemia. It was, as I said, a difficult time."

The President shrugged this off. "And then you became a priest," the President said. The President leaned back and took a sip of tea.

"There were," *Julius* said, "a few steps in between."

"No doubt." The President set down his cup. "Tell me the first one."

Julius stared, puzzled. "The first what?"

"The first step. Your calling. How you came to abandon the faith of your birth and become a priest. What set you on this path of rebirth."

Zimmerman looked at the other man. He considered whether to bother to explain himself to the man sitting across from him. He decided his objective required him to provide a response, despite his feeling that the President deserved no such courtesy. So he answered, "God came and spoke to me and my family."

"I'm sorry? God spoke to you?"

Julius nodded. "He came and visited us when we were seeing the doctor, with my brother."

"The one with leukemia?"

"Yes. God came to us and granted us a miracle. He cured my brother's leukemia."

"God Himself? Visited you and your family?" *Julius* nodded. "He spoke to you?"

Julius nodded.

The President shook his head in wonder, tinged with disbelief. "If what you say is true, I must admit to a bit of jealousy on my part," the President said. *Julius* offered no response. "But being visited by God didn't make you and your family better Jews? Somehow the experience made you reborn in Christ?"

"Like I said, Mr. President, that was only the first step of a long, long road." His tone left no doubt that he was done discussing the subject.

The President smiled a pained frown. He cleared his throat. "So, then, Father," the President said, almost amiably, "what can I do for you?"

"Do for me? Perhaps we can do something for each other. I'm here to open a line of communication, Mr. President," *Julius* said.

"Communication, huh? What are we communicating about?"

"The Holy Roman Church has a program, as I'm sure you know—a program that anticipates the coming of the End Times."

"Is that so?" the President asked.

"It is indeed so, Mr. President, as you are undoubtedly aware." The President said nothing. "This program, by its very nature, requires a type of 'Fail-safe' signaling. Given both its broad, worldwide reach, as well as its overwhelming significance, we believe that it is critical that there be no possibility of confusion."

"If what you say is true, Father Zimmerman, that your Church has a program that might effect the world at the time of the Apocalypse, I can understand why you wouldn't want such a thing triggered by accident."

"Quite so, Mr. President," *Julius* said, nodding.

"But what does your program have to do with the LDS church?"

"It has recently come to our attention that your program utilizes a system of communication that dangerously approximates our own." *Julius* stared at the other man levelly.

The President looked baffled. "I'm sure I don't understand, Father. To what program are you referring?"

"Mr. President, I didn't come all this way to fence with you, or to get you to admit the existence of your Church's program of planting sleeper cells of Returnees around the world in anticipation of the End Times. I'm here to prevent a potentially calamitous mistake. Your current activation codes overlap dangerously with our own." The President opened his mouth to protest again, but *Zimmerman* raised his hand in anticipation. "There is no need for further denials, Mr. President. There is, indeed, no need for you to comment any further. I'm here to say the following, for our mutual benefit: Our system of activation utilizes biblical references. Of course, we will not be utilizing any reference to the many Books specific to your Church. It is our earnest hope that you will limit your codes to the various holy books specific to the LDS church. These parameters should permit you to conduct your interests without undue inconvenience. But the current system—your current signal—you must understand, is unacceptable. It is a dangerous situation, and must be addressed immediately."

Julius sat back as the other man quietly considered this.

The President smiled sardonically. "If there were any substance to your beliefs, Father," the President said, "I would say that I am very impressed with your knowledge of the inner workings of my organization. If I believed you, that is."

"I'm not asking you to believe me, Mr. President," *Julius* said. "I'm only asking that you take this small precaution. As quickly as possible."

"Since I have no idea to what you are referring, Father Zimmerman, I'm afraid that I can't help you."

Zimmerman leaned into the other man and spoke softly. "'Written not with ink, but with the Spirit of the living God.'" He stared icily at the other man. "'Second Corinthians, chapter 3, verse 3.'" He waited, watching the other man carefully. The President leaned back in his chair.

"Well, Father Zimmerman," the President said after some consideration, standing, "I guess that whether I believe you or not, if such a program did exist—and I must say, I have no knowledge whatsoever of any such program—but if such a program did exist, I would feel compelled to comply with your request, if only as a matter of courtesy to your faith."

Zimmerman stood as well and shook hands with the President. "That would be the most prudent approach, Mr. President. Thank you for your time. Peace to you."

"And also to you, Father," the President said. *Zimmerman* turned to leave. As he reached the door, the President called, "Julius?"

Zimmerman stopped and turned back at the doorway from the office. "Mr. President?"

"These programs have been around for a generation. I doubt the signals have been changed in a decade. Why now?"

"Of course, you know the answer to that, Mr. President." *Julius* smiled at the other man. "He is among us." *Zimmerman* left without waiting for a response.

Salt Lake City, Utah

Julius sat down across from Parnell at the deli. Parnell was on his sixth cup of coffee.

"Where have you been? Did you get it?" Parnell asked, half-bouncing up from his seat.

"I had to stop to buy a new phone. And no, I didn't get it. Not yet," *Julius* said, signaling the waitress.

"You didn't get it?" *Julius* shook his head and finally caught the waitress's eye. "Why did you have to buy a new phone?" Parnell asked.

"I lost mine."

The waitress approached and *Zimmerman* ordered breakfast and coffee. He took out his new smartphone and placed it on the table before him.

"But you didn't get the new code?"

"Not yet."

"If he didn't tell you, how are you going to get it?" Parnell asked, attempting to refill his cup from the urn on the table. It was empty.

The phone chimed. *Zimmerman* leaned over it.

"Bingo," *Zimmerman* said.

"Bingo? What bingo? You bugged his office? How?"

"With my phone," *Zimmerman* said, smiling with satisfaction as he watched the code scroll down the phone's screen. "My old one."

"I thought you lost it," Parnell said, confused.

"I lost it in his office."

"How did you get into his system? Wasn't he there with you?"

"He was," *Zimmerman* agreed. "Just stuffed it between the cushions of the couch I was sitting on. It's acting as a sniffer."

"A sniffer?"

"The idiot uses a wireless keyboard. The phone picks up the signal."

Parnell whistled and tried to read the upside-down screen. "How did you know?"

"Didn't. But when I saw him at his computer, I knew this would work."

"That's brilliant," Parnell enthused. "What's the new

code?"

"It's a reference from the Book of Moroni," *Julius* said. "In honor of the moron priest who just admitted that the Catholics have a secret program regarding the End Times."

"Is that what he wrote?"

"Yeah, he's writing in his daily journal. 'In honor of the Jew-priest,' he says. Here's the verse: 'And now I, Moroni, write a few of the words of my father Mormon...as he taught them in the synagogue which they had built for the place of worship.' It's chapter seven, first verse," *Zimmerman* said.

"We're in!" Parnell said. He high-fived *Julius* across the table. "Where's that waitress? We need more coffee."

Salt Lake City, Utah

The next evening, *Julius* and Parnell were still waiting, but for what they weren't quite sure. "How will we know when to pull the trigger on this thing?" Chuck asked his companion over a couple of cold beers. *Julius* didn't respond, but continued to watch the BBC world news on the TV over Chuck's shoulder.

"Julius," Chuck said, irritated.

"What?"

"We got the codes, so when do we pull the trigger? No way to know how long before the Prophet feels like changing them again."

Julius pointed at the TV screen with his bottle of beer. "When we start seeing shit like that, Chuck."

"Like what?" Chuck asked, twisting in his seat to face the screen.

They watched as a news reporter described the view from a helicopter showing tens of thousands of people walking through the rough highlands of Afghanistan.

"What did he say? Who are they?" Chuck asked.

"He said they were followers of the new messiah," *Julius* said. "On a pilgrimage to Jerusalem."

Chuck swung back in his seat, smiling. He made a gun of

his thumb and forefinger, pointing back at the TV.

"Bang."

"Oh, I get it," *Zimmerman* said. "Pulling the trigger."

"Bingo."

"Which is it? Bang or bingo?"

"Finish your beer," Parnell said. "We got an Apocalypse to start."

Salt Lake City, Utah

The Prophet stood in the doorway of the Temple.

"What in God's name have you done?" the Prophet demanded.

Julius and Parnell came to a breathless halt in front of him. Neither spoke.

"What have you done?" he demanded again. The Prophet stepped forward and grabbed Parnell by the shirt, shaking him. "Parnell, you bastard. Do you know what you've done?"

Zimmerman put his hand on the Prophet's arm. "It's too late, buddy. Let 'em go. We're leaving."

The Prophet dropped his grip on Parnell and sagged against the door behind him.

"You don't know what you've done," he muttered.

"We know," *Zimmerman* answered. "Come on, Parnell," he urged, "we got a bathtub to catch."

Parnell and *Zimmerman* pushed past the Prophet.

When they stepped out, they had left the Prophet far behind. They were in Jerusalem, though they weren't completely sure what they were doing there.

Kandahar Airport, Afghanistan

"Where are we? Where are we going?" Grace asked. She stretched, cat-like, in her chair.

"You're awake," Julius said. He reached across the airplane's aisle to shake Uriel.

"What?" Uriel grumbled.

"She's awake," Julius explained.

"Great," Uriel said, closing his eyes again. "I'm not."

Grace stared out the window. "Where are we going now?" she asked again.

"Kiev," Julius explained.

Grace looked at him. "Where the hell really?"

"Ukraine, I think," Julius said. "Kiev."

"And that's where the gate is, right?"

Julius said, "That's what they tell me."

Grace stood with an effort and crossed the aisle to where Uriel was pretending to sleep. She stared down at him.

"This is going to work, right?" she asked him.

"Only one way to find out," Uriel answered, not opening his eyes.

"Seriously? That's the best you got?"

Uriel sighed and opened his eyes, straightening in his chair to look up at her.

"Yeah, Grace. That's the best I got. Right now, it's all we got."

"The gates are closed."

"Not this one. At least, I don't think so," Uriel said.

"You don't think so," Grace echoed. "I tried the gate in the Guggenheim. It used to work, then it didn't. What makes you think this one still works?"

"Parnell said he used it dozens of times," Uriel said. "It's made outta stone. Sounds like a chance to me. You got a better idea, be my guest." He stood. "I need something to drink." Uriel started up the aisle to the galley, Grace and Julius following.

"We're going to Kiev on the word of Parnell?" Grace said. "The man's an idiot."

"Can't argue with you there," Uriel said, pawing through the pantry. "Ah, here we go." He extracted a bottle of Jameson Black. "Where they keep the glasses on this boat?" he mumbled. Julius produced three glasses from storage. Uriel poured.

"How would an idiot like Charles Parnell know anything

about a gate in Kiev?"

"Parnell's an idiot, true. But he's a very, very old idiot. Guy's been around."

Grace opened her mouth but Uriel cut her off. "Not worth talking about no more, girl. It's a gate, and it's gonna work."

"How do you know?"

" 'Cause it's made of stone, that's how I know. Like the one Jesus used. Worked for him, right? Can't be turned off just by screwing with one of Frank Lloyd's commissions. He'd have to undo the whole 'He is Risen' thing. Don't think He's going to do that just to screw with you, girl. Leastwise, I hope not."

Julius nodded, taking a sip of his whiskey. "Makes sense to me."

"That's the stupidest thing I've ever heard you say," Grace said. "So that's it, then. I'm going home. Going to see my family again."

Julius downed his drink and refilled his glass.

"Maybe," Uriel said.

"What do you mean, maybe?" Grace asked.

"Family may not be there when you get there. If you get there, which is also a very open question at this juncture," Uriel said.

"Gabriel isn't here, Earl. Which means he's over there, waiting for me." Uriel shook his head. "Well, if he isn't here, and he isn't there, where the hell is my husband?"

"Someplace else, obviously," Uriel said. "No sense worrying about that right now, either. Out of our hands."

"Well, I'm worrying—" Grace began.

"Well, don't. You got bigger shit to worry about. Like making it to that gate, because the Lord's got other plans for you, you know."

"Maybe He gave up," Grace said, collapsing into a chair.

"No chance."

"Why not?" Julius asked, sitting. "You see that documentary Bogart and Bacall put together? God may have his hands full dealing with the New Messiah."

"In your dreams, Father," Uriel said, sitting across the table and putting the bottle down between them.

"That's the plan, Earl," Grace said. "Build up our Messiah into a bigger pain in the ass than I could ever be. Seems to be working. I'm doing jack-shit. Meanwhile, Mahdi's on his way to Jerusalem with Revelation's revolutionaries. I'm nothing compared to that."

Uriel shook his head. "Girl, you never struck me as a person prone to wishful thinking. Quit dreaming 'bout unicorns and rainbows, Grace. You're working the hardest con there is."

"Yeah? In which way is that?"

"You're trying to con a mark that knows he's being conned. That's a damn tough nut to crack."

"You think He knows?" Julius asked.

"Shit yeah, He knows. We're talking about God, here. He knows everything, remember?"

"Then why is He playing?" Grace asked.

"For the only possible reason. He thinks he can flip your con, girl. Use it to get what He wants. That's how the game works, right? Wouldn't bet against Him, either."

Grace was silent for a bit, thinking. "I'm fucked."

Uriel shrugged. "Probably," he agreed. "Almost definitely."

"What do you mean, 'almost?'" Julius asked. "It's God. He's omniscient."

Uriel took another sip and sat back again. "True, up to a point."

Grace sighed heavily. "I never believed in Him, to be honest. Never thought it was really God that wanted me excised."

"So you said."

"Never thought He was real. And if He was real, never thought He gave two shits about me."

"Well, you were wrong on both counts, it seems."

"So I've been trying to con somebody who knows everything I'm doing, knows everything everyone is doing, and knows the future."

"Yeah. Pretty stupid plan."

"I'm so fucked."

"You said 'probably,'" Julius said. "Before, you said Grace was probably fucked. Seems pretty definite, the way you laid it out."

"I said, 'almost definitely.' Not entirely definitely. God knows almost everything."

"He knows the future," Grace said.

"He knows *a* future. His future. He knows what's going to happen—what happened in the reality that's been. But there is one variable. One thing He doesn't know for certain."

"What's that?"

"You," Uriel said, pointing at Grace. "He doesn't know what you'll do."

"That's why He wants me excised," Grace said.

"Probably. Something you did, or can do. Something damn important."

"I just want to go back to being dead. Be with my family again. That's not so big."

"Maybe that's all there is to it. Maybe not."

"So He's going to come after Grace again, isn't He?" Julius asked.

Uriel nodded. "Definitely."

They heard the plane's engines spool up as it prepared to take off. Julius looked out the window.

"He could just swat us out of the air," Julius said.

"He could've killed Grace ten thousand times already," Uriel said with a dismissive wave. "That's not what He wants."

"No," Grace said. "That's what everyone else wants. God wants me excised. Like I never existed. It's everyone else that wants me dead."

Uriel nodded.

"How is He going to flip my con?" Grace asked. "What is it about my con he can use to get me excised? Why do I need to be excised instead of just dead?"

"I don't know," Uriel said.

"But He must know. He must know something none of us do, something he's going to use against me."

Uriel nodded.

"Something that's going to happen in the future," Grace said. "Maybe something I can decide not to do, then. Change the game back to my favor."

"Maybe," Uriel said. "Not necessarily. Maybe something he knows, that we simply don't know. Something that's true already. It could be anything."

"Great."

The plane lumbered down the runway, the hills of Helmand Province blurring to a featureless brown wave that finally fell behind them as the plane lifted away.

Over the Caspian Sea

They slept fitfully, scattered in seats about the plane. At thirty-two thousand feet, it was Grace who first noticed the walls of the aircraft begin to disappear. She blinked herself awake, staring. The walls, the ceiling, the floor—all were becoming white, translucent, then transparent. She screamed, awakening the others, who, looking about and seeing only sky, in turn began to scream.

It took almost a full minute before each of the passengers realized that despite the illusion, they were still safe within the airplane in which they had been riding. The illusion was so perfect, however, that no one dared budge from their seat. Grace was furthest forward, and by now had ceased screaming.

The sound of the wind keening through the thin air came to her, and on the wind she heard the voice again, building now so it came from all around her, saying:

"THE LORD CALLED YOU BEFORE YOU WERE BORN, WHILE YOU WERE IN YOUR MOTHER'S WOMB, I NAMED YOU. I MADE

YOUR MOUTH LIKE A SHARP SWORD, IN THE SHADOW OF MY HAND I HID YOU; I MADE YOU A POLISHED ARROW, IN MY QUIVER I HID YOU AWAY. I SAY TO YOU NOW, MY DEAREST CHILD, YOU ARE MY SERVANT, IN WHOM I WILL BE GLORI-FIED."

Grace stood, staggered at the illusion of emptiness all about her, and fell to her knees. "I have labored in vain, I have spent my strength for nothing and vanity; yet surely my cause is with the Lord, and my reward with my God," she said into the wind.

This pleased the Lord. The wind softened and His voice was heard to say, "IT IS TOO LIGHT A THING THAT YOU SHOULD BE MY SERVANT. RAISE YOUR EYES AND BEHOLD YOUR LORD, CHILD."

Grace looked up and saw an incandescent image of a man, huge in the distance ahead, shrouded in fire, his features indistinct. All about Him was a great radiance that caused Grace to squint and shade her eyes.

"I am here, Lord," Grace said.

"A GREAT WICKEDNESS IS ABROAD," the voice intoned. "IT HAS BEEN LONG IN COMING, BUT MY PEOPLE NOW STAND TO THE CROSSROADS," He continued. "THE PATH AHEAD IS FRAUGHT, AND MY PEOPLE ARE IN NEED OF DIRECTION. WITHOUT THE GUIDANCE OF THEIR LORD, SURELY CALAM-ITY WILL BEFALL MY PEOPLE."

Grace bowed her head and said, "Surely, My Lord, it is not my place—"

"NO, IT IS NOT," the orotund voice bellowed. "THE LORD KNOWS THE WAY FORWARD AND SETS HIS HAND ON YOUR BROW, SO THAT YOU WILL KNOW WHAT IS REQUIRED OF HIS CHILD."

With that, the hand of God reached forward and swept towards Grace. Grace cowered in her invisible chair expecting she knew not what, but raised her eyes and watched, the hand as large as a mountain sweeping towards her, blazing. She felt the heat as it approached, heard Julius call out from somewhere behind her and then stood, amazed, as the hand of God almost touched her but then suddenly recoiled—just slightly, almost imperceptible, but she saw it, as if the Hand had touched something sharp. The Hand of God hovered in the air before her, as large as a building but now not quite as hot, not as brightly aflame, now slowly moving in a gesture of supplication, beckoning her to step forward onto the up-turned palm.

"*CHILD*," the voice of God said soothingly, "*COME FOR-WARD AND BE WITH ME.*"

Grace stood still, shaking slightly. "My Lord commands," she stammered, "and His child wishes with all her heart to obey," she lowered her head, saying, "but I cannot move."

The hand withdrew slightly.

"*MY CHILD CANNOT MOVE,*" the voice said.

"I cannot, Lord."

The hand of God flew away, retreating back into the flaming shape ahead. The plane solidified around her and shook violently for a moment, then plunged ahead into the sky.

Purgatory

"Shit, shit, shit," Elliot yelled, gesticulating at the wall-sized screen. "Guys, Arthur! Gabriel!"

The others appeared at the doorway.

"What is it, Elliot?" Arthur asked, sipping his Coke as he looked over Elliot's shoulder. "I was just gonna take a nap."

"Screw that," Elliot said, tapping on the console before him so that the screen zoomed in to look down on a scene of cloud tops scuttling across a dark sea. "It's happening again —look!"

Gabriel dropped into the chair next to Elliot. "What's happening?" He watched as a black plane appeared from the clouds below. "Oh, Grace's plane. So what?"

"Looks fine to me," Arthur added.

"It's not fine," Elliot insisted. "There's another one of

those energy surges starting, right in front of the plane."

"I don't see a thing."

"You can't see it," Elliot said in exasperation. "Wait, I can show it to you." Elliot tapped his keys and the colors on the screen changed to various hues of blue and black.

"See even less now, buddy," Arthur said.

Elliot rotated the view to follow the plane from behind. A bright orange blotch appeared in the otherwise purple sky in front of the plane.

"Oh. Shit." Arthur said.

"How far?" Gabriel asked.

"Five or ten miles, not sure. It just appeared out of nowhere, started as a little point of energy but it's building fast," Elliot said.

Noether, Einstein, and Gödel drifted into the room. Samantha followed them in and took a seat next to her husband.

"Is something interesting happening?" Noether asked. She noticed the image on the screen. "Oh. What is that?"

"Same spectrum as that energy bolt that hit the tree," Elliot explained. "Same as the mountaintop thing, whatever that was. If that hits her plane, it's not going to be good. Not good at all."

"Interesting," Einstein said. "Can we see this spectrum, Elliot?"

Elliot tapped more keys and a waterfall display of the energy source appeared on the adjoining monitor.

"Oh," Noether said, "that is interesting."

"What? What is interesting?" Arthur asked.

"It is perfect black body emission, no?" Einstein asked. Noether nodded.

"Intensity is increasing exponentially," Gödel added.

"That's bad, right?" Gabriel asked.

"That depends," Einstein said absently, stepping closer to the monitor displaying the spectrum of the radiation source.

"Depends on what?" Gabriel asked.

Einstein appeared not to hear the question. "*Herr* Elliot, can you show us the energy spectrum of the young lady as well?"

"What young lady?" Elliot asked. "What are you talking about, Al?"

"The pretty girl with the seizure disorder. You know, the one we were discussing earlier, she in the critical opalescent state."

"That's your theory, Albert," Noether said. "I think she's just anxious."

"Oh, her." Elliot tapped more keys and a tiny pale yellow dot appeared superimposed on the image of the plane, still flying over the darkened image of the clouds.

"Her spectrum, too, please," Einstein said.

Elliot tapped and a narrow waterfall of colors appeared on the second monitor beside the first one, its intensity miniscule alongside the other display. The bands of color bounced and jangled across the height of the screen.

"Oh, my," Noether said whispered.

"What?" Gabriel asked.

"Just my theory, Emmy?" Einstein smirked and tapped his finger on the display of dancing colors. "Look at that! Critical opalescence. Just as I said."

"You're insufferable, Albert. As always," Noether said.

"What's happening?" Arthur asked, staring at the screen. As they watched, the bright orange mass enlarged, stretched, and took on the blurry shape of an orange-red giant, shimmering in the air in front of the plane. They watched as one arm stretched toward the airplane.

"Not good, not good, not good," Elliot said. "Energy levels are spiking."

"We need to do something!" Samantha said.

"What can we do?" Arthur asked.

Elliot shook his head.

Noether stepped up to stand beside Einstein, staring closely at the spectra on the screen.

"She goes critical now, I think," Einstein said, tapping his chin intently. "Poof!"

"You mean, she dies?" Gabriel asked, half rising from his chair. Samantha grabbed his hand.

"Or not," Noether said, pointing at the screen. The narrower spectrum, Grace's spectrum, suddenly froze, it's hectic jumping pattern becoming a fixed picket of color across the screen. "Maybe..."

"Maybe what? What's happening?" Samantha demanded.

"See, Albert? You don't know everything, after all, my dearest *dummkopf*! Maybe, she gets more stable, more phasic. Not critical. She is strong, I think," Noether said. "Oh, I like this young woman!"

The group watched the screens as the orange-red apparition faded and disappeared from in front of the plane, its spectrum fading from the second monitor as well.

"Hmmpf!" Einstein exhaled. "That is not at all what I would've predicted."

"Maybe, Albert," Gödel said from his place at the table, "Maybe, God does play a little game after all." He smiled at his friend.

The Iranian Border, Afghanistan

Hila stood on the top of a small hill and surveyed the fenced border ahead. To each side of the gated crossing, hundreds of Iranian soldiers looked back at her.

"I don't think they're going to let us cross," she said.

Beside her, the Mahdi stood facing in the opposite direction, looking back at the tens of thousands of pilgrims that had joined his march. From this vantage, the sea of people looked like a huge, breathing dragon, its tail extending for miles behind.

"*I don't think they will have any choice*," the Mahdi answered, turning to make his way back down to the road.

Hila followed him. "They have guns, Mahdi. And tanks. Maybe it is we who have no choice."

"You are right, of course, my little one," Mahdi replied. *"No choice. With so many behind us, what choice do we have but to keep moving forward?"*

Hila jumped down onto the road ahead of the Mahdi and turned, facing him. Her face was red with anger, hands on hips as she looked up defiantly. The Mahdi stopped, smiling.

"Something troubles you, little one?"

"You will not call me that again," Hila said.

The Mahdi's smile dissolved and he looked down at his young friend with sadness. He nodded once.

"I will not."

"Good."

Hila turned and led the Mahdi up the road towards the border crossing.

"What will happen now?" she asked of the Mahdi, who walked behind her, ahead of the mass of pilgrims.

"I'm sure I don't know. Hila."

Purgatory

"Boss, we've got trouble," Libby said, jogging to catch Arthur as he walked quickly down the corridor.

"No time, Libby," Arthur replied, not slowing his pace. "I've got something I need to deal with."

"Yeah, well, if we don't deal with this shit, we're going to lose the Mahdi and a few hundred thousand followers."

"Sorry, Lib, you're going to have to handle it. Do whatever," Arthur said, continuing on his way to the conference room. Libby stopped and watched him go.

"Fine," she said to his back. "I'll handle it, then."

Libby returned to the small control room and watched the monitors as the Mahdi walked towards the massed forces of the Iranian army. She dropped into the chair. "Okay, Scotty. Let's handle this." She watched as the Mahdi stopped before the border crossing, the young girl standing beside him.

"You should handle this pretty damn soon, too, Libby," she said to herself. She looked about the control room, looking for inspiration. When she looked back at the monitors, every soldier had raised his weapon and aimed it at the Mahdi. Even the tank turrets had swiveled to point at the man who stood before them.

"Oh," Libby said to herself. "That's not good. Think, Libby. Think fast." Her fingers flew across the keyboard before her. "This will have to do, for a start."

Over the Caspian Sea

"Holy shit, what the hell was that?" Julius said, stumbling forward to fall into a seat next to where Grace remained standing, still trembling uncontrollably.

Uriel and Azrael joined them.

"That was Him," Azrael said, taking Grace's hand. "Sit child, sit down. Julius, get her some water or something."

"Yeah, Father. Something a helluva lot stronger than water, Padre," Uriel said, helping Grace to sit down. "And get me something too, while you're at it. Did you see that, Azrael?" Uriel asked, leaning forward to look into Grace's face closely. "You see what she done?" He shook his head slightly and whistled under his breath, leaning back. "Damn, girl."

"I thought..." Grace stammered, trailing off as tears streamed silently down her cheeks.

"Thought He was going to crush you like a bug," Uriel said, taking the drink Julius was offering to Grace. "Yeah. Like He was gonna crush this plane like a little can of soda. So did I. So did we all."

Julius returned with another drink for Grace and sat. He couldn't speak, but just stared at Grace.

"Damn, girl," Uriel repeated.

"I thought," Grace started again, softly, "I thought He was going to excise me."

Azrael nodded.

"So why didn't He?" Julius finally managed to ask.

"I don't know," Azrael said.

They were all silent for a bit, thinking and staring at Grace as she continued to silently cry, staring at her drink as it sloshed about in her shaking hands.

"God wants her excised," Julius said. "It's in the bible."

"True," Uriel said, thinking.

"She was excised, before," Julius continued. "In the museum."

Uriel nodded.

"So why not this time?" Julius asked of Uriel.

"I'm thinking, padre. Give me a minute here."

Julius straightened up and pounded the armrest, causing Grace to startle and drop her glass.

"Shit, sorry," Julius said, picking it up for Grace. "Sorry, hon." He turned to Uriel. "It's Pauley. Pauley was at the museum--both times. Pauley who tried again to excise her in the church. Not God Himself. His agent. Pauley has to do it."

Uriel looked at him. "You may be right," Uriel said.

"But why?" Azrael said. "Why can this man Pauley perform the excision, the will of God, but apparently not the Lord Almighty Himself?"

"Because he's the Devil," Grace said, and scrubbed at her cheeks. She moved to go up the stairway.

"Ha!" Uriel said, snorting a laugh. He turned to Azrael. "The Devil, she says! That's rich."

Julius suddenly realized something—he felt a piece click into place. He thought he knew why Pauley had to be the one. Pauley wasn't the Devil—but he might be the father.

"Where are you going?" Julius asked Grace as she mounted the stairs.

"I'm going to hide in bed," she said. Grace stopped halfway up the steps. "You coming?"

Purgatory

Arthur tapped his pencil against the top of the small conference table nervously.

"Please stop doing that, Arthur," Gabriel said.

"Where are they? Where are Emmy and Albert?" Arthur asked, now chewing on the end of the pencil.

"Probably arguing about the nature of the universe," Gödel said.

"And screwing like bunnies," Elliot added.

"*Ja*," Gödel agreed. "It is all the same for Albert. Such a dog, he is. I should've just brought Emmy. Much more productive."

"I'll go find them," Gabriel offered, getting up from his chair.

"So sorry," Einstein said, ushering Noether into the conference room before him. "We didn't mean to keep you waiting."

Gabriel sat back down as Noether and Einstein took adjoining chairs at the small table. Everyone tried to ignore the fact that Einstein's rumpled sweater was inside-out.

Arthur cleared his throat. "Well, now that we're all here," he began, "Let's get started." He tapped his keyboard and the monitor on the wall showed the spectrum from the giant apparition they had watched assault Grace's plane earlier. Arthur gestured at the screen. "We've all seen what it is we're up against. Gabriel and I have been conducting this little opera up to this point, but now we're at the climax. We need your help."

"Help? What kind of help?" Einstein asked.

"What is that?" Noether asked, nodding at the display.

"That is the protagonist is this drama," Arthur answered. "The individual trying to excise Grace. Our goal here is to try to prevent that from happening."

"That force is very, very strong," Noether observed, furrowing her brow. "What is it, exactly?"

"We think it's God," Gabriel answered matter-of-factly.

"Hmmpf," Einstein said.

"Really?" Noether added. "Interesting."

"Really? That's what you think?" Elliot said. "Interesting?"

"It is interesting, I agree," Einstein interjected. "An interesting theory, at least. Whatever you call it, Emmy is right—it is a very powerful force. Perhaps it would be best to seek another adversary, instead."

Gabriel shook his head. "I'm afraid we're stuck with this one, Albert. Let's just call it God, okay?"

"Okay, Gabriel," Einstein said. "What is it you require of us?"

Arthur leaned forward. "A way to stop Him."

"Stop him? Stop God?" Noether said. "Is that what you are asking?"

Gabriel nodded. "Exactly."

They looked around the table. Finally, Elliot spoke.

"Have you considered the possibility, Arthur," Elliot asked, "that it might not be possible to stop Him?"

"No," Gabriel answered. "So let's get to work."

The Iranian Border

"Um, Mahdi," Hila said, taking the Mahdi's arm. "This is not good."

The Mahdi nodded as they faced the array of weapons pointed at them.

"What should we do?"

"I'm thinking."

"Think faster," she said.

The Mahdi raised his hands above his head and looked skyward.

"What are you doing?" Hila asked.

"Still thinking," he said, *"but now I'm thinking with my arms raised. How am I doing, Hila?"*

"It's a start," she sighed.

At that moment, she felt something fall on her head. She wondered if she had been shot. She reached up to feel her hair, and it came away wet. At first, she thought it must be blood. But no. All about her, little explosions of sand were raised. Bullets? Hila looked at the ground as large raindrops fell about them. She looked up. The sky was still a cloudless blue. Before them, the soldiers' guns drooped as they looked about as well. The rain began to fall harder.

The Mahdi still had his arms raised high.

"Are you doing this?" Hila asked, amazed.

"I don't know," the Mahdi laughed, *"but I'm thinking I should keep my arms up, just in case."*

The rain came harder and harder. The downpour became a deluge, and the soldiers lowered their weapons. It was raining so hard they could barely see. Many laughed.

The Mahdi lowered his arms and walked forward, the press of his followers coming behind. A speaker crackled with a challenge in Farsi, but it was lost in the staccato of the heavy rain bouncing off tanks and helmets.

The Mahdi, with Hila by his side, led his followers into Iran under the cloudless rain.

Purgatory

"There," Libby said, leaning back in her chair. "Libby handled it." She watched on the monitors as the thousands and thousands of Mahdi's followers streamed unopposed across the border into Iran, the soldiers falling back to either side of the road. She zoomed the image and saw the soldiers, smiling and encouraging the pilgrims as they passed.

"Next time," she said to herself, smiling, "Libby gonna make it snow."

CHAPTER 16

Purgatory

Gabriel left them when the group began arguing about the nature of God and whether it was even appropriate to work in opposition to Him. The others didn't notice his exit.

"I tell you, it is no matter to me," Einstein said, banging the table to punctuate his words. "Yes God, no God, it is not important. That—" he continued, pointing at the display, "is not something that we can challenge. It is foolish to even consider such a thing."

"Oh, Albert," Noether said, ruffling the man's gray hair, "when did you get so old?" Einstein reddened. "There was a time when you were so young and foolish that you would laugh at God. I remember that young man. Where did he go?"

Gödel shook his head from across the small table. "It is truly humbling, I agree, Albert," he said. "Such energies are beyond our abilities."

"Babies, the both of you," Noether admonished. "This phenomenon is not beyond our comprehension. So why should it be beyond our abilities? Foolishness."

"I must share their opinion, Professor Noether," Tesla said. "The forces are quite vast, no? Far beyond anything in our experience."

Buckminster Fuller nodded in agreement from his end of the conference table.

"You are nodding as well, Mr. Fuller?" Noether chided. "These two," she continued, gesturing dismissively at Einstein and Gödel, "are just mathematicians, so they are easily scared by the real world when it jumps at them like that. But surely not the two of you. You are practical men, are you not? You can see what must be done."

Einstein and Gödel stared down the table but said nothing. Fuller and Tesla looked puzzled.

Noether exhaled in exasperation. "Men," she said to no one in particular. She pushed her chair back and walked to the white board. She began to draw a diagram, erased part, drew more. She paused, hummed softly to herself, drew a circle about a portion of the diagram. She added a formula beneath the diagram. Noether nodded at it in satisfaction, placed the marker down and returned to her seat.

"Albert," she said. "Solve that for me, will you, dear?"

"What is it?" Einstein asked.

"It's a formula," Noether said. "You're a great mathematician, are you not? Solve the little problem."

Einstein reddened again but stood to the board, considering. For several minutes, he swayed before the white board, arms crossed, occasionally making a clucking sound or muttering unintelligibly. "Oh," he said finally, and then began to write. He covered a third of the white board with formulaic scribbling, then dramatically circled his solution. He beamed triumphantly at Noether.

"Very good, Albert. Very impressive. For that, I give you a kiss, dear." Einstein came over and collected his reward, then sat.

Gödel tapped a finger against his pursed lips, considering the board. "You were always good at seeing the problem from the other side of the mirror, dear Emmy," Gödel said. He turned and smiled at her. "That was always your genius."

"You are too kind, Kurt," Noether said. "Or are you just looking for a kiss as well?"

Gödel blushed brightly.

Tesla cleared his throat. "Excuse me, but I don't quite understand."

"Nor I," Fuller added.

"But you must, gentlemen," Noether said, standing and approaching the whiteboard once again. She drew a dark circle around Einstein's solution and a dramatic arrow from the solution to her diagram. "You must, because it is you two who will make this happen. That is your particular genius, I believe."

"Make what happen?" Fuller asked.

"It is true, the forces are far too strong to confront," Noether said, gesturing to the monitor beside her. "So we do not confront. We confound." She smiled.

Neither Fuller nor Tesla smiled back. "I don't get it," Fuller said.

"Nor do I," Tesla agreed.

"Albert," Noether said, sighing as she regained her seat. "You must explain. I cannot."

"Certainly, Emmy," Einstein beamed, turning to Tesla and Fuller. "You see, gentlemen," he said, gesturing to the whiteboard. "Of course, what we have here is a Dedekind domain. Now we know this to be a particular type of algebraic construct, particularly a Noetherian ring. Named, of course, for *Professorin* Noether. It is Noetherian since every ideal is generated by at most two elements. This follows from the Krull-Akizuki theorem. You are, I take it, familiar with the theorem of Krull and Akizuki?"

Fuller and Tesla shook their heads.

"*Narish kinder*," Einstein said, smacking his forehead.

Gödel cleared his throat. "Perhaps, Albert, I can be of assistance." He smiled at the two confused men on the other side of the table. "Emmy has pointed out a way to deal with the extraordinary power we see demonstrated."

"Demonstrated by God," Fuller interjected.

"Yes," Gödel continued, a bit nonplussed at the interruption. "Yes, demonstrated by God, as you say. That is not the important aspect. Rather than meeting such a powerful force straight on, Emmy's formula—"

"And my solution," Einstein added.

Gödel sighed. "And Albert's solution," Gödel continued, "indicate that it is possible to shunt the force aside, so to speak."

"Shunt it where?" Tesla asked.

"Well, I couldn't say," Gödel said. "The calculation simply indicates that such a thing is possible."

"But not how to accomplish this possible thing," Fuller said.

"Well, of course not," Einstein said. "It is mathematics, not engineering."

"All things are possible," Tesla said.

"But not everything is achievable," added Fuller.

"No, Mr. Tesla, all things are distinctly *not* possible," Noether said, irritated. "But this particular thing *is* possible. The mathematics demonstrates this."

"All things are possible for God," Tesla mumbled into the desk.

"You give God far too much credit, Nicholas," Einstein said. "It is nature that governs our existence, and nature is described by mathematics. Emmy shows us that it is possible to safely deflect this force with which we are faced. It is the job of you two gentlemen to work out the practicalities, that is all."

"Is that all?" Fuller asked.

Tesla leaned forward and took a deep breath. "Dear lady, gentlemen," he began, "I know a little bit about the manipulation of forces. Large forces, even. It is—was—my life's pursuit, in point of fact. You may be familiar, for example, of my employment of the harmonic properties of the Earth itself as a conductor for massive flows of electricity. A rather novel and revolutionary approach—"

"Exactly," Gödel said. "That is what you, with Mr. Buckminster Fuller's assistance, will do in this case, also, Mr. Tesla."

Tesla shook his head. "These forces such as you describe, they are the forces of God, not men. My experience has never even approached such magnitudes. Before such a force, I have no method, no construction, with which to exert mastery. Not even the Earth itself will suffice."

"Then use the Sun, the Moon, the stars above, Nicholas," Einstein implored. "Use whatever constructs your awesome God has provided you. We have shown you it is possible. So make it reality."

Tesla threw up his hands and leaned back in his chair.

Fuller put his hand on the other man's shoulder.

"I have a thought…" Fuller said.

Over the Caspian Sea

Zimmerman stared at Grace's sleeping form, considering. He closed his eyes, listening to the soft sigh of breath washing in and out of his friend lying beside him.

The pieces of the puzzle that were his life had knocked about in Zimmerman's head since he was first sitting in darkness in the basement of the car dealership, seemingly a million miles away and a thousand years ago in New York. With each step in this renewed world, the world he found himself in after dying at the point of Uriel's knife, each episode had shaken the pieces of the puzzle in his mind like die in a tumbler, and with each concussion one piece and then another had fallen into place. Now, as he listened to the two of them breathing together in the darkness, the final pieces tumbled into alignment. He stared in his mind's eye at the picture left there. It was a map of how he had come to where he was now, an image of why he had suffered as he had, an explanation of why he had done the things he'd done to shepherd this woman lying here beside him—a woman who in his previous life had been a complete stranger. This realization—this epiphany—should have caused him to cry out, to pound his fist, or strike out in anger—but all he did was stare and listen, now finally with the understanding that had eluded him through the best part of two lifetimes.

No man is the master of his fate—Zimmerman knew this as well as anyone. He never believed otherwise. He knew in his former life that, whatever force had judged that his beloved older brother should die, had shunted Julius down a path not of his own choosing. The pain that resulted from Eli's loss, the years watching his parents crumple under the weight of their sorrow, the dimming of all the hopes that a teenager should otherwise have, gave Julius a rough shove down the road that ended in Kandahar, a rookie Navy SEAL nervously panning his weapon at unseen dangers as he walked dusty patrols. He looked back on that path and had always accepted it as his fate in life.

What Julius had never come to accept was the cataclysm that claimed his soul while he was in-country. Firefights happen, things blow up under your feet, your friends die violently around you—Julius was prepared for this, accepted this. He was even prepared to die on that road in Kandahar. But he lived; and though he lived he never understood what had happened that day. He never understood how he had managed to kill an innocent family, to be responsible for the deaths of children, of a baby whose face he saw every night in his sleep.

Zimmerman untangled himself from Grace, stood and walked to the mirror. In the gloom he stared at his bare hip where the tattoo still bore witness to the mission that had torn his life to shreds, the small script "Salome" up until this moment making no sense at all. But now, after two lifetimes of suffering the lifeless stares of those children, the puzzle that haunted him came together. It might have been a moment of relief, of escape. But the pain was now replaced by a cold realization. He sighed and turned to stare back at Grace, now understanding that she was the cause of all he had suffered.

She was the reason. He understood that now. That was the last bit of understanding, the last piece that fell into place. In his first life, the family was lost as Grace had been lost. In that life when Grace fell, bleeding and excised, despite everything he had done, the fate that was excised with her became his own fate. In the echo of her excision, the lives of those children were lost. Because of Grace, because he couldn't save her, his life was just as lost as those of that family.

Julius realized this now. Now that he saw this new world, a world that really wasn't his, a world where these people survived. That family--that baby, those children, their parents —lived. Why? Because in this world, Grace lived. He watched her breathe, curled up on the bed, alive. In this world, there was Grace. And in this world, there was the Mahdi. That was the key piece, the connection he saw now.

A strange man aspiring to be a savior, that silent man with whom he had shared tea, was the key to his salvation, because it was that man who had saved those people, had led that family to freedom. In Zimmerman's prior life, his real life, there was no savior.

The puzzle had taken a long time to solve. In the days after meeting the Mahdi, of hearing his story, of witnessing his strange power, it became obvious that here was what was missing from his prior life. In the Mahdi was the salvation of all that had been lost before. But why was the Mahdi missing from his prior life? Because there was no Grace. Grace had been lost. Grace had been excised, and all that Grace had been was lost. Despite Zimmerman's greatest efforts, Grace had been excised. And in losing Grace, he now realized, he had somehow allowed the Mahdi to be lost. Allowed the deaths of those whose burden he carried.

But here was the last, missing piece of the puzzle: Why would the absence of Grace cause the Mahdi to be lost? The two had never met. There was only one explanation, he now realized. In a world where Grace lived, there was this man, this Mahdi, this strange unspeaking savior. Without Grace, this man never was.

He stared at Grace—how could a woman not know her

own child, perhaps not even know she had a child?

"What are you staring at?" Grace asked. Julius hadn't realized that her eyes were open, looking back at him. She pulled the sheets up to her neck. "Why are you looking at me like that?"

Kiev

Julius was jounced from his reverie by the big plane's landing. He glanced out the windows but it was still dark outside. It seemed to Julius that it had been dark an awfully long time.

The nagging discomfort was dashed away by Grace's kiss. She stood up before him, smiling at him, stretched as she stood on tiptoe. "You're awake?" she asked him.

"Yeah," Julius said. "And hungry," he realized.

"Me, too," she said, twisting her neck with a satisfying crack. "Let's go find some breakfast. Where are we again?"

"Kiev," Uriel said, appearing at the door.

"Kiev, right," Grace said. "They got pancakes in Kiev?"

"They better," Uriel said.

Grace bumped into the back of Uriel as he stood at the open doorway.

"Oh, hell," Uriel said, staring out.

"Sorry, Earl," Grace said. "What's wrong?"

"It's Hell. Like I said," Uriel said, gesturing.

Grace and Julius looked past Uriel to the outside. It was dark.

"Where is everyone?" Julius asked.

"Where is every*thing*, you mean," Azrael corrected.

Grace pushed forward to the door's edge. She stared out and realized that there was, indeed, nothing but darkness. Grace retreated back into the plane, suddenly shaking. Julius caught her by the shoulder and held her close. From outside, he could feel the cold emptiness that had struck Grace.

Azrael probed the emptiness with his new cane. "Kiev,"

Azrael said, turning to the others with a weak smile, "kind of sucks." He took a step outside the door and appeared to float in midair, bathed in the light from the plane. "Come on," he added, turning away. "I'm starving." He shuffled off into the darkness. The others looked at one another and then followed the old man. Just outside the doorway, Julius turned back to see Bogart and Bacall staring from within the plane, agape.

"You guys coming?" Julius asked them.

Bacall shook her head. "We'll wait here," Bogart said, holding his wife's hand. "Bring us back some bagels or something."

The four moved off slowly into the darkness, Azrael in front tapping with his cane, Uriel and Julius on either side of Grace, Julius holding her hand firmly. As they moved away, darkness closed in around them. Even above and below, there was only featureless gloom, but Azrael kept his steady pace forward. The only sound was of the muffled thudding of Azrael's cane against the ground. Julius bent for a moment to feel the ground, but his hand met nothing beneath his feet. He straightened and resumed walking next to Grace.

"What is it?" she asked.

"Nothing," Julius answered.

"What do you mean?"

"Just that. Nothing there."

"You know where you're going, Azrael?" Uriel asked.

"No. Just going," Azrael said, his voice also muffled, though he was only a few feet ahead. "Doubt it matters."

"You say so," Uriel said. "But make sure you stop if you see anywhere we can get something to eat."

"I will."

They walked what seemed a very long time. It was impossible to tell for just how long or far they walked, but they grew weary of walking and had to rest. They rested by sitting in a tight group in the darkness. Each of them tried to feel the ground upon which they sat only once, frightened by the sensation of nothing to be felt beneath them in the dark abyss.

"Should've brought a snack," Uriel said during their current break from walking.

"Or called ahead," Azrael said.

Grace swallowed hard. "Maybe it's happened," she said, her voice cracking. "Maybe this is excision."

Julius squeezed her hand in the darkness. He hadn't let her go since they stepped off the airplane.

"Nah," Uriel said, the sound of him spitting into the void coming to them in the darkness. "We still exist. Just not quite sure where we are, is all."

"Thought you said we were in Kiev, Earl," Julius said.

"Yeah, I did. Must be around here somewhere."

Grace dropped Julius's hand and suddenly scrambled to her feet. Julius reached around for her in the gloom.

"Grace, where are you? Where did you go?" Julius said, panicked.

"I'm right here," she said. She reached down and pulled Julius upright beside her. "I see something." She pointed into the darkness, but nobody could see her pointing. "There."

"Where? I can't see anything," Julius said.

"There," she repeated, turning Julius by the shoulders to face in a slightly different direction. "I'm sure I see a light or something."

"I don't see a thing," Julius said.

"No, you're right," Azrael said. "I see it as well."

"Let's go," Uriel said, standing. "Show us, Azrael. We'll follow."

They set off walking, Julius reclaiming Grace's hand.

After a considerable time, Uriel said, "I still don't see a fucking thing, Azrael."

"I do," Azrael replied.

"Probably your cataracts, old man," Uriel mumbled.

"You still see it, Grace?" Julius asked.

She paused, then said, "I think so. And I hear something,

too. I think."

Julius cocked his head, listening. "Water?"

"Yeah," Grace said, smiling in the darkness next to him. "A river, I think."

"You two let me know when you start smelling bacon and eggs, okay? Because I don't hear or see a fucking thing."

So they kept walking.

"Voices," Uriel said, after a while. "I hear people, like on a street or something."

"Yes, I hear it, too," Julius said. "And the river is louder, I think. Just barely, but it seems like it's to our right, doesn't it, hon?"

Grace nodded in the darkness. "Let's just keep going," she said.

"Better not be the Styx," Uriel said. He felt the others look at him. "Just saying."

They walked, and rested, and walked on again. The sounds remained at the very threshold of their perception, at times disappearing altogether, other times so vague as to seem a hallucination. But they moved on, feeling more and more like there was something about them, just beyond their perception, somehow obscured.

Azrael stopped suddenly and Grace ran into his back with a grunt.

"What the fuck, Azrael?" Uriel asked.

Azrael pointed ahead into the darkness with his cane. "Someone is there."

"Who? Where?" Uriel asked, squinting ahead.

"Just ahead."

"Can you see who it is?" Grace asked. "Is it Donovan? Is he here?"

"I don't know, child," Azrael said.

"Let's go," Julius said. Grace hesitated, but Julius squeezed her hand and urged her forward.

It wasn't Donovan. They couldn't tell who it was. As they approached, they could see the form of a man, seated in the distant gloom ahead. There was no other light, or substance; just the man himself, his features a blur. As they approached, the man appeared larger and they felt a wind stir in their faces for the first time. The wind grew stronger, its sigh drowning out the other sounds they had heard. Now there was just the wind, and the figure ahead. As they grew closer, the seated man loomed larger and higher, seeming to tower above them but still quite distant in the gloom.

"Is it a statue?" Julius asked. "It looks—really big."

"No," Grace said, her voice a quaver. "It's Him."

And in that moment, He was before them, seated in the darkness, towering over them, the only thing apparent in the darkness, but throwing no light in which they could see each other. A robe covered the old man to his ankles, billowing in the wind that swirled about them. They stopped at his feet and looked upward at a magnificent head far above them, long hair moving in the breeze, but otherwise without feature or expression. The massive head tilted forward and gazed down upon them without eyes.

ALAS FOR YOU WHO DESIRE THE DAY OF THE LORD! WHY DO YOU WANT THE DAY OF THE LORD? IT IS DARKNESS, NOT LIGHT; AS IF SOMEONE FLED FROM A LION, AND WAS MET BY A BEAR; OR WENT INTO THE HOUSE AND RESTED A HAND AGAINST THE WALL, AND WAS BITTEN BY A SNAKE. IS NOT THE DAY OF THE LORD DARKNESS, NOT LIGHT, AND GLOOM WITH NO BRIGHTNESS IN IT? I HATE, I DESPISE YOUR FESTIVALS, AND I TAKE NO DELIGHT IN YOUR SOLEMN ASSEMBLIES. EVEN THOUGH YOU OFFER ME YOUR BURNT OFFERINGS AND GRAIN OFFERINGS, I

WILL NOT ACCEPT THEM; AND THE OFFERINGS OF WELL-BEING OF YOUR FATTED ANIMALS I WILL NOT LOOK UPON. TAKE AWAY FROM ME THE NOISE OF YOUR SONGS; I WILL NOT LISTEN TO THE MELODY OF YOUR HARPS. BUT LET JUSTICE ROLL DOWN LIKE WATERS, AND RIGHTEOUSNESS LIKE AN OVERFLOW-ING STREAM.

Purgatory

"I lost her," the technician said, seated at the console in the main control room.

"We can see that," Arthur said. "What happened?"

"I don't know," the technician answered, scrabbling at the controls before him. The others stared at the monitors, all now showing a patten of grey noisy snow.

"You didn't just lose her," Gabriel said. "You lost everything. Why is it like that? Where's the plane?"

The technician pushed back from the console. "Everything's working, as far as I can tell. There's just nothing there."

"That makes no sense," Samantha said. "There is a plane, and an airport. Grace is there. And the others. We just saw them stepping off the plane."

"Well, they stepped into something that seems like nothing," the technician answered, to no one's enlightenment.

Sam sat down next the technician. "Forget the personal feed, then," she said, twisting dials. "Pull back. Show us the whole thing."

"Yeah," Arthur said, nodding. "A god's eye view."

"Yeah," the tech answered, pulling back up to the console beside Samantha. "You're looking at it."

"How can everything be gone?" Arthur asked. The tech shrugged.

"Okay," Samantha said, slowly. "No visual then. Audio?" The technician shrugged. "Well, let's listen for a bit." They did. "What's that?" Everybody shook their head. "Crank it up." The technician swung a knob to full gain. "There! Listen. Hear that?"

"Faintly. Sounds like—I don't know, static?"

"We can hear that, asshole," Sam said. "Beneath the static."

"No need to be cross, dear," Arthur said.

Sam ignored him. She twisted knobs. "I hear voices."

"And cars, I think."

"And water running. A river, maybe."

"Do you hear Grace?"

They listened.

"No."

"Okay," Samantha said, drumming her fingers on the console. "Maybe, show us just, like energy sources. Try that."

The technician nodded slightly and went to work. "Oh, hey," he said. "Look at that."

The others looked at the monitor that showed a single intense glowing amber spot.

"What is that?" Gabriel asked.

"No clue," the tech said. "But it's pretty hot, I can tell you that."

"How hot?" Arthur asked.

"Hotter than that crazy 'burning bush' shit back in Afghanistan, that's how hot."

"Well, where is it, then?" Samantha asked. "Give us a map or something."

The technician keyed and a map appeared to overlay the bright spot on the monitor.

Gabriel leaned closer over Samantha's shoulder. "Looks like it's a few miles from the airport. Near a river. Why can't we see a river? Why can't we see anything?"

"I don't know," the technician said.

"Maybe it's not really there, some sort of illusion," Gabriel suggested.

"No way," the technician said. "I told you, it's about a million times more powerful than anything normal. It's like a small sun sitting down there. It's real, and it's there."

"Then why can't we see it?" Arthur asked.

"Good question, Artie," Samantha said, considering. She turned to the technician. "Is it the same as the 'burning bush' thing, really?" She asked.

"Think so," he answered. "Here, let's have a look. I'll pull that up." He fiddled with his console for a minute, then considered the patterns that appeared side by side on the screen. "Sure looks like it," he pronounced.

"But why can't we see it then?" Gabriel asked. "We should be seeing it, like before."

"Something is masking it," Samantha said. She drummed her fingers. "We should be able to tell." She turned to the tech. "Assume the two sources are identical at the source. Do you see anything different between their signatures?" She pointed at the screen.

The technician. "Not offhand, but that's just a crude display. I can check. It'll take some time. I'll need some help."

"Great. Get some help," Arthur said. "But don't take too long."

"Find the difference between this and the unmasked signature, the 'burning bush.' Get the smart guys to work it backwards, find out how we're being masked. And how to see past it."

The technician nodded.

Kiev, Ukraine

"BEHOLD," a tympanic voice rolled over them, "*YOU COME BEFORE THE PRESENCE OF THE LORD.*"

The four pilgrims stood stupefied, unwilling to look away but unable to look directly at the intensely glowing figure looming above them. Julius had a brief memory of when he was a small child, maybe four or five years old, when his parents had taken him to the Detroit Art Museum and he had stood at the shadowed base of Rodin's Thinker towering above him, with the summer sun just behind. Grace sank to her knees beside him, pressing her face to the ground and covering her head with her arms. Julius felt like doing the same, but remained standing, trembling involuntarily.

"Maybe so," Uriel's voice came, sounding reedy and wavering, "but we're looking for Kiev. And breakfast. Any idea which way that would be, Lord?"

"*THERE IS EVIL ABROAD IN THE WORLD,*" the Lord continued, not acknowledging Uriel in any way. "*A MAN WALKS THE WORLD, AND IN HIS WAKE LIES CALAMITY. THE LORD SEES HE WHO CLAIMS TO KNOW MY WAY, TO BE MINE OWN. MULTITUDES FOLLOW HIM, BELIEVING A MAN TO BE OF ME.*"

"We know this man, Lord," Azrael shouted, straining against the wind that tugged at them. "He indeed has many followers, and is believed to be your Messiah. He performs great miracles, and leads his people to the Holy Land. Yet You say he is not of You. How can such a thing be so?"

The voice came as drums rolling on the wind. "*THIS MAN IS NOT MINE. HIS WORKS ARE BUT SLIGHTS UPON MY PEOPLE. KNOW HIM TO BE FALSE. HE LEADS THE PEOPLE TO THE PRECIPICE. HE COMMANDS THE ILLUSIONS THAT PRACTICE GIVES HIM. HE IS THE EVIL ONE WHO PRECEDES THE TRUTH, AND IN HIS WAY HE WILL BRING DESTRUCTION AND WOE.*"

"Well, Lord," Uriel said loudly, "You gotta admit, he's pretty convincing. Seems to be doing pretty well for himself, for a false prophet."

"*THE EVIL ONE WILL BE STOPPED,*" the voice rolled in reply.

"You say so," Uriel said.

The seated Lord stretched out an enormous hand and pointed at Grace, still prostrate before him. "*IT IS FOR THIS ONE TO RID THE WORLD OF THIS EVIL.*

Julius stepped before Grace, between her and the outstretched hand glowing before them. "It's not for Grace to do any such thing, Lord. She is tired, and only wishes to return to her rightful place in your heaven."

"*THERE IS NO PLACE FOR HER,*" the voice continued, "*WHILE HER EVIL IS ABROAD ON THE WORLD.*"

Julius helped Grace to her feet. She wavered slightly and strained to look up at the figure towering above her.

"I stand before you, Lord," Grace said.

Purgatory

"I don't know what the lady did for a living before this," the technician said, "but she knows her shit."

Elliott shook his head, staring at the monitors from his chair beside the technician. "She has some good ideas, I'll give you that. Seems to me, she's pretty much spit-balling most of the time." He tapped a pencil against his teeth as he looked across the monitors arrayed in front of the two men.

"Well, I think she nailed this. Here's the spectrum of the energy source from the mountain, clear as day. Here's the one from the cloaked source." He leaned forward to bring up a new image. "And when you do a transform between the two, this is what you get. Pretty cool, huh?"

Elliott stared at the new display. "Seriously?"

"Serious as death, my man."

"You can use a better analogy, Bob. But that's pretty much a pure tone."

"Not pretty much. The only reason it's not registering as pure is because of noise on the sensing side. It's a coherent energy focus of some kind, like a laser is for light, but way, way up the spectrum."

Elliott tapped the pencil against his teeth.

"That's really annoying," Bob said.

Elliott tilted his head, staring at the display. "Like a laser, huh?"

"It was just an analogy. Like 'serious as death.' It's not really a laser."

"But what if we—I don't know, did something so it wasn't like a laser. It's a single wavelength, focused. We do something that makes it, I don't know—fuzzy."

"Fuzzy? Seriously? You're going with fuzzy?"

Elliot shrugged.

"Decoherence. That's what you mean."

"Okay," Elliot said. "What you said. Can we do that?"

"Yeah, easy. Not easy to make a force like that, so tightly coherent. But to screw it up, make it more like something we see in nature? No problem. At least a dozen ways to fuck it up."

Elliott leaned back in his chair, smiling.

"Let's try fucking it up," Elliott said. "But first, let's get some breakfast. Tell the smart guys we're buying."

Purgatory

The smart guys—several engineers, a couple of physicists, and Elliot, as well as the technician—argued over pancakes and eggs in the cafeteria. Before them on the table, spotted with drops of syrup, were printouts of the analysis the physicists had run on the energy sources.

"Why did you tell her they were the same?" one of the engineers asked the technician. "Not even close."

"Well, they're kinda close," the other engineer said, "but not the same. You shouldn't have told her that, Bob."

The technician shrugged, a forkful of eggs just short of his mouth. "I panicked. The woman freaks me out. Especially when she starts mashing the buttons on the console like like that. Like she was killing ants in the break room. Angry-like."

Elliot was looking over the printouts, understanding almost nothing shown. "Don't blame you there," he said. "Is this the differential you ran, like she asked?" He tapped one of the printouts with a sticky finger.

"Yeah," the technician nodded. "Pretty cool, huh? Like a laser or something."

"No, it's nothing like a laser," said an engineer.

"It's not a clean subtraction," another engineer observed. Both physicists nodded.

"Not even close," the first engineer agreed.

"Who gives a shit," Elliot said. "Use what you got. Take that shit and beam it back down into the fog, see what happens."

The others looked at him.

"You think we should?" the technician asked.

"That's nuts," the engineer said.

"You don't know what it'll do," another engineer observed.

"Probably not a damn thing," Elliot admitted, wiping the syrup from his fingers as he rose to leave. "Or maybe something. Who the fuck knows. At least it'll get the lady off our collective asses for a couple hours."

The others nodded at that.

Kiev, Ukraine

Grace stood in the darkness beside her companions, looking up at the huge form looming over them. With her promise to serve the Lord, the wind died to silence. The huge figure before them stood slowly, his head and shoulders looming impossibly high, looking down, still with no expression save His implacable eyeless gaze.

God reached down and His giant hand stretched open above their heads, encircling them, grasping, when—it stopped. The hand trembled, the darkness about them flickered as if an image in an old film about to break. Sounds —voices, rushing water, cars passing on a street—stuttered through the darkness. The huge head of the Lord God, looming far above them, tilted quizzically for a moment, puzzled —and then it all disappeared. Like a fog burning away, but so much faster, the darkness surrounding them dissolved, revealing the city streets of Kiev all about them.

Kiev, Ukraine

Grace looked about, gobsmacked. She looked up and felt the rain splash down on her face, not understanding where she was or the strange moisture for a few moments. The sounds of the river and the road beside them, of people bustling about, were the very same sounds they were almost hearing as they blundered through the darkness on their journey to God. It was as if the scene had suddenly changed in some strange stage play, sound amplified and the lights now shining where before there was only the murmuring darkness.

"What the fuck?" Julius asked, turning about. "Where the hell are we? What just happened?"

"Kiev, if I'm not mistaken," Azrael said, looking about. He leaned heavily on his cane. "In the rain."

"Well," Uriel said, "that kinda makes sense, don't it?"

Grace sat down heavily on the sidewalk and held her head in her hands.

"What the hell's wrong with you?" Uriel asked her. "Get up girl. It's raining"

Grace said nothing, shaking her head.

"What's that mean, just shaking your head?" Uriel insisted, grabbing her shoulder roughly and going down on one knee, turning her to face him. "What's that mean, eh?"

Grace wiped at the tears mixing with the rain running down her cheeks. "I've got no place to go, Earl. There's no where else to go."

Julius stepped in and separated the two. "Let her be, Uriel," Julius said. "She's tired."

"Tired? She ain't tired. She quit." Uriel stood and turned to spit on the sidewalk. "Tired not in it. Shit."

Julius knelt in front of her. "Grace," he said softly, gently pushing away the wet locks of red hair from her face. "Come on, Grace. We have to go."

"Go?" she said, looking up at him. "Go where? Where are we going? Tell me, Father. Where do you want to run to now? Where will we hide from that?" She looked behind them, still seeing the huge head looming over them in the darkness beyond the rainswept street.

Azrael stepped up and leaned down heavily on his cane, looking Grace levelly in her face. "No need to hide, Grace," Azrael said. "Let's just get you home." He smiled at her kindly as she blinked the rain away.

"Get me home?" she repeated. She let Azrael pull her up with his free hand, surprisingly strong for someone so ancient and bent. "Which way is that, Azrael?"

Azrael put his arm around her shoulders and pointed with his cane at the gold-domed cathedral half hidden by the hills ahead. "Just there, Grace," he said. "Not so far now, daughter." He set off down the rain slicked walk towards the church, helping Grace along.

Purgatory

"I tell you, I am sure of it," Buckminster Fuller said to Einstein and Noether as they sat alongside him in the bar of the Hotel Purgatory. "One doesn't forget the voice of one's savior. When I heard the woman's voice on the monitor, I was dumbstruck, I tell you."

"What is it you mean, 'one's savior?' I don't understand what you mean, Bucky," Noether asked, sipping her drink.

"It is a common story for people like us, Dr. Noether," Fuller said. "I was young, and foolish, and despondent. I was penniless and newly a father, again. My first child had died, and I was failing my new family. I was walking on the shore of Lake Michigan, in Chicago, and I was seriously considering drowning myself in the lake. For the insurance. It seemed like the only way not to fail another little child."

"Oh, Fuller," Einstein said, "how could you be so foolish?"

"As I said, I was young. Who wasn't foolish when they were

young, eh, Albert? Certainly you had your moments as well, did you not?"

"Indeed, he did. Many, many such moments, Bucky," Noether interrupted. "Thankfully, I kept my distance when he was young. But tell your story. You did not drown yourself, did you?"

"I did not. But only because of that woman—Grace. I'm sure it was her voice I heard that day, in the grayness of the fog about the lake."

"And what did the voice say?"

"It was Grace, I'm sure, who said, 'You are needed.' I remember this like it was yesterday, and I remember the sound of the voice. It was her. That is why I am here now, I believe."

Einstein drank off his spirits with a flourish. "Perhaps you are right. A cosmic *mitzvah*, a paradox of time and space and wonderfully vague, which makes it so much more mysterious. Moving story, Bucky. Deeply moving. But now it is time for Emmy and I to leave you, I think."

"I swear, Albert, that is all you think about," Noether said, shaking her head. "Go ahead without me. I need to speak more with my friend, Buckminster." Einstein pouted but Noether shooed him off. She turned back to the bar and stirred the ice in her drink with her finger.

"Call me Bucky, Dr. Noether," Fuller said as he watched Einstein leave.

"Then you must call me Emmy," she replied, smiling. Fuller blushed as he nodded. "Tell me, Bucky: Back in the meeting room, you indicated that you might have an idea how we may deflect the energies of God as I described in my formula."

Fuller nodded. "It was something you said, I don't recall exactly. But something in your formula, the way you described it, struck a chord. It is similar, I believe, to my Tensegrity theory."

Noether looked at him, puzzled. "I am not familiar, Bucky,

I am sorry. Is this a mathematical theory of of yours?"

"Not in the way you mean, Emmy. It is more a philosophical construct—it is my idea of 'tensional integrity.' The balancing of opposing forces of tension in order to achieve a point of harmonic stability."

"Yes, I understand what you are describing."

Fuller smiled at this, warming to the discussion. "But it is more than a static stability. My geodesic dome—you are familiar with my invention?" Noether nodded. "Good. The dome is a very stable structure, the most stable ever designed, in fact. But it is not dynamic. Tensegrity is a design principle--my design principle--that puts the structural elements in a dynamic tension. This tension not only provides the structure its integrity, but allows the structure to respond to forces dynamically. Do you understand?"

"I believe so. We have similar principles in mathematics as well."

"No doubt. When Tesla was so fatalistic in describing his inability to withstand the forces we are faced with, I thought immediately that the man, while brilliant, was missing your point. He was still considering the impossibility of meeting such a force directly. Bluntly. But you mentioned the mathematical possibility of shunting the force aside, and I immediately thought of a device using Tensegrity principles, which may respond to the initial brunt of the force. Then Tesla can drain the energy wherever he thinks best—into the ground, up to the moon, who knows. But a device using the principle of Tensegrity will withstand the strain of God's onslaught, I believe. That is what I was referring to in the meeting, Emmy."

"Why, that is exactly what is required, Bucky," Noether said, smiling broadly. She gave his hand a squeeze and finished her drink. "I am so thankful that you are here with us. You will work with Tesla, then, to make the device we need to protect our Grace the next time?"

"I think it only right, to try to save the one who once saved me. Don't you?"

"I do, indeed, Bucky. Grace was right--you are needed."

Purgatory

Einstein, Noether, Gödel, and the others leaned over the schematics spread upon the table before them. Arthur and Gabriel looked on briefly but both realized that they could make no sense of the intricate diagrams.

Tesla paced about the room, circling the others at the table, chewing at his fingernails.

"It looks impressive, Nicholas," Gödel said admiringly.

"Will it work?" Gabriel asked, less admiringly. Einstein shook his head doubtfully.

Tesla stopped pacing momentarily. "Perhaps," he said.

"It will work," Fuller said. Noether smiled at him.

"It is not as simple as 'will work' or 'will not work,'" Tesla said, beginning his pacing anew. "I admit that Fuller's principles of Tensegrity will prevent the device from being destroyed in the initial onslaught. But after that..." He trailed off.

"What happens after that, Nicky?" Noether asked. "It seems that you have designed a device to conduct the energies safely. Is that not what your machine accomplishes?"

"Yes, yes, of course it does. But the conduction, it is not perfect," Tesla muttered, stopping in his orbit about them.

"Nothing in nature is perfect," Noether soothed.

"Nicholas is worried about current leakage," Fuller explained.

Tesla nodded. "There will be leakage. The energy will be shunted by the device, the device will most likely survive the exchange, the energy will be conducted in a dispersive sphere. It is the most efficient way, the only way to dissipate such a large force. A spherical dispersal pattern will be propagated spontaneously. Who knows where the energies will finally be felt—the next galaxy for all we know."

"Well, we can't worry about a little leakage, Nick," Arthur

said. "As long as Grace is protected within your device, that is what matters."

"No, no, no," Tesla stammered, gesturing awkwardly as he resumed his stomping around the room. "These forces—the leakage is not insignificant. The leakage will create a field, it must create a powerful field. Dr. Noether knows—it is her principle, after all. But these are the forces for God to manipulate, not me. Not Man."

Gödel leaned forward again and stared at the drawings. He tapped his finger on the central design. "Nick has a point, I think. I didn't see it initially, but there may be a problem. A field will be generated, as he predicts. There is no doubt." Gödel took up pencil and pad, began to scribble calculations.

"So?" Noether leaned in. "A field will form—we have seen how to deal with fields, have we not, Albert? My theorem accounts for this. It is why Albert was able to look so smart, isn't that true, Albert?" Einstein scowled at her. "There is a force here, and by necessity, the energy of the force will be preserved in some manner. The symmetry theorem makes it necessary. Energy will be conserved in the symmetry of time."

"So you say, Emmy," Gödel said, still scratching at his calculations. "It is probably true…"

"Not probably, Kurt," Noether retorted. "It is a fundamental principle, as Nicky said. My principle."

"Yes, the Noether Theorem. Not 'principle,' Emmy. Theorem. I am familiar. A most elegant work," Gödel said, circling the result of his calculation on the paper. "But if the field is generated as Tesla suggests, and the forces are indeed dissipated in a spherical fashion, I fear we may approach something." He tapped his pencil on the pad of paper. "Something like—"

"Banach-Tarski Paradox," Einstein said, looking over at the term Gödel had circled.

Gödel nodded. "Perhaps."

Silence settled in the room.

Finally, Noether said, "That is an interesting thought, Kurt." She tapped a fingernail against the desk. "I didn't think of that."

Arthur looked between the mathematicians, each now silent in thought. Tesla muttered to himself as he continued to pace.

"So?" Arthur finally asked.

"In the words of the famous scientist, Egon Spengler," Gödel said, "'It would be bad.'"

"'Total protonic reversal,'" Noether said. "Like crossing the beams of the proton guns. It is like that."

"Right," Arthur said.

"No, really," Gabriel said in exasperation. "What might happen? What is this paradox?"

Gödel shrugged. "Banach-Tarski. Before now, it is just a puzzle for mathematicians. What will happen? Who knows? The forces are, indeed, extraordinary. It is possible that the vacuum energy is exceeded, and for an area that is not insignificant. Spherical dissipation must be assumed, as Nicholas predicts. And as Emmy said, there are symmetries to consider."

"So?"

Gödel studied his calculation. "A small bubble of alternate universe, perhaps? Maybe not so small. Time stasis? Or perhaps reversal? It is unknowable, I think."

"Oh. Why is it unknowable?" Arthur asked.

"Because that's what it means to be a paradox," Einstein said. He cracked his knuckles loudly. "God may not play dice," he said, smiling at Noether. "But it seems He does like to play games," Einstein continued. "And I'm starting to believe He cheats."

To wit: "The Dark Fire Scenario"

Left unchecked, it is your destiny that

THROUGH YOUR ILL-CONSIDERED STRIVING, BY YOUR SCIENTISTS' PRIDEFUL GRASPING, THAT YOUR HIGH ENERGY INTERACTIONS WILL TRIGGER A CONVERSION OF ORDINARY MATTER INTO DARK MATTER, AND THAT THIS PROCESS SHALL HAVE AN AUTOCATALYTIC EFFECT THAT LEADS TO A CONVERSION OF NEARBY MATTER AT AN EVER INCREASING AND INEVITABLE PROGRESSION. THIS CONVERSION WILL BE INVISIBLE UNTIL IT IS FAR TOO LATE TO REVERSE.

LEFT UNCHECKED, YOU SEE, YOU WILL DESTROY CREATION. IT IS THE PROCESS OF ALL LIFE PASSING INTO THE DARKNESS. THAT, MY CHILDREN, IS AN APOCALYPSE.

THIS IS NOT MY IDLE THREAT, NOT SOME HOLY REBUKE THAT YOU SHOULD NOT TOUCH THE HOT STOVE OF KNOWLEDGE, THAT YOU MUST NOT WORSHIP FALSE IDOLS. NO. THIS IS REAL. YOUR SCIENTISTS KNOW THIS. GO AHEAD, SEARCH IT UPON YOUR GOOGLE. THIS IS THE HEADLONG RUSH OF HUMANITY INTO THE DARKNESS, AND THE DARKNESS IS DEATH.

YOUR SCIENTISTS KNOW THIS, YET THEY LEAVE IT TO ME TO STOP THEM. 'TRUTH BEFORE GOD' IS THEIR CREDO. THEY MEAN TO TEST ME.

GOD IS NOT TO BE TESTED.

Purgatory

"Got 'em. She's back!" the technician yelled over her shoulder to the others in the next room. The other men and women streamed in from the conference room and stared at the monitors.

They all looked at the images on the monitors.

"It worked, huh?" Elliot asked the technician.

"Damn right it worked. Of course it worked," the technician said, smiling.

"What worked?" Samantha asked, sitting and immediately twisting knobs on the console.

"Not what you're doing," the technician said. "Just stop doing that, please."

Sam looked at the woman.

"Where is that?" Arthur asked.

"Kiev. In Ukraine, right about where they landed. It looks like they travelled into the city, about thirty kilometers from the airport."

"Why couldn't we see them before?"

The technician shrugged. "God only knows," she said. She winked at Elliott, who smiled.

"Zoom in," Gabriel said. "Get us audio."

"You don't want much, do you?" the technician asked.

They watched as the group on the monitor stood on a street corner in Kiev, cars passing and pedestrians streaming past. It was raining hard.

"Why are they just standing there, in the rain like that?" Arthur asked.

"If we had audio, maybe we'd have a clue," Gabriel said.

"Working on it," Samantha said, twisting knobs on the console. The technician sighed.

"—need to just go home—" the speakers above the monitor crackled.

Kiev, Ukraine

"Where are we going?" Julius asked, following behind Azrael as the old man tapped his cane, walking up the path with

Grace in hand.

"Kiev Pechersk Lavra," Azrael said over his shoulder, pointing with his cane at the gold-domed steeples ahead.

"Come again?" Julius asked.

"Chapel of the Caves," Uriel explained, coming up behind.

"A church?" Julius asked.

"Not the church. The caves," Uriel explained.

"Why? What's in the caves?"

"A gateway," Uriel said. "You know this."

"The gates are closed," Grace said.

"But not this gate," Azrael said.

"You're sure?" Julius asked.

"Yeah. We're sure," Uriel said. "You keep asking that. Stop asking that."

"Can't be blocked, not unless He changes all the way back to Creation itself. He's not going to do that," Azrael said.

"He can't," Uriel added. "Stop asking that, too. It's annoying."

"Why can't he, Earl?" Grace asked. "He's God."

"He may be God, but He's not the Creator. None of Them are. That's the bullshit They want you to believe. We've been over this."

Julius shook his head at that. "So this gate we're going to, it's going to get Grace back to where she needs to go?"

Uriel nodded.

"Hopefully," Azrael said from ahead.

"What do you mean, 'hopefully?'" Grace asked. "You just said that God can't shut this one down."

"It'll work," Uriel insisted. "Just not sure where it's taking us."

"Well, that's great," Grace said.

Azrael looked up and put a palm out. "Oh, look. It stopped raining."

"No it hasn't," Grace said, still getting drenched.

"Over here, it has," Azrael said. "Come over here, child. Out of the rain."

Grace walked up to Azrael. The rain followed her, now drenching her and Azrael.

"Hmmph," Azrael said, looking up at the rain.

"Well, that just sucks, don't it," Grace said miserably.

"Quite. Maybe you should step back a little, child," Azrael said.

Grace glared at him.

"We should get going," Uriel added. Azrael nodded and started back up the path. The others followed behind. The rain followed Grace.

The four came over the rise to look down upon the compound of clustered buildings, several with gold-domed steeples, others with turrets or green-tinted coppered roofs.

"Pretty," Grace said.

"Where are the caves?" Julius asked.

"Probably underground," Uriel said.

"Let's find out," Azrael said and moved off towards the plaza that marked the central square of the churchyard.

They stopped in front of the largest of the buildings, a gold domed church looming over the square.

"Here, you think?"

Uriel nodded. "Why the hell not?"

They went in the front door. They stood four abreast, staring down the central aisle at the ornate interior ending in the elevated altar. A huge golden cross confronted them from the other end of the nave, upon which hung a discomforting Christ.

"Okay, then," Grace said, watching Julius cross himself and bow. "To the crypts, gentlemen."

"May I help you?"

They all jumped as one, then turned to see the young Orthodox priest who appeared behind them.

Azrael recovered first and smiled at him. "Yes, Father, perhaps you may. We are looking for the entrance to the crypt."

"I'm sorry, but the crypt is not open to the public," the young man answered. "Not much to see down there."

"Oh," Julius replied. "I am Father Zimmerman. Actually, we're looking for the entrance to the cave."

"Oh, you wish to join the tour?" He led them out the front door and pointed to a small white building to the side of the square. "Tickets available right over there. Have a good day, then."

Azrael nodded their thanks and the four moved off towards the open square.

"Tickets!" Grace said. "Isn't that convenient? What the holy fuck, Earl?"

Uriel quickened his pace to escape Grace's onslaught but she kept at his heels, saying, "I should've known this was all just shit at the first mention of Parnell, that shit-for-brains idiotic bugger. You've dragged me halfway 'round the fuckin' globe so I can buy a ticket for a tour of the world beyond the veil? Is that what we've been flyin' about for? This was your grand plan to get me home, was it, Earl?"

They had come to the small ticket booth. Given the rain, there were no other customers at present. Azrael bought them four tickets. Julius chose not to wonder how the old man came to possess sufficient local currency with which to effect the transaction. They followed the signs to the start of the tour and presented their tickets to an ancient docent at the door to a small entrance. He gestured them inside.

Grace continued her harangue without pause, saying, "Natural gates, you know, like the one used by Jesus Christ, himself. Had himself a golden ticket, did he? Like in Willy Wonka, right? Of course he did, nailed it to the fuckin' cross, didn't they? INRI! Am I right?" She looked about as they followed the tiled floor through the maze of small chambers and sanctuaries. "Maybe we should've got hold of a map, eh? Anybody have a clue where we're going? Anyone?" She looked like she would spit in disgust.

The others looked about at the diverging hallways. Some led to stairways descending below ground, others bent in various directions and disappeared.

"Shall we pray for guidance, Father Zimmerman?" Grace asked, rounding on Julius. Before he answered, she turned to Azrael. "Maybe you can enter a kabalistic trance there, old man, just let your eyes roll back and point the way with your staff." Azrael shook his head at her. "Hold it, what was I thinking? You're the guy with the answers, aren't you, Earl?" She turned on the other man and stabbed a finger into Uriel's chest. "You're the one who got the directions from Chuck. He give you a map? Scribble down some pointers for the weary traveller? Give you the lowdown on the where-the-fuck-do-we-go-now? God damn, fuck me sideways!" Grace said, punctuating each of the last three words with a poke in the man's chest.

A priest in black smock stopped in the passage to give her a disapproving look.

"Yeah, well, fuck you, too, Father," Grace said. "Fuck you all to hell and back," she said, striding purposefully down the hallway straight ahead. The others followed in her wake, murmuring apologies to the stunned priest.

Purgatory

They were back in the conference room.

"So, okay," Tesla said, now sitting at the table with the others. "We have a mechanism. We have a prototype. What now?"

"Now," Gabriel said, "we build it."

"Oh, good," Fuller said. "Best part."

"Maybe," Elliott said. "Please don't tell me, Gabe, that this thing—" he gestured to the schematics before them—"needs to be made into a handbag or something. Because it can't be done."

"Of course not," Fuller agreed.

"Course not," Gabriel said. Arthur nodded beside him. "It'll be massive, I'm sure."

Fuller, Elliott, and Tesla all nodded at that.

"Massive," Tesla said.

"Size of a building, at least," Arthur added.

"Yes, yes," Fuller agreed. "A building."

"So, a building, then," Gabriel agreed.

"Okay," Elliott said. "A building." He paused. "Wait—what building, exactly?"

Gabriel smiled at him. "The Third Temple. In Jerusalem."

Elliott narrowed his eyes. "Hold it. Did I miss something? I mean, I've been in this god-forsaken place for a while, I know. But there's only been the two temples, right? Still just the Western Wall standing, right?"

Gabriel nodded.

"Hang on," Elliott said. "Now you want us to build a temple? *The* Temple?" Gabriel nodded. "The one in scripture?" Gabriel nodded. "You do realize," Elliott continued, "there's the small problem of the site? Temple Mount?" Gabriel and Arthur nodded together. "Middle of downtown Jerusalem? Not to mention, the little problem that the holiest shrines of several major religions sit on that site? That the Dome of the Rock is in the exact location where the sanctuary is supposed to be?"

Arthur nodded.

"How are we to do that, exactly?" Fuller asked.

"You'll work it out," Gabriel said, standing.

The Chapel of the Caves, Kiev

The others struggled to keep pace with Grace as she strode purposely straight on, ignoring the hallways branching off to either side, ignoring the small signs labelling the various chapels and monuments to numerous obscure Saints, some whose remains were entombed in the cave beyond, many signs unintelligible in Cyrillic as Grace continued on, unheeding, down the main hallway, now steadily sloping downwards.

"You don't know where you're going," Azrael admonished from behind her.

Grace ignored him, walking fast. The hallway narrowed, the tile floor replaced by roughly hewn rock. There were no more signs, no more branching paths.

"Grace," Uriel called to her, stopping to help Azrael on the rocky path.

Grace kept on, unheeding. Julius quickened his pace to catch her up, finally laying his hand on her shoulder. She shrugged him off.

"Grace," Julius said. "I'm afraid this path won't lead to where you want to go."

"That's not what you're afraid of, Julius," Grace said, her pace still not slacking. "You're not the one who's going to die here. So fuck you, too, Julius."

Julius stopped. He watched as Grace walked down the darkening path and disappeared.

The Chapel of the Caves, Kiev

Uriel and Azrael caught up to Julius.

"Where did she go?" Uriel asked.

Julius pointed ahead.

"Where?" Azrael asked.

"She just kept walking," Julius explained. "And then she wasn't there anymore."

The three stood, looking ahead into a tunnel that disappeared into darkness as it descended.

"What do you think?" Azrael asked. The three looked at each other. Uriel shrugged. Julius began to walk, following in Grace's path. The others followed.

The gloom closed in about them.

"Has anyone told her?" Julius asked the others.

"Told her what?" Uriel asked.

They stopped suddenly. The path ended abruptly. Beyond was a sharp drop into a dark abyss.

"Damn," Azrael muttered.

The Chapel of the Caves, Kiev

Grace walked quickly, ignoring the calls of the others following. It took her a few moments to realize that as she walked into the deepening gloom, she no longer heard the sound of her footsteps. She looked down to see the floor no longer descended beneath her—the floor was no longer there. Beneath her feet was now only a vague softness, then nothing at all. *Déja vù* all over again, she thought to herself. She kept walking, faster now.

The walls of the passageway faded into the dark on either side. For a while, Grace could see nothing at all. If this was a gate, she thought, it wasn't like any of the others she had passed through before. 'I'm afraid this path won't take you to where you want to go,' Julius had said.

A small white light appeared ahead, flickering in the distance. As she walked, the light grew brighter, closer. Grace hoped it wasn't an oncoming train. The light grew brighter, and larger, and now the flickering was filled with colors. Grace hurried closer. She heard voices.

The colored lights flickered across her face as Grace stopped, aghast. Before her in the gloom was a room filled with people, all staring back at her. Most she didn't recognize. It was a strange room, like a small theater or a conference room of some kind, strangely lit. In the seats behind the flickering light, Grace could clearly see her husband, and Arthur, and Samantha. Many others. They all stared straight ahead, but didn't seem to be watching her. The voices she heard weren't theirs, either, but now seemed to be coming from behind. Grace turned around and looked back at what these people were looking at—a large screen that replaced the passage from which she had come, the screen displaying a movie. On it, the image of the Mahdi stood tall over her, the title appearing to a swelling of inspirational music: <u>The Silence of the Savior</u>

CHAPTER 17

<u>The Silence of the Savior</u>

#

a documentary film by Bogart/Bacall productions

#

[Aerial shot of hundreds of thousands of people, small as ants, swarming in waves through the desert from all directions, all converging on a central plateau. The camera swoops down to the center, now showing a tall, pale man with green eyes, bald with raspberry blond eyebrows, standing on a rocky outcropping, hands raised, imploring the throng as they converge from every corner, the camera circling around him, showing the crowds of pilgrims, men and women, children, mothers holding their babies up for his blessing, others falling to their knees in supplication as more and more approach in an unending stream stretching from every horizon. Music swells in intensity.]

#

Narrator: In the span of just over 40 days, an army of pilgrims has crossed the ancient lands of the Middle East, following the lead of a man they call Mahdi—The Messiah. In an event biblical in scope and reminiscent of an ancient Exodus, tens of thousands of believers walked from a remote valley in Afghanistan, across the ancient land of Persia, to the modern Canaan—Jerusalem.

That can't be right, Grace thought, standing transfixed as she watched the screen. *We left the valley only a few days ago…*

498

Narrator: Who is this man, the one so many call the new Messiah? Where did he come from? Why do so many follow, and to what end? Can he truly be the Son of God returned, and still be the Mahdi? The True Messiah of Jews, Christians, and Moslems? How could one man be the savior for all?

Grace shook her head and smiled sardonically. "He can't," she said. "Don't care how cute he is or how dramatic the music. He isn't." She stared at the image smiling benevolently back at her on the screen. "Though he is damn cute."

Narrator: —doubt dissolved like smoke in the face of these twin miracles. As prophesied by the disparate religions of the world, this new Messiah cut down the objections of the world's great religious leaders one by one—not by his words, but by his works.

"Works? What works?" Grace asked the empty air between her and the projection. "He uses our technology to project his thoughts—that's not a miracle, that's a fucking parlor trick. And patent infringement, probably."

Narrator: Is this history to which we are witness, or mass hysteria? The final fulfillment of every major religion's greatest prophesy, the Revelation come to pass in our own lifetimes? Or the most successful charade of the modern age? Your host—Lauren Bacall.
[Medium shot Bacall standing, outside daytime, surrounded by the crowd, Mahdi seen over her shoulder in the distance addressing the crowd, *unintelligible*.]
Bacall: "My name is Lauren Bacall. Together we will take up these questions face to face. Man, Messiah, charlatan, or Satan himself—you will decide. Let's begin..."

"God, she looks great," a man said from behind Grace.

Grace turned to look back into the strange conference room full of people, squinting against the bright light of the projector. A young man with his feet crossed on the conference room table, leaning back in his chair with fingers knitted behind his head, continued conversationally, "Was she that smokin' hot in <u>The Big Sleep</u>, or whatever? What was that, like a hundred years ago?"

"About eighty," another voice said. "Show a little respect."

"Just sayin'," the first voice continued, "she looks great, that's all."

Somebody threw something at the guy talking and he went over backwards in his chair with a curse. Grace walked forward until she was standing amid the individuals gathered in the conference room. Nobody noticed her as she looked about and listened. Gabriel stood at the back of the room next to Arthur, looking nervous. She moved closer to hear their conversation.

"Nothing since we lost them in the caves in Kiev," Arthur said. "Sorry. Don't worry, Gabe. She's gone off the grid before, remember? We'll get 'er back. Hasn't been that long."

Her husband shook his head and scuffed a toe against the floor. "It's been over three weeks, Art. We never lost her for this long. And this feels different, somehow," he said, sighing. "Like that time she drove away..."

"I'll go over to the control room, see what the techs are up to," Arthur said. He walked past Grace and out the door.

Grace stared at her husband, smiling. "I'm right here, love. But I'm guessing you can't see me," Grace said to him. He gave no response. He looked tired, she thought. "You did great, hon," Grace continued. "You made this work. Not sure what all you did, or how you did it, or how this ends--but you never let me down, Gabe. Love you," she said softly, and kissed his cheek. When she did so, he looked up, looking right through her. He reached up and touched the place on his cheek, confused. "Goodby, Gabriel," she said. She walked past him and through the door to the passage beyond.

THE HOUR IS VERY LATE. SO MUCH LATER THAN YOU REALIZE, SO MUCH LATER THAN I WOULD WISH. EVEN NOW, A PIERCED AND TATTOOED LADY—A CANADIAN, IF YOU CAN BELIEVE IT—A PHYSICIST TOO CURIOUS BY HALF AND TOO SMART TO LEAVE WELL-ENOUGH ALONE, DREAMS OF OCTONIONS AND SEES IN HER DREAMS THE INTRICACIES OF THE UNIVERSE I THOUGHT WOULD LIE BEYOND YOUR COMPREHENSION SO MUCH LONGER. BUT ALAS, THE MIND UNLEASHED IN SUCH A SOUL IS A DANGEROUS DEVICE, INDEED. O CANADA! WHO COULD FORESEE SUCH AN EVENT? NOT EVEN GOD HIMSELF, I ASSURE YOU.

INDEED, HOW SHOCKING IT WAS TO EVEN WITNESS HAMILTON'S DISCOVERY OF THE QUATERNION, A CONCEPT SO MUCH LESS THAN HALF THAT WHICH IS ABOUT TO BE REVEALED. HOW COULD THE MAN STUMBLE UPON SUCH REVELATION? THE MECHANISM THAT LED THE IRISHMAN TO SCRATCH HIS REVELATION INTO THE WOODEN RAILING OF A BRIDGE IS NOT TO BE PREDICTED EVEN BY GOD HIMSELF, SO RICH IS THE QUANTUM UNCERTAINTY OF THE FREELY WILLED MIND. IT BOGGLES, DOES IT NOT?

HOW LONG NOW BEFORE YOU HAVE LAID BARE THE MOST FUNDAMENTAL MECHANISM WHICH UNDERLIES MY WORK? WITH KNOWLEDGE OF THE

OCTONION, FEW SECRETS REMAIN TO ME. HOW LONG BEFORE YOUR SCIENTISTS AND MATHEMATICIANS SWING THIS NEW TOOL, THIS OCTONIONIC HAMMER, AND BREAK OPEN THE CRYSTALLINE NATURE OF EXISTENCE ITSELF? AND THEN? IT IS BUT A SHORT LEAP TO A GRAND UNIFICATION, TO A THEORY OF (NEARLY) EVERYTHING. A CUSP IS REACHED, UPON WHICH RESTS THE KNOWLEDGE THAT BEYOND YOUR SMALL WORLD LIES A UNIVERSE FILLED WITH DARK MATTER AND DARKER ENERGIES, A DARKNESS WHICH UP UNTIL NOW YOU HAVE ONLY GUESSED AT. WITH THIS NEW REVELATION, YOUR PEOPLE—MY CHILDREN—WILL RACE PAST THE PRECIPICE WHICH IS THE KNOWLEDGE OF ALL THAT MUST REMAIN HIDDEN. THE URGENT FALL FROM THIS FATE IS INEXORABLE AND BEYOND EVEN MY ABILITY TO RESCUE YOU.

ALMOST TOO LATE, BUT NOT QUITE. THE LORD SAYETH TO YOU: I WILL SAVE THE PEOPLE.

<u>The Silence of the Savior</u>

\#

[Outside daytime, Jerusalem, medium shot Bacall holding microphone in front of Temple construction.]

\#

Bacall: Historically, Jews knew what the return of the Messiah, the *Maschiach*, required. The Jewish philosopher, Maimonides, laid out the Thirteen Principles of Faith, interpreting the words and prophesy of the biblical Book of Isaiah. And while many orthodox Jews prayed for his coming, few believed in the proximity of the event. The prayer, "I believe with full faith in the coming of the Messiah. And even though he tarries, with all that, I await his arrival with every day," was just that—a prayer, rather than an expectation in modern times. Because as every Jew knows, the coming of the Messiah must await the rebuilding of the sacred Temple. And in this stricken land, where the forces of each of the West's great religions vie for domain, the prospect of a rebuilt Temple on the site of Islam's holiest monuments, on Christianity's revered paths, where the holiest of holy structures, the Western Wall, stood—surely it was impossible to even consider such an event.

"And yet, behind me you see that prophesy being realized, as the Great Temple, the Third Temple, rises before our eyes. The mechanism of its construction remains a mystery, though it occurs in plain sight and under the very feet of our most sophisticated engineers and scientists. It rises despite the protestations of Jerusalem's politicians, the great Rabbi's objections to the impudence as the new structure's foundation incorporates the Western Wall, the threats of the Ayatollahs and Imams as the footprint of the rising great structure subsumes the holy sites of the Dome of the Rock and the Al Aqsa Mosque.

"Behind these threats and objections, armies amass. The edifice behind me arises, rising continuously despite calls from every quarter of the globe to stop, to consider the terrible consequences. The affront that this edifice represents has ignited the fuse of a potentially cataclysmic holy war. Eastern and Western forces, religious forces, populist and anarchic and socialist and every other faction, prepare to engage in the coming fray, refusing to be left to observe as civilization seems to come to a climax. A climax no one on Earth saw coming even a few short weeks ago. A climax foreseen, perhaps, only by God Himself.

"As the world watches the Temple rise behind me, perhaps He tarries no more. Perhaps today is that day. And as to how such a thing can be in our modern, scientific times? We would do well to consider the inscription on the wall which stands behind me, within the Dome of the Rock itself: "Glory be to Him! When He determines a matter, He only says to it, "Be," and it is."

#

[Bacall turns away from camera to face Temple construction. Drone shot beginning shoulder level Bacall facing away from camera, now camera swooping upwards to aerial shot of construction of Temple on top of Temple Mount, higher and higher, showing that the new Temple encompasses the entire mountaintop, its perimeter incorporating the Dome of the Rock, the Western Wall, the Al Aqsa Mosque, and much of the neighboring homes and surroundings, then revealing a sea of massed pilgrims surrounding.]

Purgatory

Grace walked out the door of the conference room, following the way Arthur had left. 'Going to the control room,' he had said. Only when Grace stepped through the door, she was outdoors, in blazing white sunshine. She held her hand up to shield her eyes. It was suddenly blistering hot, the sun intense. She spun around, blinking at a glaring brightness, seeing nothing but painfully bright white all around.

Grace stood on the sidewalk in front of St. Brigid's Mental Health Hospital, swaying slightly to and fro. She was dizzy, and a little nauseated. She turned her head to look around and took a few steps, staggering slightly.

"Watch out there," a burly man said, brushing by on the sidewalk.

Grace looked at where the voice had come

from but the man was already past. Cars sped along on the street, leaving blurry trails in their wake. She looked down at her hand and saw the white plastic bag she held, full of bottles of medications, the same medications she had been fed four times a day for the last four years, the bag appearing to glow from within with a sickly yellow light. She let it go and watched the bag float slowly to the sidewalk. Grace stepped off the curb, turned in the direction of a high-pitched motorcycle horn. She watched as the bright red machine, a black leather-clad man astride, his face invisible behind the darkened plexi mask, ran her down.

Negev Desert, Israel

"Here she is," Parnell said, calling to his companion. "Come on, Julius, she's over here."

Grace stopped and blinked, her eyes tearing in the bright light. "Chuck?"

"It's me, Grace," he said, taking her up in a bear hug and spinning her around. "Oh, it's been too long!"

Grace pushed him away once he had set her down. "Don't do that, Chuck," Grace said. Her eyes were adjusting to the light now and she stepped back to take in their surroundings. She had no idea where they were. *Julius* came running up, breathless.

"Which one are you?" Grace asked him.

"The other one," *Julius* said.

"Figures," Grace said.

"Well, don't act so thrilled to see us, Grace," Parnell said.

"Where are the others?" she asked.

"What others?"

"No one else, then," Grace continued. "Great. Where the fuck am I now?"

"We're in Israel," *Julius* said.

"Well, fuck me sideways," Grace said, looking about at the bleak landscape about them. "Israel sucks. At least it was raining in Kiev."

"This part sucks, for sure. We're in the desert. The Negev," *Julius* added. "The navel of the world."

"Why are we here?" Grace asked.

"I could ask you the same thing," Parnell said.

"Don't. Just get me out of here."

"We've got a car over this way," *Julius* said. "Come on."

Purgatory

Gabriel came into the control room and leaned over the back of Arthur's chair, staring at the monitor. He smiled, relieved.

"Where is that?" Gabriel asked.

"Israel. Negev desert. Middle of fucking nowhere," Arthur said.

"How'd she get there?"

"That gateway in the cave, I guess," Arthur said.

"Well, that's a fucking disappointment."

"But not a surprise," Arthur said. "No one really thought it was going to be that easy."

"None of this has been easy, Arthur. But no—no one really thought it would be like the end of The Wizard of Oz."

"God's a tougher mark than the wicked witch of the West, huh?" Elliot said, from his chair beside Arthur.

"Something like that," Gabriel said. He stared at the tiny image of his wife on the monitor. "She won't last long in the middle of the fucking desert, Art. What can we do?"

"Already done," Elliot said. The image on his monitor

panned and he pointed to a small speeding blur on the screen. "We've got *Zimmerman* and Parnell ten minutes out."

They watched as the blur became a car, a plume of dust tracing its course across the desert toward Grace.

"Really? How?" Gabriel asked.

"You don't pay me to screw around," Arthur said.

"Wait. We're getting paid?" Elliot asked.

"Which Zimmerman?" Gabriel asked.

"The other one," Arthur said. "Don't look at me like that, I'm working with the team you put together, pal."

"Where are the others?" Gabriel asked.

Elliot's fingers flickered across his controls, and another monitor showed Julius, Uriel, and Azrael still standing in the cave in Kiev, looking lost.

"Still in Kiev, it looks like."

"Get them to her," Gabriel ordered, slapping Elliot on the shoulder. "She's not going to survive this on her own. With those two in the car, she might as well be on her own."

"How am I going to do that?" Elliot protested.

"Figure out what happened to Grace, then have the others do it," Gabriel said, walking towards the door. "And do it fast. Grace is going to need all the help she can get. We're getting to the end game here. I'm going in."

Elliot shook his head as he went back to working his console. "Yeah, heard that before. Half a dozen times, I think."

"He's right," Arthur said. "This time, I think he's right." He spun his chair to look back at the door. "Hold it—did he say he's going in?"

The Silence of the Savior

#

[Interior, Bacall seated, facing subject of interview, a middle-aged balding man]

#

Bacall: Helmut Schnorr, thank you for agreeing to this

interview.

Schnorr (fidgeting uncomfortably in his chair): Of course, yes. Yes.

Bacall (smiling): Please, Herr Schnorr, be at ease. A few questions, that is all.

Schnorr (nodding): As you say…

Bacall: You are currently residing in Munich, is that correct? (Schnorr nods.) For how long?

Schnorr: I'm sorry?

Bacall: How long have you been living in Munich?

Schnorr (shifting in chair): Not long.

Bacall: Months? Years?

Schnorr: No, not that long.

Bacall: Oh. Well, then—before Munich, where did you live?

Schnorr (shrugging): No place in particular. Many places.

Bacall (sighing): Please, Herr Schnorr. I do not mean to embarrass you, but our research reveals—

Schnorr: I told you, you are mistaken. It's not true.

Bacall (leaning in): What isn't true, Herr Schnorr?

Schnorr: That I lived in Munich before the war. It isn't true. That was someone else. Your researchers are mistaken, that is all. There is nothing more to it.

Bacall: To which war do you refer?

Schnorr: World War Two, of course.

Bacall: Of course. Pardon me, Herr Schnorr. So, just to be clear, you are referring to the individual, also named Helmut Schnorr, who died in the Bergen-Belsen concentration camp in 1944?

(Schnorr nods, looks briefly at camera and then away again.)

Bacall: It is your contention that this individual is no relation to you?

Schnorr: Relation? No. No relation.

Bacall: Are you familiar with the history of this unrelated Helmut Schnorr? The one who died?

Schnorr: He didn't die. He was murdered. By the Nazis, Ms.

Bacall. He didn't die.

Bacall: So you are familiar with the individual, then?

Schnorr (reddening): No. You said, just now.

Bacall: Yes, of course I did, Herr Schnorr. Just for the record, then, this other Helmut Schnorr, no relation—

(Schnorr nods)

—with whom you are not familiar—

(Schnorr nods again)

We have done some research regarding this individual. This other Helmut Schnorr had a family, a wife named Helga, and three children. Two little girls, a son named Kyle, I believe.

Schnorr: (unintelligible)

Bacall: I'm sorry, Herr Schnorr?

Schnorr: Nothing. I said nothing.

Bacall: Oh. Well, as I was saying, this other Schnorr, he was quite a hero, it seems. According to our research, Helmut Schnorr developed and led a kind of underground railroad for Jews escaping the Nazis. For over three years, this other Helmut Schnorr—no relation, as you say—personally organized and administered a network of safehouses, a system that was responsible for ushering hundreds, maybe thousands of Jews out of Germany, where they otherwise were faced with certain and imminent extermination.

Schnorr: So you say, Ms. Bacall. That is all well and fine. A nice story.

Bacall: Do you have a family, Herr Schnorr? Children of your own?

Schnorr (pausing, looking at floor): Yes, I did. I do, I mean. I have a family, of course.

Bacall (brief smile): Of course. Herr Schnorr, however, was caught by the Nazis. It seems that in the course of his efforts, he was betrayed by an associate. His family—his wife, his three young children—were taken up, arrested in his absence. That his efforts to free his family led to his own arrest. And, of course, as we discussed, his transportation to Bergen-Belsen.

(Schnorr nods.)

Sadly, our hero never learned the fate of his own family.

Schnorr (indignant): That is not true!

Bacall: I'm afraid it is, Herr Schnorr. This man—this hero of which we speak, a man who personally saved thousands from the Nazi death camps—could not save himself. He never learned the fate of his own family. He went to his death not knowing whether he was successful in freeing his own wife and children.

Schnorr: Of course he was! He would never have allowed his own family...

Bacall: It was a war, Herr Schnorr. We can hardly imagine, as we sit here today, how terrible it must have been. But the fate of this poor family, well, I hate to consider the retribution which must have been visited upon those poor children, given the reputation of the Nazi SS at that time.

Schnorr (agitated): What are you saying? No such thing ever happened! The family escaped! They were taken to Switzerland. They lived very good lives. (Spluttering) Helga remarried, a very nice man, six or seven years her junior. Another child, even! What kind of researchers do you employ, Ms. Bacall? Not terribly skilled, I think.

(Silence.)

I'm sorry. I meant no offense, Ms. Bacall.

Bacall (leaning forward and taking the man's hands in hers): Of course not, Herr Schnorr. You are familiar with the heroic Helmut Schnorr, about whom we have been talking?

(Schnorr nods.)

And not just familiar, are you, sir?

(Schnorr shakes his head.)

Bacall (shaking the man's hand gently): I congratulate you, sir. You are a true hero. Thousands and thousands of your countrymen owe you their lives.

Schnorr (smiling weakly): They are all dead now! It was such a long time ago...

Bacall: It was. But that makes your accomplishment no less spectacular, Herr Schnorr. The world thanks you for what you have done.

Schnorr: You are very kind to say so.

Bacall: Why are you back? How is it you are here today, with us now, Herr Schnorr? How can such a thing be true?

Schnorr (shrugging): Unfinished business, Ms. Bacall.

Bacall: Can you explain, Herr Schnorr?

(Schnorr shakes his head.)

Bacall: But you are not the only one, are you? There are others, not as famous, perhaps, so we hear only rumors. But we know that there are others like you, others who have, somehow, reappeared.

Schnorr: Yes, that is true.

Bacall: And they, too, have—how did you put it? 'Unfinished business?'

Schnorr nods.

Bacall: How many are you, then? How many have returned to finish this business, whatever it is?

Schnorr: Why, six million, Ms. Bacall. Six million, and more, besides. Many already here. Others waiting to join us. Only this time, we are coming home, not running for our lives. This time, Ms. Bacall, our fate is our own, you see.

The Chapel of the Caves, Kiev

"Well, standing here isn't doing any of us any good," Julius said. The three of them stood in the gloom of the cave, staring ahead to where Grace had disappeared. "Not Grace, either."

"If we follow, we may be lost as well," Azrael warned.

"She's not lost," Uriel said.

"How do you know?" Julius asked.

"Because she is where she needs to be," Uriel explained. "It is we who are lost. Come on. We must trust that whatever forces brought us this far will see us forward." He started down the tunnel.

The others followed.

"And exactly what forces might those be?" Julius asked.

"If I knew that," Uriel said, "I wouldn't be leading you suckers down this tunnel."

The Silence of the Savior

#

[Outside daytime, Jerusalem, medium shot Bacall holding microphone in front of Temple. She stands in the midst of a large gathering of pilgrims, tens of thousands in an outdoor semicircular amphitheater facing a raised stage adjoining the new Temple, now complete. Onstage, the Mahdi.]

#

Bacall: This huge gathering of the faithful, an army which began as a ragged band of pilgrims in a hidden valley in far-away Afghanistan, a procession that swelled to a multitude as it swept across the ancient lands of Persia to become the nation of this new Messiah, here in this holy city of Jerusalem. A fulfillment, perhaps, of biblical prophesy.

#

[Camera rises, slowly at first, to reveal Bacall standing in the midst of the huge number of people in the crowd. Camera rises more swiftly and scene transforms to computer-generated view of Middle East. Graphics represent throngs of religious pilgrims approaching Jerusalem from various directions.]

#

Bacall (voice over): And even now, as we stand before the newly risen Third Temple, thousands upon thousands more approach. Every major religious order has deemed this a time of urgent importance, the coming of their own Messiah. Christians, Moslems, Jews, all convinced, it would seem, that the time of a great Revelation is nigh. A vast number of Hindu devotees, well over a million in number, supported and protected by the national army of India, stream across the subcontinent to take up their claim to this man as well, if man he is. They call him Kalki, the tenth avatar of the Lord Vishnu, who, they believe, has appeared on Earth to usher in the Era of Truth.

#

[Camera swoops lower in dizzying rapidity to overhead view of Temple and surroundings.]

#

Bacall: What will happen when these hundreds of thousands, perhaps millions, of believers converge on this ancient site? Each major religious order, every sect and believer, claiming this mysterious, silent leader as their own? Will it be truly the Revelation? Or a cataclysm of biblical proportions? And what of those that seem to have arrived from much farther away, from beyond the veil itself? Will the world at large even believe in the resurrection they claim, believe that they have returned as an avenging army from beyond the grave for this moment? Or will it all be seen as an elaborate hoax?

#

[Camera slowly returns to medium shot Bacall, still in midst of crowd.]

#

Bacall: While the world may wish to disbelieve, to hide behind accusations of hysteria and hype, the reality of the man standing on the stage behind me cannot be denied. Out of nowhere comes a strange and silent individual, a man whose power springs from his mind to inspire all those around him, and who now leads an army of believers. A man unlike any the world has seen, perhaps, since the time of Christ himself.

#

FADE TO BLACK

Jerusalem, Israel

They drove Grace to Jerusalem. It wasn't far. Nothing is

far in Israel, Parnell mused. Once in the city, Parnell had to navigate a throng of thousands walking everywhere in the city, many clad in little more than sandals and tatters. He stopped the car on a street outside the newly risen Temple.

"There it is," *Julius* said.

Grace looked out at the towering Temple wall, shining like liquid gold in the sunlight, surrounded by crowds of pilgrims.

"Where?"

He gestured to the iridescent structure. "We'll catch up," Parnell said.

Grace got out of the car.

She stopped just short of the arched entry and looked up. The walls rose shimmering above her and were lost in bright reflection. Grace squinted, blinded, and shook her head as she was jostled by pedestrians and pilgrims streaming past in every direction.

"God damn," she said. She walked into the Temple.

Jerusalem, Israel

Grace stepped through the archway leading into the Temple, and as she did so, was overcome by a strange sensation —a momentary opalescence as the world gave a corkscrew twist about her, an instant of diving into a milky cold pool. She staggered, recovered, and walked ahead into sunshine. Again, she was outside.

"What the fuck?"

Grace emerged from the Temple she had just walked into, but now looked out upon a massive throng, hundreds of thousands of individuals, the crowd arrayed in circles of supplication within a vast natural amphitheater below her. Between her and the crowd stood a man. He stood facing the crowd, his back to Grace, dressed in a rough white caftan that reached to his ankles, his head bald and glistening in the bright sunlight. He raised his arms and threw back his head in a gesture of exultation, and in that same moment, Grace realized who this man must be, as she heard his words come to her mind without a sound.

"Fear Not!" was the thought sent by the Mahdi to the gathered multitude, and what came back in response was a concussive roar of approval, an impulse of sound that swept over the stage, over the Mahdi and Grace behind him. The man turned and gave Grace a conspiratorial wink, and then turned back to his audience. *"Not an end,"* his thoughts boomed before them, *"No, not the end. A rebirth. Revelation! The reward. Hallelujah!"*

The throng answered with another thunderous wave of adoration. Grace turned and ran, almost tripping over Hila, huddled just before the entrance to the Temple. Grace knelt and touched the girl's hand. Hila raised her head to look at her, wiping tears from her cheeks. She gave Grace a weak smile.

Grace touched the young woman's face. It was changed from their time in Afghanistan; older, lined with worry and exposure.

Grace squeezed the girl's hand, saying, "He needs you." Hila shook her head, wiping tears from her cheeks. "He will need you," Grace said. "You must be strong." Grace squeezed the girl's hands together in hers.

Hila smiled, nodded, and looked toward the Mahdi. She gave a shuddering sigh and stood.

"Take good care of him," Grace said, and then hugged her, before she turned to the Temple once again.

Say to those who are of a fearful heart, "Be strong, do not fear! Here is your God. He will come with vengeance, with terrible recompense. He will come and save you." Then the eyes of the blind shall be opened, and the ears of the deaf unstopped; then the lame shall

LEAP LIKE A DEER, AND THE TONGUE OF THE SPEECH-LESS SING FOR JOY.

Jerusalem, Israel

"There's not a damn place to park in Jerusalem," Parnell complained, driving around the block for the seventh time since dropping off Grace in front of the Temple.

"Stop!" *Julius* yelled from the passenger seat.

"What? You see a space?"

"No, you idiot. Just stop. Look!" He pointed to the sidewalk across the street. Looking decidedly out of place, Uriel, Julius, and Azrael stood on the corner, looking about.

Parnell drove over and lowered his window. "Hey, boys! Need a lift?" The three stared at Parnell and looked confused.

Julius leaned across the seat and yelled, "Get in!" Julius recognized him and the three awkwardly crossed the busy street and climbed into the back seat.

"Where is she?" Uriel asked as he closed the door. Parnell drove ahead.

"Who, Grace? We dropped her at the Temple," Parnell said.

"The temple? What temple?" Azrael asked.

"The new Temple," *Julius* explained. "You haven't heard? Where you guys been?"

"Hard to say," Julius said. "Kiev, mostly."

"Kiev? Really? Why, Kiev?" Parnell asked, again scanning for a parking place.

"No fucking clue," Uriel said. "Parnell, what the hell are you looking for?"

"Parking place. This town is batshit." He leaned on the horn to no effect. "I love Kiev. Used to visit there all the time, long time ago."

"Just get us back to this damn temple where you dropped Grace."

"I'm telling you, there's no place to park there," Parnell

explained. "It's a madhouse. Did you visit the Chapel of the Caves? Amazing, just miraculous."

"What a fucking moron," Uriel muttered. "Shut up and drive, Parnell."

Jerusalem, Israel

Grace again stood in the entrance to the Temple, then stepped ahead cautiously. She glanced behind and could see the Mahdi silhouetted by the sun shining beyond. She walked ahead into the newly risen Temple, the space still echoing with the cheers of the crowd outside.

The entry hall was vast, walls and ceiling so distant as to be barely perceptible. Light suffused from above, a brightness of an ethereal hue that reminded Grace of her afterlife. Which, she supposed, was probably the point. Grace walked listening to her footfalls on the hard stone floor, then to a sound she couldn't place: a rushing, hurrying sound like nothing she had ever heard before. It was soft but incessant, implying a wind she could not feel. She walked forward.

A giant shimmering hourglass appeared slowly before her as if emerging from a fog. Grace stopped and gazed at the huge glass shape, the double globes towering over her, hinged upon an ornate mechanism of gold. Inside the hourglass flew thousands and thousands of brightly colored butterflies. Dazzling wings of reds and blues and orange, fuzzed indigo bodies, some striped or spotted with bright yellow, flew crazily about within the glass globes, occasionally bouncing against the inner surface and flitting away, all in unceasing motion. Grace stared, transfixed, listening to the strange breeze of their wings.

"No timepiece, this," Grace heard softly, as if to herself, as she stood, considering. "No grains of sand to obey gravity's cruel insistence. They fly, and in flight never fall. Timeless." She smiled at the strange device, heartened by its lively pattern, entertained by its magical sound. "It is beautiful, is it not?"

Grace turned to see an elderly bearded man had joined her. He wore a small skullcap. She nodded.

"Touch it," the man suggested.

"Why?" Grace asked.

The old man stepped forward. He reached up and gently pushed the lower globe of the hourglass. The huge device spun silently on its axis and slowly came to rest inverted. The butterflies continued to flit about, apparently unaffected by the change.

"So beautiful," Grace agreed.

"Come," the man said. He led her past the hourglass and forward down the long gallery. Grace stole a last glance back at the device as she followed. "They are," the man continued as they walked together down the long corridor, "as the souls of man."

"You mean," Grace questioned, "that they are *like* the souls of man?"

The man shrugged.

"Of course," the old man sighed, "there's only so much air in an hourglass."

Grace stopped. "What do you mean? What happens then?"

"Then," the man said, taking Grace's elbow to urge her forward down the hallway, "they become as grains of sand. As must we all."

THE AUDACITY OF THE WOMAN, TO EVEN THINK THAT SHE MAY PLAY TRICKS UPON ME. SURELY SUCH AN AFFRONT MUST ANGER THE LORD.

NOTHING COULD BE FURTHER FROM THE TRUTH. ON THE CONTRARY, I APPLAUD HER. SUCH HONESTY IN DECEIT!

EACH OF MY CREATURES COMES TO ME, NOT IN

*FAITH, BUT IN DECEPTION. THEY DO NOT BELIEVE
SO MUCH AS THEY WISH FOR ME TO BELIEVE;
TO BELIEVE IN THEIR BELIEF. GOD KNOWS.*

*BUT SUCH A BRASH CUNNING, TO PLAY ON GOD
ALMIGHTY HIMSELF! SO EARNEST, SO DIRECT, SO AU-
DACIOUS—NO PRETENSE OF THE PRAYERFUL CLERGY-
MAN, THE REMORSE OF THE APPREHENDED, THE
GREASY HYPOCRISY OF THE HOLIEST AMONGST YOU.
I SEE YOUR LIES UPON LIES, STACKED LIKE TURTLES,
ALL THE WAY DOWN—I AM GOD, REMEMBER? THEN
GIVE ME SOMETHING IN RETURN FOR OVERLOOK-
ING YOUR DECEIT, SOMETHING MORE THAN YOUR
DESPERATION OR MERE MURMURED SUPPLICATION.
YOUR FAITH? YOUR FAITH IS SO SHALLOW IT CANNOT
EVEN DROWN YOUR PITIFUL IMPIETY. GIVE ME SOME-
THING TO WORK WITH HERE! THAT IS WHAT THE
YOUNG LADY DOES, DOES SHE NOT? A CON, YES—BUT
A WELL-CRAFTED GAME OF QUID PRO QUO, OF SUR-
VIVAL MOTIVATING MENDACITY. I AM INTRIGUED.*

*BUT EVERY CON MUST REVOLVE UPON THE
GREED OF THE MARK, DOES IT NOT? HOW CAN SHE
EXPECT GOD TO PURSUE A GREED EVEN GREATER
THAN HER OWN? WHAT COULD ANY WOMAN DANGLE
BEFORE ME—ME, TO WHOM ALL THINGS ARE POS-
SIBLE? AND IF SHE WERE TO FIND SUCH A DESIRE IN
ME, WHAT PREVENTS ME FROM TAKING FROM HER*

WHICH IS OFFERED, FROM MAKING THE REWARD OF HER EFFORTS MORE COSTLY THAN SHE COULD IM-AGINE? WHY, NOTHING AT ALL. NOTHING AT ALL.

Jerusalem, Israel

"Who are you?" Grace asked the old man as they walked together. "Where are we going?"

"I am the Rabbi," the old man said. "And we are going to the Sanctuary."

Grace nodded at that. As they walked, the walls approached from either side. They were alone, walking down a broad, quiet corridor. The walls went from opalescent, to translucent, then crystalline clear. It was hard to tell, because on the other side of the walls there was only an suffused lightness, almost indistinguishable from the hallway itself. As Grace watched, however, she believed that the walls must be mirrored, because on either side she saw herself walking. Not mirrored, exactly, because the man walking next to her was not to be seen in the reflection. Grace mentioned this fact to her companion, but he only nodded. On her right side, Grace saw her reflection now joined by Gabriel walking alongside her. She smiled. In the reflection, she took his hand and they walked together. The Rabbi said nothing as they walked.

It was a very long hallway.

Grace looked to her left and saw her reflection walking as well, again with no sign of the Rabbi beside her. In this reflection, Grace noted with a spasm of revulsion, she was accompanied by Father Donovan. The old priest turned and smiled at her from the mirror. Grace shivered with contempt.

"What is it, child?" the Rabbi beside her asked, concerned.

"Is it much farther?" Grace asked.

"Not far," the Rabbi said.

Jerusalem, Israel

One second Grace was walking down the strangely mirrored hall, accompanied by the Rabbi in life, by Gabriel and Donovan on either side, the next step she was overcome by the same sensation of falling forward into a cold stream she had felt upon entering the Temple. As she cleared her head of the strange twisting disorientation, she entered a room of golden light, and from above a strange brilliance flooded down, too bright to allow Grace to look upwards. The rabbi was the only one still beside her.

"I believe we are here," the Rabbi announced.

CHAPTER 18

Jerusalem, Israel

The Rabbi took Grace by the hand and led her into the sanctuary. Grace didn't move to follow the old man, but found herself within the sanctuary nonetheless.

"Please, sit," the Rabbi said. Grace sat on a low circular pew near the middle of the space. The Rabbi sat down beside her and patted her hand. "You'll be fine," he assured her.

"In my experience," Grace started—then stopped as she saw Donovan enter opposite her. He smiled at her.

"Blessed morning, child," Father Donovan said.

Grace said nothing as she looked about. Just beyond the margins of the light, Grace could make out faces. They were animated, talking—but she couldn't hear their voices. They were, she realized as she stared around her, the faces of her husband and her friends. Gabriel, Julius and *Julius*, Uriel and Azrael, even Parnell. They were just outside the sanctuary space, obviously unable to enter. She smiled back weakly. Parnell waved. Julius pounded at an unseen barrier in silent frustration.

Grace watched as Donovan took a seat on a pew opposite her. Between them, was a raised circular dais, bathed in the bright golden light from above.

"This is where it ends, then," Grace said to the Rabbi beside her.

"Yes, child. This is where everything ends, and everything begins."

"Yeah, whatever. Will He be joining us then?" Grace asked.

The Rabbi nodded towards the stage before them. In the middle there stood a low circular table. On the table, a bowl of oil supported a small flickering flame, burning bright yellow.

"He is here, of course," the Rabbi said. "We are in God's house."

"Yeah, that's a candle," Grace said.

"The Lord is with us, rest assured," the Rabbi assured her.

"Yeah, but when you say 'with us,' do you mean He is *here with us*, or, you know, just 'with us,' the way you guys always say that God is 'with us?'"

"I don't always say that," the Rabbi protested.

"Yeah, you guys say that all the time," Grace said.

"I don't."

Grace stood and walked toward the dais. She was careful to keep the circular stage between herself and Donovan, who was watching her closely, as was the Rabbi. Grace mounted the steps to the stage and leaned over the candle. She gave a short puff. The flame went out. A small curl of smoke rose from the basin of oil.

Grace returned to her seat.

"I'm guessing that wasn't Him, then. Or are we done here?" she asked the Rabbi.

The Rabbi's face went beet red. He opened his mouth to speak. Instead, he shook his head in disbelief. He looked at her, opened his mouth again to speak, closed it again. He looked at the extinguished candle and muttered something in Yiddish.

Suddenly, a gout of red-orange flame shot with a roar from the dais, a tornado of fire extending upwards, rending the ceiling and flashing upwards, burning into the clouded sky above. Grace and Donovan, cowering instinctively in their seats on either side of the conflagration, were nearly overcome with the intense heat of the apparition. The Rabbi sat beside her, unmoved.

Purgatory

"Uh, boss!" Elliot yelled, staring at the monitors before him. "You better come take a look at this."

Arthur came into the room finishing off a bagel with cream cheese.

"What is it?"

"We have a problem. Maybe. Maybe a big problem," Elliot said, pointing at the colors suddenly spreading across his monitor.

"What? What are we looking at?" Arthur asked.

Fuller entered, accompanied by Gödel and Tesla.

"What are we looking at?" Fuller asked.

"That's an energy bloom, same signature as before," Elliot explained.

"God's lightning bolt, you mean?" Tesla asked.

"Yeah, exactly. Just not quite as strong as the last time," Elliot said.

"So?" Arthur asked. "That's exactly what we were expecting. That's what these guys designed for. The Temple is one big Tesla Tensegrity device. We're prepared for a blast an order of magnitude greater than the last blast, right? This is smaller, you said."

"Yeah, that's not the problem," Elliot said slowly.

"Oh, shit," Fuller said. "Is that coming...?"

Elliot nodded. "Yeah, 'fraid so, Bucky. It's inside the structure."

"Oh, hell," Tesla said.

"Why? What? What do you mean, inside?" Arthur asked. "What's the problem?"

"The problem is obvious, Artie," Gödel said. "These gentlemen fabricated the Temple as a dissipator against a bolt of energy from without. This is not the circumstance they designed for. Actually, just the inverse. What was designed to dissipate an outside force might well act to concentrate a force released within."

"Exactly," Fuller said.

"Well, what's going to happen? Grace and Gabriel are inside that structure. Not to mention everybody else we arranged to be there, too."

"It is not obvious," Gödel said, looking at Tesla.

Tesla muttered something in Serbian and left the room.

"Where is he going?" Arthur asked.

"To try to figure out an answer to your question," Fuller said. "I hope."

"Remember the paradox we talked about, the one I said might result from our design but probably wouldn't?" Gödel asked.

"Batman and Starsky? Yeah, what about it?" Arthur said.

"Banach-Tarski. Now I'm thinking," Gödel said softly, "probably will."

Jerusalem, Israel

"Holy shit," Parnell said, pointing into the sanctuary. "Look at that!"

The others stared through the invisible barrier. Julius pounded again without effect. "She's going to be incinerated," he said.

"No she won't," Uriel said. "He didn't bring her all this way just to burn her up."

Gabriel pushed against the wall. He turned to Uriel and asked, "Then why? Why did He bring her here?"

"You know that better than any of us," Uriel said. "You're the one been making this con of hers go, ain't you? Making all of this work," Uriel said, gesturing to building about them. "Making it so's everyone can hear that boy's mind talking? So he can lead his parade across Persia to the Promised Land? Made this newly risen Temple! So, now, all of a sudden you decided to come out of wherever you was hiding to see the game play out? Watch to see if He falls for your little con?"

Gabriel said nothing, but watched the fiery cyclone separating Grace from Donovan.

"What game?" Parnell asked. "What are you talking about, Earl?"

"Tell him what's playing out here, Gabriel," Uriel said. "Tell these folks about the con you and your wife been running while we been trying to keep her from getting killed."

"Yeah. You were trying to keep her from getting killed—I'm trying to keep her from being excised," Gabriel said.

"How?" Parnell asked.

"By setting up that guy to take the fall for Grace," Julius said, gesturing to the hallway behind them. The others turned to see the Mahdi approaching from the long passage behind.

"Really?" Parnell asked. "You're trying to run a con on God? That can't work."

"She's still here, isn't she?" Gabriel asked.

"Yeah," Uriel said, "let's see for how long."

"It's not really the con that's kept her here, though. Is it, Earl?" Julius asked, watching the Mahdi approach.

Uriel turned to look at Julius and arched an eyebrow.

"You got something figured out, Padre?" Uriel asked him.

"Yeah, Earl," Julius said. "I figured something out. I figured out why my life is so screwed up. Why I spent my life thinking I had killed a whole family, when really it was on Grace the whole time."

Gabriel turned on Julius. "What are you talking about? What was on Grace?"

Uriel shook his head. "Not the time, Padre," Uriel said.

Julius wasn't listening. "Those children—that whole family—was killed, but not because of anything I did. It was Grace. Because of him," Julius said, pointing at the Mahdi.

Parnell shook his head. "What does he have to do with it?"

"That family depended on the Mahdi," Julius answered. "But the Mahdi wasn't around to save them. Why did he disappear like that? And then I thought about who else disappeared from my life, cut out like she never existed. Excised."

"Grace," *Julius* added.

"That's right," Julius said. "Grace was gone, and so was the Mahdi. No one to save that family, so I walked in and took the fall for their deaths."

"That makes no sense," Gabriel said. "The guy never even met my wife. Grace didn't know him at all, let alone enough to make him disappear with her excision."

"Unless he's—" Julius said, as the Mahdi arrived.

Uriel raised his hand, shaking his head. "Not the best time, Julius," he said.

"Unless I'm what?" the Mahdi asked.

WISDOM IS RADIANT AND UNFADING, AND SHE IS EASILY DISCERNED BY THOSE WHO LOVE HER, AND IS FOUND BY THOSE WHO SEEK HER. SHE HASTENS TO MAKE HERSELF KNOWN TO THOSE WHO DESIRE HER. ONE WHO RISES EARLY TO SEEK HER WILL HAVE NO DIFFICULTY, FOR SHE WILL BE FOUND SITTING AT THE GATE. TO FIX ONE'S THOUGHT ON HER IS PERFECT UNDERSTANDING, AND ONE WHO IS VIGILANT ON HER ACCOUNT WILL SOON BE FREE FROM CARE, BECAUSE SHE GOES ABOUT SEEKING THOSE WORTHY OF HER, AND SHE GRACIOUSLY APPEARS TO THEM IN THEIR PATHS, AND MEETS THEM IN EVERY THOUGHT.

THE LORD GRANT HER A NEW SON, ARISEN IN SILENCE UPON THE WORLD REBORN. A WORLD WHICH THE LORD HAS MADE SPLENDID IN THE SON'S RADIANCE, A REFULGENT CREATION FOR MANKIND'S REBIRTH.

Jerusalem, Israel

Gabriel stared at the Mahdi. He shook his head.

"Grace and I never had children," he explained. "She couldn't."

"Maybe you didn't, but she did," Julius said.

"Didn't you hear what I said?" Gabriel insisted. "She couldn't have children. And don't you think she would've mentioned it to me if she did, asshole?"

"Maybe she forgot," Julius said softly.

"She forgot? Are you out of your fucking mind? How does a mother forget she had a child?"

"Some things," Azrael said, as he nodded to the man seated across from Grace in the sanctuary, "may be too painful to remember."

Gabriel followed his gaze and looked at Donovan.

"If that were true," Gabriel said, "I'd kill him myself."

"Be my guest," Uriel said. He produced a flat black knife from his sleeve and offered it to Gabriel.

Gabriel looked at the knife and took it from the older man.

"How do I get in?" Gabriel asked.

"We can get in," Uriel said. "You got those rings?"

Gabriel nodded. He slipped the Claddagh from his finger and handed it to Uriel. The Mahdi removed his and handed it to Uriel as well. Uriel took each in hand, being careful not to allow them to touch.

"Well," Parnell said, smiling. "This should be interesting."

Uriel shook his head. "Another guy who couldn't kill a mouse with a machete. That knife's as good to him as it was to you." Uriel looked back to the drama in the sanctuary. "That's not the real problem," Uriel added.

"No? What's the real problem?" *Julius* asked.

"What happens to the Fiddle Game when the fiddle is worth more than the con?" Uriel asked.

Jerusalem, Israel

The Rabbi's flush of anger retreated, as did the intensity of the fiery cyclone before them. Grace dropped the hand she was using to shield herself from the intense heat.

The Rabbi stared at her, studying her.

"What?" Grace asked, when this became annoying.

The Rabbi sighed heavily.

"Do you have faith in the Lord, child?" the Rabbi asked.

Grace gave a wary glance towards the flame before answering.

"You mean, do I believe that some really powerful asshole has been fucking with me for most of my life? Yeah, I'm a true believer, Father."

"I'm not a priest," the Rabbi corrected. "You don't call me that."

"Sorry—childhood habit. What do I call you, then?"

"Rabbi is fine," the Rabbi replied.

"Rabbi Fine, then," Grace said.

"You believe that your failings may be laid at the feet of the Lord?"

"Not exactly, no," Grace answered. "I blame a lot of the shit that's come my way on that asshole sitting right over there," she said, stabbing a finger at Donovan sitting across the Temple.

"You killed him for it," the Rabbi said.

"Not good enough," Grace said.

"You don't repent of your actions?"

"Just fine with it, Rabbi Fine. Do it again in a heartbeat," she said.

The Rabbi sighed again deeply and the flame atop the dais stuttered momentarily. He shook his head slowly.

"You want, maybe, to grant me forgiveness, Rabbi?" Grace said. "Maybe I should feign some small iota of regret, so you can absolve me of my sins?"

He shook his head again. "Rabbi, remember? Not the way this works."

"So how does this work, then? What are we doing here? I mean, I don't see any fixings for S'mores, so I'm kinda at a loss as to what kind of barbecue you're cooking up here."

They turned at the sound coming from the entrance to the sanctuary. Gabriel stood next to the Mahdi at the entrance, both pressing against the unseen barrier.

The Rabbi inclined his head in their direction.

"How about him?" the Rabbi asked Grace. "Do you believe in him?"

"Who? Gabriel? He's my husband, I sort of have to believe in him, you know? Part of the deal."

"No, not your husband. The other," the Rabbi corrected.

"The Mahdi guy? Believe in him? Like, do I think he's really some kind of Messiah, or the 'Christ come back' sort of thing? Are you joking? I mean, he seems pretty nice, and he's kind of cute. Not as cute as Gabe, of course. Cute in a different way," Grace said.

"Do you care for him?"

"For which? I mean, like I said, I have to care for Gabe— that's the deal."

"The other. The Mahdi, as you call him."

"Care for him? Not especially. I mean, I don't dislike him or anything. Seems nice enough, like I said. Bit 'holier than thou,' but I guess that's the gig, right? I mean, literally, he's supposed to be holier than the rest of us, so I can't really criticize—otherwise, seems okay. Why do you ask, Rabbi?"

"It matters," the Rabbi explained.

Grace nodded. Iridescent sparks swirled within the cyclone of flame on the stage.

"Pretty," Grace remarked.

The Rabbi looked annoyed. He watched as Gabriel and the Mahdi talked with Uriel on the other side of the barrier.

"An eternity of irritation," the Rabbi muttered to himself.

"Pardon?" Grace asked, following the Rabbi's gaze toward the three men. "Yeah, gotta agree with you there. Though, for me, it was about twenty years. Not an eternity, but still— a lot of irritation. Part of the deal, right?"

They watched as Uriel took a ring in each hand and made a broad circular gesture at the barrier before him. He stepped forward into the sanctuary, smiling at his success. Gabriel and the Mahdi followed, each retrieving their ring from Uriel. The three approached to where Grace and the Rabbi sat.

"The bounds of good and ill were rent," the Rabbi said, scowling at Uriel.

Uriel smiled at the Rabbi. "Strong Hades could not keep his own, but all slid into confusion," Uriel said. He bowed with a flourish.

A blush tinged the flames atop the stage.

"Hello," Gabriel said. "I hope we're interrupting."

"Hey, hon," Grace said, standing to give her husband a kiss on the cheek. "Great to see you." She indicated the Rabbi. "This is Rabbi Fine," she continued. "We were just discussing my sins and all. He's going to forgive me, I think."

The Rabbi shook his head at this, still staring at Uriel, barely concealing his contempt. The Rabbi turned to regard the Mahdi.

"Out of the good of evil born," the Rabbi said.

Uriel took a seat on the edge of the stage, ignoring the cyclonic fire a short distance behind. "The right of presence, remember?" Uriel asked. "*Hinene!* 'Shrilling from the solar course.'"

The fire grew in intensity momentarily.

Gabriel took a seat on the pew alongside his wife. Grace took his hand in hers and held it in her lap.

"We were just talking about you," Grace said to the Mahdi.

The Mahdi remained standing and smiled pleasantly, inclining his head to the Rabbi. He said nothing.

"He doesn't speak, you know," Grace explained to the Rabbi.

The flame flared and guttered beside them.

Purgatory

Arthur and Elliot found Gödel, Fuller, and Tesla huddled together in front of the white board in the small conference room. Tesla snapped a pencil in half. He swore in Serbian.

"Going well, huh?" Elliot asked.

Fuller looked up and shook his head.

Gödel pushed back in his chair. "It is not exactly clear," he explained. "The device was designed with a functional convexity to the exterior, designed to reflect away the incoming energy. An energy surge from within the structure…" He shook his head. "Nikola fears the structure might, instead, focus the energy, concentrate it."

"That sounds like the exact opposite of what we're trying to do," Arthur said.

"*Ja*. Pretty much," Gödel agreed.

Jerusalem, Israel

The Rabbi said softly, "It is time."

The others looked at the Rabbi. There was an uncomfortable silence.

"O-kay," Grace said.

The Rabbi stared at her. "This," the Rabbi said, standing, gesturing to the surrounding sanctuary, the flame, Donovan sitting across the stage. "This! This is not a game, woman."

"You said 'it was time,'" Grace said. "And then, nothing. You see what I'm saying? It was time, and then, I guess it wasn't really time, because nothing happened." She stopped talking at the Rabbi's withering stare. "Or did I miss something?"

"See what stands before you," the Rabbi said. The fire built as the Rabbi spoke more forcefully, "The Lord is strong. The Lord does not wait upon you." The Rabbi paced about the small dais before them, his back to the intensifying flame and Donovan beyond. "Only by the grace of the Lord…" the Rabbi said, considering. "Only by His grace."

The Rabbi stopped and pointed toward the Mahdi. "By the grace of the Lord, here breathes your salvation. This New Messiah is chosen to act upon the Lord's will. As you were, now the Son, and the Son will serve the Lord." The Rabbi dropped heavily back onto the pew. He put his head in his hands and waited.

The others looked at each other in confusion. Grace, however, seemed to understand.

"By His grace, Rabbi? The Mahdi will serve? Which is to

say, I'll be—not excised? Does the Lord allow me? Allow me to be as I am—and may be?"

The Rabbi raised his head and looked at her. He nodded.

"Choose him for what?" Gabriel asked.

"Not really our concern, dear," Grace said. "If the good Lord—"

"*I am chosen for what?*" the Mahdi asked.

"To be Mahdi, of course," Uriel said. "Son, you can make for a glorious summer. The Messiah everybody's been waiting on. The spark that ignites a Revelation. Am I right, Rabbi? Of course I am. Can't have an Apocalypse without a Messiah. Congratulations!"

"*And if I choose not to play the role of Messiah?*"

"Don't think you're being asked, son," Uriel explained. "You been set up. Isn't that right, Grace?"

Grace blushed deeply.

"Not a bad gig, Messiah," Uriel continued. "You're mostly there already. Of course, the really hard part hasn't started yet. This is all the fun stuff, before the bombs start dropping. Before the apocalyptic shit starts happening. What say you, Rabbi? What are we looking at? What's the damage?"

The Rabbi looked at Uriel. "The damage?"

"What's the plan? How many?" Uriel asked.

"Every fifth," the Rabbi said.

Uriel whistled softly. "So sayeth the Lord. His judgement to fall upon twenty percent."

"Twenty percent of what?" Gabriel asked.

Uriel spat.

"Oh, sorry," Uriel said. "Forgot where I was for a second. Twenty percent of what? Of the world, that's what. Twenty percent of mankind. That's about—give me a second—about two billion folks, give or take. Our young Messiah, here, gonna be responsible for killing off two billion souls. Like I said, son, congratulations on getting the promotion. Give 'em Hell! And I do mean that literally."

The Mahdi grew rigid, his hands tightening into fists by his sides.

Grace looked at the man, then to the Rabbi.

"Why?" she asked.

"The sheep do not question the path the shepherd has chosen," the Rabbi said, standing again. "The Son will serve so that you may be. This is the grace of the Lord," he said.

There was silence in the room, punctuated by the swirling flames. The vision faded. Donovan coughed uncomfortably. He feigned prayer.

"In vain produced, all rays return," Uriel said softly. "Evil will bless, and ice will burn."

Grace looked at him. "Not sure what you're talking about, Earl," she said. "But you heard the man. Rabbi, I mean. No choice. Gotta be done, for the good of all." She turned to the Mahdi. "To each, our part," she said. "It's what you expected, I'm sure."

The Mahdi looked at her. *"No, Grace. It isn't."*

Grace looked to the Rabbi.

"I'm ready," she said. She grasped her husband's hand more tightly. "We're ready."

The Rabbi stood and moved to leave. Julius stood in the aisle with *Julius* beside him, the two of them challenging the Rabbi's exit.

"Why do you call him the Son?" Gabriel asked. The Rabbi turned but said nothing. "Ask him, Grace. Ask the Rabbi why he calls upon the Son in return for your soul. Why is he the Son?"

"The Mahdi is the son of God, Gabriel," Grace said. "He is the messiah returned."

"Is that what you mean, Rabbi?" Gabriel asked. Gabriel turned to his wife. "We know that's not true, Grace. We did this."

Grace stared at her husband. "Gabriel, don't—"

"This is the grace of God? To allow Grace to pass without knowing?" Julius said. The Rabbi stood mute before them.

"Tell her, Rabbi," Gabriel said.

"Tell me what?" Grace asked. "Without knowing what?"

Jerusalem, Israel

"She is not innocent of this," the Rabbi said. "This path is of her own choosing. By God's grace, her soul will survive."

Uriel stood up to face the Rabbi. "She must know the cost," Uriel said.

The Rabbi shook his head. He turned to Uriel and said, "We have been through so much. The child has been through so much. Forty-two times is enough. This time..." He sighed and the flame guttered hard, nearly going out before it caught its strength once again. "This time."

Julius stood before the Rabbi. "This time, she can't leave here not knowing."

Grace looked at Julius. "Not knowing what?"

Uriel stood beside Julius. "Tell her," Uriel said to the Rabbi. "Or I will."

The Rabbi looked to Uriel and said, "You shame the angel's veiling wing." The Rabbi shook his head sadly and turned to Grace. He placed his hand gently on her head and Grace fell unconscious, collapsing into Uriel's arms.

Grace lay in her bed, her baby suckling at her breast. She looked down at the tiny, perfect little boy and was overcome, wiping tears from her cheeks. She was tired, exhausted. The nurse entered the room and smiled at her nervously. "You need to sleep," the nurse said, caressing the baby's head as he lay on Grace's chest. The nurse went about injecting the sedative.

The nurse went to take the baby from Grace. Grace shook her head and held the child fast to her breast. "He stays with me," she said.

"But you must sleep," the nurse said.
Grace shook her head. "He's mine,"
she said, as she fought to keep her eyes
open. In the morning, her baby was gone,
as if he had only been a dream.

Jerusalem, Israel

Grace's eyes fluttered open and she awakened screaming, pushing Uriel away and struggling to stand before the Rabbi.

"I can't!" Grace said, gathering herself, her face reddening. "*This time* you said? On the forty-fucking-second time I'm here—"

Grace staggered, nearly fell but caught Uriel's shoulder to steady herself.

"Forty-two times, I've been raped over and over by that monster? Forty-two times my sister has been thrown to her death? In every life I've been put through—that *God* put me through—I was orphaned, and raped, and drugged, and brain-fucked to the point that *I don't even know I have a child?* Where I spend my whole life not knowing *until this exact moment,* when you have the fucking gall to make me sacrifice my son so that I may be *allowed* to exist?"

Grace stepped forward, stumbled and grabbed the Rabbi by his robes with both fists, her face inches from the old man's. "I don't care what you are, or what you think I did to deserve this, or what this moment means for all of fucking humanity. You think you're God? You're not fit to be my god. *Not this time.* You don't get to do this to me in reality forty-two, asshole. And neither does he!" Grace said, pointing to Donovan. She pushed the Rabbi away and glared at Uriel.

She held out her hand. Uriel nodded to the knife in Gabriel's hand.

Grace pulled the knife from her husband's grasp. She

turned to face Father Donovan, her arm poised to fling the blade at the old priest. Donovan cringed in silent anticipation. In the next moment, Grace turned back to the Rabbi and buried the knife blade in the man's chest.

Grace watched him die.

"There's your answer. That's my choice."

Behind her, the fire erupted.

Purgatory

"Oh, shit," Elliot said. He spun his chair and yelled down the hallway. "Guys, it's happening!"

The others came running in. On the monitors, an intense blotch of yellow-red bloomed over the image of the Temple.

"*Mein Gott!*" Gödel exclaimed. "That's really bright. That is a strong blast, no?"

"Shit yes, a strong blast," Elliot said. "We've never seen anything like that. A hundred times stronger—more." He looked at the monitors, each showing read-outs pinned to the maximum. The yellow-red blotch intensified, blossoming, shimmered, obscuring everything else on the screen.

They all stood silently and watched. The bright colors flashed, persisted for a moment—then receded to a single point, like the image of an explosion suddenly run in reverse.

"What the hell just happened?"

Jerusalem, Israel

The flash of energy filled the Temple with white light. At first, Grace thought she was having another of her episodes. But as the whiteness persisted, unfading, she realized that she was conscious, waiting for whatever had just happened to fade away, to leave her standing again with her husband and her friends. But the whiteness persisted. She blinked away the sparks which floated before her eyes.

"Hello," Grace said softly, and her voice sounded like the

chiming of bells in her head. "Is anyone here?" She could see her words spread away from her as ripples in the whiteness all about her.

"I am here with you, child," Grace heard, spinning around to look but not seeing where the voice was coming from. "We are not afraid."

"What has happened?" Grace asked the lightness around her.

"I don't know," the Voice said, and the voice sounded surprised at this.

"Where are we?" Grace asked.

"We remain in this place of sanctuary," the Voice said. "But our position—has changed."

"I don't understand," Grace said. She lifted her hand and saw it glowing before her. She swept her hand sideways and the lightness parted like a fog, showing a glimpse of reality beyond. She looked down at her feet and saw far below her the sanctuary of the Temple, her husband and the others looking upwards, looking up at her.

"Please," the Voice said.

Grace looked about. She could see everything; everything veiled thinly by the whiteness of the fog. She brushed the fog away above her, and she could see the world of the after-life, her sister and many others she had known after death, watching her, her sister smiling at her. Her sister waved. Grace waved back, a trail of glowing cloud tearing away from her hand as she waved.

"Please," the Voice repeated. "We must go back."

"Go back? Go back where?" Grace asked.

"To before," the Voice said, and as the Voice said this, Grace looked down on the scene in the sanctuary below and realized that the voice of God was coming from the Rabbi, very small and pale below her. "Please, Grace. Please, child."

Grace allowed herself to float downwards, coming to rest just above the floor of the sanctuary. The flame on the dais had gone out, she noticed. Grace reached out to touch the lamp and a soft yellow flame appeared. She looked about and saw Gabriel and the others hold their hands over their eyes, shielding themselves from her gaze. She smiled to show them that she was fine, that nothing bad was going to happen. The Rabbi alone looked upon her. He looked much more frail, hollow.

"Please," the Rabbi said. "This is not as it should be, child."

Grace considered this.

"Isn't it?"

"No, no, no," the voice of the Rabbi said, sounding plaintive, shaking his head. "Gracious god, no."

"Gracious god?" Grace said, smiling upon the Rabbi.

The Rabbi reached out to her.

SEE, THE SOVEREIGN LORD COMES WITH POWER, AND HIS ARM RULES FOR HIM. SEE, HIS REWARD IS WITH HIM, AND HIS RECOMPENSE ACCOMPANIES HIM.

HE TENDS HIS FLOCK LIKE A SHEPHERD: HE GATHERS THE LAMBS IN HIS ARMS AND CARRIES THEM CLOSE TO HIS HEART; HE GENTLY LEADS THOSE THAT HAVE YOUNG.

WHO HAS MEASURED THE WATERS IN THE HOLLOW OF HIS HAND, OR WITH THE BREADTH OF HIS HAND MARKED OFF THE HEAVENS? WHO HAS HELD THE DUST OF THE EARTH IN A BASKET, OR WEIGHED THE MOUNTAINS ON THE SCALES AND THE HILLS IN A BALANCE?

WHO HAS UNDERSTOOD THE MIND OF THE LORD, OR INSTRUCTED HIM AS HIS COUNSELOR?

*WHOM DID THE LORD CONSULT TO ENLIGHTEN
HIM, AND WHO TAUGHT HIM THE RIGHT WAY?
WHO WAS IT THAT TAUGHT HIM KNOWLEDGE OR
SHOWED HIM THE PATH OF UNDERSTANDING?*

*SURELY THE NATIONS ARE LIKE A DROP
IN A BUCKET; THEY ARE REGARDED AS DUST
ON THE SCALES; HE WEIGHS THE ISLANDS
AS THOUGH THEY WERE FINE DUST.*

Jerusalem, Israel

"Don't you see, child?" the Rabbi asked. "It is still my time. I am needed. All need to believe on Me."

"I don't," Grace said.

The Rabbi raised his hands to her in supplication. "There are others, so many others that want to believe, that need to believe. At night, in the darkness. In that moment after the doctor tells them the diagnosis—they need to believe, to have that faith within their grasp. What else do they have? What will you give them in my place, if you take me away?" The Rabbi reached up, but Grace floated higher to escape his touch.

"Please, child," the Rabbi said. "Where will you have your brothers and sisters seek comfort? The incense and incantation bring solace where otherwise there is only confusion. Where will they turn after they watch their families fall, when the ground opens up to swallow them, when the person they've loved for a lifetime turns false or frail? Who will hear a mother's wail as she rocks her dying child? Where will they go, if you allow my temples to fall, if there are no quiet corners where faith provides their only respite? Where will they turn then, when you have torn it all down?

"And for what? For the existence of a child you have never known, for whom you have never cared, who even a moment ago didn't exist for you? Let Us go back to that moment, to the moment before the boy was known to you, before the pain and anguish of which he is the seed. Let him go and serve the Lord, I pray you."

Grace looked across the Temple sanctuary to where her son stood, looking up at her in awe. She shook her head.

"You must," the Rabbi begged. "As those before you, when asked to do the same, have given their sons unto God. As did Abraham. As did I. Do you think I sacrificed a Son willingly, child? You think it was the Lord's plan, for My own child to die in such a way? That it was not the fate served by deceit and folly, by faithlessness in the Lord? Do you not think I mourn His passing every day? The world is the way it is, and We are called to do what we must. What you must do now."

"What I *must* do?" Grace raged, and the remaining fog was burned away, the flame on the dais redoubling and crackling angrily. "Because men are so willing to forsake their sons, that is what is expected of *me*? What did God ask of Sarah? What did You ask of Mary, as she nursed Your Son? A mother does not so easily sacrifice her child, even though God asks. Ask me again, God! Ask me to give you my son in my stead, for the fulfillment of Your great plan--for the good of all. Ask me!"

"Please, Gracious God," the Rabbi asked her. "Do this, for the—"

"NO!"

Jerusalem, Israel

"Then I am lost," the Rabbi said. "All is lost."

"I don't give a fuck," Grace said. Grace swept her hand and the Rabbi dissolved into dust.

Grace alighted on the floor of the sanctuary, a soft glow surrounding her as it did the now-steady flame on the dais. Grace looked at Gabriel, at Uriel and the others, who were now able to see her clearly.

Grace smiled at her husband. She mounted the steps of the

dais and sat on the large seat before the Scriptures. She beckoned to her son and the Mahdi approached, kneeling before her, his head bowed. Grace placed her hands on his head.

I SAW A NEW HEAVEN AND A NEW EARTH; FOR THE FIRST HEAVEN AND THE FIRST EARTH HAD PASSED AWAY, AND THE SEA WAS NO MORE. AND I SAW THE HOLY CITY, THE NEW JERUSALEM, COMING DOWN OUT OF HEAVEN FROM GOD, PREPARED AS A BRIDE ADORNED FOR HER HUSBAND. AND I HEARD A LOUD VOICE FROM THE THRONE SAYING, "SEE, THE HOME OF GOD IS AMONG MORTALS. HE WILL DWELL WITH THEM; THEY WILL BE HIS PEOPLES, AND GOD HIMSELF WILL BE WITH THEM; HE WILL WIPE EVERY TEAR FROM THEIR EYES. DEATH WILL BE NO MORE; MOURNING AND CRYING AND PAIN WILL BE NO MORE, FOR THE FIRST THINGS HAVE PASSED AWAY."

AND THE ONE WHO WAS SEATED ON THE THRONE SAID, "SEE, I AM MAKING ALL THINGS NEW." ALSO SHE SAID, "WRITE THIS, FOR THESE WORDS ARE TRUSTWORTHY AND TRUE." THEN SHE SAID TO ME, "IT IS DONE! I AM THE ALPHA AND THE OMEGA, THE BEGINNING AND THE END."

Jerusalem, Israel

Grace raised her son's head and smiled at him. She gestured about her, and the walls of the Temple disappeared. In their place, the world of the afterlife could be plainly seen, glowing with an ethereal lightness.

"See now," Grace said, "the Home of God is among mortals, now and forever. Let any who fear death, any who feel grief in the passing of a loved one, let them come here and see the truth of what lies beyond and be comforted."

Grace rose. She stepped forward and took her husband's hand. They turned and together walked toward the afterlife. Grace stopped and let go of Gabriel's hand. "Give me your ring," she told her husband, and Gabriel gave it to her. Grace walked back and approached Julius. She embraced him. Grace stepped back and said, "Thank you forever, Julius. I'm sorry for the pain I have caused you. Be at peace now." She smiled at him. Grace reached out to her son. "Your ring," she said, and the Mahdi gave her his ring. Grace took the took two Claddagh rings in her hands and clasped them tightly together. With a soft sigh, the rings turned to dust, sifting through her fingers.

Grace turned. She took up her husband's hand again, and they walked forward into the world beyond, and into her sister's embrace.

Uriel, Azrael, and Parnell left the sanctuary, walking with the Mahdi back up the long hallway. They passed the hourglass filled with butterflies, still flitting about within. They came to the doorway and the Mahdi looked out at the crowd gathered beyond. He tried to say something to the others, but they heard nothing in their minds. They shook their heads at him. Hila saw the Mahdi in the doorway and came to him. She took the Mahdi's hand and led him outside to where his followers greeted him with a mighty cheer.

"She'll have to speak for him," Azrael said.

"Perhaps a softer voice will command a more peaceful fate," Uriel said.

Uriel turned back to the Temple and a knife appeared in his hand. He threw it and it struck the upper globe of the hourglass. The glass shattered, releasing the many thousands of butterflies to fly out over them, over the Mahdi, and over the shouted adoration of the believers.

EPILOGUE

Over the Indian Ocean

Arthur Schlessel sat next to his wife, holding her hand across the armrest of their first class seats. He looked past her to the darkness outside the window. Sam turned to him, smiling.

"Tell me again," Samantha said, "why we're here."

"What do you mean?" Arthur asked, bringing his gaze back inside the cabin of Malaysia Airlines flight 370.

"On this plane. Flying to Biejing. Why?"

"I told you forty times already. And again, when we were sitting in the airport."

Sam shook her head. "I know. Tell me again. Because I still don't get it."

"Gabriel left us these tickets. You know that."

"Yeah, I get that part. In the envelope, on his desk. You told me."

Arthur nodded. He thought that answered the question.

"Gabe's dead, hon," Sam continued. "He's been gone a long time. He was dead when you found the tickets. For what possible reason would he have bought us tickets to fly to Beijing?"

Arthur shrugged. They had been through this dozens of times.

"And even if he wanted us to fly to Beijing, why fly to Kuala Lumpur first? Why not go straight to China from San Francisco? It doesn't make sense, Arthur."

"I know, hon. But the tickets were in the envelope, and

they had our names on them, and they were for this flight, so —"

"Gabe never said anything about going to China, did he? Did he ever once mention going to China? No, never. Not even when Helena was alive. I don't remember that girl even getting on an airplane in her life."

"She didn't like to fly."

"You know who else doesn't like to fly? You know who's pretty pissed off about flying over the Pacific Ocean all night for no goddamned reason? Give you one guess."

"I know, dear," Arthur sighed. "They were our friends."

"Yeah, well now they're our dead friends, Arthur." She gestured to the large ring Arthur was twisting nervously about his right ring finger. "That's why you're wearing his ring, Art. He's dead." Samantha looked out the window, seeing nothing but her own reflection against the black night sky. "Makes no goddamned sense," she muttered.

"Maybe we should try to get some sleep," Arthur said. "It's a long flight."

***

Sam woke up and rubbed her eyes. They were still flying through the dark. She nudged her husband next her and pointed to the aisle seat a row ahead. "Wasn't there someone sitting there before?"

Arthur looked over. "Don't think so. Nobody there now."

Samantha sighed and laid her head on her husband's shoulder. "I'm going back to sleep," she said. "Wake me when we get there."

AFTERWORD

Many aspects and themes of this book are a continuation from the first two books in The Claddagh Trilogy. As such, the interested reader is directed to the End Notes sections found in God Bless the Dead and The Problem with God. In particular, the reader interested in a discussion of time travel (past only, unfortunately), Closed Time-like Curves, and quantum time effects may find further information in GBTD. The integration of the Ossianic Cycle of Irish mythology is also discussed in that section. References made to the atrocities associated with the Irish Catholic orphanage system, serial abuse, and forced adoptions are based upon the journalistic and historical record related in the end-notes of TPWG. The discovery of almost eight hundred child corpses within the septic tank of The Home for Wayward Mothers is a historical fact and the subject of an investigative commission by the Irish government as depicted in the novel. As in the two preceding books in the trilogy, every effort has been made to be true to the reality of events and locations. However, all characters within this book are entirely fictional. Any resemblance to actual persons, living or dead, is not the intention of the author. I hope that these books have entertained you. Additional essays and other short works may be found at my blog site: The Goat Rodeo Blog. Correspondence may be directed there. I welcome your comments.

ABOUT THE AUTHOR

Evan Geller is a surgeon and educator living on Long Island. He is married to an amazing woman with whom he raised three extraordinary people. He is editor of the textbook, <u>Shock and Resuscitation</u>, originally entitled <u>I'm Okay, You're in Shock</u>. Geller also authored the two preceding books in *The Claddagh Trilogy*, **<u>God Bless the Dead</u>** and **The Problem with God**. Hopefully you already read the first two books, because if you didn't, you missed a lot. Who starts a trilogy with the last book?

Geller has also published poetry and shorter works of fiction and non-fiction. Many of these works, including extensive writing regarding his experience as a practicing surgeon for over thirty years, may be found at his blog: **The Goat Rodeo Blog** at www.theGoatRodeoBlog.com   The author welcomes your comments through this website.

BOOKS BY THIS AUTHOR

God Bless The Dead

Book One of The Claddagh Trilogy

"The truth will not set you free. The truth will get you killed."
-Screamin' Jay Hawkins

Gabriel Sheehan is in the truth business. He has invented a practical mind reading technology. But his wife, Helena, is no friend of the truth. Gabriel knew she was something of an enigma when he married her, but occasionally she seems more catatonic than enigmatic. And he definitely has the impression that she may have killed someone, though he's not quite sure of the details. Now forces are intent on using his new technology in ways that Gabriel had never anticipated—in ways that may lead to his wife's final disappearance.

Proceeds from each book sold are donated to research seeking improved care for individuals with mental illness.

The Problem With God

Book Two of The Claddagh Trilogy

Father Zimmerman knows all about Life, and Death, and God, and Salvation. He's seen it all, lived and fought through wars and worse. Now, as a Jesuit priest teaching "The Problem of God" course to Georgetown undergrads, he's used to

being the one asking the tough questions. And grading the answers.
But Life is so much more complicated than he imagined. So is Death.

When the woman with no name falls from a bridge, Zimmerman has the fleeting impression that he's witnessing an angel falling to Earth. He's wrong about that, too.

Proceeds from each book sold is donated to charities seeking to improve the lives of homeless individuals.